Sarah Armstrong is the author of *The Insect Rosary* and *The Devil in the Snow*. Her short stories have been published in magazines and anthologies, and she teaches undergraduate and postgraduate creative writing with the Open University. Sarah lives in Colchester with her husband and four children.

Also by Sarah Armstrong

The Insect Rosary
The Devil in the Snow

THE WOLVES OF LENINSKY PROSPEKT

SARAH ARMSTRONG

SANDSTONE PRESS

First published in Great Britain by
Sandstone Press Ltd
Dochcarty Road
Dingwall
Ross-shire
IV15 9UG
Scotland
www.sandstonepress.com

The publisher acknowledges subsidy from
Creative Scotland towards publication of this volume.

ISBN: 978-1-912240-46-3
ISBNe: 978-1-912240-47-0

Cover design by Mark Swan
Typeset by Iolaire Typography, Newtonmore
Printed and bound by
CPI Group (UK) Ltd, Croydon, CR0 4YY

To Mum and Dad
thank you for all those books

Remember the country and the age in which we live. Remember that we are English, that we are Christians. Consult your own understanding, your own sense of the probable, your own observation of what is passing around you. Does our education prepare us for such atrocities? Do our laws connive at them? Could they be perpetrated without being known, in a country like this, where social and literary intercourse is on such a footing, where every man is surrounded by a neighbourhood of voluntary spies, and where roads and newspapers lay everything open?

Jane Austen, *Northanger Abbey*

1972

I

I still had about twenty leaflets to hand out from my twenty-five. Harriet was walking up to people, asking them, 'Fancy smashing the patriarchy today?' She wasn't getting rid of many either, but she was getting attention. Not good attention, like people agreeing that they were benefiting from a rigged system, but we hadn't expected that. We weren't so persuasive, yet.

I loitered quietly by the gate, hoping to sneak the paper into the hands of men passing before they realised what it was. They just rolled their bicycles right past me.

'Equality for all!' shouted Harriet.

'Oh, do stop screeching,' said one of the passing men, flapping his college scarf at her.

Jack, Harriet's boyfriend, had moved from the shade of the gate to the patch of sun before the avenue of trees. It looked marginally warmer there. He was holding his leaflets awkwardly at his side, and I felt a pang of sympathy. He hadn't been eager but, when we discussed it in the pub, he'd agreed. We knew he'd agreed for Harriet, but no one had made him.

We'd already been moved on from Trinity Street, and the

rear entrance by the River Cam had seemed a good idea, but the porter was already walking up and down behind the cream stone gate, keeping an eye on us. He adjusted his bowler hat every time he tipped it to a student walking through. It looked like he was waiting for someone to move us on again. It was a bright, clear day, but chilly, and I was hoping we'd be sent away fairly soon so I could warm up.

There were fewer people coming down the Avenue from the Cam now, but a couple, dressed rather more warmly than us, were walking together. I hoped they were important visitors and Trinity would be forced to explain to them why women weren't allowed to study there. I held up my leaflet, hoping they would at least read it: *Stop Economic and Sexist Exploitation.* The woman pulled out a camera from her handbag and took a photo of the gate. Tourists. I sighed.

Harriet came over to me and beckoned Jack. 'It's dead round here.' She flicked through her papers. 'Shall we go back to Trinity Street? We could give them out to shoppers, just to get rid of them.'

My fingers were stiff and I could see hers were red with cold. Jack had folded his leaflets into his pocket and put his hands in the opposite sleeves.

'I'm pretty cold,' I said. 'Maybe we could get a cup of tea first.'

Jack nodded. 'Great idea.'

'Oh,' Harriet said. 'Look.'

I turned. There were two policemen talking to the porter, and then they looked at us.

'Run!' shouted Harriet, and we ran down the Avenue, across the Cam and halfway around South Paddock before we realised we weren't being followed. We stopped and Jack laughed nervously.

'Pub?' said Harriet. I'm not sure who was more relieved,

me or Jack. Harriet took our leaflets and put them in the next bin we passed. 'When we see the others,' she said, 'the others who didn't bother to turn up, we need to tell them how great it was.'

I looked at Jack. He smiled.

'We'll come up with a story.' Harriet took Jack's hand. 'But the police are going to chase us in that version.'

A few days later, Mr Anderson was just closing the gates as I got back to Girton, and he asked me to wait before handing me a letter from the college. I got back to my room where there was a note pinned to my door saying that my father would be here at 9 a.m. That was odd, and I had a tutorial at that time. It had to be a mistake, but it was too late to phone home and check.

I sat on the bed, too tired to take my shoes off. My books were open, unread, and my essay unwritten. I tried to work out what time I'd have to get up to give it a decent go. It would be another embarrassingly rushed job, even if I finished it. Another pep talk with Dr Faulkner. My cheeks flushed at the thought of it.

I bent over to undo my laces. I had to find my gloves, wherever they'd ended up. I hope they were in here. The magazine was still on the floor, folded to the article about the Angry Brigade I'd shared with Harriet.

'That's exactly what everyone needs to do,' she'd said.

I frowned. 'Bomb people?'

'No, protest what's important. We spend so much time talking, but who cares about that? Look at what they say. Fascism and oppression do need to be smashed. Don't they?'

I nodded.

'We all need to look at what is around us, identify what we don't like and act to change it.'

To be honest, handing out leaflets sounded so tame after that I was pleased to do it.

I lay back on the bed, then remembered the letter in my hand. I ripped it open, read it and sat up. My heart was beating as it had when we'd run from Trinity. I read it again. I had been sent down. My protests outside Trinity for their ban on female students had brought Cambridge University into disrepute, it seemed, and after the previous warnings they had no choice.

The letter fell to the floor as I looked around the room. My books, my unfinished essay, my life all had to be packed up.

I had to go home.

2

I had been ignoring the calls from downstairs for too long, it seemed. Someone was coming. I heard the swish of carpet as the door opened, and pushed my face into the pillow. A cold hand sneaked under the sheet and grabbed my ankle. I screamed, sitting up.

'Kit, you arse. When did you get here?'

He jumped onto the bed and lay down next to me. 'Hours ago, darling. Your mother sent me up.'

I lay back next to him. 'Did she tell you?'

'Yes, but David had already told me the unvarnished version. Hers was a little more polished.'

I threw one hand over my forehead with a dramatic sob. 'And now I'm trapped here, back home, forever.'

'A sad spinster.' He pouted his lips, which always looked bee-stung without this added effect.

'And you a confirmed bachelor.'

'Perfect for each other.' He kissed my forehead and smiled. I stroked the hair from his eyes. He'd let it grow, just a little, and it suited him. I snuggled into his armpit.

'You're as bony as ever,' I said.

The birds which had woken me were silent now. The

room was bright through the pale floral curtains. I could hear David opening drawers in the room next to mine and, downstairs, my mother was on the phone, ordering a delivery of coal.

'I know what day it is. I know that there are a lot of deliveries, but I want mine before three. If it's any later, I won't see the mess they've made until the morning. I remember last time, you know.'

'They dropped some dust outside the coal bunker and then it rained,' I whispered. 'She swears the stain never came off the stone.'

'Poor Peg.' Kit whispered. 'It's a hard life without staff.'

'They both insisted on a whole ten days off this year. I hope you're ready for defrosted offerings tonight.'

'Can't we eat at the pub?' Kit smiled. 'No, maybe not. I'll survive.' He sat up. 'But what are we going to do with you, Martha?'

I pulled the sheet over my face again, and he teased it off.

'Darling, you've been in bed for three weeks as far as I hear. It's time to get up, get dressed and start looking ahead. New year, new plan, new everything.'

He pulled the rest of the sheet off and took my hand, holding it until I was standing.

'I've messed it all up,' I said.

'I know. But it will be the making of you.' He kept hold of my hand, kissed my cheek and squeezed my fingers. 'Don't make me come back in here, Martha. I'll go and put the kettle on for you and Peg.'

I sniggered. 'She'll catch you calling her that one day.'

'She loves me. The second son she never had.' He paused in the doorway. 'Ten minutes and I'll be back.'

He closed the door. I opened the suitcase and took the

last of my clean clothes out. Time to do a wash, and accept that I wasn't a student any more.

In the kitchen, Ma was defrosting an apple pie Cook had left in the freezer. The last of the turkey had been mixed with coronation sauce. Same as every New Year's Eve that I could ever remember, turkey sandwiches, apple pie and champagne, but each time with a little less excitement about the coming year.

I put my washing in the new machine and tipped the powder in. I hesitated as I looked at the range of programmes, but Ma came across and selected one before pressing the button.

'Christopher made you tea, and you can have your breakfast for lunch,' Ma said, and pointed to a plate with two pieces of curling toast.

'Can I fry an egg to go with it?'

'I don't know,' she said. 'Can you?'

I grimaced at her little grammar joke and took my toast to the table. Frying an egg would just mean a fuss about the pan, the mood she was in. Ma lifted my mug to wipe the table with a cloth, and began to wash up some plates.

'How long is Kit down for?' I asked.

'Christopher is going back to London tomorrow, I believe. He's driving David too.'

So, I'd be alone with the parents again. I took a bite of toast, rigid with cold butter, and put it on top of the range to warm up while I tried to chew through my mouthful, aided with sips of tea. I flicked through the *Radio Times* to see what films were on later. David and I would work out when to distract Pa from the television, and what was safe. I noticed I'd thankfully missed most of the National Folk Ballet of Korea, but there was a second ballet later.

'I wish they were staying longer,' I said.

'You need to stop worrying about other people and concentrate on sorting yourself out. And stop reading the television guide. You'll have to get a job, Martha,' she said, not bothering to look away from the washing up. 'You won't be spending the rest of your life in bed.'

'I know, but I couldn't look over Christmas, could I? I'll go into London next week and sign up at some agencies.'

'You don't think you should look around here?'

'The pub?'

She turned around to tut at me, and went back to the plates. 'The school. David's old school. You managed a whole year and a term in Cambridge. You must have learned something.'

'I didn't learn how to teach.'

'You don't need a qualification to teach in a private school, Martha. You could do something useful.'

'But I don't want—'

'Daddy has already spoken to Mr Arnold, so it's all settled.'

I stood up and put my empty mug at the side of the sink. She looked at me in a way which showed she was tired of looking at me.

'Ma, I don't want to stay here.'

'Martha, if you are going to act like a badly-behaved child and throw away every advantage you've ever been gifted, then we will keep you where we can see you.'

'I've been punished. I've left university and I won't get my degree. I don't need to be watched.'

She threw the dishcloth onto the side. 'It was in the newspaper, that ridiculous protest. You can't change things by going around shouting about them. You will not make a fool of us again.'

'But I wasn't charged with anything. I'm not a criminal, and things do need to change.'

Ma took a step towards me and grabbed my shoulders. 'You're so childish. We have saved you from yourself, and now you do what we say.'

I staggered away to the table and sat down again.

'I need to know what is happening with my friends. I need to phone them.'

'No, no phone calls, no contact. You need to move forward, and you've proven you choose friends very poorly.'

'Harriet has my number from before. If she calls, can I speak to her?'

'No one has called. No one.' People had been calling. There had been so many 'wrong numbers', according to Ma, that I began to wonder if they ever had real phone calls. Ma lowered herself into the chair next to mine and grabbed my hand. 'I don't know, and I don't care, why you did it. We did what we could for you, Martha, and you can't say you've been hard done by. We all need to move forward. This is very important to us, and you can't say we haven't allowed you leeway to make choices. But now you have to promise that you won't contact anyone from Cambridge. All right?'

There were tears in her eyes, very unlike her. It disturbed me. I nodded.

'You can concentrate on getting a job and we'll make sure that you meet the right kind of person. People that aren't going to make things difficult for Pa.'

She cleared her throat, stood up and walked back to the sink. Pa, who did who knows what, at GCHQ. Government Communications Headquarters. My life had been full of warnings not to embarrass him and, by default, the whole government.

'Why don't you find David and Christopher, see what they're up to?'

I left the room and leaned against the wall in the hallway. For weeks I'd been home and, until now, they'd avoided talking about why I was here, just exchanging looks of miserable resignation.

There was a cough from the stairs. Kit was sitting about halfway up, the light shining through the window behind him.

'We could grab a drink before the pub closes,' he said. 'What do you think?'

They'd called last orders just as we arrived, so Kit went straight to the bar and came back to the table with three halves.

'That's a bit sensible for you,' I said. 'Halves?'

'I'm pacing myself,' he said. 'It's going to be a long night.'

'You didn't get a better offer than us for New Year?'

Kit looked out of the window. 'I got many offers, but not with such old friends.' He pointed out of the window to the grey streets. 'And such terrible weather.'

'Ah,' said David, putting his arm around Kit's shoulder. 'And we love you too.'

Kit sighed. 'It's important to remember one's roots.' He picked David's hand from his shoulder and dropped it on the table. 'And I have my first foreign posting coming up, so I had to choose carefully.'

I slouched on my bench, back against the sticky wallpaper. Everyone was moving forward but me. Twenty, and back at home in the pub which had no one discussing physics or poetry in the corner. No danger of being entertained with stories of Harriet's latest plan. Just Bert behind the bar, his wife glowering at the end of it, and the prospect of teaching small children to fill my days.

At least when David came back, he had people nearby to visit, like Kit. Best friends at eleven, they had kept in touch lightly over the years, with none of the expectations of birthday cards and all the pleasure of meeting up again. I had no friends from school that I wanted to keep in contact with. I'm not sure whether that said more about me or them, but Kit was a friend to both of us now. And about to leave the country. I'd missed him saying where.

'Sorry, where are you going?' I asked.

'Aren't you listening?' asked David. 'He's going to Moscow.'

'Oh, how brilliant. Dostoyevsky, fairy tales, snow. You're so lucky.'

David looked appalled. 'What? There's no decent food and everyone's under surveillance. It's a very tricky posting.'

Kit frowned. 'It will be difficult, but very good for my prospects. So I'm told. As long as I don't end up doing anything illegal.'

'You should take Martha,' said David. 'She would attract all the trouble away from you. She can't help it.'

I grabbed Kit's hand in both of mine.

'Kit, listen to him,' I said. 'Take me with you. You would be my saviour and I would keep you out of trouble.'

'Ha!' David nearly choked on his beer.

'Drink up!' Bert had been roused by his wife and was doing the rounds. 'This one dead?'

'Let's walk down by the river,' said David. 'I miss seeing a nice, clean river. Do you know how many bodies have been pulled out of the Thames in the last six weeks?'

'Is that all you do in Westminster, count the bodies?' asked Kit.

'It's how we like to start our days.'

David had been a Secretary, Personal Secretary or even

13

a Private Personal Secretary for so long now that I really couldn't ask him again. I could have asked our parents, but I tried not to ask them anything. The slightest enquiry would end up in a lecture about how successful David was, how proud they were, and thank God for boys. I found it best to answer questions, rather than ask them, in the hope that one day they wouldn't roll their eyes, ever so slightly, when I came into the room.

It was cold down by the river, but clear, and we held out as long as we could.

'Better get back. It's the hour between dog and wolf,' Kit said.

I said, 'What hour?'

'Dusk,' said Kit. 'My grandmother always called it that. Was it connected to Odin? January is the month of the wolf, but that's something different. Or is it French?'

'Never mind that,' David said. 'We need to give you some instructions, Kit. An updated list of things not to discuss this evening with my Pa.'

'Decimalisation,' I said.

'Is he still against?' asked Kit. 'Even Pa has stopped moaning about that.'

David tutted. 'Still against, obviously, seeing as it's a communist plot. See also centigrade and centimetres. Miners, they're a no. What else?'

I said, 'Women having a national football team. He read about that in the paper and Ma nearly called an ambulance.'

Kit said, 'It's OK, I've got this. I'll just pretend he's Pa.'

He offered me his arm, and I offered my other arm to David. In a line, we walked up from the river. No one was in a hurry to get back.

I knew it was my fault we needed to be more careful

around Pa. Being kicked out of university, after he'd been so proud of the first girl in the family with brains. Ma said he'd caught a cold, but she looked at me like I'd broken his heart. I'd noticed that she jumped to answer the phone, but left it to ring just a little longer before she answered it, as if she was steeling herself. I stayed in bed for as long as I could. But I had no one to blame but myself, as she reminded me.

'I feel we should be singing something,' said Kit.

David patted Kit on the back. 'Let's save our voices for midnight.'

It was too late: Kit and I rearranged our arms and launched into Auld Lang Syne. By the chorus, David was with us.

1973

3

David went to bed at quarter to one, after the National Anthem, when the screen went black. Kit and I were the only ones left up, small glasses in hand. 'Desperation sherry,' I'd called it. My parents weren't ones for stocking up on alcohol, just keeping a dozen bottles with an inch or two in each. Kit was stretched out on the sofa and I was on the floor, near his head so we could speak quietly. I was unsure how well we were doing with that.

I took another sip and pulled a face. Kit smiled and closed his eyes.

'I wish I could go back to school,' he said. 'Your father has put me right off getting old. I'm not ready to be an adult.'

'We could run away with the circus,' I said.

'Can we?' He sighed.

'But you have a great job. It's all,' I put a finger to my lips, 'secret, and everything.'

'Darling, don't be ridiculous. I'm just a boring old secretary.' He opened one eye and we both laughed.

'And you get to go to Russia. You get paid to go there, and I will be teaching small boys to not pick their noses. Want to swap?'

Kit opened both eyes and smiled. 'Maybe we should have got married, like you said. What were you, twelve?'

I laughed. 'Too young to realise it was David you wanted, that's for sure.'

'Ah well, I grew out of him.'

'Poor David.' I leaned my head back against his stomach. 'But maybe I have a chance now.'

He stroked my head. 'You little optimist. That's making me feel sick, though, your head on my stomach.' He lifted my head, struggled onto his side and put the glass on the floor. 'It's a shame we can't marry. It would make a lot of people very happy.'

'People at work?'

'Yes. They like everyone to be nicely paired off so they have control over them when they inevitably have affairs. And my poor old Ma and Pa.' He groaned and used the sofa arm to push himself up to sitting. He placed both hands on his face and mumbled, 'Are you sure you don't work for the Ruskies? I haven't been this drunk for years.' His legs fell to the floor and I clambered up backwards to sit next to him. I put one hand to my head until I stopped feeling sick.

'Let's get married, then.'

He laughed. 'Yeah.'

'Really.' I turned him by the shoulder to look at me. 'A marriage of convenience. You need an understanding wife and I need to not be a teacher. And I need to go to Russia. Even if I never realised it before. This is why everything has happened. It is fate.'

'Married.' He was clearly having trouble focusing, and

closed one eye. 'That's some proposal, Martha. Shall we sleep on it?'

'OK.'

The hangover started early, before dawn, with a terrible thirst. I tried to negotiate myself back to sleep, but had to drag myself and my head, which felt detached somehow, downstairs. I drank four glasses of water, one after the other, which made me feel sick again.

I opened the back door and sat on the doorstep, clutching the fifth glass that I couldn't quite face, but was convinced would sort me out. The cold air made me shudder, but it was working on the nausea. My body was a series of balances which I needed to respect. That I should have respected last night, before mixing champagne with gin, then sherry and every type of drink my parents had ever bought or been given.

I closed my eyes as a dream started to seep back to me: Harriet standing in the university library with her torch on, shining it on the ornate ceiling, and then straight at me. Harriet. I needed to know what had happened to her, and Jack, but I couldn't ask. If I phoned anyone, the next phone bill would show Ma and Pa that I had broken the very last rule which mattered to them. I would have lied. There were phone boxes in town, of course, but someone would see me and report back: I saw your Martha . . . did you know?

My eyes throbbed. My stomach gurgled. Now I needed to go back upstairs to the toilet. I used both hands to pull myself up the door frame, picked up the glass and locked everything back up.

I slid against the wall, as if my feet were fighting the stairs, trying not to spill the water. I needed to stop drinking so much. I needed to get away. I needed to show my parents that I wasn't the total failure they thought. But, oh God, just getting to the toilet was too much.

Back in bed, my feet icy and my head pounding, I knew that there was no way I was going to live at home and work in a school. But my choices were limited. My parents wanted to punish me, or educate me or however they'd phrase it. I might deserve it, but that didn't mean I wouldn't fight it. I had no money to go to London myself and look for work. I would have to ask for everything.

I tried to turn onto my side, but changed my mind when the room started spinning. I thought back to what I'd said to Kit. I was only half joking. I would go. I would go for him, but I would go for me too. A million miles away from home.

That sounded good.

4

We managed to squeeze in a quick engagement drink in London before Kit left. His advice had come by letter after a few weeks: 'Soap, shampoo, washing powder, lady items, tea towels. Learn temperatures in centigrade. And bring lots of things to read – empty the library.' It wasn't the most exciting advice, but I hoped that it was down to my love of books rather than an absence of anything else to do when I got there.

My copies of Dostoyevsky were first in the pile. I thought about *War and Peace*, again. It would keep me busy, but maybe there were more modern Russian novels that would give me a better understanding of where I was going.

Kit often referred to my stock of books as 'the library', yet it gave me the idea to look for some new ones. I walked down to the library in town. It was sunny but still cold, even for March. I would have to start thinking about what I wore a lot more carefully, my mother kept saying. 'It won't be funny when you freeze to death.' Only, her saying that did make it sound funny.

The library wasn't as useful as I'd hoped, although the librarian did her best. I was shown a copy of a new poetry collection, *Stolen Apples* by Yevtushenko, and wrote it down on my list to order from Foyles. Ideally, I would have travelled into London and browsed in person, but I still wasn't trusted to travel alone. All the librarian's other suggestions were Chekhov, Pasternak, Tolstoy, Pushkin and Dostoyevsky. All a bit old and classic, but I wrote them down.

I had a quick look on the shelves for awkwardly spelt names. Not for the first time, I thought back to the beautiful university library and the comprehensive knowledge of the stern librarians. My favourite, her blonde hair bobbed, always seemed to give me the very book I didn't know I wanted, and which turned out to be crucial.

The librarian here was arguing with an elderly man over whether he was allowed to take more books out when he hadn't paid his fine.

He waggled his finger at her. 'I didn't fight the Nazis just so you could stop me using the library, young woman.'

'You didn't fight the Nazis, Mr Blake, you went to Ireland to work on a farm.'

'I never did,' he said, but his voice was unsure now. 'I was at Passchendaele.'

'That's the wrong war. So, this eight pence that you owe?'

The last twenty-eight years were clearly a blur for him, or longer. Maybe he'd made up so many stories about where he'd been and what he'd done in the war that he honestly couldn't remember. Most people knew exactly what had happened and where they had been. I'd been born in 1953, but David had been born seven years earlier, in 1946, and remembered rationing. It felt a million years ago now, but it wasn't. Our father had stayed in London, but whenever the war was mentioned he clenched his teeth. I'd never know why. He wasn't the kind of man you could just ask.

The librarian put two more books on the table, and made me jump.

She spoke quickly, a little out of breath, one eye on Mr Blake. 'I knew there was another. Bulgakov. However, I would check whether these are OK to take because *The Master and Margarita* is only published in a censored version, and *The Heart of a Dog* is banned.'

'In Russia?'

'Yes. That is where you're going, isn't it?'

I nodded. Everyone knew, it seemed. 'Thanks.'

She went back to her desk. Mr Blake was by the doors, looking confused.

'I think you're right. I should read these now, rather than take them with me.' I took my library card from my bag and she stamped them for me.

'There are non-fiction books on Russia too. Geography, sociology, politics. When do you leave?' she asked.

'Next month,' I said, still surprised by her interest.

'Don't forget to return them.'

I didn't forget. In fact, I went back and consulted the other books she'd mentioned. I read about the economy and the politics, how the party elite was rewarded and those with an aristocratic background punished. I read about dachas, the summer chalets, which rewarded the good communists, and the many people slaughtered by Stalin on a whim, or sent to the Siberian gulags to die a little more slowly. I was almost sidetracked by a book on Rasputin, but forced myself back to Soviets.

The librarian came over to me in the history section, holding out a thin booklet.

'I think you left this on the table the other day,' she said. 'It was where you were sitting.'

'Thanks.' I took the booklet. *The Wolf Sleigh* by E. V. Mann. It had seven very short stories, and a tiny paragraph inside the front cover: 'E. V. Mann has lived in Russia for over twenty years, working as a literary translator. This debut contains modern fairy tales from the land of the bear.' Hardly a book, I thought, but I checked to make a note of the ISBN. There wasn't one. No publisher either, just a plain, stapled card cover.

I took it back to my table near the window, where there was a small pile of books. I sat down next to it, feeling the heat of the sun much more through the glass than I had on the walk over. I flicked through the stories. They looked interesting, but it wasn't mine. It wasn't a library book either. I closed it and placed my hands on top, and then slipped it into my handbag. I would read it at home and then return it. I felt the urgent spring heat and wondered when spring would arrive in Moscow.

I was accidentally learning my first Russian, and how good friends would talk 'soul to soul' – 'dusha v dushu'. I wondered how I'd slip that into conversation. And how did all the mentions of the Russian soul fit in with the destruction of churches? There were pictures of an enormous cathedral on the Moskva river, white with gold cupolas, that Stalin had knocked down for a palace. When that didn't get built, they turned the space into an outdoor swimming pool. I could track how things changed, but I found it hard to understand why. From cathedral to swimming pool. It wasn't what I'd expected to learn. I compared pictures of Leningrad to Moscow and tried not to wish I was going to Leningrad.

By the end, I felt more prepared. Leonid Brezhnev was in charge, and things were pretty stable. People had money, if little to buy, free education and health, zero inflation, no unemployment and no crime. Supposedly. But every country cooked their statistics, and I suspected there were many people in the US who would be grateful for free medicines, as long as they didn't have a hammer and sickle printed on them.

I had a better idea of where I was going, but less of an idea about what I was going to do there. I'd read about British diplomats and journalists, but they were all men. They'd brought their families with them. But what did their wives do if they didn't have children to raise? I was starting to have doubts that I would fit in.

My university trunk, still with my father's initials engraved on top, was sent on to Moscow three weeks ahead. I always wondered whether I had been given his initials to save on brass plaques. It felt odd knowing that the likelihood was I'd still get to Moscow before it did. My books were inside, but no Bulgakov. Just in case. The rest of the room was taken up by bathroom and kitchen supplies, and my woollen winter coat, scarf, gloves and a pair of boots.

My suitcase held two sweaters, two skirts, one pair of jeans, my cotton dress, a jacket, a notebook and some pens, as well as a couple more books. Kit had enclosed in one of his letters a list of clothing and emphasised natural, breathable fabric. I'd shown it to Ma. She'd taken the nylon blouses back to Marks. I put two cotton ones and a T-shirt back in, and I sent a little blessing to Kit. I hated nylon, and had no money to buy my own clothes.

He didn't have a phone yet, so we had a strangely formal engagement, letters full of endearments which made me snigger and Ma smile. I had a horrible feeling that Kit had asked for my hand, or some rubbish like that, because she was very happy about it all. I knew that Kit had had a long chat with Pa, supposedly getting his blessing but, more likely, Pa filling him in on my multiple failings and the great sin of pride. Pa had connections, ripe for extricating errant daughters from police charges, and probably knew exactly what Kit's job was. As there was nothing outside the local paper about the protest, I suspected that he wouldn't be telling anyone else at the office, but his sense of fairness meant he had to tell my husband-to-be. Which still sounded weird.

David knocked on my open bedroom door, and closed it behind him. He kicked the suitcase with his foot.

'So, you're really going ahead with this?'

'Yep.'

He sat on my bed, and sighed. 'Martha, I have to tell you that he's gay.'

'I know.' I sat next to him. 'I fancied him when I was twelve, but he fancied you.'

David looked surprised. 'Did he?'

I backtracked. 'No, not really. But I have known for a long time.'

David shook his head. 'It's not right. You're fooling our parents, and his parents. You know they put an announcement in *The Telegraph*? They're nice people, Martha. And his job. If anyone found out, he'd be in terrible trouble. They could blackmail him or extort information. You really don't want to end up in a Russian prison. An English one would have been bad enough. Your judgement is always a bit off.'

I folded my arms and tried to remember that I wouldn't be seeing David for months.

'That's a bit unfair. David, I haven't pushed him into this. I like him and I think we'll get on. I'm excited about going to Russia, and it's a posting. It's not forever. We can always get divorced if we want different things. That could happen with any marriage. Right now, he's in a dangerous position whether he's married or not. I don't mind being part of keeping him safe.'

'Don't you think he'll take more risks if he thinks he can hide behind this stupid marriage?'

'No. We trust each other, and he's had time to get used to Moscow and set the scene. It's going to be great.'

David stood up. 'OK. Well, I had to say it. What time does he get to Heathrow?'

I looked at my watch. 'About an hour. His parents are collecting him and booking into the hotel. They're having dinner here, and you're going out, aren't you?'

'Yes, I have to meet the others from the train and then we're off for his last night of freedom.' He smiled weakly. 'Ma and Pa are happy, at least. If they were going to pick anyone for you, it would probably have been Kit. Right parents, right kind of job. They seem to have persuaded themselves that it was all their idea in the first place.'

'I know. Everyone is happy, I think. It will work because we like each other.'

'I do hope it works. I just want you both back safe.'

I jumped up, hugged him and then stood back, arms at my side. 'The last time we hugged was probably ten years ago.'

'Ah well, we can hug again when I get married.'

'You're twenty-seven. You can't wait that long.' I hesitated. 'You'll write, won't you?'

'Have I ever written to you?'

'We don't have a phone yet.'

'You'll just have to come back to visit.'

I watched him open the door and give a little wave. My eyes filled and I realised for the first time how much I would miss him. Even Ma and Pa. A clean break, a tiny wedding for close family only, and then I'd be off. It wasn't a day I'd dreamt of and planned for, but still. And it was saving me from my probable future of frustrated teacher, living at home until some dull man took sympathy.

I could have walked down to the library for the last time and called Harriet from the phone box. I didn't. I tried to justify it to myself as the wrong time, now I had to focus on other things. But I knew it was just guilt that stopped me calling. I had something wonderful to do, and I was pretty sure that she wouldn't be in the same position.

I put the strap of the suitcase through the buckle and pulled it tight. My stolen pamphlet of short stories was on the bed, ready to go in my handbag. The librarian had never mentioned it again, and neither had I. A little piece of Russia to take back to its home.

5

Perhaps we should have felt guilty, but neither of us had any remorse about standing in my small local church and telling lies, probably because neither of us saw this as something real and legal and binding. Our parents already seemed to know each other, or just slipped into that pretence of doing so. I'd been over to meet his parents a couple of times while he was away, so at least they weren't complete strangers. They seemed surprised by the marriage, but pleased. His mother had bought an enormous pink hat, and it seemed she was determined to wear it throughout the meal.

We introduced each other to the couple of grandparents left between us and shook hands with a few people both of our fathers knew, but we didn't, and everyone posed as some photos were taken. That was it. We were married.

As we walked back to the house, I heard one of the older women commenting on the wedding. 'Not even a flower girl,' she said, 'let alone a veil. And the dress.' I intended to dye it, a simple tea dress, to wear it again.

In the living room, David and Kit's sister, Olivia, both highly disapproving in a reserved way, carefully avoided the subject of the wedding, despite their roles as best man and chief bridesmaid. Instead, they talked about Moscow and how Kit found it.

'It's warming up a bit now, but the snow was a bit of a shock to the system.'

'That's what I'm most looking forward to,' I said. 'Is it still there?'

'No, we've had the thaw and tons of slushy mud. It was unbelievably cold in January, and the wind is a whole other thing. Stop looking all excited, Martha, it's hard!'

'I know, I know.'

Ma clapped her hands. 'Shall we go through?'

I had no idea what the meal would be. Ma had chosen the flowers, the food and the guests. I didn't mind and she was trying to pretend I would be missed. As long as no one brought up Cambridge, she'd be happy.

The chicken in wine sauce was served. Cook's staple for mass catering. It could have been worse.

My father was on my left and Kit's mother next to him. I let them get on with it while I tried to work out who the other people were. I'd been introduced when we shook hands on entering the house, but the names meant very little. My father had always worked in Cheltenham, driving down the A40 every day, and it struck me that I didn't really know what he did. I was sure I must have asked him at some point. Somewhere with lots of posh men, it seemed, who all greeted him as Brigadier. I heard him address them, Mr Ellis, Mr Cocks, Mr Williamson, but had no idea who was who.

One of them leaned around his wife to speak to my brother. 'Well done on your job, David. I keep meaning to call in on you when I'm in London. Maybe we could have lunch one day.'

His wife muttered, 'Not a liquid lunch. You know what the doctor said.'

They started to bicker quietly, and I leaned backwards to catch David's eye. He was too grown up to join in. I sighed and went back to my meal. My mother was giving Kit instructions on how best to hand wash clothes in the bath.

'There are no laundrettes?' I asked.

'You can technically get things dry cleaned,' he said, 'but you have to remove all the buttons first. And then, of course, you can't buy needles and thread.'

'You can take some with you this time,' my mother said. 'Martha can sew them back on for you.'

I said, 'And darn his socks?'

'If necessary.' My mother leaned closer to Kit. 'She will claim not to know how to do this kind of thing, but I assure you she can.'

'Can you write me a list of her skills?' said Kit. 'I wouldn't want to feel I hadn't got my money's worth.'

My mother smiled. 'Very funny.'

The plates were taken and dessert arrived. Eton mess. My favourite. All of a sudden, I became a bit tearful. Why was I doing this?

My father took my hand and squeezed it.

'It's a long way,' I said.

'Nowhere is that far, nowadays. I'm sure your mother will write and tell you all the news.'

'You could write.'

'I'm not one for letters.' He squeezed my hand again and let go. 'Eat up. You might not see fresh fruit again for a while.' He broke the meringue with his spoon. 'I've assured everyone that you're going to behave.'

I stiffened, glaring at him. Why would my father have to make assurances about my behaviour? Who would he make them to?

'This is Kit's future you're stepping into, a fresh start for you. He's a nice chap and you'll be happier with him than you are here. He'll be kind, if nothing else.'

I blinked back sudden tears, and looked to see if Kit was listening, but my mother had his ear.

'What do you mean, you assured everyone?' I said, but my father was dinging on the glass and standing to make his speech. Kit turned to me and smiled, eyebrows raised. We've done it, he seemed to say, we've fooled them all. But I didn't think we'd quite fooled everyone.

'We Run'

by

E. V. MANN

I hear the howling at night. It wakes me sometimes. I think, I must speak to them. They should know that these apartments are too small to leave a dog in for long. But no one has heard of anyone getting a dog.

I walk through the snow to the Metro, feed my hard coins into the metal machine and take my ticket. I find myself thinking, oh, I must get two, but, of course, there isn't anyone else. I look behind me, just to check. Yes, on my own, as usual.

Over time, I get used to the feeling of company, hold the door open at work just a little longer than it takes me to get inside. I pick food off my plate and hold it, wondering what I was going to do with it, before slowly eating it and licking my fingers. I murmur things, not quite to myself.

I work, I eat, I sleep. Same as ever.

One night after work, instead of getting on the Metro, I walk to the park. I sit on a bench near the boating pond, hunched over for warmth, but the cold is settled so deep it doesn't help. Behind me, the sun is setting, casting a glow on the windows in the grey building opposite.

It's on fire, I whisper. The people don't know, but they're

all going to perish and blow away in the night. I look at the pond, and I know I have to find a deeper one.

Then there is movement at my side and I see it. Startled, I can't move. My heart, already beating in panic, starts to hurt. The wolf just looks at the pond, and the last boy trying to get his boat out with a long stick. There are other cold people on benches, trying not to go home. No one else notices the wolf.

I'm just imagining it, I think, but I see its fur move as it breathes and I smell it, pungent, overwhelming. It smells both death-bearing and full of life, beyond my imagination.

Maybe it doesn't know I'm here. I push myself along the bench with my frozen hands, away from the teeth and the fur, but it looks so warm and soft. Now the sun has almost used up the last of its heat and my fists hurt with the cold.

The wolf turns to me. 'Eva, I am with you,' he says.

I think then, I've gone mad. Too long by myself. People were right to talk about me.

I stand, a little unsteadily, and walk towards the Metro station. I don't look around. I can feel him by my side, smell his warmth and hear the panting. As I walk, my shoulders straighten and fall back. People move for me. My steps become a stride. I arrive at the station entrance and I don't want to go inside, I don't want to stop.

I look down at my wolf and he looks up at me with cool, blue eyes. I hold my hand to his muzzle. He licks it, lets me run my fingers over his skull, through the heat of the universe. He yawns, showing his teeth, and I nod. I have always heard the howling.

I take off my shoes and coat, roll up my trousers, and we run.

6

Sheremetyevo Airport had the most bizarre observation building, a pillar which looked as if it supported a giant UFO on top.

'It's beautiful,' I said.

'Really?' Kit checked to see if we were looking at the same thing. 'It looks like a sombrero. If you're impressed by that, then you're mad.'

'How can you not love it?'

Kit shrugged. 'OK. Soviet modernism has a new fan.' He smiled. 'I must say, I've been worrying about what you were going to like about this place, but maybe it's a great fit.'

My high hopes for architectural wonder had been dulled by the fact that the interior of the airport stank of cigarettes. Not normal cigarettes, like Kit's Players, but something more pungent, acrid. Kit noticed my expression.

'They're called papirosy, filterless and pretty foul. Half of it is empty card, but they like smoking them in Russia for some reason. You'll have to get used to the smell.'

We collected our suitcases and Kit took mine from me. I hoped this was an act, rather than him taking the husband idea too seriously.

A short woman was shouting, 'Line up! Against the wall!'
Our planeload shuffled as close as it could while some passengers, better ones, were ushered past us and out. Some passengers shouted back in Russian.

'This bit takes ages,' said Kit.

We shuffled forward while the customs officers went through the baggage of all but the lucky ones, sifting through books and clothes and, in one case, removing the entire person for a more thorough examination.

'Does that happen a lot?' I murmured. I didn't want to be examined. I didn't know what they would make of the washing up liquid, dishcloths and selection of plugs that Kit had pushed into my suitcase.

'Don't worry,' said Kit, but I could see he did worry. Now I worried whether I'd brought the wrong books, bad ones, by accident.

When it was our turn, we were separated, with our suitcases. I tried to look unconcerned, knowing that I had assumed the sweaty, fearful appearance of a smuggler. The officer's hands turned over the kitchen and bathroom supplies, flicked through my books and the Mann booklet, pulled clothes and underwear onto the table. That booklet, it wasn't right, was it? I'd only read a few pages of the stories, but it was critical, undermining, dangerous. My hands started to shake.

'Go!'

I felt I had escaped sentencing despite being guilty.

I followed Kit through the airport doors, where a man in a checked shirt and baggy grey trousers left the pillar he was leaning against and nodded. Kit handed him the cases.

'Martha, this is Pyotr. He's our driver.'

'Hello.'

He nodded.

'He doesn't speak English,' said Kit. He let Pyotr walk ahead and then more quietly, 'They don't like them to speak English when they work with foreigners.'

'So why are you being quiet?'

'I'm not totally sure that he doesn't understand English, even if he doesn't speak it.'

'And how is your Russian coming on?'

'Otlichno.'

'Excellent. I assume.'

We had reached the outer doors. I was surprised it was still daylight; everything seemed to have taken so long.

'Ready?' said Kit.

I did my coat up and we walked through.

'It feels the same temperature as at home,' I said.

'Today, that is true. You've got until winter to say that.'

Pyotr opened the door of a black limousine.

'This is a bit posh, isn't it?'

'He is our driver and this is our car.'

Kit looked at me strangely and I thought, oh, this is one of those moments. Our journey began with me reviewing all of the warnings he'd given me on safe ground. Don't ask questions in public. Don't start conversations as you may get people into trouble for talking to you. Equally, remember that if they're not suspicious of you, you need to be suspicious of them. Everything on paper is of interest to someone. You may think that you don't know anything, but you're wrong. Don't assume that because we are alone no one can hear us. I had thought he was just saying what he'd been told to say, but now I could see he believed it. I found myself reviewing what I was going to say before I said it.

'Do we get the tourist route?' I asked.

He smiled, and I was relieved I hadn't messed up.

'You'll see some of it.'

We got in the car and drove away from the airport. Kit talked.

'OK, so this is Gorky Street, and we're about to hit the ring road. The zoo and US embassy are over to the right, theatre, theatre, theatre, on the left the Kremlin.'

We drove past the high, red walls, and over a bridge.

He pointed left, 'The embassy is down there.'

Then another bridge.

'Where's St Basil's?'

'Back the other side of the Kremlin.'

I could barely believe that I would see the domes: red, gold, green, white, blue, zigzags and ice cream swirls, stippled and criss-crossed, like an edible house in a fairy tale.

'Can you go in?' I asked.

'Yes, it's a museum. The opening hours can be flexible, so you may need to go more than once to get in.'

'This is amazing.' I found Kit's hand and squeezed it. He smiled at me and checked Pyotr's reflection in the rear-view mirror.

A man started crossing in front of our car, and I grabbed onto Kit's arm as Pyotr seemed to speed up. The man just looked at us speeding towards him, and Pyotr had to swerve, beeping, at the last moment.

Kit patted my hand. 'It's one of the strictest driving tests in the world. Safer than it seems.' He changed the subject. 'This is Gorky Park on the right, and our apartment is down this road, about six miles. But they use kilometres here. This is Lenin Avenue, in Russian Leninsky Prospekt. They use it for parades, important events like Castro's visit. This,' he pointed again at another park, 'is named after Yuri Gagarin.'

'There are so many parks.' The road was wide, but it had a green strip down the middle which softened it. Regular blocks of five storey apartments were made attractive by the angling and the space between them, all green and full of flower beds. A large furniture shop sat in its own green space.

'We've just had Lenin's birthday, where everyone has the day off to clean and beautify their environment. Some of the flowers won't last much longer, but it's nice for a while.'

'There's so much space. I imagined everything to be much more cramped.'

'Well,' Kit searched for the right words, 'there are a lot of things which aren't here any more. And they're spreading right out in a giant circle. We are almost on the edge of the city.'

I looked at him. He was nervous. I wanted to phone David and say, he's definitely not a spy. We'd never spoken about it, but the way David spoke about Kit's job, I'd just thought he was putting speech marks around 'secretary'.

The car drove through a gateway, past a guard in a small security hut, and pulled up outside an apartment block.

'This is us,' said Kit.

'Why is there a guard?'

'A militiaman. For our security, of course,' Kit said tersely.

I should have waited with that question. I got out of the car. It was one tall, grey tower block of a group of three. Around us, other giant buildings were finished and some still being constructed from concrete slabs. Grey towers in their own empty spaces.

'Not quite as impressed by this architecture?' said Kit.

'Um, no. What floor are we on?'

'The eighteenth. Don't worry, they have lifts.'

Kit picked up the bags, said something to Pyotr, and led the way. The entrance hall felt airtight once the door had closed behind us and he called for the lift. It came straight away and we got in. I held my hand to my nose.

'It always smells of cabbage, I'm afraid. You get used to it. But, to be honest, we struck lucky with the apartment. It belonged to an American journalist and he had a kitchen shipped over from Finland. Unfortunately, he sold the oven when he left. You'd be amazed at how many of the people here get by with little hot plates for years. And concrete floors instead of lino. But I warned you it was small.'

'I remember.' I was looking at the lights showing which floor we were on. The smell was more than cabbage, there was a vinegary element too. It was feeling real for the first time. A bit late, maybe. How long could we pretend we were married? Even friends fell out.

The eighteenth floor. The doors slid open and Kit turned left along the corridor. Third door along.

'Ready?'

I nodded. He put one of the suitcases down, opened the door and gestured for me to go inside. I took a step forward. It was dark. He flicked a switch and a single bulb lit the hallway.

'Two cupboards on your left,' he said, 'and then the bathroom and then the toilet. The kitchen is ahead.' He put the suitcases down and closed the front door.

I walked through and opened the door. The light streamed in and I finally breathed out. Ten-foot square, it had a fridge, an electric hot plate with two rings, and cupboards, as well as a small table by the window.

'No oven, as I said, but you didn't strike me as the cooking type. I tend to eat a big work lunch, so I've never needed to cook much in the evening. Natalya tends to leave me things I can heat up.'

'God, Kit, I was beginning to think there were no windows. Why did you leave all the doors closed?'

'That was Natalya. She always does that.'

'Oh, she has a key?'

'Of course. She's the housekeeper. The other rooms are through here.' He went back to the hall and opened another door. A large room, maybe fifteen-foot square, had been painted cream and I realised how brown the rest of the apartment was. There were books on shelves and a record player on a sideboard next to a rocket-shaped money box made of tin. A large poster on the back wall, over the dark green 1930s style sofa, showed a man and a dog in helmets, who both looked happily and confidently into space as a planet, an asteroid and Sputnik filled the darkness behind them. Two armchairs faced each other, and there was a small pine desk near the window.

'This is lovely.' I walked into the centre of the room. 'And a balcony?'

'Yes.' He walked ahead and opened the door. 'The height means we should be quite protected from the mosquitos. I hear they're a bit of a problem in the summer. You can take the chair out here if you want to sit. It means that you can't see anything.' He crouched down, as if sitting. 'But no one can see you either.'

Behind our building was a large pond, and behind that, up a slope, a small wood, half birch and half fir. The view to the centre was obstructed by large apartment blocks and giant cranes. Some buildings were grey, some yellow; one looked as if they had run out of grey brick and continued with yellow. The building on the left was still being constructed. A group of other buildings to the west had words stretched out over their roofs.

'What does that say?'

'Workers of all countries unite.' Kit smiled. 'Comrade.'

As we stood there, I heard the sound of glass breaking. I shivered.

43

'They break a lot of glass,' said Kit. 'They make it as thin as possible to save money and then it breaks. When it does get fixed in,' he pointed to the balcony door, 'it's very efficient. A double layer of glass keeps the heat in. And the sound.'

Until then, I'd forgotten the warnings and now all I could think of was people listening, and all the things I could say wrong.

'And the bedroom?' I asked.

'I'll show you that later. Right now, you choose a record to put on and I'll make some tea.'

I relaxed again. We could talk when the music was on. Kit had given me many instructions but I was feeling so tense and foreign that they were only coming back gradually. I flicked through his records and realised that, if I really knew him, I wouldn't have been surprised that they were all classical. I vaguely recalled liking Pachelbel at one point, and put that on. Ciacona in F minor. I closed my eyes and was instantly in a dark, cool church. I was reminded of Harriet. She had played this for me. It was too much.

I sat in one of the armchairs and pressed my fingers together in front of my mouth. Kit came in with two teacups.

'Are you praying?'

'Not yet. Is this a terrible mistake? You look so settled here. I don't think you need me at all.'

'I didn't think you were just coming for me.' He handed me a cup. 'I thought you wanted to come.'

'I did. I'm probably just a bit anxious.'

'You're overthinking things. As far as I'm concerned, we're good friends doing each other a favour while we do what we want to do.'

44

I drank my tea. 'You're right. So, what's the deal with the bedroom?'

'It's up to you. I had this wall put up to make one.' He pointed to the poster wall. 'There's no window, so it's a little like a monk's cell, and there's the sofa. I thought it would make more sense for you to have the bedroom as I'm out more, but it would work either way.'

'You can't sleep in here,' I said, and pointed at the windows. 'The light will keep you awake.'

'Ah, you can't buy curtains in Russia,' he said. 'There's a two-year waiting list, I heard. That's why my suitcase is mostly full of curtains with blackout powers.'

'You could make a fortune selling curtains.'

'I couldn't. No one can sell anything without being arrested for profiteering. You can get some excess crops from special markets, but that's it.'

'And I won't need any more money?'

'There's nothing to buy, darling.' Kit came over and knelt next to me. 'If I found a nice man, I couldn't bring him here, so you won't be getting in the way. The people at work want to meet you, and that's the limit of their interest. You get to spend some time here, you can go back to England whenever you like. Some wives just don't get on with Russia, and it won't surprise anyone. This will work for as long as it does, and then we'll both do something else. OK?'

'OK.'

'So, you take the bedroom, put your clothes in the drawers, have a nap or a bath or whatever, and we'll go out for dinner.'

I threw my arms around his neck and he hugged me back.

'It's all right to feel different here. It has a funny effect on people. I like it. Some don't. It's not the end of the world either way.'

'OK. So, what is the guard really for?' I whispered.

'Oh, to stop Russians coming in and to keep track of us. Nothing terrible.'

I let go of his neck. A bath and a rest and it would all be exciting again.

I woke up in the dark with panic gripping me. I didn't know if it was day or night, where I was or where I should be. I heard a noise from behind the wall and started to remember. It's Kit. I'm in Moscow. It's OK.

I pulled the blanket from me and edged my legs out of the bed. They felt leaden, as if I'd run all the way here. I rubbed my face and stood up, then edged my way to the handle and opened the door. Now I could see the room, I remembered that I had thought the chest wasn't going to fit. The bed was pushed along the wall which ran along the hallway outside the apartment, next to the drawers which held a mirror and a lamp. A further, taller set of drawers was hidden behind the door when it was opened. There was hardly room to walk to the bed. Maybe we could use the chest for a coffee table, I thought, and yawned.

Kit was drinking tea in the kitchen.

'There's enough water for you,' he said. He pointed at what looked like a silver trophy.

'Thank you. What is it?'

'It's an electric samovar, but it's basically a kettle.' He got a cup, put a teabag in and turned the small tap on the front of the samovar to pour the water.

'That's so clever.'

I joined him at the window, looking out into the dusk. The forest looked thick with night already. I remembered his little phrase from before, at home.

'Between dog and wolf,' I said. 'Or wolf and dog.'

'Let's go out with the wolves.'

I noticed that he had changed and looked fresh. I looked down at my creased skirt and blouse. Ma had persuaded me to 'dress like a respectable grown up for a change', in case there were any upgrades going. There weren't.

'Do I need to get dressed?'

'No, you're fine.'

I drank my tea and he finished his.

'Pyotr should be there,' he said.

'So, whenever we go out, the car takes us?'

'We pay, of course. They like to know where we are, and it makes life easier. It's all arranged through the embassy, and the foreigners' service, UPDK, like Natalya.'

Natalya, the housekeeper, whom I would meet the next day. The thought made me nervous. I expected her to see right through our pretence and tell everyone. She must have got to know Kit a bit, even if it was just by going through his things. Three days a week, she bought the shopping with the coupons foreigners got to spend in special foreigners' shops, took the sheets to wash, and cooked small meals for him to reheat. With such a small fridge, it wasn't possible to go just once a week, or maybe she didn't want to carry too much.

Kit put the cup down. 'Let's go.'

The Metropol was a strange introduction to Moscow, full of talkative foreigners and silent Russians. I hadn't believed Kit when he told me you could see the difference, but you could. The Russian men were all slightly the wrong shape for their rumpled jackets, or vice versa. The Russian women wore muted dresses: dark blue, brown and grey; and sometimes dark skirts with white blouses. They all looked like the same shapeless pattern, just with variations on sleeve length, and skirts just above the knee. When they lifted their faces, their make-up was bright and child-like, blue eyeshadow and red lipstick, red cheeks, like dolls.

The clothes of foreigners were too bright and their voices too loud, their faces plain.

The waiter escorted us to a small table for two and presented us with large menus. I hung my jacket on the back of the chair, then flicked through. 'Four languages?'

'There are a lot of foreigners here,' said Kit. 'I was here until I got allocated an apartment. Each floor has its own dezhurnaya, like a little old lady minder, and a small shop for the long-term residents. I met some interesting people.'

I looked around. The tables weren't so close that it would be easy to listen to us, but each of them had people talking to each other. 'So, we're OK here? To talk?'

'Martha, you're going to drive yourself mad if you keep thinking about things like that. That's for me to worry about.' He smiled. 'What signal would you like me to give if we need to be careful?'

'Just kick me,' I said. 'Don't try to be subtle.'

'Trial run?' he said. He put his menu on the table and leaned back.

'No, I'll wait.'

He was right. I was overthinking things again. Everything I'd ever heard about Russia, without even being aware of it, had been circling in my head. Parades of guns and rockets, the tales of Siberia and starvation and murder.

'What do you usually have?' I asked.

'When the waiter comes back, I'll ask him to point out what they actually have in. Whenever I choose from the menu, they don't have it. I started to take it personally until I realised that the menu is more of a wish list. It can take an hour for them to take the order, and then half an hour

48

later you'll find they don't have what you ordered. Quite maddening.'

'Ah.' I put my menu down too and began to look around the bright room. The stained glass ceiling was two storeys high, lit by enormous upside-down chandeliers mounted on slender pillars, an extravagance I'd assumed had been destroyed in the revolution. I gazed at the green and grey floor-to-ceiling stained glass window and wondered how it would look in the daytime. I'd assumed that old Russia had been erased and replaced with utilitarian concrete blocks, so I was struck, for the second time today, by the playful beauty of Moscow, enhanced by the sense that it was clearly fading like a great lady. The gold paint had peeled off the sweeping coving, and the fabric of the chairs had worn through. The chandeliers, created with rings of different sized bulbs, had some which needed replacing. But the height and the swell of the room was still there, right over the marble fountain in the centre, and the colour of the glass canopy was clear, even at night.

The waiter returned. Kit spoke to him in Russian, and translated for me.

'Beef fillet or sturgeon?'

'The fish please.'

'And wine or vodka?'

I laughed. 'Wine tonight, I think.'

The waiter left.

'I'm going to have to learn some Russian,' I said.

'Oh, they speak English here, but I asked him to speak Russian as I need the practice. I've already asked UPDK to sort a teacher out for you.'

'So, whatever services you want, they'll find something? It's a great idea.'

'It just matches people like us up with the right people.' Kit raised his eyebrows.

I leaned across to whisper. 'I thought you said it was OK to talk here.'

Kit whispered back. 'It is, but you're so jumpy and you don't even have anything to feel guilty about. I thought if I said "spy on us", you'd be weird.'

I immediately looked at our neighbouring tables.

'See?' Kit rolled his eyes. 'Listen, we might have to wait an hour for our food. Let's talk about good old England and drink some wine, yeah?'

I rolled my shoulders to relax them. 'Sorry. I had no idea I was so uncool.'

'It's no surprise to me, darling.'

I kicked his leg.

'Don't abuse the secret code.'

Kit looked around. 'There are so many people who were on the same aeroplane as us.'

I looked. I recognised nobody. I needed to be much more observant.

Dinner was OK. I'd had better, but I'd never spent so long eating. After the cabbage soup, there were cheeses, then the main course, the sturgeon having been cooked in mushrooms and sour cream, and then stewed fruit and coffee. All of it just slightly overcooked. The wine was good, though, and I'd relaxed a little too much. The food, wine, flight, fierce lighting and tension had all done their work.

'You didn't warn me to pace myself. It's the size of a Christmas dinner.'

'I suppose. There's a lovely Chinese restaurant at the Peking Hotel. We can go there another time, but they do Russian sizes too.'

Kit had spotted a colleague dining with his wife earlier, and told me their names, which I promptly forgot. They came past our table as they were leaving and I tried to hide how drunk I was, resolving to keep my mouth shut.

'Charlie,' the man said as he shook my hand. He pressed a little too hard on my palm with his thumb, like a message. 'This is my wife, Alison. We've been dying to meet you.'

'And now I'm here,' I said, smiling too much and killing the conversation dead.

Charlie turned to speak quietly to Kit, and Alison drifted just out of earshot. She looked pale and tired, at the end of a long night. I forced myself to stop staring at her and looked around at the other tables. It was gone ten, and most of them had emptied. There was a lone woman dining at a nearby table, and she seemed to defy my nationality guessing. She wore a simple brown dress (Russian) but with a purple felt hat with ribbons on (British). She was older, maybe sixty, and reading a book as she ate with the free hand.

I thought, if I went to the toilet, I might get a glimpse at the book, but the route would have been so obviously to do that, I might as well have just asked her.

Charlie and Kit had finished talking. They both looked at the woman in the purple hat, and then Kit nodded. I turned back to her. She seemed to be smiling at her book.

'So, we'll see you next week, then,' Charlie said to me. We shook hands again and they left. I slumped back in my chair.

'I'm knackered,' I said. 'Where am I seeing them?'

'We're going to dinner at their apartment.'

I yawned. 'Do all the foreigners eat here?'

'No, there are lot of restaurants.'

'That was a coincidence then, bumping into them.'

Kit put on a Russian accent and said, 'In Russia, there is no such thing as a coincidence.'

'Is that from the Moscow rules?'

He looked at me strangely. 'Where did you hear about those?'

I thought. '*From Russia with Love*, maybe.'

He laughed. 'Oh, Fleming? No, that was *Goldfinger.*'

'You read Fleming?'

He flushed a little. 'I used to. A long time ago.' He signalled to the waiter to pay. 'Of course, those rules allow for the second time being a coincidence, and the third time is the suspicious one. I think they're a bit lax, personally.'

I looked around again. The woman in the hat had gone.

'I'm cured of my paranoia. Or, maybe I'm just drunk.'

'Lovely, darling. Let's go home.'

He stood and picked up my jacket to help me into it. I'd adjusted to the temperature and it no longer felt too much.

'I love this room. Moscow is wonderful.'

'This is a delightful room,' he said. 'You'll have fun finding all the beautiful bits, I'm sure.'

He held out his elbow and I slid my arm into his. In the lobby, I pulled him to the lift to look at the seven panels of delicate stained glass flowers.

'I wish I'd brought a camera. Do you think I'd be able to get one?'

'No, I don't think so. They sell some in the foreign shops, but they aren't any good.'

'Can you take me to a foreign shop tomorrow?' I asked.

'No. It's Sunday. Back to work for me tomorrow.'

'That was a short honeymoon. I'm going to be a terrible housewife, you know.'

Kit kissed my forehead. 'I wouldn't have it any other way.'

Just before we got to the door, he stopped.

'I want you to enjoy it here, Martha, but I don't want you to be deceived. There's a reason I put that poster up.'

I thought of the poster, man and dog, dreaming of the stars. 'The astronaut?'

'Cosmonaut. It's to remind me that I'm dealing with the kind of bastards that would shoot a dog into space to die. If it's beautiful here, it's for show. For every palace for the people, there's a gulag in Siberia. Don't forget what they're hiding.'

I shuddered, suddenly sober. 'Understood,' I said.

'And no camera, OK? There aren't any camera films, in any case. We'll find you something fun.'

I nodded, but felt that this huge world, which had been open to me, was closing down.

In the car, Pyotr silently driving, I thought of how we'd giggled in bed on our wedding night, remembering the happy faces of our parents who all thought that they'd got shot of a troublesome child, their relief that convention had won out and happiness and stability were ahead.

I looked at Kit's profile. His eyes were closed, his mouth fixed. Was he regretting it? I hadn't come here to create more stress for him. I would take the next few days to find my feet and behave. I might even develop a Russian soul.

7

The chest arrived ten days late, which Kit assured me was a bloody miracle, so I applied myself to placing everything around my small room. Clothes in the drawers, books on top of the drawers. It felt like I was starting a new term at university in a windowless room. I realised that buying a new lightbulb might be tricky, so I tried to leave the light off when I could.

I poked around the flat. I looked at the view. I wondered at the electric samovar, resolved to get one back to Britain somehow, and drank too much tea. I read a bit and wondered why Kit didn't have a phone. Or a TV. I had grown fond of the schools programming during my workless months waiting to come here, and I knew they would seem equally odd to a Russian viewer. Or maybe not, being a kind of communal learning with pupils all over the country learning together. The more I thought about it, the more Soviet it seemed. Still, it would have been useful to immerse myself in TV and pick out words. I fiddled with the radio, but I couldn't find the shortwave BBC World Service that Kit had mentioned.

Kit had expected me to accompany him to ballets and

operas, but nothing had been arranged yet. I knew the Bolshoi Ballet was world famous and I'd regret it if I didn't go. I went through Kit's books again. History, geography and politics that I wasn't quite in the mood for.

I went through the small fridge in the kitchen and the cupboards but, unless Natalya had been shopping, there was little in there. She arrived three mornings a week, the time depending on how long she'd spent queuing in the commission shops. They weren't as bad as the shops for Russians, and she was allowed to do this because Kit left out the hard currency vouchers for her to use. It seemed to go against the idea of communism, where everyone had the same, but foreigners were singled out as almost beyond hope. Strange guests, allowed to skip queues and buy rare items, but also expected to pay more for their privileges.

There were also Beriozkas, Birch Tree shops, which only foreigners could use. Some sounded like gift shops, with Matryoshka dolls and filigree glasses. It was all hypothetical to me as I found myself utterly unable to venture outside by myself. The fear of doing something wrong and embarrassing Kit was paralysing, and I exaggerated the slight cold I'd caught to explain it away to him.

I went back to the window and looked at the tops of the birch trees, just seeing some of the dappled white trunks and the pond below. I looked directly out to the north-east and knew that Siberia would send wind and snow, and I would see it all coming from here.

I sat on the sofa, looking at the man and the dog, ready for space. The kind of people who would kill dogs, Kit believed. I didn't know if we were much better.

I couldn't concentrate on reading anything. I got the biggest book from Kit's shelves and opened it to look at the photographs. One of Siberia struck me. It looked like early morning or evening, the windows of the simple cabin in the centre glowing bright orange from the fire within. A woman stood in the foreground, wrapped in furs, two rabbits hanging from one glove. Other than the window, the colours were cold, white snow still unshaken from black boughs, their shadows casting the snow blue. The forest which surrounded the cabin could have hidden anything – bears, wolves – and that woman, fur hood pulled low, would have known the tracks of each of them. Light was everywhere, in the sky, reflecting from the snow, illuminating the trees she would cut for her fire. I envied her mastery of the wilderness, knowing that I would last two hours before getting lost or eaten.

I did fear getting lost. I looked out of my window at the straight, wide rows and carefully spaced blocks of apartments and stretches of green leaves between them. The buildings were so similar, the trees masking any landmarks. Kit had told me that the city people still foraged in the bits of forest for mushrooms and berries, still loved the disordered nature of their wild spaces, however small.

I'd been out for a couple of short walks, but they felt aimless. All the interesting buildings were right in the centre and I wasn't ready for that. I wanted to see it all, but I feared that Moscow was not going to live up to the photographs in his books, and those I'd seen in the library, of rich churches and carved wood dachas. I was torn between my expectations and what I might find. I told myself that, but I wonder if it was really the thought of the militiaman guarding the building making notes about me that worried me most. Only, when I thought about it, I was excited. To be so dull and at the same time so interesting. Anything I did would be noted. Maybe I had performance anxiety.

I waited for Kit.

In fact, I'd been waiting for Kit for so long that the soup was in danger of evaporating away. He'd been so regular about coming home that, now he was late, I had to remind myself he'd warned me this would happen sometimes. A drink with Charlie, and work meals; things cropped up. But having him not come home made me feel vulnerable. I could hear people in the hallway, voices next door, footsteps above me. I put a record on and watched the sparrows settle in the birch trees.

8

I heard the banging in the kitchen and dressed quickly. It was Wednesday, I reminded myself. I needed some weekly structure to hold on to. I felt guilty if Natalya got here when I was still in bed, and I dressed quickly. She would know. I could tell she knew. I picked up my book and wandered into the kitchen, as if I'd been up for hours.

'Natalya Ivanovna, dobroe utro.' I said 'good morning' because I still couldn't make out the sounds of 'hello', let alone make it into words.

Natalya turned her beautiful face towards me and flicked on her thinnest smile. 'Marta,' she said, and nodded.

It was my Russian name, too close to Martha for anyone to make further changes. I wasn't going to argue with Natalya, or anyone else, about it.

'Kofe,' I said, but I pointed at the jar of coffee, in case. It was running low, but I needed coffee rather than tea this morning. Natalya loudly snatched the sweeper from the corner and sashayed through to the front room. Kit was using my chest to store his bedclothes, tipping them in on the weekdays when Natalya was here. Natalya probably had looked in there and knew exactly what was going on. I was supposed to stay around, keep an eye on her, but I hadn't yet been able to be up in time.

'Lots of couples sleep separately,' I'd said, and Kit shrugged.

'I suppose. It will just go on a file somewhere.' He looked resigned.

I wondered if I had a file yet.

I picked a mismatched cup and saucer from the shelf. Most of the things in the kitchen were hand-me-downs from ex-colleagues, chipped and loved. I was on strict orders to grab any new ones I saw, and Natalya was going to teach me to shop. I was too scared to arrange this with her.

'Is it that hard?' I'd asked.

'Wait and see,' said Kit. 'You have no idea.'

I took my coffee to the window, listening to Natalya's continual muttering as she swept the next room. I smiled, thinking that, when I learned Russian, I could spy on her for a change.

The wood below the window looked inviting in the sun, casting hard shadows on the scrubby grass. There were small patches of bare earth. The night before, Kit had pointed out where the flowers had all been torn up.

'Teenage hooligans,' said Kit. 'They spend all day drinking vodka in the forest.'

The militiaman on the door was supposed to keep them out of our building, but some of them lived here. There were important Russian families in with us foreigners. The guard was only there really to take notes on our Russian visitors, and to scare them off whenever possible.

I refilled my cup and took my book into the front room. Kit had left his scarf on the back of a chair. It was the one he'd been wearing last night when he came back smelling of papirosy and an aftershave that wasn't his. I folded it and placed it on the record player.

Natalya sniffed, smoothed down her apron, and went back to the kitchen. In her early twenties, she was slim, as if she hadn't succumbed to the pastry and bread diet of older Russian woman. I sat in the armchair and looked at the poster again. The kind of bastards who would kill dogs. The only Russian I had met was Natalya. She was grumpy, but not in a way that made me think she was untrustworthy around small animals. It could just be that she disliked that I couldn't speak Russian, so she talked to herself instead.

I looked at the chest. The tin money box Kit always placed on top was how it should be, the gaudy rocket pointing towards the ceiling.

The kitchen door slammed closed, and Natalya closed all the other doors to the hallway too.

'Proshchay,' she said, as she closed the door to the front room.

'Spasibo!' I shouted, but too late.

Pyotr waved at the guard on the gate and pulled up to let us out. We stood together as he drove away to park.

'What do you think he does while he's waiting?' I asked.

'He probably drinks. That's generally how they fill in spare time.' Kit looked at the building numbers. 'This one.'

I was relieved that numbers were the same in Russian. The alphabet was so odd, familiar letters making unfamiliar sounds, that I relied on numbers more than ever. We walked to the entrance, and an elderly lady turned away from us as we passed, pushing a mop and bucket. We took the lift to the eighth floor, the stink of vinegar overwhelming.

'At least our lift only smells of cabbage,' mumbled Kit. 'Someone must have dropped a whole bottle.'

Charlie opened the door. There was the sound of whining nearby, then a slap and a wail.

'Sorry about this,' said Charlie. 'Bobby is playing up. Let me get you a drink. Wine OK?'

He led us into a front room slightly smaller than our own, filled at one end with two sofas, underneath which toys had been crammed, a tiny television and a round table next to the balcony. There were two chairs and two stools of different heights. Elton John was on in the background.

'So, the tallest person goes on the shortest stool.' He manfully grabbed Kit by the shoulder. 'Martha, who is tallest?' There was nothing in it, but I disliked how he manhandled Kit.

'Christopher, just.'

Charlie looked put out and slapped Kit rather too hard on the back.

'Right, then. I'll get the wine.'

I grimaced at Kit, but he looked confused. I'd misjudged that. He wasn't in competition with Charlie. He actually liked him. Kit lit a cigarette and followed Charlie to the kitchen.

Alison came in looking even more tired than at the restaurant. She slumped onto a chair.

'It's been a long day.' She tried to smile. 'It's nice to have visitors, though. Have a seat, Martha. No, have a proper chair.'

She pointed to the one opposite her, and I felt pushed away.

'How old is your son?'

'Bobby is four.'

'Oh,' I said.

'I know.' She sighed. 'This flat is far too small for three

people, but we're not allowed anything bigger. We have to make up our bed on the sofas every night. I can't wait to get out of this sodding place.'

'The flat or the country?'

'The country. It's so hard. The kid, the flat, there's no way to replace anything or get anything new. I just want a proper bed and some new clothes. God, I hate it.'

Her eyelids flickered. I wasn't sure if she was going to cry.

'Christopher tells me that a lot of people go to Helsinki to shop.'

She spoke slowly, 'But I have Bobby. And Bobby ... well, we can't eat out any more because he won't have sauces. And then they say, well, it's cooked in a sauce, you can't have it without a sauce. And then if we get something else it will be wrong. The sausages are the wrong colour or smell, or – oh God.' She put her face in her hands.

I could hear Kit and Charlie chatting in the kitchen, the remnants of sobbing through the plywood wall behind me, and I felt like hiding too. The cigarette smoke filling the small flat began to sting my eyes, and Alison stayed quite still. I didn't want to pull her out of, maybe, the first peace she'd had all day. But the longer the silence went on, the more uncomfortable I felt. I looked out of the window at dozens of other blocks, all the same as this one.

'Alison!' Charlie shouted. 'Are we going to eat, then?' More quietly, I could hear him say, 'She burns everything given half a chance.' Kit laughed gently, but I cringed.

Alison lifted her face from her hands and I could see her composing it to still tiredness.

'Don't go,' I whispered. 'He's in the kitchen, make him serve it.'

She glared at me, pushed her chair back and walked away.

I'd overstepped already. I was as bad as him, telling her what she should do.

Charlie and Kit came back through with their glasses and one for me.

'So,' said Charlie, sitting on the tallest stool, his knee touching mine, 'tell me about yourself, Martha.'

'Oh, I'm just a housewife now.'

'Christopher says you were at Cambridge. What were you reading?'

'Classics.'

'Clever girl.' He moved a little closer.

I looked to Kit for help, but he was gazing out of the window. 'I'll just see if Alison needs a hand.' I pushed my chair back and felt his hand brush against my leg.

Alison had filled two plates with a kind of pie.

'Looks good,' I said. 'I'll take these in.'

There was still a distant sob coming from behind the closed door of the bedroom. I put the two plates in front of the stools.

'Ladies first,' said Charlie, as he moved the plates in front of the chairs.

In the hall, I stood between both rooms, cursing Christopher for bringing me here to these unhappy and lecherous people. I smiled, realising that using his full name when I was cross was probably as close to a normal married couple that we would get. I looked into the kitchen.

'I'm finished,' said Alison. 'Just sit down.'

I returned to the table and took my place between Kit and Charlie. Charlie's knee slid back into place against mine as he poured the wine.

'This is kulebiaka,' he said, as if he'd cooked it. 'Alison likes to try out the local recipes.'

Alison looked at him, then started eating.

'So, you and Kit work together,' I said, unsure of how to break the awkwardness.

'Yes, but we've been here for eighteen months. Old hands now,' said Charlie.

'And does Bobby go to nursery?'

'No,' said Alison. 'Bobby does not go to nursery. Bobby stays at home with his mother because that's what women are for.' She looked at no one while she spoke, cutting and overcutting the pastry to crumbs.

'Well, not everyone is destined to be a Classics scholar.' Charlie winked at me. He turned to Alison. 'And you are the one who said you didn't want him mixing with the bloody Americans.'

Alison stared at him. I looked at Kit, who made a minute shake of his head.

'Where do you take Bobby?' I asked. 'Are there parks and entertainments?'

Again, Alison didn't answer.

Charlie chuckled. 'Bobby is quite headstrong. It's tricky to leave the house if you're not doing something that interests him.'

'What interests him?'

'The woods. He doesn't like to hold hands, and it's hard for Alison with all the busy roads.'

'So, you stay here?'

'Yes, we stay here.' Alison still hadn't looked at anyone.

'I got them a television,' said Charlie.

'How marvellous,' I said, and then I worried that I hadn't conveyed any sarcasm and that Alison would think I meant it. 'I need to explore the area. I could take Bobby out with me.'

Her head jolted up. 'Yes. Yes, please.'

'OK. I can do it tomorrow.'

'Yes, yes. Tomorrow.' She looked at me, as if trying to work out what the catch was. I smiled.

Charlie seemed to be waiting for her to change her mind. 'Are you sure that works?' he asked her.

'Yes.' She flapped her hand at him.

I said, 'Noon?'

'Noon.' Alison closed her eyes and a small smile flickered on her lips. The record ended and the stylus lifted itself off, and back to the rest.

'High noon it is, then,' said Charlie.

He looked at Kit and raised his eyebrows. I anticipated some attempt to talk me out of this. Kit looked back at him, and when Charlie lowered his head and Kit's expression changed, I realised that he fancied Charlie. I looked away. I was drinking too much wine. Alison was examining my face, as if she knew something too.

'Do you go to the Metropol often to eat?' I asked her.

'Hardly ever.'

'Is it hard to get a babysitter?'

'Charlie has a constant string of secretaries who seem willing.'

Everything about this man made me feel sick. I had to get the subject away from him, but he had tentacles everywhere. His knee was beginning to hurt my own, like a bruise. He filled my glass again. He looked at Alison, who kept her head down, then back at Kit, who nodded at another unspoken comment. It reminded me of the Metropol. A different subject at last.

'Did you see the woman in the purple hat when we were at the Metropol? I wondered if she was English.'

Alison nodded. 'That's Eva Mann.'

Charlie let his cutlery fall to the plate. 'OK, that's enough about work.'

What did it have to do with work, I wondered. And Mann? My mind had automatically gone to the booklet author, and Eva was similar to E. V.

'Let's put some more music on,' said Charlie.

He lit another cigarette, and I watched him flick through maybe twenty albums before he pulled out *Never a Dull Moment*.

'Can't go wrong with Rod Stewart,' he said.

I said nothing, but flicked my eyes to see Alison's reaction. Her eyebrows were raised and it caught me as so comical that I laughed.

'You don't like him?' asked Charlie.

'Not much,' I said. 'I'm more into Cat Stevens.'

He went back to his stock. 'Simon and Garfunkel?'

I waved my hand in a 'sort of' motion.

'Andy Williams?'

'No.'

'Credence Clearwater Revival?'

'They're OK.'

Charlie clearly thought that was as good as it would get, and put on *Green River*. He sat back down, looking shaken.

'Maybe your tastes are getting old,' said Alison. 'The young people aren't as impressed as they used to be.' It was the first real smile I'd seen from her. 'Martha is too young for your records.'

'They are all classics,' Charlie mumbled.

'Charlie has his brother ship over the most popular albums at great expense so he can keep his finger on the pulse. Like the classic, 20 *Dynamic Hits*.'

'Well, we have this on now, which Martha does like, so that's fine.'

Alison was on a roll. 'And 20 *Fantastic Hits* has The Osmonds and Chelsea Football Club.'

'It was a successful compilation which got to number one for five weeks,' said Charlie.

Alison laughed.

'Christopher has only got classical music,' I said. 'I think I prefer that.'

'You can't go out of date with classical,' Kit said. He sounded apologetic.

Charlie put his cigarette out and pushed his chair back. 'Shall we go out onto the balcony for a cigar? The ladies can tidy up.'

They went out and pulled the door closed behind them.

'Oh dear,' I said, 'I don't think I played the part Charlie had written for me.'

Alison moved to his stool and filled my glass and her own. 'You're not what I was expecting either. The wives here are generally one type, quiet and keeping their head down. It's like they all went on a course.'

'Why haven't you looked into the kindergartens? Don't the embassies run something like that?'

'I have looked at it, but it's Anglo-American, and full of American children. Ghastly. He'd pick up all sorts there. But it's all been a bit much recently. Maybe I need to think again.'

'Well, I'll come around tomorrow and we'll see how it goes.'

'You'll really come? Bobby is a handful. That's the polite way of saying it.'

'I'll live. I want to have a walk around, and this is a good excuse. In the morning, I have my first Russian lesson. Do you speak Russian?'

'I don't see any Russians.' Alison drained her glass.

'Shall I help you get this washing up done?'

'No.' She yawned and rested her head on her hand.

67

There was a burst of laughter from outside on the balcony. Charlie had an appreciative audience once more.

When I looked back to Alison her eyes were closed. I looked out to the balcony. I could hear the murmur of Kit's voice as he leaned back, his face to the sky. Charlie was looking directly at me, not smiling, just staring. Charlie was going to be a problem.

9

Two days ago, it had been 24 degrees. This morning it was cold. I went out onto the balcony over the wood behind our apartment and shivered. It had snowed a little, and the trees looked frosty. It was May so the heating was off, and couldn't be put on until the whole building was switched back on. I started to think properly about how I was going to cope in the real winter.

I'd just made a cup of tea when someone knocked on the door. I froze and crept towards the door. I was imagining police or burly Russian soldiers, but when I opened the door, it was to a slender woman in a black roll-neck top and grey wool skirt.

'Galina Dmitrievna Belinskaya.'

I stared at her.

'UPDK.'

I shook my head.

She shifted her weight and sighed. 'Russian lessons. I am your teacher.'

'Ah, sorry, yes. Come in.'

I stood aside for her to pass me, but she stepped over the threshold and crouched down. I took a step back to watch as she removed her shoes. She looked so young, hardly old enough to be a teacher. Her reddened fingers struggled with the knots of the double tied laces. She stood up and handed me her coat, smelling fresh with cold. I fumbled to close the door, and hung her coat up.

She slid on tiny slippers and smoothed her hair, tied back in a tight ponytail. 'Shall we?'

I led her into the front room. I moved my teacup to the kitchen and sat down. Two lessons a week of two hours' duration by this language professor from the university, with my background in Classics? I'd be speaking Russian in no time.

'Zdravstvuyte.'

A word I recognised. I sidestepped it in my usual way. 'Dobroe utro.'

Galina leaned forward, her finger pointing to me. 'You repeat what I say.' Her finger pointed to the table. 'This is not conversation, it is lesson.'

My heart sank.

I thought about my failings as I left the apartment and turned right to walk along Leninsky Prospekt. One of the most embarrassing moments was not being able to say where I lived, not because I didn't know it in Russian, but because I didn't even know it in English.

'What if you are lost?' Galina had said. 'You think everyone will know who you are?'

I recited it to myself. Leninsky Prospekt, area 121, building number 1. Three buildings with twenty-four floors: there were a lot of people on our little corner of Leninsky. I should definitely have known which building it was. Had Kit given my parents the address in Russian or English? I hadn't had a letter yet. It took three weeks, Kit said. I had sent one to my parents, and one to David, although I had no hopes of hearing back from him.

I looked at my watch and started to speed up a little. The two and a half miles had taken no time in the car, but I hadn't thought about the distance until half past eleven. At least it wasn't too warm to rush.

I tried to make sense of my lesson with Galina. I'd had great hopes that I might be good at this, with a working knowledge of Latin, no matter how poor I was in Greek. The Greek would have served me better, with its links to Cyrillic. No 'a' or 'the', no 'H', and the alphabet was bewildering. I was never going to learn Russian.

I got to a crossroad and crossed over to the other side. Left onto Lobachevskogo and right onto Vernadskogo Prospekt. I couldn't get lost, I repeated to myself. Vernadskogo ran parallel to Leninsky, before tapering back towards Leninsky, right by my apartment. I just had to break Moscow into manageable sections.

This section of Leninsky had thick lines of trees on both sides of the road. I turned left onto Lobachevskogo and realised the trees didn't stop. The road cut right through a small forest. I couldn't quite get my head around Moscow, or my bit of it. It was a mix of wide roads built for giant armies and what looked like ancient forests. It made me feel as if this really was a place of magic, even with all the concrete blocks and tiny apartments and queues for bread. My nervousness was balanced by excitement. It was staying inside and close to home that was the problem. Whenever I went out, I knew there was something special here.

I knocked on Alison's door. She was red-cheeked and looked exhausted. Bobby was sitting quietly, cross-legged, in the hall, shoes and coat already on.

'Sorry I'm late,' I said.

'Never mind,' said Alison, her teeth clenched. 'You're here now. Bobby, this is Martha.' He didn't move. She dragged Bobby up by one arm and pushed him out the door. 'Off you go. Take your time. Behave yourself, Bobby.' She closed the door.

I looked down at Bobby. He was round-faced, and his dark blue eyes held mine with an unnerving confidence. I was being assessed.

'So,' I said, 'fancy going to a forest?'

He shrugged.

'OK.' We walked down the stairs, and I wondered whether I should be holding his hand. Did four-year-olds need to be guided like that? I decided to let him choose. When he took off and I had to chase him along the dual carriageway twice, I decided not to let him have any other choices.

'Just hold my hand until we get to the forest, OK?'

He scowled. We crossed Lobachevskogo and took a path across the open park towards the trees. He started wriggling, trying to twist his hand from mine. I crouched down.

'Bobby, I need you to listen to me. It's very important.'

He twisted his face away so I knew he didn't want to be seen to listen.

'I need you to stay near me because I've been here before and I know that the bears in this wood are very hungry.'

Now he looked at me, eyes wide and mouth slightly open.

'Do you know what a bear looks like?'

He nodded.

'So, we have to keep close together.'

His eyes narrowed as he weighed me up. I kept my face as still as possible until he slowly nodded. I let go of his hand and he made a little fuss, holding it as if injured. Then his eyes narrowed again and he ran towards the trees full pelt, before stopping and waiting for me to catch up with him. I smiled, letting him lead.

Did he speak? His angry silence was unnerving and he was bound to notice an absence of bears at some point. I just hoped there wouldn't be any big dogs running around.

We walked into the trees. There was still a dusting of snow in the dark hollows and the coolness of the shade made me shiver. Bobby walked in front but he was very aware of me, looking back now and then. It was a long, straight track, but it had been made by feet rather than a prepared surface. I'd noticed that the woods behind my apartment had dead straight paths, designed. I preferred these purposeful tracks in the silence of birch and pine. The rosebay willow herb was starting to achieve some height, and I saw a butterfly which had survived the snow.

The occasional bird fluttered from a branch. I caught the monochrome flap of a magpie, and could hear a woodpecker somewhere. I looked in the top branches, wondering what kind it was, but I couldn't spot it. I looked down and Bobby wasn't there. I turned in a circle, but he was so small that most of the tree trunks would have hidden him. I listened but there was no tell-tale crackle of twigs. He must be on a path. I ran in the direction we'd been heading, only to find there was another path which doubled back on ours. I ran ahead. Three choices, left and right, and straight out onto a road.

I undid my jacket and tried to calm my breathing. I knew I should shout for him, but the forest was oppressive and I didn't trust my voice to carry. Hooligans, drunks, who knew what was hidden here?

I spoke as normally as I could. 'Bobby, are you with the bears?' No answer. Which way would he go? He would have tried to keep an eye on me, at first, anyway. I doubled back on the other path, my heart hurting and the breaths stuttering in my throat. I couldn't even ask anyone if they'd seen him, I couldn't shout for help. I was running when I found another path turning left. I stopped. All that way with no turns, and now there was nothing but choices.

I took a breath to scream for him, and saw him, crouched down a little way up the path. I was going to strangle him when I stopped feeling faint.

I walked up behind him, and he gestured for me to get down.

'Bears,' he whispered, his eyes bright, and pointed with a stubby finger through the trees.

Three men were at the bottom of a tree, two of them asleep on the ground and the other leaning up against it, finishing a bottle which was wrapped in a paper bag.

'Bears,' I whispered back. 'Well spotted, Bobby.'

He looked at me and grimaced. 'You're all sweaty.'

'I'm quite hot now.' I shrugged my jacket off and tried to flap some cold air under my jumper. 'Which way should we go so the bears don't see us?'

Bobby pointed and we crept away. Now that he'd scared me silly, we'd broken the ice. We saw trolls and imps, chased a butterfly (possibly a fairy) and kept an eye out for more bears.

'Maybe next time,' I said.

'We can come back?'

'There are lots of forests to explore. There's another one over on my road.' I pointed back in the direction we'd come from. We were nearly back.

'And there's one on my road.' He pointed past his apartment block. 'I can see it from the window.'

'Let's go back and have a drink now, though.'

'We can take a picnic.'

'Maybe Mummy can come.'
He looked at me. I could see Charlie in his sneer.

'She didn't hold my hand on the roads, and we saw bears.'
'So you had a good time.'
Bobby nodded.
'The television is on. Go and sit down.'
Alison went into the kitchen to put the percolator on: bulbous steel bowls in the style of a futuristic space colony, topped with the Atomic label in black and white. I liked to think that cosmonauts would use this. I waited in the hall, expecting to be told off, but Alison gestured for me to follow him. Bobby was sitting in front of the television watching a programme about farming. Occasionally, he looked over at me and gave a little smile. He looked exhausted. Alison brought back the coffee in delicately painted teacups.

'The coffee is British, don't worry. We get it from the embassy. Russian coffee can be anything, from acorns to roots. If you have the money, it's not in stock. If it's in stock, you don't want it. These teacups are for the export market, not for the people who live here. Don't you need new ones?'

'It's not important.'
'Ha. You're like the Russians. They never apologise for what they don't have. They think it's anti-communist, being concerned with private property.'

I wasn't sure if she was insulting me, so I smiled.
'We have some old saucepans you can take. Charlie says Kit's kitchen is empty.'
'Thank you. Did Charlie visit Kit much? Before I came.'
Alison turned away. 'He said he did.'
I had to change the subject. Everything that came out of my mouth was wrong. 'Do you know many Russians?'

'No. I told you, I don't see any. I just know what Charlie tells me. We had a cleaner, but she didn't last long.'

Her face looked strained as she aimed for nonchalant. I changed the subject.

'Why didn't he let me ask about Eva Mann last night? Who is she?'

Alison sat down at the table. 'I'm not sure. She's British, and she works as a translator. Novels, mostly, but some poetry. Nothing famous.'

'So, why won't they talk about her?'

Alison sipped her coffee, and frowned. 'She married a Russian, I think. There was some trouble in Berlin, but I don't know what it was about. She's not "one of us", that's for sure. I haven't met her, but I've seen her around. She doesn't go to any embassy parties, which is odd as most British people end up there occasionally, just to talk English with no one listening for a change. Have you seen Mrs Highfield yet?'

'The ambassador's wife? Christopher gave me a letter from her, inviting me to call, but I haven't yet.'

'Oh. She won't like that.'

'I don't really want to be an embassy wife. I don't have to, surely?'

'It makes this run more smoothly if you let Emily High-field take charge, I know that. Her Russian is excellent too.'

I drank my tea. 'Can you understand any Russian?'

'Some bits and bobs. I had lessons before we came. Didn't you get offered that?'

'No. There wasn't much time to organise things.'

Alison smiled and looked away, out of the window.

'What?'

'Your relationship with Christopher.'

'What about it?'

'It wasn't what I was expecting, that's all. Have you known each other long?'

I didn't want to be quizzed on that. 'I said last night. Were you in the kitchen? Oh, look at him.'

She looked across to the other end of the room. Bobby was sprawled on one sofa, his head back and mouth open.

'So,' I said, 'Bobby would like to go back to the forest and find more beasts. He says there's one on this road. Did you want to come?'

Alison's posture stiffened and she looked down at the table. 'No, I don't want to do that.'

'Don't you ever go out?'

'Not without Charlie. Charlie will let Christopher know.'

I sat back and waited for her to expand on that. She smiled weakly but said nothing else. I imagined her, stuck in this flat, waiting for Charlie. Her face was still now, tightly closed up.

'I'd better get off, then,' I said.

'Yes. Thanks for your help.'

On my way down the stairs, with the saucepans, I wished I'd said something else. I didn't know what.

Kit put his spoon down.

'It must be the pans. Everything has that weird taste.'

'Chicken noodle soup, with added zinc. No wonder Charlie wanted rid of them. I'll go back to the old ones.'

Kit poured more beer into his glass, then mine. 'How did it go with crazy Bob?'

'I like Bobby. After he nearly got run over and attacked by drunks, we had a good time. Do you have a map so I can look for more forests?'

Kit frowned. 'You took him to a forest?'

'Kind of, a small one. You know the wooded areas either side of the road?'

Kit turned his glass in his hands. 'They're not very safe, Martha. Even if you talk Russian, you can't reason with someone who only drinks vodka. Then you have the problem of rabies. Ticks.' He put the glass down. 'And hooligans.'

'Hooligans?' I laughed. 'Why do you always call them that?'

'That's what they call the teenagers who don't work, don't study, don't do anything but drink vodka and mug people. They don't believe in the party but, if you're not in the party organisations, you don't get the right jobs. Right down there,' he pointed out past the balcony to our little wood, 'a couple of girls were attacked last week.'

I shuddered. 'Why didn't you tell me?'

'I didn't know you'd be hanging around the woods with the drunks.' He hesitated. 'Of course, there is a lot of foraging that goes on, so chances are there will be normal people around. If you had to shout.'

'That doesn't make me feel much better. I don't know what "help" is yet.'

'Pamagil.'

'Now I'm ready. I suppose.'

The record finished and I got up to turn it over and replace the needle. Maria Callas started up again. We weren't talking about anything worth recording, but I found myself still incapable of talking and relaxing without background noise. Plus, the eavesdropper got to listen to something.

I sat down and picked up my glass. 'I thought there was no crime and no unemployment.'

'Yeah, it won't be funny when you're explaining to Charlie and Alison what happened to their first born.'

'Kit, that kid seems to be trapped in the flat all week. Alison says she only goes out with Charlie.'

'Well, that's not true. Charlie says she's always out with the other mums, visiting and stuff.'

'Charlie says that, but Alison says something else.'

'There's no point arguing with me about this. We've got a trip planned at the embassy dacha in June. You'll meet some other wives. Ask around.'

'Spy on Alison?'

'Ha ha.' He opened the balcony door before lighting his cigarette.

'But do you have a map I can use?'

Kit drained his glass. 'I think we have a few. I'll have a look. If you go to an Inturist bureau, you can pick up a really basic one of the tourist places in the centre. The Russians aren't keen on maps, or not on people having access to them. Every one of them is intentionally wrong in some way. But, really, if you head into the centre, you'll find lots of parks which are a bit more open and safe to visit. Have you worked out how to use the Metro yet?' He pointed to the tin with the space dogs. 'Roubles are in there. Five kopeks will get you anywhere on the Metro or the bus.'

'I don't know. I feel happier staying local with Bobby. And she might not even ask me again. I can't understand her. She was desperate for me to take him out, and now she's gone cold again.'

'She just thinks that every woman is going to end up in bed with Charlie. She's very jealous. Don't worry about it.' He stood up and raised his eyebrows. 'Unless you're intending to go to bed with Charlie.'

'Ha! So you'll get me a map?'

'I'll try. I'm off for my bath.' He fetched his pyjamas from the chest and turned to me. 'But, Martha, you need to remember where you are.' He pointed to the poster: man and dog in space. 'They'd spend millions to send wolves to

Mars just for the hell of it, just to be first while the people drink themselves to death because there's no freedom and no hope. And remember why we keep the music on.'

I said nothing. He shrugged and left the door ajar. This had become our routine. A late supper, and Kit went for his bath. I tidied up and the room was his to make his bed up and do whatever he used to do before I arrived. I gathered the bowls and glasses, and took them to the kitchen. I strained out the noodles, emptied out the soup and filled the sink. I stood by the window, looking into the dusk at our wood. I'd walked around it on my way home and seen how it wasn't wild, but planted rows of birch and pine. Organised. Purposeful. Made for the people.

I'd walk around it tomorrow.

IO

After Galina had gone and the apartment had fallen quiet, I grabbed my bag and ran down the stairs. A few days after the snow and the temperature was back to 23 degrees, though it was cloudy. Just like England, you never knew what the weather would be like.

I took the tourist map that Kit had found for me from my handbag. I hadn't heard anything about taking Bobby out again, but the map was no good for parks anyway. It didn't even cover where we lived. I had, though, found out the nearest Metro station from Kit, and I headed to Yugo-Zapadnaya, on Vernadskogo Prospekt.

The station was a glass box with a slab of aluminium stretching across one set of stairs down, and one up. My five kopeks got me a small paper ticket and I waited. The long platform reminded me of New York subways I'd seen on films, the square pillars every six steps and rails either side of the platform. I worked out which way I wanted to head, and within two minutes a blue train had pulled up. I got on and stood by the door. My Metro map had the Russian station names in English, and I'd made Kit scribble Russian versions next to them so I knew where I was. As it was, the stations were announced, but I couldn't always catch the name without reading my notes. I had been trying to do my homework for Galina, I really had, learning that a C was an S, an H was an N and a B was a V, but I didn't believe it. I would learn how to write something while I was out, like ленин. Lenin. That would make her happy.

The stations grew grander as I travelled, with cool white marble and tulip-shaped chandeliers. The journey was smooth and fast, every platform pristine. At Biblioteka Lenina, there was a central platform with a wide, sweeping ceiling, shaped like square panelling. The stairs led sideways from the platform and the sun shone down. I stood there for a moment as Natalya and Galina and Alison all faded away. There was only light and this space and everything out there, built for its own beauty and magnificence.

There were stalls, a stout woman in a white apron selling ice cream, a small man in a brown apron ready to shine shoes. I left the station to find more stalls selling pink water, tobacco, flowers, magazines and books. I saw so many people reading books, all over the city. Russians.

I was going to walk this city until it became mine.

People approached me constantly, so I realised that I stood out. Women said something while pointing to my shoes. Men switched to English to ask if I had cigarettes or dollars. I needed to look more Russian.

When my feet started to hurt, I had to find a place to sit. There were too many choices, so many views I hadn't seen. I decided to cross to the island created by the river and the canal and look back at the Kremlin. The Great Kremlin Palace, white and yellow, towered over the line of trees which hid the high red wall. There were towers, cupolas and trees right along the river bank. On Naberezhnaya Morisa

Toreza, there were no benches. Instead, I found myself walking past the mustard building with the green copper roof that I had seen when I was standing beside the Kremlin wall. I looked at the sign. The British Embassy. I turned and walked back the way I'd come, cursing myself for not just continuing onwards. How suspicious that must have looked to the guard standing outside. All the way back to the bridge, I waited for the sound of a police car screeching up to me, but when I got onto the bridge and looked back, it was quiet and empty.

The sun had gone in, but I was feeling too hot to keep walking. Now that I wanted to stop there, all the benches were taken. I carried on over the bridge and, with relief, remembered from the map the Alexander Garden which ran alongside the Kremlin. I found a bench, the only empty one, and sank onto it. My feet were throbbing now. I'd been fairly sedentary since I arrived, apart from the walk with Bobby. Now I felt like falling asleep in front of the television as he had. And I was thirsty. And it was way past lunch.

I leaned back against the bench and flexed my feet inside my shoes. When I closed my eyes, the scene from *The Master and Margarita* came into my head. There were so many places I hadn't looked into yet, and the Patriarch Ponds was one of them. I kept having to remind myself that I wasn't on holiday. I had months to explore, and the lack of maps was interesting. Moscow was clearly a place that both invited and resisted tourism.

I opened my eyes. I was in a line of benches which made it hard to look at other people without being obvious. I wondered, my back to the Kremlin, how many meetings had been arranged here, under the red wall. My stomach rumbled. I'd seen another ice cream stall in Red Square, and thought about walking back over there, although I knew I needed something more substantial than ice cream. There were other stalls, but I wasn't sure what they sold. I should have arranged to meet Kit for lunch, but I knew that he mostly had meetings while he ate. I remembered Kit talking about the Arbat as a good area for food. I was sure it was nearby.

I got the map from my pocket. It was from 1957, from the World Festival of Youth and Students. The city centre, white roads on a brown city, was on one side and the other was pale blue, with a very basic Metro map with names next to pictures of buildings. It folded into eight pieces, but some of the text from the Metro map bled over onto the front page, which annoyed me. There were very few street names and, as I'd discovered, only the main roads. Kit had added to the four Metro lines, extending our line out to Yugo-Zapadnaya. I found the short wall of the Kremlin where I was sitting and saw that Arbat Square was just one road to the left. As I gave my feet an exploratory flex, I noticed a man standing nearby. He had stopped to light a cigarette, but I had the impression that he had been standing there for a while. He put the matches back in his trouser pocket and checked his watch, before slowly walking towards the river.

The feeling that I was under surveillance thrilled me. It was definitely only a problem when I was in the flat. Out here, I felt fine.

I watched him walk slowly away, then my eye was caught by an older woman coming towards me. Next to her was a huge, black dog, its head level with her waist. It looked powerful and alert, watchful. I realised how much I missed having pets, and how a big animal like that would come to dominate your life in those small apartments.

I looked up at the woman's face. The sense of familiarity in such an unfamiliar place unsettled me. She was in her sixties, I thought, her hair all hidden under her hat, apart from some dark strands under the brim. She had dark rings under her eyes, and no colour in her face, but that seemed to be fairly standard here. Where did I recognise her from?

She smiled at me.

'Zdravstvuyte.'

My tongue fumbled for my greeting. 'Um, dobroe utro.'

She gestured to the bench. 'May I?'

Her English shocked me, but I nodded. 'How did you know I was British?'

She sat down carefully, and the dog settled next to her tidy feet, pressed together. 'Ah, a few things. Your accent, of course, the little "um" at the start, and it is no longer morning. Dobry den is better as an all-day greeting, if you're having trouble with "hello".' She held out her hand, 'Eva Mann.'

Of course.

'Martha—'

I was still not used to saying Kit's surname, and mine felt odd now that we were married, so I left it at that.

'You'll find the Russians will use a more Russian version of your name. I'll call you Marta, to get you used to it.'

I nodded. 'What's your dog called?'

'She's called Vorona. It means crow.' The dog looked up at Eva, and then set her gaze outwards again. 'She's a Black Russian Terrier. Soviet scientists combined seventeen different breeds to create this dog.' Eva looked at me intently, as if gauging my reaction to each word.

'She's really beautiful.'

'Clever, too.'

I couldn't think of anything else to say. We lapsed into silence, not companionable, but comfortable enough with the dog to focus on. A few people walked past and I watched

them, waiting for the man with the cigarette to return. I
didn't see him. Eventually, Eva spoke.

'I should get back. Would you come and visit me? I don't
see many English people nowadays. It would mean a lot to
me to find out what is happening in England, and to stretch
my tongue again.'

My heart sank. She was excluded from the British contingent for some reason that I hadn't discovered, but the way
she'd phrased it made it hard to say no. And I was interested.

'That would be lovely, thank you.'

'Have you got a bit of paper so I can write directions? It's
not far from here.'

I opened my bag, but the only bit of paper I had was the
1957 map. I didn't think Kit wanted it back, so I pulled it
out.

'Maybe along the side of this?'

She laughed and unfolded the map. 'Well, I don't know
how you can use this. I'll get you a better map. One that at
least takes the sixties into account.'

She slid a pen from her coat pocket and added some lines
to the map, then a long arrow to a specific junction. Along
the edge of the map, she wrote the address in Russian and
English.

'Myaskovskogo?' I said.

She nodded, and added a cross. 'This is Arbatskaya Metro
station, and next to it is a cinema, the Khudozhestvenny. I
think that watching films in any new country helps you to
get an ear for the language. And it can be a good way to
spend an hour or so, if you have little to occupy yourself. I
often go myself.'

'Thank you.'

'Shall I put my telephone number?'

'We don't have a phone yet. I mean, I don't have a phone.'

'So, would you like to come in a week? Next Tuesday? Any Tuesday afternoon, in fact. If you come at noon, I'll make you some lunch. You must eat, Marta. You look hungry.'

She smiled and patted my hand. I smiled, but it felt odd, as if she was acting like someone older than she was.

I said, 'Did you know I saw you on my first night in Moscow? In the Metropol.'

'What a coincidence,' she said. She stood and the dog stood with her. 'I'll see you next week.'

I watched her walk away, remembering Kit's warning. There were no coincidences here. And I was glad. Only then did I think about the stories. I would have time to ask when I visited. If I visited.

I hadn't even taken my coat off when there was a knock on the door. I quickly shrugged it off, then opened it.

'Hello, Martha.' Charlie was posing, hands in his pockets.

'Oh, hello. Christopher's not home yet.'

'Oh, I know. He's had to go out with a gentleman. For a drink.' He looked so smug. I knew he was suggesting that Kit was having more than a drink. Was he trying to drop Kit in it so that I'd jump into his arms in revenge?

I crossed my arms. 'Right. Well, he's done that before for work. Did you just come to tell me that?'

'I could come in and keep you company.' His hands were still in his pockets. 'He might be some time. You could tell me what you've been up to, maybe show me some of the records you like so much.'

He took a step forward and I wedged my foot behind the door.

'Kit goes to the record shop on Gorky Street. I'm sure you could pick some up.'

'How about a bit of company, then?'

'I'm fine, thank you. I was just going to have a bath.'

His eyes lit up.

'I could—'

'No, you can't,' I said, and slammed the door shut.

When Kit got home, we decided to eat off our laps on the balcony. I had decided not to mention Charlie, but I couldn't think of anything else to say. Kit also seemed distracted. He finally came out with it.

'Charlie asked me to ask you something, and I'm not sure how you're going to take it.'

My heart sank. He was negotiating on Charlie's behalf? 'Go on.'

'He, and Alison – well, it's her idea. Alison wants to know if you'd be Bobby's nanny.'

That was better than I'd dreaded, but stranger. 'What?'

'I know. Not really your thing.'

'It's not just that. She said she'd be in touch, that she'd get Charlie to ask you to ask me to go around again. And she didn't, and now she wants me to be his nanny? I only spent an afternoon with him.'

'So, I'll say no?'

I groaned and put my feet up against the balcony. 'This should be a face to face thing, not Chinese whispers between husbands. It's just weird.'

'Maybe she thinks you're bored. Or you could do with the money.'

'I never said either of those things. And I'm just finding my feet. I had a brilliant time today.' Then I remembered. Kit noticed. He closed the balcony door and leaned forward, elbows on his knees.

'What?'

'I met Eva Mann.'

'What do you mean?' He clasped his hands together.

'She was walking past with her dog.'

'She's invited you around, hasn't she?'

I nodded.

'And promised you something?'

'No. Oh, yeah, a map.'

'But you can get your own map.'

'I know. But I'm interested in her. And that's your fault. You won't tell me anything about her.'

'I don't know anything, but I know,' he lowered his voice, 'she's not on our side.'

I glanced at him. 'She has a nice dog.'

He huffed, 'It's probably not even her dog. You can't go there, Martha. I bet you anything you like, she gets you to do things for her. She'll butter you up, and then you'll be running around, doing little jobs, feeling useful. And all the while she'll be getting information.'

'But I won't say anything. Apart from,' I waved my hand between us, 'that I don't know anything. And the point is, I don't want to be at her mercy or Alison's. I want to explore Moscow. So few people get to do that, and Eva knows Moscow. She lives here.'

Kit sat quietly for a while. 'Just tell me everything, OK. And if the map doesn't look like a tourist map, don't take it.'

'Got it. And I'll go around to Alison's soon, sort this out. Maybe I'll say that you said, what with rabid hooligans and crazy drunks, it's best to stay inside.'

'Hmm.' He picked up the plates to take them through. 'How was your lesson this morning?'

'Otlichno.'

He raised his eyebrows and went inside. But I felt I had improved today. I had started to get an idea of sounds from around the map. Prospekt looked a bit like 'in pocket', -skaya looked like 'ckar', just the R was backward. The letters T, O, M and A were safe. I stood up and leaned on the balcony, looking over the trees to the dark, north-east skies.

'Toma,' I said aloud. My safe letters that wouldn't trick me. But I would work hard to learn the rest. And maybe see a film.

The door behind me opened and I jumped.

'Guilty conscience?' asked Kit. 'I just wanted to say, can you talk to Alison about the picnic when you go?'

'OK.'

I thought of the militiaman, noting down all the comings and goings.

'Kit?'

'Yes?'

'Someone knocked on the door when I got back. It was really loud. It sounded official and I got nervous.'

'Who was it?'

'I don't know. Should I have opened it?'

'No. Best not, if you're not expecting anyone.'

I was pretty sure that covered me if Charlie tried to stir things up. I went to bed, eager to read through Eva's stories again.

'Cherry Stones'
by
E. V. MANN

There are so many similarities between this landscape and home – the oak, hawthorn, pansy and violet. And nettles. There is even a cherry tree at my dacha. I sit underneath in the snowfall of petals, watching tiny pips of green swell and ripen. I have never belonged to anywhere else like I belong here.

The wolf watches me from the gate, occasionally sifting news from the wind. He watches, but he says nothing. He feels far away. I miss the heat of his fur.

That first summer, the cherry tree has a full crop, heavy in the low branches. I water them and pick bugs from the leaves. I shoo any birds from my garden. The sound of trees rustling sends me to sleep, and I dream of the cherries. The wolf watches me as I sleep.

I check the crop every day, sometimes squeezing a cherry between my fingertips and sometimes eating a slightly bitter one. But less bitter than last time. One more night, and I will pick all the cherries.

I wake to the sound of feathers. When I get up, I can see from the window that the birds are finishing off the last of the cherries. I run outside, but it is too late, they have all gone. I throw damp stones everywhere and shout.

The wolf looks at me from his place near the gate. 'Why are you shouting at the birds?'

'They've eaten all my cherries,' I cry.

The wolf shakes his head. 'Do you see the flowers which grow by the gate?'

I go and look. Their tiny robustness pushes up through the stones, and from the wall where the pointing has crumbled away.

'And how about that damson tree?' he says. 'Did you plant that?'

The damson had grown while I wasn't looking, near the dacha.

'They were all planted by birds,' he says. 'We are surrounded by the work of others; we are guardians, not owners. And you begrudge them a share of their own work.' He lowers his head, but I can see a glint of resentment, as if he knew it was a test I would fail.

'They have taken every last one,' I complain. I can't help it.

'You ate some while they were green. We saw you. Would you let the birds do all the work and eat their fruit?'

A blackbird flew down and sat on the gate to address the wolf.

'Comrade, I congratulate you on providing such lovely fruit for the citizens. We are sorry to say that we believe your companion does not have the right kind of soul.' The wolf nods. I watch the bird fly away.

The wolf opens the gate and I know it's for me to leave. I fling my arms around his neck. He speaks gently and I feel the rumble of his words.

'You have been denounced. You can't stay here.'

I whisper, 'Please let me stay. Forgive me. I love you.'

'You do, citizen, but your soul needs to be fixed. You must live in the city and learn to love us equally.'

I walk back to the city alone, noting the position of every bird in the sky and how they follow me with their hollow bones and shrill voices. My tears fall like cherry stones, hard and bitter.

II

After Natalya arrived with the shopping, I walked the other way to Alison's, crossing over Leninsky by my apartment to where it met Vernadskogo Prospekt. It was no quicker, but I liked going past Christopher the Archangel, no longer a church, of course. Kit had told me that most churches were used as storage now. I felt that it was an excuse not to knock them down, although some had gone from the centre. Kit said that, just down from where I'd been on the river, a huge cathedral right on the Moskva had been destroyed for one of Stalin's dreams, which never came to anything. The massive space was now an enormous outdoor swimming pool, heated through the winter. It was the one I'd read about in the library, but I had no idea I'd been so close.

It was one of the many moments when I thought, Alison could take Bobby there. There were so many grand, stunning places for the people, it seemed odd for her not to see the grand Metro stations and run through their parks.

I was hot by the time I got to apartment block 79, and tentatively passed the militiaman. Hot could look like guilty. He didn't stop me. I decided to take the lift, but Kit had been right. They did all smell of cabbage, day and night.

I paused at Alison's door before knocking. She'd said she didn't go anywhere, so I supposed this was a test of sorts. I knocked. A few seconds, and she opened the door, hand on one hip.

'Ah. So you're interested? You really should get that husband of yours to install a phone.'

I shifted my feet. Not staff, and already I was being kept on the doorstep. 'Shall I come in?'

She stood aside and I walked into the hall. She closed the door but didn't go anywhere else.

'I don't want to be a nanny, Alison. Sorry. I'm happy to take Bobby out as an informal thing, but I don't want to be tied down.'

Her eyes widened. 'But it's not like you'll be having any of your own.'

I tilted my head. 'Why not?'

She paused, blushing slightly. 'Well, you probably feel too young.'

She knew about Kit. I'd known she was fishing the other day. If he'd told Charlie, he was a fool.

'Yes, well, I think that's our business.'

I put my hand out to open the door and she placed a hand on my shoulder.

'Please don't go. I feel like I've lost all my social skills. I used to have friends, honestly. Come in.'

She went into the front room. I hesitated and followed her. I couldn't see Bobby. Then I looked out at the balcony and gasped.

'Alison!'

He was sitting on the concrete wall, his back to the

sixty-foot drop, his feet dangling. Both hands were on the book he was reading.

'Oh, for God's sake, not again,' said Alison. 'Bobby, get off that wall!'

He looked up and smiled at me. I held my breath as, somehow, he jumped forward off the wall. He walked in, waving his book at me.

'I've been reading about wolves,' he said.

I took the book. 'Fairy tales are brilliant.'

'Can we look for bears today?'

I looked at Alison. She nodded.

'Could we have a chat first?' I said.

She looked at her watch. 'OK.' She sat down at the table. 'What do you want to talk about?'

I didn't sit down. I wanted to ask what the problem was, why she switched her friendship on and off, what I'd done that was wrong. I didn't say any of those things.

'Christopher said to ask you about the picnic.'

'Yes?'

'Well, he said it as if I knew what that meant. What picnic, where, when? Do I have to do something?'

'It's at the embassy dacha, on the 9th.'

I looked blank.

'It's a week tomorrow. The embassy provides the food. Maybe he wanted to share a car out there, but there'd be too many of us. But he and Charlie probably just think the wives do it all.'

'OK. I'll ask him what he meant, then.' She was so snappy again. I could never predict if she was going to be friendly or not. I turned to Bobby. 'Do you want to put a jacket on?'

'No.' He threw his book on the sofa and ran to the front door. I heard it click open and rushed to catch him up.

'We'll be a couple of hours,' I shouted back.

Nothing. I closed the door.

This time, we turned right and soon saw the red M of another Metro station, Vernadskogo Prospekt. There were more buildings being constructed along the road. At the bus stop, people physically pushed each other onto the bus through the rear door, and Bobby turned to me.

'They should wait for the next one,' he said.

'Yes, I would.'

I wondered how long we'd walk before I could see the university properly. We crossed over at the crossroads and, just as I started to doubt we'd gone the right way, a thin line of trees appeared along the road.

'Oh, this isn't a forest,' I said. The park stretched out with clumps of trees, running uphill to copses and downhill to streams. It was designed for people, with wooden pathways, and yet it felt natural. 'What kind of beasts are we going to find here?'

Bobby was quiet as we approached the trees. 'Could be Giant Land,' he said.

'Giants.' I nodded. 'They eat small boys, you know.'

'I'm going to find a sword.' Bobby started to scour the ground for sword-type sticks, while I looked around. A couple of people were examining the earth around the base of a tree, and I immediately thought, spies! But they don't normally come in pairs like that, and soon I could see that they weren't collecting secret cash payments or dropped off tapes, but mushrooms. Like Kit had said.

Bobby came back, armed.

'If we go up the hill,' I pointed, 'I think we'll see the giant's castle.'

Bobby nodded and started running. I hoped the running

would wear off pretty quickly. I was hot enough walking uphill, and sure enough Bobby sat down halfway up.

'Thank you for waiting. You're the only one with a sword.'

'Don't be scared, lady.' He pushed himself to his feet.

'Bobby, do you know my name?'

He shook his head. 'I forget it.'

'I'm Martha.'

'Daddy said, say hello to Martha. And you're Martha.'

'Yes. I am.'

We continued our search for footprints, past pink lilac and striped birch. Bobby was ready to smash a cluster of mushrooms until I stopped him.

'People pick those to eat them.'

'But I hate mushrooms.'

'We'll leave them for the giants, then.' I looked north. 'Bobby, I can see their castle.'

The huge tower of the university shone creamy in the sunlight, like a slightly squat Empire State Building, rising in tiers. As we went a little higher, the four shorter towers were visible too. I turned around. It had reminded me of Richmond Park, but the tower blocks surrounding it made me now think of Central Park, which I'd only seen on films and always struck me as a dangerous place. Here, I felt utterly safe. I remembered about drunks and rabies, but it was impossible to feel any danger with so many people walking and sitting, just enjoying the space.

'Charge!' shouted Bobby, running full pelt down the hill, past squirrels, thin pine trees with vibrant purple cones, a patch of dandelions, until we reached the small stream at the bottom.

'Those sneaky giants have got a moat,' I said.

Bobby threw his stick down. 'Can I take my shoes off?'

I hesitated. It was only ankle deep, but I knew what a

nightmare it was to get anything washed by hand in the sink. But it was just socks. If Alison got funny, I'd wash them myself. I stuffed our socks deep into the toes of our shoes, and knotted all the laces together

We both waded in barefoot, the water running fresh over the stones, and began to search for tinier beasts. Further along, the banks grew higher and we could hide from the vibrations of giants. After a while my toes started to feel numb, and I climbed out, pulling Bobby after me. We lay in the sun and allowed our toes to dry off a bit before pulling the socks back on. They felt wrinkled, a bit gritty, no matter how tight I pulled them.

Bobby's cheeks were a bit flushed with sunburn, and the back of my neck was starting to feel tender.

'Time to go home,' I said.

Bobby nodded, so I knew he was really tired. On the way back, along the hot street, I told him about the red castle of the biggest giant that I'd seen the other day.

'You mean the Kremlin,' he said.

'Yeah. Have you been there?'

'I've seen it.'

'You know Christopher? He was telling me about these underground caves which are so beautiful. They might have trolls or bears, I'm not sure what kind of caves they are.'

Bobby didn't respond.

'Do you want to have a ride on my back?'

He nodded, and I bent down for him to climb on. He was some weight. I hoped he didn't have sunstroke.

Alison wasn't worried. 'He didn't sleep much last night, and he always catches the sun.'

'OK,' I said. I'd laid him down on the sofa, where he was flat out asleep.

'Do you want a cold drink?'

I felt my cheeks, burning hot. 'Yes, thanks.'

'Beer or kvas?'

I was putting off kvas, some kind of fermented bread drink. 'Beer sounds perfect.'

'Go and sit on the balcony. It can get a good breeze, sometimes.'

I went outside, wondering exactly how bad I looked. The flat faced west and, while it was fresh now, the afternoon sun would soon fill it.

Alison brought me my beer. She had water.

'Pregnant,' she said, to answer my look. 'That's why I'm so tired and cross with him all the time.' She nodded back inside towards Bobby. 'And probably why I've seemed a bit off with you. I'm not sleeping well at all. The white nights. It will only get worse.'

'I was looking forward to that. Is it a problem?' I asked.

'I need total darkness to sleep, and there's no actual night. No real darkness. Do you know about twilights? Astronomical, nautical, civil?'

I shook my head.

'It's about the levels of the dark. And where we are at this time of year, there is no absence of light. Charlie got me an almanac. Today we have no night, over an hour of astronomical twilight, nearly four hours nautical, almost two hours civil twilight and seventeen hours of daylight.'

'Oh,' I said. 'I've never heard of these kinds of twilight.'

She went inside and brought back a thin book. 'After the 3rd June, we only have nautical and civil. And it isn't until the 8th August that we get half an hour of night. Actual darkness. And we've had no night since the 6th May. Three months. And I know it isn't like Greenland, and I know,' she waved the almanac, 'that there is technically no night in

England for two months. But we never have less than three hours of the darkest twilight and,' she dropped the book on her lap, 'in England we do have bloody curtains.'

'Can't you get an eye mask?'

Alison tutted. 'A rolled-up flannel is the best I've come up with.'

I looked at the sofas which she and Charlie slept on, by the large balcony window. A wall made of glass, and no curtain at all. We had a thick curtain in the room where Kit slept, which he'd brought over.

'Does it keep Charlie awake too?'

'Of course not, but he can have a beer or two to make sure it doesn't. Now that I'm pregnant, I feel like my eyes are pinned open all the time. It makes me feel sick to drink since that night you came over for dinner.'

'We sleep in the bedroom, like Bobby. No windows,' I said. 'Can't you sleep in there with him?'

'No. He's so hot and wriggly.'

'Why don't you go and stay in a hotel for a couple of nights? Get Charlie to watch Bobby, and just have a rest.'

'You can't just book a hotel. Everything is organised and I've been allocated my space here. And I don't trust them.'

'Them? Russians?'

Alison smiled weakly.

'I went into the centre a couple of days ago. It's amazing, Alison. Won't you have to go shopping for the baby?'

'They don't have anything to buy.'

'Can you get stuff sent over?'

Alison laughed. 'There was a girl at the embassy who asked her family to send over her thick winter coat. I don't know why she hadn't brought it. No room in the suitcase, I suppose. She had to trek out to Ostankino to collect the package, where the guy opens it and then tries to charge her three times the cost of the coat. They assume anything remotely useful will be sold, and they want their cut.'

'What are you going to do? You have to allow yourself out of this flat.'

'I do go out with Charlie. I just go to see other English people.'

'Think about it. There are so many parks and they're amazing. You can almost see where we went today. There's a circus up this road, a zoo.'

'You could take him.'

'No, I can't, because I hate circuses and zoos. Get Charlie or UPDK to get you tickets, and you won't have to speak to anyone. Your driver can even take you there. You need to wear Bobby out, and you'll sleep better too.'

Alison slumped back in her chair and yawned.

'Anyway, think about it. I'm going to leave now so you can go and have a sleep in Bobby's bed.' I stood up to leave. 'For God's sake, lock this door, though.'

Alison nodded but didn't move. I let myself out.

I walked along Lobachevskogo and, when I reached Leninsky, I crossed over. This was the other half of the wood which I'd been to with Bobby. This half was Yugozapadny Lesopark. Yugozapadny was the area I lived in. Leso meant forest. So, Yugozapadny Forest Park. I had been making Galina talk about my area and the parks. I pretended to be very interested in trees and, as a result, learned a lot of species which I had now forgotten. I sketched out rough maps for her to fill in the names of parks and forests and was amazed that south-west, beyond the edge of the city, was an enormous forest park, Troparovo. It was my aim to get Alison out there. I could make her love Moscow too.

But here, at the edge of my forest park, I was stuck. I

couldn't see a path into the wood. I could see a lake and I walked around it, finding the path behind it. I stood at the edge of the trees, my hands slightly clammy. I realised that it wasn't the heat. I was afraid to go in without Bobby. It was all Kit's fault, talking about rampaging teenagers and drunks. I would stay on the path, like all good children in fairy tales.

It was instantly cooler in the trees. I closed my eyes and breathed in the smell of soil. It felt odd to be so completely by myself outside. I hoped I was completely by myself. The trees, although clearly planted in lines, were different thicknesses and heights, which made it feel more wild than when I looked down on the trees outside my window. Their combined canopies let in very little light.

After a while, I started to ignore the smaller rustlings, and only looked around on the bigger cracks and movements. But I didn't see anyone, neither drunken wolf nor angry giant nor aggressive bear. I missed Bobby's distracting chatter and, when I saw a good sword, I picked it up to whack the bushes, bravely.

I was happy to get out into the sunshine again. I found myself near Lumumba University, and instantly knew that if I turned left and right twice I would approach my apartment block from the other way, on Ostrovityanova. I had been north, east and west of my flat. Another forest called to me from the south, across the road. I wasn't going to get lost, after all. I was starting to feel at home.

Kit had arranged the first opera tickets for us, and Pyotr was waiting in the car park for me when I came down. I hoped that a blouse and a skirt were going to be smart enough.

I said hello to Pyotr, he grunted, and that was our first conversation. I was on a roll.

This time, alone, I paid attention to the car, to the soft leather seats and the clean chrome ashtrays. The ride was smooth, and we sped down the central lane which was reserved for important people. I did feel important as we drew up at the Bolshoi and Kit was waiting on the steps for me, a rose in his hand.

'Cinderella,' he said as he bowed, and I imagined Pyotr writing that down in a little notebook as my *nom de guerre*.

I took Kit's arm, and we went inside.

'What are we watching?'

'*Khovanshchina* by Modest Mussorgsky.'

I bowed my head. 'Should I know this?'

'No, you're quite all right, darling. Only the Russians have heard of this. It's the Shostakovich revision, which will sound good if you put it in a letter.'

We climbed the stairs to the embassy box, where we found a couple already sitting. I was introduced to Mrs Highfield and her husband, Sir Alec, who I realised was the ambassador.

'Are you an opera fan, Mrs Hughes?' asked Mrs Highfield.

'No, this is my first,' I said.

She whispered something to her husband who smiled, but not at me.

Kit and I took our seats as the orchestra tuned up, I put my rose on the floor and waited for the gold and red curtains to open.

After about fifty minutes, the curtains closed, the applause was loud and long and the audience began to stream out.

'There are drinks and snacks downstairs,' Kit said. 'Do you want to stretch your legs?'

We joined the movement down to the lobby. Many women had sweeping, vibrant evening gowns under fur collars, and

I felt very underdressed. The queue for drinks was long.

'When does the second half start?' I asked.

'Ah,' said Kit, 'there are five acts.'

'Five? How long is it?'

Kit looked concerned. 'Didn't you eat before you came?'

'No.' My stomach had already been rumbling.

'But I've played operas for you. They are all long.' He sighed. 'Darling, I find the best thing to do is just let it wash over you. I could tell you what's happening, but sometimes it's best to just guess. It can be more fun that way. And stop you falling asleep, if this isn't your kind of thing. I'll get some food.'

'I'll wait here.'

I watched Kit join the crowd and looked at the lucky people who had snapped up crackers with red caviar. One man seemed to be watching Kit, but I wasn't sure. He was tall, almost military with his cropped dark hair and straight shoulders, but didn't have the heavy jaw many of the soldiers were distinguished by. I would have thought he was Russian, but his black jacket fitted properly. He looked around and then approached Kit, talking close to his ear. Kit shook his head. The man walked away, through some double doors.

When Kit came back it was time to go back up. I crammed the hors d'oeuvres into my mouth and drank the champagne as we climbed the stairs.

'Who was that man?' I asked, wiping my mouth.

'No idea,' he said, very quickly. 'Let's go.'

12

Pyotr picked us up from the apartment. I tried to say hello, but he didn't even grunt this time. Kit smirked.

'Do you need me to say it for you?'

'I have a teacher, thanks.'

'Otlichno,' he said.

The dacha was half an hour north-west from the apartment, at Serebryany Bor. We drove along the wide roads until we got close, where the roads narrowed to lanes and there were more guards.

'It's not just our embassy here,' said Kit. 'There are lots of different ones, as well as the richer Russians. Do you know you can make 150,000 roubles from a book here? They really like their writers.' He lowered his voice. 'The right kind of writer, obviously.'

We passed by more guards and stopped at a barrier for our papers to be checked, then drew up to the dacha. I got out of the car to hear so many English voices that I felt quite homesick. The big old wooden building was in a pine forest. It looked a bit run down, the paint peeling, but loved.

'You can hire it for the weekend,' said Kit, steering me to follow the others. 'This is the way to our private beach.'

The Moskva ran through the forest, and stretches of sand were visible on both sides.

'This is beautiful,' I said. I almost wished that we weren't surrounded by people, but could sit here on our own and enjoy it.

'Martha!' Bobby ran up. 'I saw a dinosaur in the water!'

'Quick, let's see!'

We ran down to the river, and Bobby squatted down. I copied him.

'It was there.' He pointed.

'Bobby!' Alison came down to the river. 'Daddy wants you. Food first, then monsters. Can't keep you from the monsters either, I see, Martha.'

'Someone has to keep an eye on them.' I stood up. 'This place is amazing.'

Alison looked around. 'Wait until you get trapped in conversation with some old git.'

I put my arm through hers. 'Let's stick together.'

I saw Kit and Charlie, drinks in hand, deep in conversation away from the others. It wasn't how I'd normally seen them talk. Charlie was not laughing at his own jokes, and Kit looked worried.

'What are they up to?' I asked Alison.

'No idea,' she said, but she said it slightly too quickly and kept her eyes on them a little too long.

'Picnic' wasn't quite the word I'd have chosen. There were lots of cooked dishes: coronation chicken, potato salad, sausage rolls and hors d'oeuvres. I filled my plate twice, realising how dull my diet had become.

'Do they ship in all the ingredients?' I asked.

'I suppose so. The embassy shop is quite varied. Have you been there yet?'

'No. I have barely bought anything since I got here.'

'What do you do for food? Our driver takes me to a Beri-ozka, or the embassy shop, which is the only place to get decent milk. Didn't you get an introduction to all this?'

'No. Natalya just brings things and I see what I can make.'

'You don't choose anything?'

Alison's astonishment made me feel embarrassed. 'I never thought.'

She thought for a moment. 'Maybe they should only send students over here. You're used to making do. Let's get some more food.'

'You can't still be hungry. Where's Bobby?'

Alison pointed to a blanket where he and six other children were sitting. He was crossed-legged and cross-armed.

'He won't stay there long, but they try to keep the kids together.'

Alison moved to the end of the line and filled her plate again. 'So, ready to meet some other wives?'

I took a breath. 'OK.'

'Watch out for Emily. It may all be first names here, but she's Mrs Highfield everywhere else.'

'Ah, I met her last night.'

She led me to a small circle of women by the river, two on chairs, one on the sand. I wondered if there was a hierarchy in this.

'This is Martha,' said Alison. She swept her cutlery to point at the two oldest on the chairs: 'Jessica, Emily' and 'Sandra', on the sand.

Emily held her hand out for me to shake. 'How did you find the opera, Martha?'

'Very interesting, thank you. The costumes and sets were very impressive.'

I was conscious of being watched as I settled onto the

sand. Their eyes drifted away, and I wondered what they had been talking about. Food shopping, I guessed.

'So, what did I miss?' asked Alison.

'We were talking about yetis,' Jessica said. 'Again.' She was the most smartly dressed, a pink cardigan topped by pearls.

Alison turned to Sandra. 'Have you found anything new?'

Sandra put her plate down and tucked her hair behind her ears. 'No, I'm still trying to persuade them that it explains the deaths at Dylatov.'

'It was a bear,' Emily said, and shook her head. Despite the heat, she was wearing tights and, unlike Sandra, had kept her shoes on.

Sandra leaned forward. 'It might have been a bear. And it might have been a yeti.'

I said, 'What's a yeti?'

Sandra looked at me bright-eyed. 'Have you heard of the Abominable Snowman?'

I nodded. 'From an episode of *Doctor Who*.'

'Urgh. OK. Like that, a type of gigantic ancient man which is half man, half ape.'

Oh God, I thought, they're all mad.

'Ha!' Emily pointed at me. 'Even she doesn't believe you.'

Sandra turned to me and away from Emily. 'I read the news reports. There is loads of documented evidence. There was an official scientific hunt in 1958 by the Soviets in Siberia. The next year, nine students were killed in a mysterious accident. And,' Sandra looked pointedly at Emily, 'British explorers have also seen them. The *Daily Mail* sent an expedition in 1954.'

'Now, you see,' said Emily, 'that's just going too far. I read the *Mail* and I don't remember this at all. And, surely, it would have been to disprove the theories of the Soviets.'

She winked at Jessica, who rolled her eyes. 'And didn't you say 1958 the last time we discussed this?'

Sandra turned back to me, 'The fifties. Anyway, every month the research is presented and assessed at the Charles Darwin Museum right here in Moscow. I have a friend who goes there and takes notes for me.'

Jessica cleared her throat. 'I know you enjoy having a new audience, Sandra, but maybe we could let Martha tell us something about herself.'

Sandra continued, 'Do you know that the whole lit side of the moon that we can see is as big as Siberia? Can you imagine being so short-sighted as to say you know everything that is there? And it's not just the Soviets and British looking. Last year, two Americans in Nepal—'

'OK,' said Alison. 'Once we bring in the Americans, you've lost me too.'

'But, I'm just saying that people who have not even been looking—'

Emily clapped her hands. 'Martha, it's very nice to finally meet you. Unfortunately, it seems that Christopher did not pass on the message to you about meeting with me so I could make you feel a little bit at home.'

There was a slightly odd intonation to the way she said Christopher that I would replay in my head. Had he got into trouble when I ignored her letter?

'Never mind,' I said. 'It's lovely to meet you all now.'

'And how are you finding everything?'

'I love Moscow. I think it's an amazing place.'

Now it was my turn for Emily to shake her head at me. 'Oh dear, Jessica, they've got her hooked.'

Sandra, though, agreed. 'Isn't it brilliant? It's like the nineteenth century, when there was no real definition of what science was, so they just looked at everything. Alfred

Russel Wallace came up with evolution at the same time as Darwin, while he was also investigating mediumship. There were no rules and everything was up for grabs. Have you heard of Nina Kulagina?'

'No.'

Emily and Jessica both let out audible sighs and began to speak to each other. Alison put her arms back and raised her face to the sun, eyes closed. I could see the small bump under her dress and quickly looked away.

'I've just read a paper by Professor Ullman. It's very short, if you want to borrow it. So, Nina can move and lift objects without touching them. There are films that Ullman has seen, and they're careful about showing it's not a trick. Because years ago, no one would have believed something as simple as the electrical fields we all have. So why can't they believe in Kirlian photography? Especially when you can actually see the photographs.'

'I have no idea what that is,' I said.

'Basically,' Alison said, eyes still closed, 'the Soviets and the Yanks are trying to find ways to control everyone by trying to exploit our minds and bodies without even having to persuade us or bully us into believing what they tell us.'

Sandra paused. 'Yeah, that's probably true.'

'Good job it's all rubbish then.'

'But the evidence—'

'Is faked.' Alison lifted her head and opened her eyes. 'It's a distraction from what we should be looking at, all this paranormal stuff and racing to space. Nixon's government, right now, is under investigation for trying to tap the opposing political party. It's pure Soviet techniques. Listen to your enemy, especially when they're talking to their friends. As if Nixon didn't know.'

Jessica sat forward, 'We've talked about this, Alison. I

met Richard and Pat when they visited here last year, as you well know, and I won't hear a word against them. You can talk about all the monsters and flying balls you like, but the Americans are our friends and allies. That's enough.'

'I'd better go and check on Bobby,' said Alison. She sat up and then struggled to her feet. 'Oh, I feel sick.'

'It's not the chicken, is it?' whispered Jessica. 'I do worry about the food being left out like that for hours.'

'No, I'm fine. I'll just check on Bobby and go inside for a bit.'

She walked away, one hand on her stomach.

Jessica and Emily watched her go and looked at each other.

'Pregnant,' Emily said. Jessica nodded.

'I'm going to get a drink,' I said. 'Would anyone like one?'

'Oh, white wine all around, please,' said Jessica.

I collected the plates and walked back to the table. I could still hear Emily when she started talking.

'She knew. Did you see her face? I've got so many questions to ask her. She clearly can't lie for toffee.'

She laughed with Jessica. I carried on walking.

Jessica and Emily had both acquired parasols by the time I got back with the wine. Alison didn't return for some time, but Sandra was good, if challenging company. She promised to lend me *Psychic Discoveries Behind the Iron Curtain*.

'Is that a permitted book, dear?' Emily had asked.

'It's an American book,' said Sandra.

Later, she'd been telling me about Scanate. 'Scanning by coordinates. So you give someone a coordinate and they can project their mind, or soul, or something, and tell you what they see.'

From the corner of my eye, I saw Emily jump up and

walk over to some men standing by the silver pines near the shore.

'I'm not sure I believe that,' I said.

'Well, you don't have to. I just think it's fascinating. Imagine being able to lie in bed and imagine yourself anywhere, see what people are up to.'

Emily came back with a tall man. He held his hand out before he got close, so I scrambled to my feet. He seemed like a headmaster. He had a strong handshake.

'Martha, how lovely to meet you. I'm Edward, I work with your husband.'

'Nice to meet you.'

He smiled and looked down at Sandra.

'Sandra, dear, would you mind coming with me? There are some gentlemen to whom I promised to introduce you.'

Sandra's face paled. She slowly stood up, brushing the sand from her skirt.

'I'll see you later,' she said to me, but she didn't sound certain.

I stayed standing as I watched them walk away, Edward's hand around Sandra's shoulders. I knew that if I sat down, I would be at the mercy of the best British spies at this picnic. With relief, I saw Kit walking across. He kissed me on the cheek.

'Darling, I see you've met Mrs Johnson and Mrs High-field. Ladies, I'm going to steal her away, there are so many people to meet.'

Jessica and Emily smiled and nodded. Kit guided me towards a group of men, including Charlie.

'Are you OK?' he whispered.

'Yes, but I think Sandra's getting told off.'

'Where's Alison?'

'Inside. I think she got a bit too much sun.'

'Well, darling, I hate to say it but your nose is looking a little rosy.' Then he put his mouth next to my ear. 'Don't say anything about all that until I bring it up, OK?'

I nodded.

In the apartment, I felt the tender sunburn on my forehead and nose. What an idiot. But the breeze from the river had been so lovely, I hadn't noticed the heat.

Kit gestured with the wine glasses to go out onto the balcony. I let him through and closed the door behind us. The sun was still high above the horizon, but it felt as if it should be dark.

'You can't say anything about what Sandra said.'

'Any of it?'

'I don't know. Definitely not whatever she said last.' Kit slumped over the balcony rail and took a long drink. 'They're usually quite fun events.'

'I was enjoying it. Is she in trouble?'

Kit kept his gaze on the trees and nodded.

'I'm guessing that—'

'Don't guess.'

I was guessing that Sandra had been given information that was classified, that she shouldn't have heard the word Scanate. And who would have given her that but a spy? I thought about the excitement on her face as she led me through her strange thoughts and interests. Every woman who was brought out here needed to find their own way through. Her way was the best I'd seen – just investigate everything that you find fun.

'What were you and Charlie being so serious about?'

Kit laughed. 'Oh, it's all a mess right now. A few things at work. I wouldn't try to guess them either, darling.' He crossed over to me and put an arm around my shoulder. 'It is good to have you here, Martha. After a day like today, it's good to have someone to talk to, who you can't talk to about things. Does that sound stupid?'

'No. I get it. It forces you to be grounded in the real world and talk about real things.'

But I felt that, if he really was my husband, I would be furious at this secrecy. As it was, I couldn't shift the image of Edward's arm on Sandra. The men were all steering the women to ignorance. Some of it might be necessary, I supposed, but they didn't have to enjoy it so much.

Kit drained his glass and went back inside for the bottle. It seemed he didn't have any real things to talk about, after all. He came back with three airmail letters.

'I'm just off for a bath, but I forgot about these,' he said. 'Your father has been handing them over for inclusion in the diplomatic bag, but there's been some kind of delay and they've all come at once.'

'Oh.' I felt guilty. I'd only sent one letter the whole time I'd been here. 'I haven't finished mine. I'll do it now.'

I held them in front of me and wondered what I was going to write. I fetched the thin blue airmail paper I'd brought, and started writing: 'Moscow is great – can't wait for the snow.' When I wrote to them before, Kit reminded me that my parents would not be the only people reading it, and the thought of trying not to offend both the Russians and my parents almost scuppered my feeble efforts. In the end, I made it into a touristy list of places I'd seen, even just from a distance, as if they would ever be here to take up my recommendations.

Now, my head was full of names I'd learned that I was sure I shouldn't write down. I hesitated, chewing the end of my pen. I wanted to write about Sandra most of all. I hoped she would be all right. I'd get her address from Alison so we could have a proper conversation.

I put my pen back to the paper. I could write about the weather, the food. What I mostly thought about was, what does Eva think about all those things Sandra talked about? She lived here. Did she know about the yetis and scanning distant lands with your soul, and strange photographs? I had been reading through Eva's stories and there seemed to be something behind them. Something hidden that made me want to ask her questions. And she'd approached me, I realised. Unlike Kit, she must want to answer them.

13

Kropotkinskaya station was on my Metro line. I turned off Gogolevsky Boulevard onto Sivtsev Vrazhek Pereulok. The buildings were old, each three or four storeys, and I didn't think it was just the word Boulevard which made me think of Paris. Doorways had intricate art nouveau canopies, sections of the first floor which jutted out with Juliet balconies. There were window boxes on window ledges, sometimes with crusts for the birds, and plants inside on window sills. The paint was peeling from the mouldings, the wrought iron rusted and masonry cracked, just as it had been in the area of Paris I'd stayed in the previous summer. It made me think of Harriet, but I put this out of my mind because I didn't want to come out with any names in front of Eva. I wanted information from her.

I checked Eva's map, and crossed the first road. One building ran from it to the second turning, five storeys high, and thin windows along the bottom showed there was a basement too. It was the grandest so far, with wall lanterns in between each ground floor window and three large balconies on the corner. As I neared, I could see that they ran right around a narrow angle, less than a right angle.

I gazed up, then crossed the road to the small park opposite for a better look. A man, who had been standing on the
corner with his copy of *Pravda*, walked into the park and
sat down on a bench. I waited a moment, to see if he'd look
up at me as I pretended to check the map again. He didn't.

When I turned back, I saw how the building looked like
the prow of a ship. I imagined Eva, disguised by the reflections of grey sky and neighbouring buildings, watching me.

At the entrance, I looked for a buzzer. There wasn't one.
I turned the door handle, the door opened, and I walked
up the sweeping stairs to the second floor, one hand on the
dark, polished handrail.

I knocked on her door and it opened to show Eva, one
hand on her dog's head. She must have known I was going
to knock. The light shone from behind her so I couldn't see
the expression on her face clearly, just the impression of a
small woman with her dark hair pulled back into a bun, like
a ballerina. Her fitted blue dress was slightly longer than
the general style here, well below the knee. I held my hand
out and she shook it.

'Mrs Mann, I hope this is a good time to call.'

'Marta, please call me Eva. We don't use such terms as
Mrs here. No masters, no mistresses. Do come in.'

She stood aside. The hallway was long but the chandelier
was sparkling, and I could see large, expensive looking
furniture: a console table, a low chair next to the grey
telephone, a high occasional table with a large blue vase.
Again, I got the sense of being in Paris.

She closed the front door and opened another, into
a large, high-ceilinged room. I realised it was one of the
rooms I'd looked at from outside, the prow of the boat,
narrowing to an expanse of glass and light.

'Please sit. I'll make some tea.'

She left the room, but her dog stayed. Had she told it to? I looked around for somewhere suitable to sit, but it all looked so clean, and I was conscious that I hadn't washed my skirt for days. It took so much effort to hand wash in the bath and took so long to drip dry into it. I had sometimes left clothes on the dining chairs, but with no direct sunlight it didn't speed up the process. I had a new appreciation for mangles.

I settled on the edge of a gold sofa and gazed around. The bookcase, the sofas and the writing table were all ornately old in a heavy, dark wood, but the art was new. Women in factories or in the fields, sleeves rolled up and determined expressions. Women in pilot uniforms striding out. One caught my eye and I stood up to examine it.

There were four figures, against a bridge with red carriages running high across the background. One man in khaki with huge black boots had his back to the viewer. Two other men faced forward, one in beige and one in blue. But the woman – not only did she face forward in her brown jacket and skirt and red top, but she swaggered, hands on her hips, one foot raised on a piece of wood. Her cream headscarf framed her stern face. And at her feet was a dog.

'Ah, you've found my favourite,' said Eva as she came in. 'A reproduction, of course. Nikolai Ivanovich Andronov. It's called *Plotogony*, which means the rafters.'

It was then that I noticed the watery background, the reflection of the bridge support, the mountains, the boats.

'She's so striking,' I said. 'And her dog is wonderful.'

I smiled. She had already sat down, so I took a seat opposite her. The blue and gold teapot had a matching set of cups and saucers, even a milk jug. She leaned back and folded her hands in her lap.

'I like to think it's a wolf,' said Eva.

'It's funny you should say that. Before I came to Moscow, I found a book of stories about wolves.'

She shook her head, interrupting me.

'Here, you need to try tea the Russian way.' She fetched from the sideboard a glass with a silver filigree holder, and poured tea into it. 'No milk, just sugar.'

I pushed my milky tea aside, added a sugar cube to the black tea and stirred it. She waited for me to take a sip, then continued. 'So, Marta, what do you think of our country so far?'

'I think it's astonishing. The buildings and the parks are all so impressive.'

Eva nodded. 'Have you seen our best Metro stations? Novoslobodskaya, Komsomolskaya, Arbatskaya?'

I shook my head.

'I'll draw you another map so you can go back via Arbatskaya.'

'I saw the swimming pool from Kropotkinskaya. It's so close. Do you go there?'

'Only in the winter. It is a steady 28 degrees, and I love the steam coming off it. Are you thinking of going? You know you have to wear a swimming cap? We're very keen on hygiene here.'

'I didn't even bring a swimming costume.'

Eva looked disappointed. 'Oh, what a shame. Well, should you find one to borrow, I can lend you my cap.'

'The shopping is a real problem, isn't it?'

'No.'

She spoke so sharply that I expected her to suddenly laugh or – I wasn't sure. She held my gaze, waiting for me to speak first. I thought of all the things I wanted to ask about, fairy tales, yetis, and failed to find anything which I didn't think would enrage her.

'I, um, haven't actually been in a shop yet. It's just what people have said.'

'People? Russian people?'

'No, my Russian is appalling. British people.'

'British people with their Beriozkas and special shops?'

'Aren't there special shops for Russians too? For the elite?'

'Ah, I see.' Eva sat back and sipped her tea.

'You see what?'

'You're attempting a provocation.'

A provocation? That was what spies did, tricking foreigners into currency violations or unlikely seductions. I suspected my expression had revealed that I knew the implications of the word, but if she was going to play dumb, so would I.

'I have no idea how I'm provoking you. I was interested in talking to you about your writing and translations. Your stories really helped me to make sense of the scale of Moscow, that sense of gods and giants.' I didn't say that I saw the gods as silence and the giants as fear.

Eva's eyes glittered. 'You are mistaken. I don't write, I only translate.'

My mouth opened and closed.

'I would like to talk about my translations, as there is a lot of work that I've done which deserves much more attention in the West, but it seems you've come here with preconceptions that you want confirmed, and misconceptions about my work.'

'I didn't. I'm sorry if I offended you.'

The dog, which I had forgotten about, walked over from the doorway and sat at Eva's feet. Could it hear the anger in her voice?

'I will tell you the truth about us. The Soviet Union is huge, on a scale not seen since the Roman Empire. And, like the Roman Empire, it has to have strict rules to govern such diverse peoples and to ensure that everyone has the home, food and care that they need. Not want, need. While we are currently a socialist state, we are aiming for Communism, when the people are ready to put their wants away. And, like the Romans, our advances and sophistication are resented because people want to return to their tribal loyalties. But we know, don't we, that the Romans benefited Britain. Now we can see it, and we care for their ruins and wish for their organising principles.'

I drank some more tea, feeling the tannin thick on my tongue. 'The British Empire was pretty big.'

'But it tried to make everywhere British. The Soviets have a Union in which we all have a voice.'

There was no point trying to drag this back to a pleasant chat. 'And the dissidents? What about their voice?'

'Dear Marta, I know you are very clever, but you are so fixed in your ideas. In the natural world, the wolf hunts the deer. Is it bad that they do this? No. The wolves pick off the weak deer, and the herd improves overall. They are stronger and healthier. In the Soviet Union, we have some weak minds, woolly thinking, that we try to help. They are welcomed back, aren't they?'

'Like Solzhenitsyn?'

Eva nodded. 'You always have to remember the scale of our mission, from the Black Sea to the Arctic. Unlike the Romans, we aren't stopped by the cold.'

'Because you're the wolves?'

'I think university has made you too cynical, Marta.'

My spine prickled. 'How do you know I went to university?'

Eva raised her eyebrows. 'It would have been a catastrophe if you hadn't, a clever woman like you.'

I was starting to feel dizzy. Compliments followed insults, but I had the sense that she was trying to impress me too.

'I think I should go now.' I stood up.

She led me to the front door. 'You really should tie your hair up, Marta. We see loose hair as nekulturny, uncultured.'

She opened the door for me.

'Maybe I should get a headscarf.'

She smiled, a genuine smile this time. 'Maybe.'

I stepped into the hallway. 'Maybe I could come back and we can talk about fairy tales.'

'You know where I am,' she said, 'but in Russia we bring a gift when we visit each other,' and closed the door.

Now I felt really ill. I made it to the top of the stairs and slid to the floor. My head was spinning and I thought I was going to be sick. I closed my eyes and slid my feet onto the step below so I could concentrate on breathing and feeling the pressure through my shoes.

I was OK. I was OK.

She couldn't have had such a physical effect on me, I thought. Maybe this was a panic attack. I breathed, hands on my knees, head bowed. I don't know how long I was there for, but eventually I felt well enough to go back down. Fresh air would be the best thing.

I staggered out of the door, closed it behind me, walked carefully to the corner and crossed over to the park. I desperately wanted to lie down on the bench, but I knew it would be the worst thing to do. I just had to sit out this weird attack.

I sat, shaded in the tiny park, forcing my eyes to stay open, and I waited. But Eva had faded away and all I could think about was Harriet.

We'd been to Paris in our long summer vacation, teaching English to some eager students in the day, and wandering around the city at night. I think we thought that's what writers did, hang around the Moulin Rouge and wait for inspiration. It was Harriet who wanted to write. I was just there for her, and the moules-frites. This little bit of Moscow looked just the same, and every time someone passed behind speaking Russian, it was a jolt. I wondered where Harriet was now.

The sickness was fading a little and I felt less dizzy. I remembered feeling like this the year before I went to Cambridge, a sudden unwellness that turned into flu. I couldn't get sick, or worse, make Kit sick. We'd have to lay in the same bed being ill together, while someone nursed us. It would be a nightmare.

I became convinced that I was being watched, and turned around to look at the building over my shoulder. That caused another wave of nausea and I slowly fumbled for my map. I unfolded it slowly, thinking how I must look drunk, and traced my way back to the Metro.

I was woken by a ringing telephone. I sat up, still groggy, thinking, I've missed it. I don't know who called. But we didn't have a phone. The room was dark, but a little daylight seeped around the edge of the door. I dragged myself to the kitchen. Kit was eating a sausage sandwich.

'Darling, what's wrong?'

'Please can I have some water?'

'Go and sit down, I'll bring it to you.'

I lay down on the sofa and stared up at the man and dog, who in turn stared up to space.

'Here you go.'

I sat up and drained the glass.

'Are you sick?'

'Yeah. I don't know what it is. I just feel awful.'

'Were you out today?'

I nodded. 'I went to see Eva Mann.'

Kit went over to the record player, placing the needle on the record. *La Traviata*, again. Then he came at sat on the floor by my head. I put the back of my hand over my eyes, partly because of the light, and partly so I didn't have to look at Kit.

'What did she say?'

'She was angry with me. She said I didn't understand and that the Soviet Union was the new Roman Empire. Or something like that.'

I heard Kit blow air from the corner of his mouth. 'Right. Did she give you anything to eat or drink?'

I uncovered my eyes. He was serious.

'Tea.'

I felt sick again. She had put something in my tea. She had done this.

I whispered, 'She poured all the tea from the same teapot, though.'

'It doesn't mean that there wasn't something already in the cup. Could you see?'

'No. Not from that angle. Oh,' I realised, 'she changed cups. She was going to use china and then used glass. But, no. That's silly. Of course she hasn't poisoned me. I think she's lonely, Kit. I don't think she'd poison me. She wants me to come back. I think.' The end was all a bit hazy.

Kit stood up, went to the writing table, and came back with a piece of paper.

'Draw her apartment for me. Everything that you can remember. And write down what she said.'

'Kit, it doesn't make sense anymore.'

'Never mind. We can go over it tomorrow.'

'She must be important to get a place like that to live. It was really stunning.'

Kit snapped his fingers and pressed the pencil into my hand.

'Martha, do it now, before you drop off again. I'm going to get you some bread and water. I think that's all you should have tonight.'

'OK. I will.'

14

I felt weak for a long time. Kit phoned the UPDK office to cancel Galina for the week, and I didn't even hear Natalya come in on her days. We'd been taking it in turns to leave our sheets for Natalya to wash, but Kit didn't want to move me. He put his sheets out to be washed again.

When he sat on my bed with soup or tea, I tried to answer his questions about Eva, but it was all fuzzy.

'You won't go again, will you, Martha?'

I shook my head, but I couldn't hold his gaze. I noticed that the way Kit looked at me had changed, and I wondered if I had spoken aloud when I was ill. The next time I opened my eyes, he'd gone again.

I dreamed of wolves in birch forests, the trees growing cherries and stars. Sometimes, I woke convinced that I wouldn't go there again, and sometimes I was desperate to go back. Eva was one of the most interesting things about Moscow. That little seed of the booklet, which I read and reread, was a riddle I wanted to solve.

Eva was special. She knew both what it was like to live in England and in Moscow, and I wanted to know what it was that had made her jump from one to the other. Was she a communist? It was so hard knowing that she couldn't speak freely, but she wanted something from me. She'd given me the booklet. But then, I'd realise, she hadn't. It was a trap. I'd walked into it and she'd poisoned me. I'd get to a point when I couldn't process any more questions, and fall back to sleep.

When I could stay awake for more than a few minutes at a time, I thought of home. I imagined Pa coming in from work to sit at the table for dinner, while Ma discussed the village gossip. Her letters had covered nothing of note, but it seemed so much more informative than mine. The neighbours' gardens, the local history group and the latest on the bypass. I'd read them all three times, but learned nothing about my parents' lives.

I finally made it out of bed and into the kitchen to find a pan full of scarlet borscht. Either Natalya had been here this morning, or it had been sitting there since the day before. I touched the saucepan. It wasn't warm, but I heated it up and took a bowl to the table. After I finished, I went back for more, but this time I looked for the sour cream in the fridge and rye bread to wipe the bowl clean.

That made me feel much better. I checked the time and saw Kit should be home in an hour. I hoped I'd left enough for him.

I opened the doorway to the balcony for some fresh air. It was very fresh indeed. I pulled my cardigan tight over my nightdress, and quickly closed it again.

I heard the key in the lock and was pleased Kit had come home early. But it wasn't Kit. Charlie stood in the doorway to the front room, swinging Kit's keys around his finger.

'What are you doing here?'

'Christopher lent me his keys.'

'Why would he do that?'

Charlie sat in the armchair and smirked. 'He explained how sick you were, and I'm pleased to see that you are better than he suggested. He knew he was going to be late, so I said I'd call in on you. And here I am.' He looked at my nightdress and I pulled the cardigan tighter.

'Thank you for calling, but I'm still not feeling very well, so I'd like you to leave.'

Charlie stood and took a few steps towards me before putting the keys on the table and holding his hands up. I was trapped by the balcony door. If I screamed, would anyone come?

'You didn't tell him that I called before. Why would you keep that a secret, unless you like,' he smiled, 'secrets?'

Another step, and he held me by both wrists.

'Charlie, get off me.'

'Oh, Martha, you don't mean that. I saw the way you looked at me, and Christopher – well, he's Christopher. Isn't he?'

He pulled my wrists behind his waist so I was holding him. I twisted, but I couldn't free them. He leaned in to kiss me. I turned, and I could hear him breathing. And, I realised, people were listening to this.

'I'm being assaulted!' I shouted. 'Help me!'

He let go of one hand and grabbed my face. 'There's no point to this, Martha. Everyone knows you don't have a proper marriage. I can do things for you that Christopher can't.'

He pulled my face towards his and I screamed, tried to knee him in the groin, and pulled away. He still held my right hand, but with my left I picked up the tin money box and held it up.

'Listen! Someone is trying to kill me!'

'Why are you saying that? Come on, Martha, I just want a kiss.'

'His name is Charles! He's married, he has a child and he works for the British Embassy.'

He let go. 'You little cheat. Is there someone here?'

He went into the hallway to check the kitchen and the bedroom. I slammed the door behind him and pressed myself against it. He turned the handle and pushed back.

'Martha, come on. It was just a bit of fun.'

'Get out of my house!'

There was a final bang against the door, and then I heard the front door open and close. I stayed where I was, the money box cutting into my hand where the tin hadn't been smoothed off on the edge. I waited until I had stopped shaking, listening. He wasn't that patient. He must have left, but still I waited.

The room grew darker, but not dark. I was glad it wouldn't go dark, but I thought of Alison raging against the light and stuck with that pig of a man. And I thought, thank God for the KGB.

Eventually I got up, stiff and shaky, and sat on the sofa to wait for Kit.

I woke up to banging, and it took me a while to work out it was the front door. I held onto the money box, went into the hall and listened.

There was laughter, and then I heard Kit say, 'No, I really can't find them.'

I opened the door.

'Oh, darling, thank goodness.' Kit fell towards me and I held him up.

'Ow, you scratched me.' He half stood, examining the

long scratch on his hand. 'Why are you holding that thing?'

I looked at the money box and put it on the floor so I could hold him with both hands. He stank of papirosy and drink. Behind him stood a man whom I recognised from the opera, the man who had spoken to Kit at the interval. Kit turned to him, losing his balance.

'I forgot. This is Martha. I have a wife. This is my wife. I suppose you don't want to come in.' He held a hand to his mouth. 'Excuse me.' He staggered to the bathroom. The man and I listened to him vomit over and over.

'Who are you?' I asked.

'Sergei.' He gestured, as if touching a cap. 'Good night.'

I shut the door and fetched a glass of water, which I left by the sofa for Kit. I thought about making up his bed but decided not to bother.

I sat against the wall on my bed and left the light on, my knees under my chin. Silence again. They would be recording this too, this embarrassment of Kit, and who knew what he'd been doing before he got home. They'd know. I expected he didn't even remember giving the keys to Charlie.

Charlie. I looked at the marks on my wrists. I was furious.

I picked up a fresh piece of paper and wrote about what had happened with him. I could give it to Sir Alec and he'd have to send him home. Wouldn't he? But that could mean making things worse for Alison, stuck with him, for now at least. I finished writing and put the pages inside *The Brothers Karamazov*, with the short stories.

15

By the following Wednesday, I was much stronger and desperate to go out, so I'd asked Kit to arrange a time for me to pick up Bobby on Friday. I did think about whether this was a good idea, but I liked Bobby and Alison, and I wasn't going to let Charlie ruin that. And I wanted to check that he hadn't taken it out on her.

It was a lovely temperature, about 22 degrees, after the rain the day before. I didn't want anything to happen while I was in charge of anyone. I walked slowly, testing my body after so long inside, but there were no signs anything was wrong.

I knocked on the door to the apartment. Alison answered, Bobby next to her.

'Let's go,' she said.

'Oh, you're coming?'

'Yes. I got Charlie to get Inturist tickets and everything.'

'For what?'

Alison put one finger to her lips. 'We're going to see that statue of Lenin, and then we're having an ice cream.'

The mausoleum – but Bobby couldn't know it was a body. Bobby led us to the Metro station, pointing in the

direction of the park we'd last been to. I'd since found out
from Galina that it was named for the 50th Anniversary of
the revolution. Or the 'Great October Socialist Revolution',
according to Galina. So it was only six years old. I could
only assume that there had been some kind of park there
earlier.

We got off at Prospekt Marksa and I looked at Alison to
see if she was impressed by the silvery marble, but her eyes
were on the people around us.

'No one's smoking,' she said.

'They're not allowed to on the Metro.'

She looked stunned. 'It's so clean.'

The battalions of old ladies who kept the floors swept
and cigarettes unlit had done their job.

We left the station and turned around to get our bearings.
A large red building was in front of us and, to the right, a
corner tower of the Kremlin. We walked up to the statue of
a man on a horse and saw to the left another enormous red
building.

'Do you know what they are?' asked Alison.

'No. The maps are a bit rubbish, so I draw little ones for
my Russian teacher and she tells me what the buildings are.
If I'm allowed to know. One time she just said, "There's no
building there." Like I'd hallucinated it.'

'Is Inturist not any use?'

'They might be, but they just want you to go to certain
places too. I like exploring.'

Alison pulled Bobby's hand towards her more tightly and
spoke quietly. 'There might be a good reason for keeping to
their directions, Martha.'

I lowered my voice too. 'I only take him where I tell you
I am going.'

Bobby was looking from one of us to the other.

'This way,' I said.

We walked between the first building and the Kremlin wall, along the grey cobbles. There were a lot of people standing in line. They queued everywhere here.

'Oh, St Basil's,' said Alison. 'It always makes me happy to see it's still standing.'

More of the domes were revealed as we walked up the incline, and then the square opened out and we walked into the middle of it.

'Wow,' said Alison.

The red wall of the Kremlin faced the creamy walls and arched windows of another massive building.

'Don't you think it looks really French?' I asked.

'What is it?'

'It's GUM, the department store.'

'That is GUM?'

'Goom,' repeated Bobby. 'The goom of doom.'

'Isn't it weird? All those pictures of the politicians standing on the Kremlin wall, and they're facing that shop,' I said. 'We can go in after.'

'Are we allowed?'

'It's a shop, Alison.'

I turned to look at the mausoleum behind us, and worked out what the queue was for. It bent in right angles, up the side road, along the back of the first red building, then at a right angle into the square, and another right angle to the entrance itself. Some people had flowers, and I was relieved to see not all the women had headscarves. I hadn't thought about covering my head.

A guard in a blue uniform was patrolling the line, telling people off for having their hands in their pockets or for talking.

'Do you have the tickets?' I said.

Alison looked through her handbag, pulled out the tickets and a piece of folded paper. 'Sandra's address.'

I nodded and looked up and down the line.

'Alison,' I whispered, 'there are no children in the queue.'

'I noticed that.'

The guard spotted us, walked back in our direction, and took a man's hat off on the way. We stopped talking. Alison still had hold of Bobby's hand, but he was starting to jiggle.

'Stand still,' Alison hissed.

'What is the man shouting for?' Bobby shouted.

'Shhh!'

Did I have my passport? Did Alison?

'Inturist?' he said, pointing at the tickets which were still in Alison's hand.

She nodded. He tapped his watch.

'Sunday,' he said. 'Nine forty-five.' He pointed back to the cobbled hill we'd first walked up. 'Nine forty-five,' he said again, and made a cutting motion with his hand.

'Spasibo,' said Alison.

Someone further up the queue lit a cigarette. Our guard ran over, snatched it from his mouth and threw it to the ground while shouting with such rage I found myself thinking it must be an act. Could you get that angry every day about the same things?

'Can you use the tickets again?'

'I'm not sure. I'll ask Charlie. It's free really, just foreigners can pay $5 to jump the queue. So, technically we could line up now and wait for hours, but I'd rather not.'

'Are you disappointed?' I said to Alison.

'Not really. Charlie must have forgotten to pass on that bit about timings. He's been really distracted.'

Good, I thought.

She continued, 'But I'm a bit relieved. It was stressful

enough coming here with Bobby, without actually going in to see a man in a box.'

'A man in a box?' repeated Bobby.

'How about an ice cream?' I said, pointing at the stall near GUM.

'Yes.'

We crossed the square, and I ordered three white ones, which I hoped were vanilla.

'This is disgusting,' said Bobby.

Alison had already creased her face up, and was rummaging in her handbag for a tissue.

'Spit it out,' she said.

I was trying to think what taste reminded me of. Art classes, brushes.

'It tastes of turpentine,' I said. 'Well, how turpentine smells. The one I had the other day was lovely.'

We took them back to the stall, and the man held out a bucket for us, full of discarded cones.

'It happens quite often,' Alison said. 'Not this, exactly, but things made near the end of the month are dodgy. It's the monthly targets, they'll do anything to hit them. I get that. But why does he keep selling them?'

'He can't imagine what else to do with them, I expect. Shall we go in?' I pointed to the GUM doors.

'Yes,' said Bobby, and dragged Alison after him.

It was like entering a magnificent train station, the glass roof flooding the place with light. Bobby ran his free hand over the reddish-brown surround of the fountain.

'I want to go in this,' he said.

'No way,' said Alison.

He pulled her back. 'I want to swim in this.'

'Well, you can't. Can you see anyone else swimming? It's just for looking at.'

Bobby dipped his hand in the water.

'Oh, God.' Alison scrabbled in her bag for the tissue again. 'Don't put that hand in your mouth.' She grabbed for his hand, but he wiped it on his trousers.

'Let's go this way,' I said.

We wandered in and out of some shops, but there was little to remind me of shops at home. What was on sale looked poor quality, but still women queued to choose their goods, queued to pay for them, and queued again to have them wrapped in old copies of *Pravda* or waxy paper.

'Let's get out of here,' whispered Alison.

We stood under an opening to look at the bridges between the balconies on each side of the first floor, and the thinner balconies above, all surrounded by ornate green railings.

'Ah!' shouted Bobby.

'Shh,' said Alison. 'We're just looking.'

'Ah! Ah!'

'It won't echo,' I said, 'it's not that kind of space.'

He took a deep breath. 'Ahhhh!'

People who hadn't turned around yet, now began to look at us. Old women in headscarves started to rebuke us, and a policeman was heading over. We went back out past the fountain and into Red Square. I checked behind. The policeman had stopped at the doors.

Alison exhaled. 'OK, I think we need to have a walk. He's been in one place too long. Which way should we go?'

'Probably not that way.' I pointed past St Basil's and mouthed 'water'.

Bobby pointed at St Basil's and said, 'Daddy works near there.'

'That's right,' said Alison, 'but we can't see him today.'

'Let's go to the square by the Metropol,' I said. I was still attached to the Metropol, it being my first experience of Moscow. We walked back towards Prospekt Marksa station, and turned right at the Moskva Hotel. In Revolution Square, I saw a stall selling pirozhki.

'We could get a pie,' I said, unsure whether this was a good idea after the ice cream.

'Yes, pie,' said Bobby.

'Just get two,' said Alison. 'I don't think I can face one.'

I bought two. It was too early for lunch really, so there was plenty of space to sit, although many benches, as always, were already occupied by older people, glumly wrapped up in their scarves and hats despite the warmth.

Bobby eyed up his pie.

'You go first,' he said.

I took a bite and tentatively chewed it, ready to spit it into my hand. I didn't have to. 'It's really nice,' I said. 'I couldn't tell you what it is, some kind of meat and onion, but it tastes good. You should get one, Alison.'

Surprised, she went over to the stall and got her own. We sat quietly on the bench, watching the cream buses, some with a red stripe, some with blue, drive past the Metropol on one side. Over the road, past its own square, we could see the Bolshoi. Behind us, Karl Marx emerged from his granite base to urge the workers to unite. I heard something over by the Metropol, someone shouting. Looking over I saw a man being bundled away from the entrance by two men. A car drew up, and they pushed him into the back seat, one with him and one in the passenger seat. The car sped off.

'What's happening to that man?' asked Bobby.

'I expect he did something naughty,' said Alison, 'and they're going to tell him off.'

Another man had caught my eye. About twenty-five, he was shabby and very thin. I could see his cheekbones and the architecture of his wrist protruding from the jacket sleeve. After the car left, he'd pulled his cap down and started to walk over in our direction. He leaned against a tree, shuddering, and I realised that he was staring at us.

'Alison, we need to go,' I said, and stood up. I nodded my head in his direction, and she glanced up and stood too.

'Let's go, Bobby,' she said, and tried to grab his hand.

'I'm not finished,' he wailed, wriggling from her grasp.

She crouched down next to him. 'I said we need to go, so let's take it with us.'

The man started walking again, focusing on me, because I was the idiot who refused to stop watching him. I forced myself to look down. Bobby was now lying on the bench, holding his pie in the air with both hands and slowly, so slowly, taking a bite.

'He's coming over,' I hissed. 'What do I do?'

'Just don't take anything,' whispered Alison. 'Hands in your pockets.'

She sat down again, next to Bobby, resigned to his immobility. I wanted to sit down, but it felt safer to be standing, to meet this man on his own terms. I kept my eyes fixed on Bobby, calmly nibbling his pie.

The man was behind me now. I could hear his breathing.

'Pozhaluysta,' he said.

He sounded young, his voice cracking. I didn't turn. I couldn't. I could just pretend that I didn't know Russian, that I didn't know the simplest of words.

'Pozhaluysta,' he said again, and then he made a noise like a sigh. I turned and saw two more men, darkly dressed like the others, approach and lead him away. One plucked from his hand the envelope which he must have been holding out to me.

'Martha, sit down.' Alison held my hand to pull me down to the bench.

'That poor man,' I said.

'What man?' asked Bobby, sitting up. He held out his pie. 'I don't want any more.'

'Let's go home, then,' said Alison. 'I remember why I stopped leaving the apartment,' she muttered to me.

I felt I'd let her down. 'Can I take Bobby to some more parks? Gorky Park, maybe?'

'I'll think about it, Martha. To be honest, every time I come into the city I am reminded how terrifying this place is. Give me a couple days to let it fade. See you later?'

'Will I?'

'The meal with the Americans.'

'Oh, yes.'

I'd begged Kit to let me skip this, but he'd been in a state since the night with Sergei. He couldn't remember what had happened and talked rather hopefully about being drugged, as if that would get him off the hook. I hadn't wanted to add the story of Charlie to his distress, and I wasn't sure whether Kit would completely believe me. He liked Charlie, thought he was a funny womaniser who meant no harm. All I could do was hope to avoid Charlie in a natural way.

Except for tonight, it turned out. My presence was required. I had a meeting arranged with Emily Highfield the next day, so I couldn't even drink my way through it.

Boy, girl, around the table, and no spouses next to each other, meant that I was stuck between Charlie and Mike. Mike's wife, Carrie, had thought this was the best idea. I didn't like Carrie for this reason, as well as the butterfly blue eyeshadow she continually flashed with exaggerated blinks. On the plus side, she had Charlie's full attention.

We filled a table at the Ukraina restaurant, to Carrie's relief.

'They put people on the same table as you,' she said, eyes wide and slowly blinking. 'I mean, look at this place. Never more than a quarter full, and they make you share tables.' She shook her head.

Mike chuckled, and checked to see whether Alison was finding it funny. Alison gave him a stiff smile.

'I mean, they're from all over here,' Carrie continued. 'All different colours. They keep the darker people at the top though, and the elevators take an hour just from the twentieth floor. It's such a long time that they don't come down very much.' She nodded as if we'd all agreed that this was a good thing.

Kit cleared his throat. 'This is a popular hotel for delegates from the central and southern republics, as well as the Chinese and Africans. I always find it fascinating how the Russians like to divide everyone up into groups when they're so concerned with everyone being equal.'

Carrie looked at him and then addressed Charlie again. 'Can you believe that they chew garlic?' She threw her head back to laugh, and Charlie forced some accompaniment. There was, indeed, a scent of stale garlic mixed in with the papirosy and the beeswax which was applied to wood and linoleum nightly in all public places.

'Hey, Mike,' she said, 'have you told them about those business cards?'

'Oh, honey, this is why I invited these two good men to dine with us. They helped us out.'

'Well, tell the ladies, then, Mike.' Her eyes skimmed over me, and then lingered on Alison's protruding stomach, before looking back at Charlie and patting his hand.

Mike did his best. 'We have a number of businessmen here in Moscow,' he drew the 'cow' out unnecessarily, 'and one guy had come up with this plan to bribe officials.'

Kit shifted uncomfortably, trying to catch Charlie's eye. Charlie's hand had disappeared under the table and Carrie was looking ahead in a strangely fixed way.

'So,' Mike said, 'he had these business cards manufactured with two strips of card and a thin layer of gold in between them. Heavy as anything, no one could fail to notice. And he got caught, of course. What Nixon has been achieving is so incredible that people have forgotten to be careful.'

Charlie said, 'Didn't you have a planeload of people who turned up without any visas?'

'Ha, yes. That Nixon sure has changed how people see the USSR. They're all coming over, thanks to him and Kissinger.'

Kit shuddered at the mention of Kissinger. I took a large drink of wine, went back to watching Charlie and Carrie and stopped trying to follow the conversation. The men were on vodka by now, and I suspected that the bland, lukewarm vegetable soup, and grey meat stew with hard potatoes would be easier to forget with a good slug of vodka. The ice cream desserts were melting in the bowls.

Mike was still talking. 'Of course, they hate the East Germans here, call them old Nazis.' He lit a Marlboro. 'And they are, of course.'

I stifled a yawn.

'I'm going to powder my nose,' Carrie suddenly announced. 'Ladies?'

Alison and I got up to escort her. There had probably been a sign I had missed, meaning the men could quickly talk about important things.

In the powder room, as Carrie insisted on calling it, she really did powder her nose. Looking at Alison in the mirror, she asked how far along she was.

'I'm due in November.'

'Your husband's a card, isn't he?'

Alison ignored her. Carrie then turned to me. 'Your husband's a queer, I'd say.'

I was thunderstruck, mouth open and no words coming out. Alison quickly put her arm through mine. 'You're so provincial, darling. All the best husbands are queer. I wish mine was.' She squeezed my hand, and we went back to the table. I was so glad I hadn't told her about Charlie. She knew quite enough.

As I was getting ready for bed, something struck me as different – the order of my books or the arrangement of my clothes, I wasn't sure. I picked up *The Brothers Karamazov*. The story booklet was inside, but the report I'd written about Charlie was missing. I felt sick as I picked up all of my books and shook them, knowing that I would remember where I put it. I hadn't touched it since that night.

I pulled myself to my feet, went to the kitchen and poured a glass of wine. This was really bad. Whoever had taken it, and I knew it wasn't Kit, could do terrible things with it. They could make it look as if I'd given them a statement. They could use it against us. They could use it against Alison.

I looked out of the kitchen window to the dark blue of the night sky. It was the early hours of Saturday, but Kit had to work Saturday mornings and wouldn't be back until after midday. I could take everything apart in my room and be definite it had gone and have everything back by the time Kit got home. Then I remembered about Emily, summoning me to her apartment at eleven, sharp. Pyotr was picking me up and I couldn't phone to cancel. I would have to go.

'Always Been There'
by
E. V. MANN

I was walking past Kazan Cathedral, on the corner of Red
Square, when I noticed that there was no cathedral there.

I asked the officer, 'Where has the cathedral gone, citizen?'
I pointed to the corner where it had stood.

'There was never a cathedral there, citizen.'

I looked at the rubble, still smoking, and nodded. 'I see.'

'You don't remember a cathedral there, do you, citizen?'

'No.' I shook my head. 'Not at all.'

I kept walking. At the cool Moskva river, I turned right.
Behind the wall of the Kremlin, I could hear the roaring of
flames, and smoke billowed up. I put my hands over my ears
and walked more quickly past Kremlin Hill.

I stopped at the Cathedral of Christ the Saviour to catch
my breath. I spoke to the ice cream seller there.

'Citizen, have you seen anything strange today?'

He shook his head. 'I never see anything, citizen.'

'Heard anything?'

'Never hear anything, citizen.'

I nodded. 'Me neither.'

He looked to the side of me and I looked down along
the river. A band of people was walking towards us, pulling

three long chains. At the end of the chains was a large, green Slavic dragon, walking upright on its back feet. Each of its three heads writhed, trying to escape the chains which I could hear chafing against their scales.

The leader of the band, his uniform grey with ash, pointed at the Cathedral of Christ the Saviour. I quickly turned for my last look. The large gold central dome, and four smaller ones, swelled up to heaven. The white body opened itself up with slender windows and peaked wide arches of the frontage. My eyes took in the sweeping steps which welcomed in both the city and the river. I saw it all.

There was a great inrush and the dragon's three heads all spat fire at the cathedral, streams of light and heat, until the very stones had melted and the gold ran past us into the river.

The leader consulted his papers and shouted, 'The church of Saint Paraskeva in Pyatnitskaya Street!'

The band moved forward, the dragon roared, and they were gone. I stood in the falling ashes and noticed how the flowing gold had already cooled, like the spilt blood of gods.

I turned to the ice cream seller. 'Good afternoon, citizen.' He nodded, and started to push his cart somewhere which was there, and had always been there.

16

I woke up to banging on the door. I looked down at the clothes I'd fallen asleep in. Too late to change now.

I opened the door to Pyotr. He tapped his watch. I mimed brushing my teeth, and rushed quickly to use the toilet and do that.

We went down in the lift, and the sudden jolting did my stomach no favours. I wished I'd taken the stairs. I got into the car and closed my eyes. When I opened them, Emily was waiting for me outside the embassy. I had a sudden urge to fake illness and make Pyotr take me home. Instead, I got out of the car.

Emily looked me up and down. 'Martha, dear.'

'Emily, I'm not feeling very well but, as I don't have a phone, I couldn't let you know. Can we rearrange?'

Emily shook her head. 'No. This way.'

We went through the embassy, past people and doors, until we reached a sitting room with two armchairs facing each other, angled away from the windows. There was music coming from a small record player on a shelf in front of the window. On an octagonal table was a teapot, small triangular sandwiches and a two-tier cake stand with jam tarts.

Emily gestured for me to sit in one chair. She sat in the other and poured the tea.

'So, Martha, we finally get to have a chat.'

I smiled and took my teacup from her. I had no idea where this was going.

'Alison has told me that you asked for Sandra's address.'

I frowned. 'Yes?'

'After the picnic, I thought it might be a good time to review our little rules. Because I feel that you were somehow missed in the process. After all, you didn't take up my invitation. People assumed that, your father being who he is, you would understand how this works.'

My father being who he is. My father, frequenter of GCHQ. These people knew who he was. I tried to keep my face steady, but Emily realised she'd strayed from her intention to be authoritative and set an example.

'Let's take Sandra,' she said, moving quickly on. 'A very bright and interesting girl, it is certain, but recently her desire for knowledge has led her to some tricky subjects. And dubious friends. The problem is, dear, as I'm sure you'll appreciate, that friends make demands on one. Often, they don't even realise it themselves. And friends from different cultures, well, their intentions are always harder to read somehow. Yet, by the fact of being friends, we give ourselves up to pleasing them, without meaning to. Sandra needs to come back to us.'

I sipped my tea.

'And we thought about you, dear. You're bright and interesting, like Sandra, and you seemed to get on very well.'

She raised her eyebrows, and I nodded.

'So, we'd like you to spend some time with her. She has

odd ideas, and we don't mind that, but we need to keep her focused on the West.'

'I don't feel very comfortable being instructed to be friends for your sake, Emily.'

'Oh?'

'I was going to make contact with her. That's why I asked Alison for her address. I don't see why you felt I needed another push.'

'Well, we were rather hoping you would give up your recent acquaintance in order to spend more time with Sandra.'

I frowned. 'Who do you mean?'

'Eva Mann.'

I stared at her. She must have known I'd only seen her twice and had likely been poisoned the second time.

'You are an embassy wife, Martha. You should attend the parties, you should accompany Christopher to the ballet and the opera. Speaking of which, you have not been doing your cultural duty there. You keep your husband content and occupied, and everyone is happy.'

'That's not quite what I had in mind. I think it's important to explore new places, rather than make everywhere you end up look as much like home as you can.'

'Yes, I'm quite sure you'd be at home cross-legged on a dirt floor. We are here as representatives of Britain, not as individuals. We set an example.' She folded her hands into her lap. 'Did you know about the embassy choir? That might be something you would enjoy. Do have a sandwich, dear.'

I picked one up and held it in front of me, as if uncertain what to do with it. Could she tell all her embassy women exactly how to be wives? I cleared my throat.

'I'm not being paid to be here, Emily. I think how I spend

my time is my business.' I put the sandwich back on the plate. 'Kit can comment on what I do, if he wants. He's paying for my home.'

She leaned forward. 'I keep hearing about you, Martha, and that's not how it should be. You're not supposed to be evident in any way, other than to ease your husband's path through these strange lands we end up in. Meeting with people like Eva Mann is getting you noticed by the wrong people. I'm sure that isn't what you want.'

'It seems I can't stop you watching me, and whatever I do, I'm watched. But if I want to spend time with another British person, or Russian person, I will.' I stood up.

'She's not really British, you know. Just a leftover from the Second World War.'

I walked to the door, then stopped to look back at her. 'Thanks for the tea.'

I went downstairs and stopped on the steps at the front. Kit was waiting for me.

'Everything all right, darling?'

I hooked my arm through his, and swept one arm dramatically in front of my face. 'Take me away from all this.'

'I sent Pyotr off.' He smiled. 'You look terrible.'

'Does anywhere do a fry-up, by any chance?'

'No. Not that I've found.'

I remembered the pie. 'Take me to The Metropol, darling. There's a brilliant stall that sells pies. That is just what I need.'

We sat on the grass and discussed my failings as a wife.

'It is true, though,' Kit said. 'There has been a lot of interest in you.'

'Meaning?'

'I noticed that first night you were being watched.'

I swallowed too fast, and coughed. 'By which team?'

'Their team, the Soviet one.'

'And you didn't say?'

'Do you remember what a paranoid wreck you were?'

I forced myself not to look around for someone here and now. 'So, way before Eva?'

'Eva is what got our team interested. Only because they were watching her anyway.'

I tried to imagine going to see Eva and not saying all of this straight away. 'Don't tell me any more, Kit. I'm going to stuff it all down so I forget it.'

He nodded, scrumpled up the wax paper the pie had been wrapped in and flopped flat onto his back, hands above his head. 'What a week.'

'Anything you can tell me about?'

'If I look like the world is going to end, you can bet there is one of two things behind it. I've either got another prov-ocation to deal with, or Kissinger has been busy stirring the pot.'

I felt relieved. 'I haven't got you in trouble, then?'

'To be honest, there's so much other stuff going on that this won't be a priority for anyone but Mrs Highfield.' He turned towards me. 'By the way, she arranged *Eugene Onegin* tickets for us for tonight.'

'Is that an opera?'

Kit laughed. 'Yep. A long one. She wants to keep you busy.'

I lay down next him, my bag under my head. 'Do you know what I fancy? A film.'

'They show them at the American Embassy, but that's on a Saturday morning. They are terrified of sitting next to a Russian, so they have their own cinema.'

'I don't mean there. A Russian film.'

'Oh.'

'Oh, yes. You can't say it doesn't count as cultural.'

Kit closed his eyes. I found I couldn't, even being so tired. Not now I knew I really was being followed.

Kit propped himself up on one elbow. 'You're worrying now, aren't you?'

I was, but about something else. 'How easy is it to get a key cut here? If you lost one.'

'Oh, you haven't, have you? You just can't get them cut. You'd need a whole new locking mechanism.'

'No, I just wondered.' I nodded. Ever since Charlie, I'd wondered. I saw a man lurching towards us and I tensed, but he was drunk, not making an approach. He managed to turn himself around and leave in the opposite direction. I tried to relax my shoulders.

'Do you know what I think? The Moskva, over there,' Kit gestured behind him, 'has a cocktail bar on the eleventh floor. I say we go there, have a few drinks, see a film, get the last tube home. Just as if we were in London.' He waved his hand over my face. 'There are no Russians here. You can't hear Russian or speak Russian or see Russian.'

I smiled. 'OK. Let's find a hair of that bloody dog that bit me.'

Kit stood and hauled me to my feet. I tried not to look, but the movement of the man across the grass caught me and I couldn't help it.

Being in the Moskva Hotel helped. The number of English speakers meant I didn't try to pick out words that I knew all the time, and just let it wash over me. Kit made sure I paced myself with regular glasses of soda water, and by the time we reached Kalinina Prospekt, I was numbly happy. I half wanted to bump into Eva, to see what she was like with Kit.

I decided to go and see her again. I missed her in a weird way.

Kit pointed to four tower blocks. 'This is where they use lit windows to make a huge illuminated CCCP at night, the Russian letters for USSR. Have you seen pictures of that?'

'It rings a bell. I didn't know that's what they stood for.'

We continued walking. I was doubting that the small back streets he'd led me down were anywhere near the industrial sized Kalinina Prospekt, but then Kit turned left and there was the cinema, grey and rectangular.

'The Khudozhestvenny cinema,' he said. 'Built in 1909, would you believe?'

I wouldn't. It was squat and plain and dull. I shrugged. Then he pointed at the sweeping curves of another building nearby. We walked around it.

'Is it in the shape of a star?' I said.

'Yes. It's one of my favourite buildings.'

I stood back. 'Mempo.' I still had to try to read in English first, knowing full well that I couldn't. 'It's a Metro station?'

'One of the best. It's even more amazing inside. But first,' he looked at the posters on the cinema, 'we have *Planet of Storms*.'

'Oh good, sci-fi.' I had been a little worried it would be a deep conversational piece that I wouldn't understand at all. 'I can do alien planets.'

Kit looked surprised. 'I love sci-fi too. *2001* was one of the most amazing things I've ever seen. How did we not know this about each other?'

I raised one eyebrow, and looked back at the poster. Five male cosmonauts looked thoughtful underneath a strange dark shape. 'Is that a pterodactyl?'

'Maybe. That's a robot.' He pointed to a dark shape which I could now see was a rounded head with glowing eyes. 'I've heard of this. It's quite old,' said Kit, 'at least ten years. Maybe it's an anniversary showing.'

'Why is it all men? They have female cosmonauts, don't they?'

'Well, they do, but who wants to see them?'

I hit Kit on the arm as he dodged away. Then I thought how that would look to our follower, or followers. And then I thought how it might be nice for them to have a night off in the cinema for a change. Maybe that's why we were supposed to go to the ballet and opera, to give everyone a nice break.

'You're thinking about it again, aren't you?'

'Can we sit at the back, so there's no one behind us?'

'Afraid not, darling. I am going to do something naughty and blag our way in.'

'What do you mean?'

'You need to buy tickets in advance for everything, and we didn't. So, I need to pretend we're visiting from a Czech-oslovakian delegation, and that will mean the best seats.'

'Is this what they mean by "blat"? Corruption and influence?'

Kit rolled his eyes, and went to buy the tickets. I kept close to him. He was speaking for a really long time to the girl in the booth. I heard 'Festival nauchnoy fantastiki' a few times. She was writing something for him on a piece of paper. He turned and smiled at me.

'We're in luck. There's a whole series of sci-fi films on. We have to see *Solaris*. It had great reviews, but I never got to watch it.'

It wasn't what I'd been looking for, but I did feel a sense of purpose when he said that. Or was it just a way to keep me occupied and away from difficult people? Who cared, if it meant missing another opera?

'OK, you're thinking again. Let's go in.'

As we passed into the hall, with the uncomfortable chairs I would grow quite fond of, I turned to see the girl writing another list for a man. He kept his back to us, and I tried not to notice his dark blue jacket and the black hat in his hand.

17

At the door, I held out my seven roses, one rouble each, which I'd bought at the Metro station.

'Marta, how thoughtful,' she said, and smiled.

'Oh, someone mentioned that it was customary here.' I smiled back.

'Come in.' She kissed me, once on each cheek, and I could smell her face powder. 'Do go through, Marta, while I make the tea.'

My stomach turned. I felt her hand on my elbow, and I looked at her.

'I do hope you weren't unwell after your last visit. I was very ill indeed. The doctor said it was a virus, and I've been worried that you could have caught it too. I have sterilised everything in the kitchen, and I'm sure we'll be quite safe.'

She shuffled away with her flowers and I went into the same room as before. The dog, ears up, lifted her head to watch me. I walked up to *The Rafters*, again surprised by the woman's stance.

Eva had mentioned the illness, which I hadn't expected. I had been intending to pretend to sip the tea. Maybe she had really been sick. It could have been a virus. I winced, imagining what Kit would think of me if I said any of this to him. I regretted not leaving him a note telling him where to find my body, should I not return. Emily Highfield would know where I was.

Eva returned and placed the tray down. 'I thought we'd have it Russian style again today. You must be getting more used to our ways.'

Two glasses with silver filigree surrounds and handles, a saucer of sugar cubes to plop into the black tea. There would be little chance to pretend to drink this. Was this an admission of guilt, or a test of faith? Or both?

'I don't think I will today, thank you,' I said.

'Please sit. I will drink from both glasses, if you like.'

We were back in the same places, but Eva seemed happy to see me this time. I didn't want to mess this up again. I wanted to know about her.

'How have you been?' I said.

'Very well, thank you. There is a lot of work at the Novosti agency for translators. It might be something you consider one day.'

'They employ foreigners?'

'Oh yes, but we always welcome new Soviet citizens as well. I've found, the longer you spend here, the easier it is to see the problems back in Britain. Have you found that, Marta?'

I was so conscious of the background silence, the recorder whirring away out of sight. 'I think there are problems in any system.'

'Right now, in England, it's inflation that's a terrible problem. Isn't it? How much has butter gone up?'

'I don't know.'

'Forty-eight per cent. Fish, forty-three per cent. Cheese, thirty-eight per cent. Do you know how long you have been able to buy half a litre of milk here for sixteen kopeks? Ten years, Marta. The Metro has been five kopeks to go anywhere you like for twenty years. It runs every four minutes. Have you been making good use of it?'

'I've been a few places, yes.'

Eva shuffled forward on her chair, and poured the tea. 'And have you managed to see any films?' She put two cubes on each saucer next to the teaspoon, and gestured for me to choose one.

'Yes, we saw a few from the science fiction festival.' I put two cubes in the glass and stirred them slowly.

'We?'

'My husband and I. We saw *Planet of Storms* and *Cosmic Voyage*. And *The Sky Calls*.'

'And what did you think?'

'I really liked *Planet of Storms*, but it was distracting having it translated into my ear, so I'm trying to watch them myself. I thought *Aelita* would be a good one, because it's a silent film, but it seemed to be two films jammed together, one on Russia and one on Mars. And then the man woke up, so the Mars bit wasn't even true. So that felt like a cheat.'

'That was *Aelita: Queen of Mars*?'

I nodded.

'I didn't think that was shown nowadays. Do you remember where you saw it?'

'No.' I didn't want to report anything. 'Great special effects, for the twenties, though.'

Eva nodded. 'They're all pretty old. Did you know that *Solaris* is on at the Mir cinema? It won at Cannes. It's the cinema on Tsvetnoy Boulevard with the wide, curved screen. Something new for you both. You might have to wait for tickets, but I hear it's very good. You haven't been married long, have you?' She drank from her glass.

'No.'

Eva smiled at me, waiting for me to say something else. I smiled and sipped the sweet black tea. I assessed myself. I felt all right, so far.

'Is it too cold? I can get some fresh tea, if you'd like.'

'No, it's good. Thank you.' I sipped again. 'Can you tell me about your translation work? Do you translate work for children, fables or fairy tales?'

'No.' The word was spoken with such force that her dog lifted her head and looked from her to me. 'Adults. Novels for adults.'

She was so determined to get me to believe that the E. V. Mann of my booklet had nothing to do with this Eva Mann. I couldn't understand why. Hadn't I said how much I liked them?

'And what hours do you work?'

'I'm lucky to be able to take some of my work home. I tend to go into the office on Monday and Friday, for collection and delivery. Most of the time I'm here, but I like to keep Tuesday afternoon free. A little hangover from the old days, having an afternoon for reception. Does your mother do that?'

'No, she doesn't have set visiting hours.' I didn't know anyone who did. She'd said the 'old days', but it seemed more nineteenth century than her living memory. 'I expect your dog likes having you at home.'

'Dorogaya moya, Vorona.' She looked at me, an eyebrow raised.

'My darling, Crow,' I translated.

'Very good,' she laughed. 'Your lessons are working. If you wanted to spend some time with Russians for conversation practice, I can help.'

'Oh, no. Thanks.'

Eva smirked. 'You're still scared of us. You think we're all scary and different. But I take Vorona to the Chelyabinsk dog club, like any little old lady in Chelsea.'

'Eva, why do you always refer to yourself as being old? You don't look very old to me.'

She sighed but looked pleased. 'Ah, I've lived three lives. It's too many.'

She looked unbearably sad then, and I realised she still thought England was a place where dogs joyously run from the butcher's, in their mouths a string of sausages waving in the wind. I wanted to take her out for a cream tea, with clotted cream and raspberry jam, and let her pretend it was still like that in England. Because it wasn't. It was power cuts and strikes, the House of Commons lit by candles and paraffin lamps, rubbish in the streets, a million unemployed, men fighting police for the right to decent pay and people living in condemned houses with the promise of nice new flats that never came.

Her expression was curious when I drew my eyes back to hers. She stood up and gestured to the door.

'Thank you so much for coming, Marta. Please do come again.'

I was back on the stairs, but not dizzy or sick, just surprised. I hadn't even finished my tea, but I liked her again. I wondered how many versions of Eva there were.

18

I kept thinking about my meeting with Emily, and I had become more annoyed that Alison had told her I'd asked for Sandra's address. In the end, I decided to stop moping about it and go and ask her. And I was missing my days out with Bobby.

When I knocked on the door I was surprised to see Alison was ready to go out.

'Oh, I'm sorry, we're off in a minute.'

'Where to?'

'We're meeting a couple of mums and going to the Puppet Theatre. Andrea organised it all. Do you want to come? You can't come in, but we're going to the Hermitage Garden after.'

'No, I'm all right.'

Alison turned to Bobby. 'Can you go and put your shoes on the right feet?'

He disappeared into the front room.

'What's the matter?' she asked.

I didn't know I was so transparent. 'I got summoned to see Emily because you told her I'd asked for Sandra's address.'

'And?'

'And why did you tell her?'

Alison frowned. 'Why wouldn't I? I didn't go and tell her especially. We were talking at the food store and I mentioned it after she brought up Sandra. I thought it was a good thing for Sandra to have someone else to talk to. Everyone else has children and, now it's the school holidays, it means women without children can feel left out.'

'So we can't go anywhere?'

'Of course we can. It's just I can't today. Why don't you go and see Sandra?'

'I might.'

'Well, she lives on Sad-Sam. That's near the puppet theatre. Get a lift with us.'

I couldn't think of a better idea.

Sandra opened the door and put her finger on her lips. She grabbed her bag, hanging beside the door, and led me outside, past the overpass and onto a long strip of grass and trees between two rows of buildings. Yet again, I was reminded of Paris.

She looked terrible, hair lank and feet dragging. We walked on until we were nearly at the other end and she looked around before sitting on the grass in an open area, away from the trees. I sat down next to her.

'No, you sit facing me. Then we have a full view of what's happening.'

I moved to face her. Her eyes were dark and sunken, her hands holding each other tight.

'Are you OK?'

She shook her head. 'They say I've been given classified documents. They say I have been colluding. That time at the picnic, that's the only time I've ever spoken about those things. No one was interested before you.'

'I'm so sorry, Sandra. I didn't mean to get you into trouble.'

She laughed. 'It wasn't you. They've been watching me. My own people. And now it seems that if I don't spy for us, I'll be charged with treason.'

'They said that?'

'No, not straight out, no. It's just all, "Who's Sasha? Where does he live? How do you contact him?"'

She looked behind me, tracking someone going past. I wasn't sure that she knew what was going on. Her mind seemed split between the place we were and somewhere entirely separate.

'Has your husband said anything?'

'Albert? No. I can't talk to him. He was so jealous that I had things to do, and things to read. I'm sure he told them to watch me.' Her hands worried against each other. 'And they keep trying to get me to sign papers to say I can't say anything, but if I do that and I am charged, no one will know, will they? I'll just disappear.' Her focus drifted. 'Like the river.'

'The river?'

'The Neglinnaya river that was here, before Tsvetnoy Boulevard.' She patted the ground. 'They hid it under the ground. It went right past the Kremlin, where the Alexander Gardens are, and into the Moskva. It's still there, but we can't see it any more.' She placed her hand flat, as if she could feel the rushing deep underground.

She turned back to me. 'Who knows you're here?'

'Alison gave me your address, and Emily knows I was going to see her. She made me go to see her and she wanted me to visit.'

'To report back?'

'I won't tell anyone what we talk about.'

Sandra closed her eyes and rubbed her temples, then opened them to scan the area again.

'Did Alison tell Emily about the address?'

'Yes, they met in the shop.'

'Coincidences, eh. Alison used to be OK, before her husband had that affair.'

'With who?'

'With the nanny. That's the one she knows about anyway.'

I held one finger up. A woman, bent over, her face hidden by a loose headscarf, was shuffling past, behind Sandra. I kept my eyes on her until she was out of earshot, all the while thinking that Alison had had a much worse time than I thought.

'I don't think she meant to meet up with Emily.'

Sandra rolled her eyes. 'Yeah, she's made you feel useful, looking after her kid, and it worked. Now you're loyal.'

'But you can take any situation and track it back with the right mindset, and lots of things look deliberate from that angle. There was no intent on my side to do anything but get Bobby out of the apartment for an hour or two.'

'Did you ever ask him where he goes when you're not there?'

'No. That would be weird. I'm not going to question a child.'

'How did you get here today?'

'Alison dropped me off. I'm not trying to hide anything.'

'You don't know anything. You're being used.'

She was utterly serious. Her hands were shaking, and she planted both palms on the ground and breathed more consciously, more slowly. The sun went behind a cloud and the buildings behind her darkened. Small birds flew between trees. Her hands stilled, and she gathered them in her lap.

'It's not your fault. I'm angry because we're all being used.'

'I know.'

'Albert has been in such a terrible mood with this thing that's going on at work. He's been foul. How's Christopher been?'

'He's fine. He shrugs things off quite easily. He's been tired, but he's spending a lot of evenings out.'

'And you don't mind?'

Her expression suggested that there was something else I should mind.

'I don't mind.'

'Moles, thieves, spies. It's a ridiculous way to live, isn't it? It attracts the ridiculous, that's for sure.'

'What are you going to do? I mean about what they've asked you to do.'

'I can't look Sasha in the eye and pretend nothing has happened. He calls and I don't answer. He knocks and I don't answer.'

'How did you know it wasn't him when I knocked?'

'I watch from the window. All day. I see everyone leaving for work and for nursery and school, and I watch them come back. I watch the sun rise and the night fall.'

I was suddenly struck by the similarity to Eva's stories. Maybe they weren't fables, but just a symptom of what Moscow did to everyone. I thought about the story Alison had told me about the previous summer. Early in August, the city had been filled with smoke and for a week the press denied it. She'd got clay from *Children's World* to seal all the gaps around the windows. People were coughing and suffering, but no one would admit it was a problem. Nothing on the news, nothing to see. And finally, it was announced that there was smoke in Moscow, and it became real: a peat bog had been on fire for a month, sixty miles away. Plane crashes are kept secret, murders don't happen, rivers don't flow and no one watches each other all the time.

'How long have you been in Moscow, Sandra?'

She laughed. 'All my adult life. I'm not sure any more. How long has Moscow been in me?'

I was going to have to break my promise. Sandra needed help.

'Could you go home for a break?'

'Why?'

'I think this place is intense. Being watched all the time, it gets to you, and we're not used to it. We're used to being free.'

She leaned forward. 'But it's the same in England. We're just better at hiding it, and not looking for it. Everyone's in their boxes, they know whether they get that privilege or can go in that place. We are just more polite about it, but you protest on the streets and you could still be beaten to death. It just depends on where you come from and who you know.' Her eyes were bright. 'It's no different. The people in power are the same here and in London.' She looked away from me and blinked. 'We're here because they think we're the right sort. We'll sit tight and keep quiet, and keep our husbands from the beds of Russian temptresses. They don't care that we have nothing to do. I liked finding out things. I'd rather think about yetis.' She swallowed. 'They've taken my books.'

Her hands went to her face and she started to cry. I moved beside her and put an arm around her. Her face moved to my shoulder, and I felt her body shudder. People walked past on the path, not hiding their interest. I stared the first few down, and then closed my eyes to them.

Eventually she stopped, pulled her jumper sleeves over her hands and wiped her face.

'Sorry. There are no tissues in Russia.' She gulped a kind of laugh, and her head drooped again. 'This isn't the first time I've made a friend and they've disappeared. I see them in the streets and they run from me. They're afraid and I don't know what happened to change things. I must be a bad person.'

She moved away and wiped her face with her sleeve again.

'What can I do, Sandra?'

She dug into her skirt pocket. 'You could take this to Sasha for me.'

I looked at the crumpled envelope. Shit. She pressed it into my hand.

'I meet him at the Apothecary's Gardens on Prospekt Mira, the small botanic garden. By the lake. Fridays at noon.'

I took the envelope. 'What does it say?'

'It just says goodbye. It says what he means to me and how much I'll miss him. I don't mind if you want to open it, read it. I don't mind at all. He might not even come. I haven't been able to go for weeks.'

'So, he never had your address?'

'No. I just like to think he's calling for me. If he had, I'd have left with him.'

I didn't know what was true and what was fantasy any more. I knew that I really didn't want to deliver this letter.

She wiped her eyes one final time, stood up and smoothed her skirt down.

'Thanks for coming, Martha.' Her voice was controlled, almost back to normal. She pointed south. 'You can just follow the Neglinnaya back to the Kremlin.'

I nodded. I could follow the underground river? I watched her walk away, and realised that I was also watching for anyone watching her. The old people on the benches, the women pushing prams, the men with hats tipped slightly forward. No one moved.

I stood up and looked at the letter. I put it in my bag and headed south. I looked at the road name – Neglinnaya Ulitsa. A street named after the river.

I walked slowly down Neglinnaya, and was relieved to see the familiar shape of the Metropol mosaic silhouette. I crossed over and walked up to it wanting superstitiously to touch it and ground myself. As I approached one of the large arched windows, I saw a man crossing the road, his face turned to me. Blue jacket, black hat. He waited while I watched him, then turned and walked away. My fingers, resting on the window frame of the Metropol, could barely feel a thing.

Kit asked me how Sandra had been the minute he got back from work.

'How do you know I saw her?'

He sat down at the table. 'Well, Alison told Charlie that she'd dropped you off, and then Bert overheard and asked me to ask you how you thought she was. So I'm asking.'

'We went for a walk. She's not good.'

'Do you think you should contact Mrs Highfield about her?'

'No. I think her husband should do that. I've met her twice. I don't know what normal is for Sandra.'

'Sometimes people are more open with strangers. There's nothing you could add?'

I'd thought about the letter all afternoon. I wasn't sure that I was going to deliver it by any means, but I didn't want to get Sandra in any more trouble by handing it over.

'No,' I said. 'I can't add anything. She'll be all right.'

19

One Friday had already passed and I had failed to go to the Apothecary's Gardens. I regretted it straight away. I didn't want to keep the letter. It wasn't something I wanted to have to guard while Natalya was wandering around the apartment. I had to decide to throw it away or deliver it to Sasha. I also had to decide whether to read it, but I felt bad thinking that. I kept it inside Eva's book of stories.

Her tales were becoming such a strong part of Moscow. The longer I stayed there, the more I understood. I wanted to ask her about them, to ask how she'd got here, what she thought of it all. There was the small issue of the possible poisoning, but I was unsure about that. Alison was busy with the other mothers, but I had got out with Bobby a couple of times, and we had a late lunch booked for this Friday. I made it late in case I went to the Apothecary's Gardens. I wanted to see Sandra, check how she was, but I couldn't face her before I'd decided what do with the letter. Behind it all, I needed to know, one way or the other, what Eva wanted from me, but she was never going to tell me.

I decided I'd been alone too long. I needed to be around

people, even if I couldn't speak to them. I set off for the university. I was coming to Leninsky Gory, Lenin Hills, and I decided to walk up to the observation point, past the ski jump. Kit had been up here at night, before I arrived, and told me about the lights along the river and beyond, around Lenin Central Stadium.

At the paved area, I walked up to the marble balustrade. I was amazed at how low Moscow looked from here. Lines of trees led to the stadium, and the small dark windows were picked out again and again in the creams and greys of the concrete blocks of apartments. All was softened with the green of parks and grass.

I turned and sat on the balustrade to look back at the university, an encircled star right at the top of the cathedral-like tower. Kit had told me how it was almost impossible to navigate inside, that the students were endlessly lost in identical hallways and stairways.

I noticed, to the right, a woman in clothes that weren't Russian. Denim jeans, a red and white checked scarf tied at her neck. They didn't quite look British either. American, maybe? But quite 1950s in style. Her curly blonde hair was pinned back, and made her eyes look large, childlike. She was taking photographs of the view across the river, but I had the distinct impression that she was aware of me. She was going to approach me. I could sense it. I looked around for my blue jacketed shadow. I eventually spotted him, far to the left, also gazing towards the stadium, but in a brown jacket for a change. I wondered if he'd bought another, or if he had swapped jackets with a colleague. It was impossible to tell from the fit, as so many Russian clothes didn't fit well. He would always be Blue Jacket to me.

He was leaning with both hands on the waist-high balustrade, quite still. I wondered what he would do if I approached him and said hello. I walked towards him. He didn't move, and then I went back down to Leninsky Gory Metro, and got on the train into the city.

Eva never looked surprised to see me, no matter how much time had passed between my visits. I had remembered flowers again, so I got a smile. This time, she didn't send me into the front room alone, but hobbled in first, letting herself sit heavily on the sofa.

'Are you all right?' I said.

'Just a stupid accident,' she said. 'I twisted my ankle.' Her dog looked up at her, and she stroked it slowly. 'Poor old Vorona hasn't had much of a walk today.'

She looked at me sadly. I swore even the dog looked at me sadly.

'I wonder if you could do me a favour,' she said.

My shoulders stiffened. Just like Sandra, I was going to be given an envelope or something worse, and a mission. I had to say no. Then I realised what she meant.

'Would you like me to take her out for you?'

'Would you? I would be so grateful.'

The acting was so poor, I almost felt that she couldn't bother to be convincing. 'Where's the lead?'

'She doesn't need one. She knows where to go.'

The dog was going to take me for a walk. Great.

'Vorona,' I said, hoping the dog would want to stay with Eva. The dog stood, shook herself, and waited by the front door. 'You're sure there's no lead?'

'You'll be fine. She'll look after you.'

I followed the dog out of the door, down the stairs and right, along the way I'd come from the Metro. I tried to walk beside it, rather than behind it, but it was quick, determined to get where it wanted. It waited at crossings, and walked, and then in Alexander Gardens, it stopped by a bench. I tried to work out if it was the same bench I'd met Eva on, all that time ago, but I couldn't be sure. I stood next to the dog for a bit, then I sat down.

This was quite one of the most stupid things I'd done. Not only was I stuck here at the whim of a dog, but I'd also ceded something to Eva. I was starting to believe that the dog would behave the same way, whether I was here or not.

I leaned back on the bench. I wondered where my blue jacket was, behind a tree or a newspaper, laughing at me. I looked around, feeling we'd got past the pretence where we faked ignorance. To my astonishment, I saw the checked scarf woman from Lenin Hills. Map in hand, she was looking at the Kremlin walls behind me, and down at the map. I thought about that map Eva had promised me, and wondered if that's what I had looked like those first couple of times with my useless map.

She caught my eye and smiled, before coming over.

'Hello.'

A British accent. Was it?

'Didn't I see you earlier?' she said. 'Up on the hill?'

'I don't think so.'

'What an impressive dog. I didn't see him.'

'It's a her.'

'Sorry.' She shifted her weight from one foot to the other. 'I was wondering if you could help me get to GUM?'

'It's pronounced goom, not gum.' I cringed at my patronising tone. She might just be a version of me, landed here, as if on Mars, trying to make the best of it. I should be wary of coincidences, yes, but God knows it would be nice to have someone to talk to. I changed my tone. 'You just follow the wall. It's on the opposite side of the Kremlin.' I held my hand out for her map. 'The river here,' I pointed, 'is just over there.'

'Oh, I know,' she said, flopping down beside me. 'I just wanted an excuse to talk to someone. Do you mind?' Her accent veered from British to Australian, with bits of something else too.

'I don't mind. I just have to warn you that the dog is in charge, and if it goes, I have to follow.'

'Does that mean leave me alone, in some weird way?'

'No, I'm afraid it's true. It's not my dog. I'm doing someone a favour.'

'Is that right?'

I nodded.

'OK. Well,' she held her hand out, 'I'm Leila, on a student exchange here.'

'Martha,' I said. 'An exchange with?'

'The British Council. Trying to work out where's where and what's what.' She looked around and back at her map. 'I'm sharing with a girl from Georgia and it's all a bit intense right now. Most of the other exchange students are waiting for the term to start in the autumn, but I arranged a short language course to be with my boyfriend, who's an Australian journalist, and he's been sent away for a story. I don't know when I last had a normal conversation in English.' She threw her hands up, and they landed neatly on her lap as if she'd practised that display of casual frustration along with her life story.

'He's a journalist?'

'Yes, freelance, but works with Reuters a lot. They got the visa sorted.'

'But he doesn't live at the university?'

'No, I can't even let him in for a cup of tea. He has an apartment I can go to, but he's barely been around so I'm trying to occupy myself. Have you got a good map?'

'No, they're all rubbish. You should make your own and sell it. You could make a fortune before they arrest you.'

Leila nodded. 'That's an idea. What brings you to Moscow, Martha?'

'Dogs,' I said. 'Big dogs.'

'You have a thing about big dogs?'

'I like to keep it quiet generally, but you caught me.'

She patted my leg. 'You know, the way to make people not interested in you is to give a pretty boring answer, rather than a funny but clearly evasive one?'

I crossed my legs. 'When you've been here a while, you might find you're doing the same.'

'I don't have anything to hide.'

I corrected her. 'You don't have anything to hide yet.'

'Ha! Those KGB wolves. I can smell them. Can't you?'

She turned to face me fully. Wolves? I stared at her. This was like something out of Eva's stories.

'I can't smell anything.'

Leila turned away and smiled. I ran through our conversation, thinking whether I'd given anything away. Dogs, evasiveness. That was OK. I just had to not say anything else, and hope the dog got bored and went home.

Leila wasn't moving. The unfolded map fluttered in her hand and she raised her eyes to the sky.

'He's off chasing down a holy man, Seb. My boyfriend. In Siberia. Ha! Seb is in Sib. Have you been?'

I shook my head.

'No, I suppose you need a reason for a travel permit. And a country this big, it's amazing how they keep track of everyone, but it seems to work. It's so organised.'

She looked at me, but I didn't react.

'I think so.' She shrugged. 'No one has too much or

too little. Everything is just more fair. It's just those damn wolves that put everyone off. Because ours are better at hiding what they're doing.'

The dog, bless her, stood up.

'I guess you're off,' said Leila. She rustled in her pocket and pulled out a card. 'Here's my boyfriend's details, if you'd like to meet up. I stay at his place more than I stay at mine. There's no one to watch me there. He should be back at the start of August though.'

I took the card. 'Thanks. Nice to meet you.'

She held out her hand again. I shook it quickly.

I followed the dog, thankfully, in the direction we'd come. I didn't turn around, although I really wanted to know if she was still sitting there. I thought she was interesting, but I didn't trust her. The dog and I waited to cross. I took the card out. She'd written her name and an address on the back. That was odd. She must have done it before, but surely she wasn't going to hand out her boyfriend's address to everyone she gave a card to. I read it – 121 Leninsky Avenue, building number 1. My building. I heard her strange barking laugh, ha! No such thing as coincidences.

Against my better judgement, I turned around. She waved. She'd been watching me, watching which way I went, waiting for me to turn around.

I decided that I wouldn't mention her to Kit after all. One dubious contact was enough. Unless our side was watching me too. I hoped I'd be able to read on his face whether there was something I should tell him.

No, I should just tell him.

When I got back, I cut some rye bread to go with the noodle soup. I was laying the table when I noticed a dark shape on the balcony. I opened the door to find it was a crow. It looked like it had a broken neck; it must have flown into the window. I shuddered. I was pretty sure that was unlucky.

I was still looking for something to wrap it in when Kit got back.

'Hold on, I have a *Pravda*.' He fetched it from his brief-case, and unfolded the six pages to wrap up the crow. 'Just put it in the bin for now, I'll empty the bag later.'

I took the floppy body and opened the bin lid. There was no bag.

'Argh! Kit, why didn't you put another bag in? I hate that.'

He came out of the bathroom, drying his hands. 'I didn't empty it.'

'But Natalya wasn't here today, and there was a bag last night.'

Kit gestured to the ceiling and the walls. 'I wonder what happened then,' he said.

They would take our bin bag? I gestured to the bird. He nodded. They could have left that too. I put it in a new bin bag and washed my hands repeatedly. Then I heated the soup and brought it in.

Kit had put Bach on. If I ever took a classical music quiz I would beat everyone now. He switched it up a little and sat down.

I passed over my scoop of the day.

'I was approached by a spy, I think. I saw her twice in different places. She's pretending to be British but the accent is all strange.'

Kit looked at the card. 'Oh, she's with the British Council. I met her when she was in the embassy today, trying to get a decent map.' He pushed it back to me. 'Why has she written our address on it?'

'Oh, she said her boyfriend lives here.' I drank some wine. 'Don't you think that's odd?'

'I suppose, but they do cluster foreigners together.'

'I think I might have been a bit rude, in that case.'

Kit laughed. 'Better safe than sorry. She really didn't strike me as someone who would take it personally.' He cleared his throat. 'Darling, I have something a bit awkward to ask you.'

I sighed. 'Yes, I went to see Eva again today.'

'What?'

'Oh. I thought you meant that.'

'Did you eat or drink anything? How are you feeling?'

'I had some black tea with sugar. I'm fine. It was much better this time.'

Kit sat and stared at me for a few moments. 'Christ, Martha?'

'Is it about Sandra?'

'No. No, it's about Alison. We are going to go back to Eva, though.' He looked genuinely shocked. 'It's not funny, Martha.'

'I know. Sorry. What about Alison?'

Now he looked shifty. 'If she was to ask whether I was out last night with Charlie, could you say yes?'

Now I was shocked. 'You want me to lie, for Charlie?'

'I'm asking you to lie for me.'

'What do you get out of it?'

'He's my colleague and my friend.'

'He's an arsehole. You've fallen for his smarm.'

'I have asked you for a favour. It's now up to you.' Kit dipped his bread into the soup. 'And Eva? What can you tell me about her?'

'I'm so angry with you.' I put my spoon down and crossed my arms. 'You know she's pregnant?'

'It will blow over.'

'Like the others?'

'Not our business, Martha. We can't go throwing stones.'

'So, he knows about you, and is holding it over you?'

'Martha. Darling. Let's not fall out over this.'

'All right, but you have to tell me something about your day. What's Kissinger up to?'

He stared at me, and had a spoonful of soup. I thought I'd offended him, but eventually he spoke.

'Have you caught any news about Afghanistan recently?'

'I can't get the radio to work.'

'There's been a coup. The Afghan king was in Britain for eye treatment, and then went to Italy for a holiday. Wasn't it lucky the coup happened when he was in Italy?' He winked at me.

The music was still playing, but I lowered my voice. 'Was Kissinger pushing for it to happen when he was in Britain? Was he trying to involve us?'

'I never said anything of the sort, darling. It's only what you can read in the newspapers.' He frowned. 'Not *Pravda*, obviously.'

We ate our soup and I thought about the million different impacts that Kit was having on the world, unravelling threads and exposing truths, and I was jealous. I wanted to know everything.

Kit fetched a bottle of Georgian white wine, which was particularly vile, and Bach carried on in the background.

20

It had started raining the day before, and not stopped. On the way to the bread shop, I'd seen drivers get out of their cars to attach wipers. I wondered how many would forget to take them off again and lose them forever. It was one of those rainstorms where the drops feel much larger and wetter than normal. My coat still wasn't quite dried out from then. I gave it another ineffectual shake and put it on.

I was due at Alison's for two, but it was a Friday. I'd promised myself to go to the gardens today, and I couldn't let the rain stop me. I wanted to see Sandra again, but I needed, at least, to try to deliver the letter before I did.

My Metro line went to Prospekt Mira, so I didn't need to change. I walked over the wet chessboard floor, past the cream marble and gold mouldings, and carefully negotiated the steps up to the street. The dezhurnayas had kept it very clean. I held the letter inside my sleeve, having found out that nothing stayed dry in the pockets.

Already drenched, I continued through the rain until I found the entrance for the Apothecary's Garden. The tanker trucks which washed the dust from the streets every day in summer, were washing the streets in the thunderstorm. On the wall was some graffiti I'd recently learned to translate: 'Ленин Жил Ленин живёт Ленин будет жить'. Lenin lived, Lenin lives, Lenin will always live.

A large double gate was closed, but the single gate on the right was open. I paid and went into the garden. There were paths to the left and right and a pond in front of me. I'd grabbed a simple map, and saw that there were two ponds, one rectangular and one more natural in shape. Which one would Sandra have called the lake? I decided it would be the larger, natural one, the one out of sight of the entrance. At least I could tell her I tried, but I hoped this was a waste of time.

There didn't seem to be anyone else outside. I checked my watch – ten to twelve. If I went in the greenhouse I'd seen on the map, someone might decide to take me on a tour. I headed to the lake.

The rain was not letting up at all. I kept my hood up and my head down, but the rain didn't roll off because my coat was so wet already. I stood under a tree next to the lake and tried to look like a tourist. Now that I thought about it, why would Sasha approach me? Sandra hadn't been able to meet him to say that I would be there in her place. I could, at least, have waited until the following week and not come in a rainstorm.

I shivered. The cold was soaking right into my bones. I heard a noise behind me and turned, but I couldn't see anyone.

I stared at the lake, watching the splashes on the surface, watching it for so long that it started to seem like a rippling, monstrous lizard skin.

I checked my watch again. The smell of the rich, damp earth and beaten flowers was fading as I stood there. Either I was getting used to it, or I was getting a cold. This was ridiculous. Sasha wouldn't know me, I didn't know Sasha. I had no idea what Sandra wanted to pass on. There was still a few minutes before twelve, but I left, heading towards the exit.

The rain got even heavier, and I didn't hear the man approach me. His hand rested on my shoulder and I turned in alarm. He was much older than I expected Sasha to be, easily late fifties, with heavy eyebrows and a serious expression.

'Sandra?' he said.

I shook my head. He looked away searching for words. The rain ran from the brim of his hat.

'Sandra go?' He mimed away, with his hand. 'Informat-siya Sandra?'

His face was slightly tense. The fact that he didn't speak English made me trust him more.

'Ya skuchayu po ney.'

He missed her. I pulled the soggy letter from my sleeve and held it out to him. He took it, nodded his head, and walked back the way he'd come.

I regretted it instantly. Shivering, I headed back to the Metro.

Alison looked at me in horror.

'Strip off,' she said. 'I'll get you my dressing gown.'

I was shaking all over by now, wet through to my bra and pants. I went into her bathroom and stripped, wringing each item as much as my stiff hands could. I towel dried my hair, and emerged to a cup of tea.

'I wasn't expecting you to come out in this,' she said. 'You really need a phone.'

I knew that. Kit had finally told me that he didn't have a phone because in the hotel he'd been called at night by women wanting to come to his room. He tried leaving the phone off the hook, and the receptionist knocked to insist he replace the receiver as it was messing up the switchboard. As if. His only respite was to wrap it in clothes and put it inside his suitcase. I didn't know whether Charlie had been alone in a hotel before Alison arrived, and I didn't think that Charlie would have been as resistant to the phone calls. So, I didn't explain why we really didn't have a phone.

'Kit says there's no point having something you're reluctant to use.'

Bobby was sitting on the sofa with a book. He waved and then ignored me; we wouldn't be exploring today. I sat at the dining table.

'So, what have you been up to?' asked Alison.

'Um, learning Russian. Reading. Not much.'

'Have you seen Sandra again?'

'No.' I moved my hands around the cup, trying to soak up more heat. 'Have you been up to much?'

'Yes. It's much easier in the holiday. Everyone has been planning for this the whole school year. Maybe when Bobby goes to school, I'll become an organised mother.'

'You're sending him?'

'Yes, well, with number two coming along, I think it's for the best. Charlie said he'll get a car so I can drop him off at school.'

'When are you due?'

'November. So, if it's anything like last time, I'll be active until the end of August, and then it will all start slowing down again. Quite good timing, really.'

I was glad I had Sandra. If I'd been relying on Alison to keep me company, I'd be stuck.

Alison refilled my cup. 'So, I was going to ask you a favour. While I'm mobile, I wanted to plan a trip to Helsinki to stock up on baby stuff, and clothes for Bobby too.'

'And toys,' said Bobby.

'And toys. And I'm sure there are things you could do with. Maybe for the kitchen? Or books? They have a good English selection in this shop I've heard about.'

'That sounds great. So, Charlie can't go?'

'No.'

Alison looked away, and I wondered what he had planned for that time. She blinked a few times. I hoped she didn't ask about the night he was supposed to be with Kit. I couldn't lie for Charlie.

'Will you get UPDK to organise it all?'

'Either them, or the Russian department at the embassy. I don't know, Charlie will sort it out, hotels and stuff. To be honest, it would just be nice to go away for a bit and not worry about what you say or who you speak to.'

I noticed the silence, then. Alison saw me look at the record player.

'He won't have any noise when he's reading.' She nodded her head towards Bobby.

'You're being noisy with the talking,' he said.

'Not that noisy.'

'You're going to be busy,' I said.

'Yes. What are your plans? You really need one for when it gets cold. You won't want to explore quite so much in the autumn.'

'I want to get much better at Russian, maybe do some translations. I see Galina twice a week, but it's not much. So, I'm going to look at doing a proper course, like a degree.'

'I'm not sure you can, with your visa.'

'Maybe I can just get more hours with Galina, then. And I really need to go shopping. I've totally avoided it so far. I can't face asking Natalya to let me go with her.'

'That's her name? Your maid is called Natalya?'

'My nanny was called Natalya,' said Bobby. 'She played with me.'

Alison left the table and began to bang plates around in the kitchen.

'It's probably not the same one,' I said.

Alison coughed and cleared her throat, then shouted through. 'Charlie got hold of some baked beans. I'm not sure how they will go with rye bread, but that's what we're having for lunch.'

'Perfect,' I said.

I could hear Alison sniffing occasionally as she opened the can and poured it into a saucepan to heat. Nice saucepans. That's something I could get from Helsinki.

The rain continued to fall against the balcony window. I got up to look out of the window. The cars drove along Vernadskogo, some with their lights on, and I was sure a couple were missing their wipers. There was a lot of surface spray and I could see sitting water on the road, where they hadn't built in a proper camber.

It was peaceful watching the cars, imagining the noise and cold, without being a part of it. My clothes were probably still dripping in the bathtub, and I had yet to walk home. But not right now. I pulled the dressing gown more tightly around me and thought, I could get a dressing gown too. That was one of the things I never thought to pack. A swimming costume, swimming hat. Once I started writing a list I could see it being way too much. I'd been content until I had the chance to get more. Maybe that's what it was like, living here. If you can't get it, you don't think about it. Somehow, I doubted it. I still felt as if I was on holiday. It was a temporary state for me.

The phone startled me.

'Can you answer it?' shouted Alison. 'It'll just be Charlie. Tell him I'll call him back.'

I grimaced and answered. 'Hello, it's Martha.'

'Ah, Martha.' Charlie hesitated. He didn't even sound embarrassed. 'I was ringing to speak to my wife. Is she there?'

'She says she's busy with lunch and will call you back.'

'Well, this applies to you as well, I suppose. Can you tell her, when Bobby isn't around, that I have some bad news.'

'What is it?'

'Can you tell her that we have retrieved Sandra's body from the river. As I say, when Bobby isn't around.'

'Has, um, has her husband confirmed this?'

'Yes, of course.' He sounded distracted. 'Thank you.'

He put the phone down. Shaking, I stood there, blinking. Bobby was pretending to read, his eyes flicking towards me. I gathered the teacups and took them to the kitchen, closing the front room door and the kitchen door. Alison was buttering toast.

'What did he say?'

I whispered, 'They found Sandra in the river.'

'In this weather? What was she doing?'

'I mean her body. She must have drowned.'

Alison looked at me. 'On purpose?'

'I don't know.'

'Was there a note?'

'I couldn't ask anything. He doesn't want Bobby to hear about it.'

'Well, I can't say that is a surprise.'

I watched in disbelief as she just carried on. Alison took the pan and spooned out the beans onto three plates. She looked completely normal as she took them in.

'Table, Bobby.'

We all sat, but I couldn't eat my beans. I'd only just seen Sasha, or someone who I hoped was Sasha, and Sandra was found dead. It had to be a coincidence. Whatever Kit said, there was such a thing. There had to be. But there was one line which cut through the rest of my thoughts, the questions, the guilt, the uncertainty – Lenin lived, Lenin lives, Lenin will always live.

I tried to go back to talking when Alison spoke to me, but only single words seemed to make it out of my mouth.

'You're taking this quite hard, Martha. Or are you sick? My uncle died after being caught out in the rain.'

I looked at her, wondering what she was talking about, and why she wasn't surprised by any of this.

'I'll phone Kit, shall I? Ask him to send the car for you?'

The rain was still falling as if there was never going to be an end to it.

'Please.' I went to put on my wet clothes, then I waited for Pyotr in the doorway of the building.

Sandra's body was sent back to England. We had a service for her in the embassy before she left. The Anglican Chaplain came over from Helsinki for it, as St Andrew's was closed. For that week of reflection and preparation, I was expecting someone to come to me and say they'd found a suicide note and I was mentioned in it. I deserved to be blamed for something, but no one ever mentioned a note. In fact, no one ever mentioned suicide, or anything but a tragic accident, a slip and a fall.

Emily stayed next to Sandra's husband, Albert, throughout the service, and her husband made an odd speech about Sandra that seemed to be applicable to ninety per cent of diplomatic wives in Moscow, but not that one. I thought back to the excitement of her yeti tales and manipulation of the physical world, and remembered her in my own way. We followed the coffin to the airport and, tight-lipped, Albert accompanied his wife home to Britain.

I asked Alison whether he was coming back.

'I hope not,' she said. She wouldn't say anything else about him.

The temperature had dropped to about 14 degrees. It felt as if summer was over. I knocked for Leila a couple of times at her boyfriend's apartment, just to speak to someone who didn't know Sandra, but she was never in.

Kit took me to the bar at the Metropol and we sat on the sofa in the corner, with a clear view of the room, drank too much and held hands. It was the closest I'd felt to him since I got here, and I felt a fraud.

'No more tears, Martha,' he said.

'But all the women here, Kit. The men have jobs that they want to do. Why do the women come here?'

Kit kissed my hand and leaned back. 'Most think their marriage will be better if they do. Which doesn't always work. Some think they will be valued for their sacrifice, just part of the job description. I don't think they understand what an impediment boredom is. Maybe they don't get bored. I don't know. But are you all right, darling?'

'Yes. I really am. Sometimes it gets a bit much, but I wouldn't have missed being here for the world.'

He squeezed my hand. 'I'm glad.'

My heart was beating hard as I sipped my drink. 'What have people being saying about Sandra? About why she did it?'

'Just lonely.' He smiled in that tight-lipped way that suggested the end of the conversation.

'She didn't seem lonely,' I said. I struggled to phrase my question. 'Was her husband nice to her?'

Kit looked away. 'I don't know him. No one knows why she did it. Emily thinks it's because Sandra refused to be one of the embassy family. Turned down a chance to be in the choir.'

'Oh. So did I, but you won't find me in the river.'

'Good.' He patted my hand. 'You might get a bit more attention for a while, trying to draw you in. But as long as you're not lonely, I'd ignore her. You're not, are you? I know I have long hours sometimes.'

'I like reading, I like learning, I like exploring. I haven't been lonely. I don't think I'll be seeing Alison as much, after Helsinki. She seems to have got into the whole mum scene. Which is fine, as it's all going to be about the baby for months.' I shook my head. 'I will miss Sandra though. I thought she was really interesting. Did you know her?'

'No. It's very much a men over here, girls over there kind of place.'

'Women.'

'Yes, women.' He smiled and closed his eyes.

'Some men seem to cross that line.'

He opened his eyes. 'Did Alison ever ask about that night?'

I shook my head. She didn't need to ask. There was nothing I could tell her about Charlie that she didn't already know.

'Running'
by
E. V. MANN

Snow falls on the streets and I find myself repeatedly tracking back to the Apothecary's Garden to seek out the palm house, the glass dome of heat which stinks of orchids. I walk slowly around the tropics until I get so hot that it begins to feel like I am being suffocated, as if wrapped in fur, and I go back outside.

I walk the paths under fractured wooden arches and around a solid pond, see leaves frozen into place on the trees until the thaw, when their reflections will return. A fox sits next to the slab of ice, yawning, a stopwatch in one paw. He wears a black beret.

I turn away. My hearing is muffled by my hat pulled low, and I don't hear the runner before he hurtles past me. I lift my hat to listen to his feet drumming. As the runner passes, I hear the fox talk to him.

'You will never be a cosmonaut.'

'I will,' says the runner, circling back. 'I am the fastest of my class and strong as a bear, and we can be anything if we try hard enough.'

The runner sprints away and I walk down to the lake. The shallow edge of the lake is white with snow and I can't see where the land ends and ice starts. It takes me way back to an imagined shadowless world of giants, queens and magicians. That is where I thought I was going all that time ago, not this grey city of concrete and fumes, occasionally made bright like death. I keep walking, marking my trail in the snow, looking for the entrance to that other land.

I see the fox, the same fox, is waiting on the far side of the lake as the runner approaches.

'You will never be a cosmonaut.'

'I will,' says the runner. 'I study engineering and learn about the stars, and we can be anything if we try hard enough.'

The runner takes a winding path away from the lake. I notice he's a little slower than before, his steps a little heavier.

I go back to the palm house and I see the fox standing upright, waiting by the door. The fox doesn't look at me. He puts the stopwatch down on a stone, leans back against the doorpost and yawns. I wait for the runner.

The runner approaches, his cheeks reddened, and stops in front of the fox.

'You will never be a cosmonaut,' says the fox.

'Why do you keep saying that? I've dedicated my entire life to being accepted for training. I've done everything I was expected to, and more. I'm fit and I'm dedicated and I have the right kind of soul.'

'Does your father have the right kind of soul?' asks the fox, standing upright and stretching his forelegs. 'Is there anything we should know about him?'

The runner opens his mouth and closes it again. I know that he wants to defend his father, but that he will condemn himself because they don't ask if they don't already know. Yet he can't denounce his father either. His future hangs on this moment. His head sinks downwards, his arms fall to his sides. He nods.

'Good answer. Follow me, comrade.' The fox picks up the stopwatch and saunters away. The runner stumbles after him.

I shiver, but I can't go back to the orchids. I walk away from the runner, back to the bleak honesty of the slushy streets.

21

I began to be quite excited about going to Helsinki. Thinking about Sandra, and being unsure about my part in it all, made me feel that my small circle was beginning to close in on me. A trip away would allow me to reset and see everything afresh. But there were still a couple of weeks left to wait as Alison had chosen to go in the middle of August.

So, I waited. I didn't go to see Eva. I worked hard at my Russian and started to go to the bread shop on the days Natalya didn't come. And Kit and I had our films.

Kit had to wait for the *Solaris* tickets to come through. A Cannes prize winner, yet there was barely anywhere to watch the film in the whole of Russia. It was sold out for weeks, but he managed to get tickets for an afternoon showing after work on Saturday.

I waited on the grass, where I'd sat with Sandra nearly five weeks earlier. The summer had come back for a last fling, and I leaned back on my arms, head raised, making the most of it. I wondered if my blue jacketed friend would remove his jacket. It wasn't always the same man following me. I'd got much better at spotting them, but he seemed to be the main one.

With my hands on the grass, I couldn't stop myself thinking about the river hidden beneath me, and Sandra ending up in the Moskva. Albert had come back to work, Kit said. He hadn't been up to much, but he was there. He didn't speak about Sandra.

Kit had been working very late, but I didn't think it was connected to her. He didn't speak when he got back. He would just open a bottle of wine and pick at some bread. I suspected something was going on at work, and now what Sandra had said about moles and thieves came back to me. It was such an intense place to work, I could imagine everyone being suspicious of everyone else would be exhausting. I couldn't ask Kit, and he couldn't tell me. All we could do was try to interpret each other.

I looked at my watch. The film started at two. Kit was late. I looked around for him, but he wasn't in sight. I'd stopped at the stall by the Metropol for pies, but there wasn't going to be much time to eat them before we went in. I unwrapped mine and tasted it. Cheese this time, rather than the minced meat from before. I preferred this. I'd also found small bottles of soda water at the Metro kiosk, and opened mine.

I checked my watch again. The film started in twenty minutes. He should have been here forty minutes ago. I stood up and looked past the trees towards the cinema entrance, but he wasn't waiting there. I was in the open. He couldn't have missed me.

There wasn't anything I could do. I sat down again. I noticed someone walking towards me, and realised with horror that it was Sasha. He crouched next to me and held out an envelope.

'Sandra,' he whispered.

I shook my head. 'Sandra gone.' I waved my hand and

struggled for words. I didn't know what 'died' was. I pointed in the direction of the Moskva.

I fumbled for words. 'Vody. Moskva.'

Water. Moskva.

He shook his head, and held it out again. He didn't believe me, or he didn't understand.

'Pozhaluysta.'

I was reminded of the man outside the Metropol saying please. I couldn't help Sasha either, just repeat myself and push the envelope away.

'Sasha, Sandra Moskva. Vody.'

He looked angry then, pushed his envelope back into his pocket. I heard a clock nearby chime twice.

I looked down, watching him from the corner of my eye. He didn't run. He just walked up the boulevard, back towards where Sandra lived. Maybe she came here a lot with him. Then I saw Blue Jacket approach him from the side and begin to argue with him. Sasha turned back to me and was shaking his head. Blue Jacket was demanding the envelope, then he marched him to the side of the park, where a car was waiting. He took Sasha's arm. As they walked towards the car, Sasha seemed to realise what was happening and pulled away, shouting and pointing at him. Another man in a grey jacket got out of the car, and Sasha gave in. He was pushed into the car without another sound. Grey Jacket drove him away.

My hands were shaking as I packed everything away. I stood up and walked towards the Kremlin thinking, if Kit is late, I'll bump into him and it will be OK. But there was no Kit, just the familiar shadow behind me by the time I got on the Metro at Prospekt Marksa.

Alison's face fell when she opened the door.

'I thought you were Charlie.'

'Isn't he here? I was supposed to meet Christopher at the cinema and he never showed.'

'Oh. So they might be together?' Her face brightened. 'I'll call the office for you, shall I?'

'Please.'

I was still holding Kit's pie and drink. I put them in the kitchen, and waited by the window while she was on the phone. One hand ran over her stomach.

'They're both in the office. Emily didn't say much, just not to expect them back any time soon.'

'Does Emily usually answer the phone?'

'Never.' Alison put her fingers to her forehead.

'What does she suggest we do?'

'Stay in and wait.' She came close and whispered. 'I don't like this, Martha. This doesn't happen. Bobby is sulking in his room because Charlie promised to take him to the zoo this afternoon. And I know he did mean it, this time.'

Whatever had been building for Kit was now here. I clasped my hands together.

'They've got keys. Shall we take Bobby out?'

'Martha, something bad is happening. I have to stay here. I just want to know.'

'Shall I just go home and wait?'

'Yes. I think it's probably best.'

The apartment was a mess. Kit's bedclothes were piled on the sofa, and I wondered why he'd done that. And then I realised he hadn't been here. He'd gone to work before I left.

I went into my bedroom. My clothes were all on the bed. I closed the door.

Kit had warned me that this could happen. People came into your home or hotel room and made it obvious they had been there. I wasn't prepared for how sick it made me feel. I went back into the front room. The heat had been building in there all day, even though it faced north. I opened the balcony doors, but there was no breeze to speak of. I went into the kitchen and opened the small window in there too. The only way to get any through draught would be to prop the front door open, but anyone could walk in. They clearly had a key, but I didn't want to make it easier for them, and they would know I was at home on my own.

I wanted to leave, to go and see if Leila was down on the twelfth floor, but I didn't. I put the radio on for a bit, thinking I might catch some news that would explain things, like a disaster they'd have to deal with. The BBC station was too full of static to make out anything. The buzz unnerved me.

I watched the sun set in the west and the sky stayed that deep dusk, not quite black. I thought of Alison and her almanac. The temperature cooled gradually, and I stood on the balcony watching the cars on Leninsky. I saw a group of kids go into the woods behind our block, and heard them whoop with laughter. I went back inside. I waited all night.

He didn't come home. By the early hours of Sunday morning, I was cursing him for our lack of a phone, and cursing everyone else for not coming to tell me anything.

At just after six o'clock, an hour and a half after dawn, Kit came in, face pale and drawn.

'Are you OK?' I asked.

He shook his head. 'Charlie's gone.'

The image of Sandra's body crossed my mind. 'Dead?'

'No.' Kit smiled weakly. 'They're sending him home.'

I looked at the record player.

'They know, and I can't even tell you,' said Kit. 'I need to go to bed.' He looked at the bedclothes, still piled up, and his shoulders fell.

'We've had visitors.'

Kit shrugged. I noticed his eyes were red. I left him alone. This could have been my fault. The report I'd written about Charlie could have been taken anywhere and used as evidence against him for a provocation. Kit couldn't tell me, even if it was linked back to me. After Sandra, it all felt too much. I didn't feel anything for Charlie, but Alison – poor Alison.

22

Kit couldn't tell me what Charlie had done, but I knew it must be bad. A step up even from his affairs and general sleaziness. A provocation, they called it, when the other side tried to expose our underbelly. People did turn away from their wives and families, and get blackmailed into doing bad things, or just did them for the money. That was my best guess, but it probably said more about what I thought of Charlie than what I knew about how things worked.

They had two weeks to sort things out and arrange to move back to England. In the meantime, I carried on as usual. Almost as usual. Natalya seemed different from before. She came in on Monday with a look in her eye, and a swagger to her hips. If I was going to bet, I'd have said that she knew something about Charlie. Much more than I did. She left the shopping in the kitchen and instead of starting in there, as always, came in the front room. I was sitting with my coffee, the balcony door open, when she came in and started picking things up and putting them down again. It was as if she was testing me. She pulled out the books, flicked through them, picked up the money box rocket and shook it. Next, she opened the chest in which the bedclothes were hidden.

I stood up. 'Stop it. What are you doing?' I'd spoken in English, suspecting that she did speak it. All spies spoke it.

Natalya put her hand on her hip and turned to me, eyebrows raised.

'What are you doing?' I repeated in Russian.

'I am sick. I have to go home.'

'Yes, go home.'

She swaggered past me. She wasn't sick, but something was going on. I couldn't make her stay.

I heard the front door slam and went into the kitchen. The coupons for Wednesday's shopping were still there, and I realised that she wasn't coming back. In fact, I suspected she had another job to replace this one.

I went back to finish my coffee. This wasn't good. I'd have to do the shopping now, and more cooking. I should have gone with Alison and seen how it all worked. I didn't even have my own bags. Maybe Kit would expect me to do the cleaning, and I'd have to wash the sheets in the bath and somehow hang them up. Suddenly, Natalya felt a crucial part of my happiness in Moscow.

I would ask Kit if we could get someone else, but as he paid for everything, I knew I should be offering some work in return, at least in the meantime.

The following day, I lost Galina as well. She came in with a furious look, and I was shocked because we'd been getting on so well. That's when I knew she was going to walk out too. There was no way I was going to let her do this easily.

I agreed with her every criticism of my pronunciation and understanding. I agreed when she said that I would never become fluent, that I didn't have a talent for languages. I apologised for my failings, but I could tell it wasn't working. She knew that we both understood the game, and neither of us meant what we were saying.

At the end of the lesson she said, 'I am being sent to long conference far away. I cannot come here for some time.' She tried to convey something with her eyes, and I knew we couldn't use any words. I saw the pressure in the way she pressed her lips together. I wished I had something to give her, but we had to pretend that she'd be back. We hugged quietly in the hallway.

That was Sandra, Alison, Natalya and Galina all lost in less than three weeks. And Bobby, my fellow explorer of the wilderness.

When I'd stopped crying, I tried to read more of Kit's books, the historical ones distanced from this Moscow. Everything seemed the same. The time of Tsars had the same secret police, the same silence when officials attacked the powerless, the same random cruelties and Siberian exiles. It wasn't the communists that were responsible for thinking up ways of tormenting people. They were following a well-established model.

I began to jump at every noise in the hallway, every yelp from the children outside. I began to think of going back to England, just for a visit, but just thinking that made me furious. I would decide when I left Moscow, no one else. I just had to get out of the apartment.

I never even thought of going in the woods any more, now that I knew I definitely wouldn't be alone. I stayed on the streets and the Metro, keeping in clear sight. Not that this was any protection. If I was bundled into a car, no one would say anything. They wouldn't want to be next.

I walked to Alison's, half thinking I should knock, but I decided against it. Charlie was bound to be there, packing. I kept walking up Vernadskogo. I walked for three hours. I crossed into Gorky Park through the arch with the grand columns Stalin loved so much, and walked to the Moskva where I leaned on the railings and thought about Sandra.

Now that the shock had worn off, I couldn't see how she could be regarded as suicidal. Despairing, yes, but for specific reasons: the loss of her books as well as her relationship with Sasha. Would someone have done this to her? One of the KGB jackets was unlikely, but what about her husband? She could have been having an affair with Sasha, or her husband could have thought she was. That would be useful information to the jackets. I would bet on her husband, white-faced, but not inconsolable. And back at work. I'd tried to ask Kit about him, but he wouldn't say much.

I turned so my back was to the river and picked out my blue jacketed friend from the people on benches. He held a newspaper in front of him, like a spy from a film, but his hat wasn't as low as usual. I could see his face, young, with the hollow eye sockets and slight grey tinge of the average Muscovite. I imagined him clenching his jaw, wishing me to look away. Maybe this was the best job he'd ever had, and to stare at him meant he could be removed, sent to work in the depths of Lubyanka.

I let my eyes drift to the bridge, and past it where the river split off to the canal, leaving the British Embassy on a long, curved island. Where had Sandra been pushed into the river? Had she fallen? Was anyone asking?

From the corner of my eye I saw a shape coming towards me and I flinched, turning to face them. It was no one. Just a couple of men in conversation, who looked at me with the vaguest curiosity. My heart was beating – run, run, run.

There was little point pretending that I wasn't thinking about it. It was Tuesday. I went to see Eva.

I think she could tell that things weren't great with me. She didn't even tell me off about not bringing anything. In fact, she hardly said anything, just settled me down in the bright room. For the first time since coming to Moscow, I felt homesick.

She spoke gently.

'How are your lessons going?'

'They were going all right, I think. I have a long way to go.'

'We can always speak in Russian, if you'd like the practice.'

'I'm not ready for that, but thank you.'

She poured the tea. 'I think I may be able to get you a job at the Institute of Foreign Languages, when your Russian is good enough.'

I was scared by that. I realised I was expecting the police to charge in and arrest me for planning to break my visa conditions. 'I don't have the right visa.'

'Visas can be changed. Don't worry, it's just a suggestion. You can think about it.'

'Sorry. I'm finding it all a bit much today.'

'Living abroad is hard.'

I flinched.

She added, 'Even when it's temporary.'

I put my cup back on the saucer. My shaking hand made it clink.

'Any problem,' she said, 'is just a series of steps. It's overwhelming to look at the whole picture.' She made a frame with her fingers. 'Look at each part separately.'

'I'll try.' I could feel tears welling up and I really didn't want to cry, but my voice was cracking.

Eva leaned forward, as if to whisper something, and then sat back. 'Would you like to sit here quietly, or would you like to walk the dog for me?'

I felt the tension in my shoulders give a little. The only uncomplicated relationship I had in Moscow. 'Oh, yes. I'd like to walk your dog, please.'

The dog led me back from the Kremlin and up to the apartment. Eva had a teapot already on the coffee table, and six crackers, each with a smear of blackness.

'Is that caviar?'

She nodded. 'Your first?'

'Yes,' I said. 'It's not expensive, is it? I don't know if I like it.'

'Don't worry,' she said. 'There's only one way to find out.'

She poured the cups, side by side, and waited for me to choose one. I appreciated this subtle nod of apology every time since the illness. Or, that's how I read it.

'Do you like the way she takes you to the bench? I need to rest so we always stop there.' Eva stroked Vorona's head. 'It's easy to feel isolated in a big city, and sometimes it's nice just to sit and watch people.'

I nodded, trying to relax.

Eva smiled. 'Shall I tell you about Black Russian Terriers?'

That sounded a safe subject. I sank back against the sofa. 'That would be lovely.'

Eva gave me a gift as I was leaving. I tied the headscarf at the back of my neck and smiled. I wore it on the Metro, and walking home, but took it off when I got back to my apartment building and pushed it into my coat pocket. I should have asked her for a bag, I realised. If it came down to it, I could pick up some essentials using my new head-scarf as a little bag, even if it would look as if it belonged over my shoulder, on the end of a stick.

I stopped off at the twelfth floor and knocked for Leila, on the off chance. I'd knocked before, but she must have been at the university, or out with her boyfriend. This time the door opened.

'Oh, you're in,' I said.

'I'm in. Do you want to come in?'

'Your boyfriend's not here?'

'No. Way over east, somewhere.'

'OK. Yes. Thanks. I just knocked to ask whether you have a bag I can borrow for shopping. I can't seem to find one to buy.'

'Sure. Follow me.'

Leila went into the kitchen, which was exactly the same as our one, and emptied the vegetables from a brown string bag onto the cupboard she was using as a worktop.

'You've got an oven.'

'Haven't you?' She looked surprised. 'Well, Seb is luckier than I thought. I've also got some string, if you wanted to make your own bag.'

'I can't do that.'

'I'll show you.' She grimaced. 'My mum is into macramé. Do you know when the heating comes on in the building? I'm freezing.'

'I think it's October. It's related to the temperature outside, I remember that.'

'A bit of a wait, then. Do you have time for a coffee? I'll look for the string while it heats up.'

'That would be great. Thanks.'

I allowed myself to be guided to what seemed to be the front room, but it was a single room containing both table and bed. The same size as ours, but there was no dividing wall. Her table was more of a desk, covered in books and a typewriter, but there were two chairs. She took the clothes from one, and I sat and faced the balcony.

When she brought in the coffee, and moved the other chair near mine, I realised what was strange.

'Don't you put music on when you're talking to people?'

'I have a radio, but I don't have many visitors. I don't think about it much.'

I looked at the pile of clothes by her bed. So many hats and scarves and coats. Twice as many clothes as me.

There was nothing in what she said to make me doubt her, but there was something odd about Leila. Or maybe Moscow had just altered me permanently and I would never trust anyone again.

'Are you all right?' asked Leila.

'Yeah. It's been a difficult few days. How's the studying?'

'Good. It's the other stuff, trying to keep occupied while Seb is away. I mean, it's difficult to find out anything inter-esting, but I like a challenge. I met some poets, saw some operas, went to a student art exhibition. I found a couple of cocktail bars, so it's been good. How do you fill your days?'

'I have no idea. Walking, watching Soviet films, rereading books I brought with me.'

'Have you tried the House of Foreign Books?'

'No. Is it in Moscow?'

'Of course. I can take you, if you're not sure about getting around.'

'I can get around, if you draw me a map.'

'You and your maps. I got Seb onto that, and he found

some good ones. I asked him to get me a spare in case I bumped into you, or someone else who needed one.'

She rifled through a drawer and pulled it out.

'That's brilliant.' I felt quite ashamed to have been doubting her. It was a proper, full map, with an index. 'I am sorry, about our first meeting and then just turning up. I thought...'

'You thought it was a provocation. I get it. We were warned about that too. It would be nice to have someone to go around with though. I'll take you to the shops I go to. It's not too bad at the hard currency places. I have some rye bread you can have, if you want. It will go stale before I finish it. Hey, you know that the Universiade is on at the Lenin Stadium?'

'What is it?'

'It's like an Olympics for universities. You haven't heard about it? The British are expecting to do all right in athletics, and they might win something.'

'No, sorry, I haven't heard anything. Things are quite busy at the moment.'

She nodded. 'Well, it starts in a week. If you could get any tickets, I just thought we could go together.'

'I'll ask.'

With my shopping bag, bread and map, I felt much more positive when I arrived back at my apartment. I sliced some kind of smoked sausage that Natalya had brought and the rye bread. Kit came in, tired again. I put Bach on. He opened the Bulgarian white wine I'd left in the fridge. We sat at the table and I ate while he drank.

'Any news on Charlie?'

'Not public news, no. But Alison and some of the mums are going to the exhibition centre at VDNKh with the kids as a final outing for Bobby to say goodbye. After he'd just started getting to know them and talk about school. Two weeks to sort everything out and leave. It's tough on him.'

Had Bobby entirely changed his character in the last couple of weeks? I doubted it. Maybe Kit meant that it was tough on Charlie, but I wasn't going to agree with that. I knew it was his fault.

'Can I go along?'

'Oh, yes, you're invited. This is your invitation, times, date.'

He pulled an envelope from his pocket. I put it next to my plate. It reminded me that I really should write home again.

We ate for a while, shrugging off the day.

'Have you heard if there's any replacement for Natalya?'

'Not yet, darling. That could take weeks, or months. They'll decide in their own sweet time.'

'I think Galina won't be back either.'

'Hmm. Did you do anything?'

'No! She's been sent away.'

'It's like the Soviets are trying to isolate you, now that Alison's going. And after Sandra, of course. Or push you in a specific direction.'

Was it connected to Sandra? My actions at the Apothecary's Gardens were looking more reckless as time went on. I still hadn't told Kit.

'What are you thinking about?' he said, suddenly. 'Anything else I should know?'

'I walked Eva's dog for her today.'

'Remember when I said Eva would get you to do things for her?'

'Yep.'

'Good. Did you ever get that map from her?'

'Nope.'

'Remember that. It's always one way.'

'I know. I am being more careful. And Leila gave me a map. The student with the British Council. She asked about tickets for the Universiade.'

'Did she bump into you somewhere?'

'No, I knocked for her, downstairs.'

'She asked you to get her tickets?'

'No, she just offered to go with me. If I was going.'

'Do you want to go?'

'I'm not desperate. I'm just trying to tell you everything that's going on.' I felt such a liar. I was covering up the very thing he should be told, about Sasha.

Kit put his hand on mine. 'You know I said that Leila was with the British Council? It doesn't mean that you shouldn't still be careful about what you say to her.'

I pulled my hand away. 'I know that. I'm not allowed to speak to anyone about more than the weather. Please trust me, Kit. You get to go out and see people every day. I just want someone to go shopping with, maybe see a film. That's all.'

Kit thought for a bit. 'So, you've been dog walking.'

'It's a big one, a Black Russian Terrier.'

Kit raised his eyebrows and opened his mouth.

'And I know all about the breed and everything, so there's no need to fill me in. I think I could probably write a paper on it and be considered an expert.'

'Is she boring, Eva?'

'No, not at all. Before we were dancing around each other, both trying not to say anything meaningful. It was exhausting. But today she was kind. I think I'd really like the real Eva. I needed her to be exactly as she was today. It's been shocking with Alison and Sandra, just gone like that. It was preying on my mind.'

'You'll find a way through it, darling. Just remember you're on a different side to Eva, but you understand her in a different way to anyone else here. She might feel she needs you to access that British part of her life. You don't need her, though. You'll find new friends. And I will always love you.'

He held out his hand across the table again and I squeezed it.

23

We arrived in our chauffeured cars, six of the embassy wives with assorted children. As we passed the VDNKh Metro station on Prospekt Mira, the Monument to the Conquerors of Space soared up behind us. A hundred metres high was a tiny rocket, leaving the curve of burned up energy on the earth.

We turned left, and the archway for the VDNKh came into view. The All-Soviet Exhibition Centre. I said to Alison that it was an odd way to say goodbye to Moscow.

'Bobby's choice,' she said. 'He wanted to see something to do with space. The planetarium is being used to train cosmonauts, so we came here.'

She ruffled Bobby's hair, and he leaned towards her, resting on her bump.

'It's a shame we never made it to Helsinki,' she said, and stroked his head. 'I won't be going anywhere for a while.' She began to blink and looked out of the window.

Our cars drew up in a line. Alison struggled from the car, and we assembled around Taisia, our short young guide. She projected her voice as if she had stage training.

'We will be going to the Foreign Department to register, and then to the Cosmos building. Follow me.'

Her male companion hadn't introduced himself; he took up a position behind us, his hat pulled low almost to his sunglasses. Taisia waved us through the entrance gates and marched ahead of us while shouting out names. Right hand – 'Central, Atomic, Coal, Friendship of Peoples, Press.'

The landscape was highly sculptured, like the architecture, with flower beds and huge ponds with high fountains. It was sunny and warm, and I half expected to see Bobby launch himself into the water. For a long time, I could see KOCMOC ahead of us, signalling the Cosmos building, domed like a cathedral with a giant rocket suspended in front of it. All the buildings were grand, belying the names Taisia was still shouting – 'Consumer goods industry, Electrification of the USSR.'

She left us outside the Foreign Department and fetched our paperwork. 'This way, please.'

After half an hour Bobby was the only child still interested. The mother of brown-haired brothers had a tight grip on their hands to keep them from running around. A black-haired girl was sitting on the floor, ignoring Taisia's attempts to get her to stand. I couldn't see where that mother had gone. Alison was standing in a corner with the other two mothers, whose names I had also forgotten, deep in conversation. I caught a sentence, 'I can't believe he had the nerve to come back,' and then they saw me and were silent.

I joined Bobby by the rocket engine. 'Do you think they built the dome and then found a rocket that would look good there, or had a rocket and built a dome for it?'

He thought for a moment. 'They built the dome for it.'

'It's pretty amazing, isn't it?' I looked around. 'I like the Sputniks. And the Vostok 1. Would you go to space in one of them?'

Bobby shook his head. 'I'll wait until they get bigger.'

'They look a bit flimsy, don't they?'

Taisia appeared behind us, her jacket over her arm. 'We have a very good safety record with travels in the cosmos, very good results. Many firsts.'

'Have you been on the moon?' asked Bobby.

Taisia's mouth tightened. 'We have done many, many things. We sent the first man to space, Yuri Alekseyevich Gargarin. He has a square, Gagarinskaya, named for him on Leninsky Prospekt. Two years later, we sent the first woman.'

'What was her name?' I asked.

Taisia didn't hesitate. 'Valentina Vladimirovna Tereshkova.'

'Does she have a square?'

Taisia fidgeted. 'She's still alive.'

'The man died on the moon?' asked Bobby.

'No. In a very terrible accident.'

Bobby pressed on. 'So, you haven't been on the moon?'

Taisia took a deep breath. 'We did send the first life to the moon on Zond 5. It went around the moon and came back, completely safely.'

'Was it a dog?' I asked.

'No, two tortoises, some worms and flies. There were also plants, as it was a proper scientific exploration of the effects of space travel. We are the scientists who proved it was possible.'

Bobby was still gaping. 'You sent tortoises to the moon?'

'All life plays a part in science.'

I cleared my throat. 'First dead dog in space?'

'You sent a dead dog to space?' asked Bobby.

I felt ashamed, almost ruining his last memory of Moscow. 'No, it was a stupid joke,' I said.

Taisia half smiled, and then walked away towards the man who accompanied her, or us, or both.

I took Bobby's hand. 'I'm being an idiot. Let's have a last look around. Are we doing something after this?'

He shrugged. 'We go home tonight.'

'I know. Are you sad?'

'I don't think so.'

I looked around for Alison and saw her across the exhibits, red-eyed. Bobby saw her too, but he turned away without saying anything. I couldn't imagine how bad things were in their house. Alison should have been resting but her husband was a cheat at best, and a spy at worst. She'd never liked being here, but now she had to move her whole life and start again.

'I'm going to space,' said Bobby. 'Do you want to come?'

'I think I'll stay with the wolves and bears,' I said.

'I don't like stories any more,' he said. 'I'm not a baby now. I have to like big boy things.'

'You can like stories and not tell anyone.'

He looked at me. 'You won't say?'

'Cross my heart.'

'Daddy is going to come later,' he said. 'He has some things to sort out.'

'Right.'

'But soon. Or later. He won't forget, will he?'

'No. He'll never forget you.'

Alison took Bobby's other hand and he let mine fall. 'Time to go,' she said.

I expected to see more of Kit now that Charlie had gone, but he came home later than ever. He looked terrible, wasn't washing as often and had taken to drinking gin at night instead of wine. It embarrassed him when I asked about the papirosy-scented nights, and he didn't offer any information, even when Mozart or Bach accompanied our silence, but stared into his glass and ran his hand through his hair.

'You don't fancy going to the cinema?' I said.

He shook his head. It had been days since Natalya had walked out, and we were eating the last remnants of tinned food Kit had brought from the embassy shop. I needed to go to a hard currency shop with the vouchers Kit could get, but I hadn't managed to catch Leila yet.

'I'm going shopping with Leila. Could Pyotr take us? Then I could get more than what I can carry.'

'No. Things have changed. The drivers are for embassy use only.'

'Since when?'

Kit lifted his head and looked at me properly for the first time all night. 'Since you.'

I sat back and twisted the stem of my wine glass. 'I'm sorry, Kit. Do you want me to go home?'

He shook his head. 'I know it isn't your fault. I think it isn't deliberate, anyway. It's just that everyone has their eye on you. You're supposed to be here to distract attention from me, but it's not working right.'

He kind of laughed and I realised how drunk he was.

'First there was Eva and then Sandra.'

'I didn't track down Eva. I'm only polite to her. And I didn't know what I was walking into with Sandra. I liked her.'

'Did you do anything for Sandra?'

It was too late to confess anything. 'I think I was the only one who didn't judge her. Is that what you mean?'

He filled his glass again and spoke into it. 'Nope.'

'Anything else?'

'Yep. You didn't tell me that Charlie came here.'

'You never mentioned that you gave your key to Charlie. We probably didn't mention quite a lot that we should have.'

'I don't remember anything about a key, and there's nothing to tell about Charlie.'

'No. You wish there was.'

Kit banged his glass down. I waited to see which way the argument would go. He closed his eyes and smiled. 'Yeah. I do.' He covered his face and patted his cheeks hard. 'I need to stop drinking so much. There'll be other Charlies.'

'You could even aim a bit higher than that.'

'Maybe. And you know the most stupid thing? They all knew I was gay. All of them in Moscow, and probably in London too. And by bringing you, I'm the one who's drawn attention to it. Not you. You're not allowed the car because they want to keep you busy with shopping and cooking. That's how it seems to me. I don't think we've got any chance of another maid, and you wanted to discover a bit more of Moscow than the interior of this apartment.'

'I wish there was a pub we could just walk over to. Can we go out somewhere after work one night?'

'I can't plan anything at the moment. We have a lot of cleaning up to do, so to speak. Or even actual cleaning. Charlie's bloody mess.' Kit put his glass down. 'I have to go to bed.' He pushed his chair from the table, stood suddenly, and wavered. 'Sorry, darling, to spill my guts out like that.'

'It's fine. I know it's not how you expected.'

'What did I expect?'

I didn't know what to say.

He swayed, grabbing hold of the door on his way out. I watched him walk away and then I picked up *The Idiot*.

It was OK, but not my favourite Dostoyevsky. Better than Solzhenitsyn, Nobel Prize or not, but not as fun as Bulgakov.

I tidied the table and closed the balcony door. It was beginning to cool quickly at night, the sun falling away behind the buildings. The glass on the balcony door already needed cleaning. I looked around the room to all the places that Natalya must have dusted. A couple of hours every other day couldn't be that hard.

24

A week later, the temperature had halved. The frost made the treetops look more solid, somehow, the green leaves yellowing. I had been to the two storey food store on Arbat, as well as to the pirozhki stall near the Metropol for more savoury pies. The two-ring hot plate was a challenge too far when it came to anything other than soup or stews.

Leila brought back a sense of fun to my life in Moscow. She'd roast a chicken in her oven on Sundays and run upstairs with it while we boiled up some vegetables on our hot plates. The corridor grannies were not happy about that at all, and this always made her laugh. She'd enter with her best impersonation of their impotent rage. Kit would burn the cork and draw heavy Brezhnev eyebrows on us all, so the ash would sprinkle onto our food. He seemed to be relaxed around Leila, laughing and full of stories of Moscow, but I had the impression that it was all for me.

I was starting to get used to the rude pushiness of the Moscow shopping experience. I wasn't above a quick elbow, it turned out.

I nearly forgot about Eva.

Leila's map and its index had opened Moscow right up for

me. Today, I intended to try the Beriozka shop for cottage cheese, and to see what else had come in. I was getting used to shopping most days; there was little else to distract me. I wrote letters full of half-truths to the parents and tried to read between the lines of my mother's letters. I would buy *Pravda* and listen to people in the parks, thinking that immersion would somehow continue my language education, but it was hard to concentrate.

My map was spread out on the table. I'd worked out that a lot of the parks and forests were missing from it. I intended to fill them in and write descriptions of each of them. They were all so different, some with buildings taken from the aristocracy and some left wild. I was just waiting for some more paper to start making notes, but hadn't reminded Kit enough times, it seemed, so I couldn't make a start yet. My watch said half past ten. I could catch a film matinee, if I left now.

As I went downstairs, I looked around for Blue Jacket as I left the building, and just resisted saluting his dipped hat.

The cold thrilled me. This was what I'd expected from Moscow. This was what I wanted, and I yearned for snow.

Emerging from the Metro station, I crossed over to the cinema. It was closed, for a 'sanitation day' the sign said. That could mean anything, and any length of time. I hesitated at the doors. A figure was walking on the opposite side of the road, head lowered, a big dog at her side. Her stride was long for someone so short, quite different from how she walked before. I was certain.

Eva lifted her head to cross the road and her eyes fixed on something. I moved from the doorway to see what she was looking at. Mr Blue Jacket. She knew him. I watched her scan the pavement for me. She raised her hand and crossed the road, slightly slower than before.

'Were you coming to see me?' she asked. 'I do hope you haven't been waiting around.'

'I was going to see what film was on, but it's closed today.'

She looked at the doors. 'It's been closed for just over a week. It will open again when it's ready. So, what are you doing now?'

'I don't know. I was just deciding.' I looked around, as if for inspiration. Blue Jacket had gone. 'Have you been OK?'

'Of course.' She didn't move.

'Are you going home now?'

'Oh, no. Vorona needs a longer walk. You can come with us.'

I nodded. There was something different about her expression, as if she was trying to lead me somewhere. I wasn't sure. Something was bugging me. Her voice seemed different. Again. Not the considerate and caring Eva of my last visit, but not the official voice she'd used on other visits either. And why couldn't we go to her apartment now? Why was she only available on Tuesday afternoons?

'So, which days are you at work, Eva?'

'Every day. Have you thought about working with us at the Institute?'

'I lost my teacher, I'm afraid. She went away. I've applied for another, but I think it is going to take time.'

'I could teach you.'

Ah. Kit had said I was being pushed towards their solution.

'You look worried,' she said. 'It's quite all right. I'm registered with UPDK. You won't be breaking any laws.'

'Thank you. I'll speak to Christopher about it.'

It was the first time that I'd mentioned his name, and she didn't blink.

'Do you really call him Christopher all the time? Never Chris?'

'Why?'

'In Russia, we use familiar forms for all names. So, Mikhail would be Mishka or Misha. Nikolai would be Kolya.'

'I just stick to Christopher, really.'

I wasn't going to give her any new information. Or confirm what she already knew. What I wanted to do was run and leave her here, and see who answered the door to her apartment when she wasn't there.

She could tell I was thinking about other things.

'Tell me about your university,' she said.

'Did you go to university?'

'I didn't, no. I went to a language college.'

'What languages can you speak?'

'English, French, German, Russian and Polish.'

'And did you always live in Britain before you came here?'

'There's no point learning all those languages and then staying in one place. I know you studied Classics, but do you speak any other languages?'

'French, badly.'

'Have you been to Paris?'

'Yes, I went with a friend.'

'A boyfriend?'

'No. Someone I knew at university.' We were waiting to cross to the Alexander Gardens.

'My daughter went to university.'

'You have a daughter?'

'Of course. Why wouldn't I?'

'You never said, and I didn't see any photos. How old is she? What does she do?'

'Irina is twenty-two, training to be a cosmonaut.'

Surely this was a story? No patronymic meant there was no father's name. Was that because I was British or a deliberate evasion? I thought back to the tiny capsules from the exhibition and shuddered. 'Seriously?'

'She's very clever and very brave.'

'She must be. Is she training here in Moscow?'

'No. Far away.'

As we approached a bench, the same bench we'd met on, I was sure, two men stood together and walked off in different directions. Eva sat down, her dog at her side. I watched them go, then turned to Eva.

'Isn't this the bench we met on? Didn't you think that was odd that they got up?'

'No. A lucky coincidence. We like to sit here.'

Her voice had that slightly clipped quality again. I sat next to her.

'So, you will talk to Christopher about having lessons with me?'

It was strange, like she was recapping our conversation for someone else. Could those men have bugged the bench for her? I looked around at the other people on benches, at the people passing, at the men standing with newspapers by trees.

'Marta?' she said.

'Maybe.'

'Are you feeling well?'

I ran my fingers under my side of the bench, looking for something that moved, something that could be a bug.

'Is someone listening to us?' I asked.

'Oh, Marta,' she laughed. 'You are still falling for the

propaganda. You think someone would be interested in your Russian lessons?'

'I think they would.'

'Why?'

'Because it's information. All information is interesting to someone.'

Eva nodded. 'That's true. Did Christopher tell you this?'

'No.'

'Did you know his college, St Anthony's, is one of the main recruiting places for British spies? Didn't your brother go there too?'

'That's not true.' I felt I should say that. I had no idea what went on in Oxford, and I was fighting hard not to look surprised that she knew anything about Kit or my brother.

'So, who told you?'

Our relationship had changed. She'd told me about her daughter, and that made her a real person. I needed to know what she wanted from me. Eva was the link to everything that had been going on, I was sure. I had nothing to tell her in payment for what I wanted to know, but clues about myself.

I looked back at her. 'Who is Irina's father? What's his name? How did you end up here?'

Eva nodded. 'We both have lots of questions, and that's because we are interested in each other. It's good, isn't it? You don't have many people left to talk to, but you can talk to me.' She checked her watch and stood up. 'Would you like to come back with me now?'

I folded my arms and focused on the tree opposite our bench. Eva laughed.

'OK. You can sit here, but I'm getting cold.' Her dog shook herself and they started to walk away. Eva paused and asked, 'I've been wondering, who is Tomas?'

Tomas? I frowned, but kept my eyes on the tree. I heard her talking to the dog as they left.

It was cold. My cords were thick enough when I was walking. Now my thighs were freezing but if I stayed here, they couldn't collect the bug from wherever it was on the bench. It was definitely here. The difference in her speech was so noticeable. I shifted along to Eva's side, and ran my fingers along that edge. Then I gave up and went home.

It took me a while to shake off how angry I was with her. Maybe she was cross that I hadn't been around when it seemed as if we could be friends after all. Whatever the reason, she'd gone back to how she was before and I wasn't interested any more.

Tomas.

That name made no sense. I thought about it all the way back and scowled at Blue Jacket as he loitered outside the bread shop, walked faster than normal home and tried to slam the door at him. It closed annoyingly slowly.

In the lift, I remembered that evening on the balcony months ago, when I was talking to myself, saying the letters which still made sense to me. TOMA. Tomas. They could hear everything on the balcony. And Kit didn't know.

25

We were on our third or fourth cocktail. I'd lost count, and
it wasn't even three o'clock. The sun shone and we looked
at the way Moscow's cream stone glowed and the windows
glinted.

'We should be outside,' I said. 'It's beautiful.'

'Oh, we can see it's beautiful from here,' slurred Leila. I
thought she'd had a head start. She lifted her glass. 'What
are these again?'

'I've forgotten.' I rested my head back against the worn
velvet chair and looked around. Were our jacket watchers
trying the cocktails? I hoped so. I was feeling well disposed
to them today. 'Where's Seb gone off to this week?'

Leila screwed her face up with the effort of thinking.
'Kiev?' she said. 'Maybe.'

'Did he ever find that holy fool in Siberia?'

'Not a fool, more of a second coming type thing.'

'He thinks he's Jesus?'

'His followers do. Seb thought he was quite impressive.'
She finished her drink, whatever it was, and hunched over.
'I think it might be coming to an end with him. He's never
here, and I made such an effort to get here to be with him. I

should have gone to Leningrad and then he'd want to travel to see me.'

'He's just busy with work,' I said. I had no idea. I still hadn't met him. When he was in the flat, Leila liked to keep him to herself. She was becoming maudlin now. 'Maybe we should eat something.'

She nodded. 'Soon.'

'There is a restaurant here.'

'Urgh, we can't eat at the Natsional.'

She spat her words loudly, and I looked around anxiously.

'Seb says it's the worst place in Moscow.' She grinned and sat up straight. 'He was placed here before he got the apartment.' Her eyes brightened. 'He was here at the same time as David Bowie.'

'Did they meet?'

'No. I think by the time he gets back to Australia, in his stories they will have spent a whole evening together.'

I knew I should ask about that, but when she was a bit more sober. Seb had told Leila all sorts of information about dissidents and protests and covered-up deaths. I hoped she wouldn't get onto more of that now, with so many people around us.

'Come on,' I said. 'Let's get some food and we can get some more drinks at the Metropol.'

Leila sighed, nodded, and we walked out, arm in arm. It was mostly for her sake.

The sun was warm on our faces and we walked slowly.

'How's your lovely husband?' she asked.

'He's OK.'

'He can't join us?'

'Maybe later. He can't take time off without any notice, and he works Saturday morning so he doesn't like to drink much on Fridays.'

She stopped. 'Now, why is that? The Saturday thing.'

I started walking again, pulling her with me. 'Soviets are asked to contribute Saturday morning working hours as a kind of tribute to the state. They're not paid, but they have to do it. So, the embassy works too.'

'Do they get paid for it?'

I thought. 'I have no idea. I've never asked.'

We arrived at Ploshchad Revolyutsii in front of the Metropol and I settled Leila on the grass before getting two pies. When I came back she was looking up at a man and talking loudly.

'I don't understand you.'

He crouched down next to her as I hurried over.

'No. I don't understand.'

I said, 'Ukhodi.'

He stood, grey faced and exhausted, and walked away.

'What was he saying?' I asked.

'He wanted hard currency.'

'Here?' The park was full, as it always was on sunny days, the older people on benches, younger people on the grass. He was walking away, around the Metropol.

'The toilets behind there are for picking up men,' said Leila. 'He'll have more luck there. Loads of Westerners.'

I shuddered. If Leila knew, the KGB knew.

I changed the subject. 'We should have some water before we start drinking again.'

I pointed at the metal machine on the corner. I hadn't known what it was when I was here with Alison, but it was a self-service drinks machine. You rinsed the glass, put three kopeks in and filled it with flavoured fizzy water. Then you left the glass for the next person. I had tried to imagine the glass not being stolen or smashed in London, but I couldn't.

Leila didn't answer. All her attention was on the pirozhki.

I bit into mine. Minced beef and onion, maybe. It was so good. I hadn't realised how hungry I was.

She finished and lay back on the grass. 'Are you having fun with your map?'

I laughed. 'Yeah, I am.'

'Filling in your parks?'

'Some of them. I don't want to draw on it, so I've been tracing parts of it onto typing paper and taking them out. I can cover Moscow in about eighteen months, at this rate.' I joked, but I was feeling filled with purpose for the first time since Cambridge and it felt great.

I finished my pie and wiped my fingers on the newspaper wrapper. Leila was very still. I thought she'd fallen asleep. Then she spoke.

'Do you know anyone else in Moscow?'

'I did meet some people from the embassy when I first got here, and someone else called Eva.'

'Do you still see her?'

'I decided she was a provocation. The whole thing was more dangerous that it was worth.'

'Why did you think that?'

'I had this booklet of stories, and I thought that she'd written them and they were autobiographical in a coded way. She said she hadn't written them. Well, didn't say that exactly, because she wouldn't speak about it at all. Then I started to believe that she didn't even live in the apartment that she invited me to. I don't know. I think it was for show. It all got too strange.'

Leila rolled onto her side and pushed herself up. 'That sounds fascinating. Can I read the stories in the booklet? Look for clues?'

'OK. You can't take it to the university, though. Your roommate will definitely read it.'

'Oh, she's so annoying.' Leila got to her feet and held out a hand to pull me up. 'I have my second wind. Let's go.'

Arm in arm, we walked into the Metropol, past the doormen and the men in hats with newspapers and stern women at desks, and knew we were untouchable.

On the way home, Leila made me get off at Universitet and we walked east.

'Where are we going?'

'Shopping.'

I groaned. Shopping with Leila was easier, but it was still a slog. And that was after we'd avoided the teenagers hanging around outside the Beriozkas, asking for chewing gum. But this place was different. Like an aeroplane hangar, it spread over a huge area.

'Cheremushkinsky rynok,' she said.

A market. 'This is where the farmers sell their surplus?'

'One of them.'

We entered through one of the large entrances and inside I could see there were four in total, large paintings above each of harvests and goods. The tables were emptying, but there was still more variety than in the commission stores. Fresh greyish-green squash, polished onions, white bulbs of garlic shone under the skylights, and jars of pickled fruit and vegetables. One woman had honey and cottage cheese, but I hadn't brought any empty containers to fill. I picked up a jar of what looked like sour cabbage in vinegar, recognising the smell of every lift I'd been in. They pickled fruit, too, and even salted apples. There were so many ways to preserve food through the long winter in the absence of cans.

Leila carefully put six eggs into her bag, wrapped in sheets of *Pravda*, then negotiated a price for some poisonous looking mushrooms.

'How do you know they're OK?' I whispered.

'They've been collecting mushrooms their whole lives. They wouldn't get it wrong.'

I looked at the woman selling them and she looked away from me, towards the women still circulating with their bags ready to fill. There were plants too, and I picked up a potted jasmine. The old woman behind the table held her hand out and I counted the money out.

Leila laughed. 'I've bought a fried breakfast and you get a plant? Your poor husband.'

'Oh, he eats in the city a lot.'

'We can share the eggs and mushrooms. Like good communists.'

'Oh, don't worry. I'll come back another time with bags and jars. I never knew this place was here.'

'Don't buy too much, comrade. We still have a way to walk home. It's nice now and then.'

'Space'

by

E. V. MANN

I always expected to carry a child, feeling within my centre the heat of summer, of the wolf's heart, of the dragon's fire, of the bear's fur. This place of marble palaces promises tiny shoes and fresh cut dreams. It is a place to bear a child. And I am promised.

But each summer passes, hot like melted silver. My wolf says he will come back. I force myself not to hold onto his fur, and collect it from the bed when he leaves. While I wait for him, I avoid the bears, flash drunk in the gutter, polluting the streets with unsanitary sounds.

I have grown good at waiting. I am so still that I can see the grass growing.

When he finally returns in the dampness of autumn, he hands me a heart-beating bundle, hair as black as the night sky and eyes as blue as dusk. A baby girl, plucked from the dust of a comet, blessed by stars. I love her with the heat of burning rocket fuel, and never leave her side.

I watch in awe as she learns to eat and smile and walk and play. I make her ice shoes and frost cloaks for her to dance in before the bitter moon. She doesn't need the heat of the sun. She burns, my only brightness, and I need nothing else, not even my wolf. But he comes back with stories of brighter, further stars and her eyes glitter. I am dull in comparison.

In no time at all, she is strapping on her boots, checking the clasps on her helmet. She waves to me as she flies up to the silent heavens. I blaze with pride. But she doesn't come back. I breathe in and out, watching for her return, and my heat fades.

I cry for her to come back. The wolves pull me away on my glass sleigh, ever further from the heat of cities towards the starlight. Now I have nothing but remote views of shifting glaciers, those pure gods of the Arctic, harder than death. The clouds they leak snow in the quietest of calamities.

All I have left is space, a falling emptiness within my centre, the cold vapour of a child's breath which sparkles like ghosts. It's a prison of air and absolute stillness, the landscape bitter with frost. I scream and it echoes back to me, again and again, like an ache.

Slowly, I transform from woman into a cold fox fire, trying to feed the residual heat of her memory that radiates deep within me, knowing that it leaves me weak and sleepless. I whisper her name into my hands, place a kiss on my fingertips and send it flying to her. Sometimes I feel the flutter of a moth against my cheek and I wonder if she has sent me back a kiss.

In the dark, I keep my eyes on the stars, hoping I will catch a glimpse of her in the frosty midnight of space. This world has no heat left in it and cold can burn almost as much as loss. The space in my chest is darkly shrinking and I wrap my heart in fur to keep it warm for her.

Because she promised to come back.

And I promised to wait.

And if it is that wolf that I see first, I will rip his heart out with my teeth.

26

I picked up a copy of *Pravda* on my way to the university to meet Leila. I flicked through it as I walked. I needed the practice as I hadn't been reading much, but I had been listening to the radio.

Soyuz 12 was being launched today, a big deal after the catastrophic failure on re-entry of Soyuz 11 two years ago. The USSR didn't want to be known as having the only people to die in space. But they weren't the focus today. Vasili Lasarev and Oleg Makarov were already being declared heroes.

I folded the paper and put it under my arm, then immediately removed it, feeling like a spy in a bad film. Whichever way I held it, it felt like a signal to someone watching.

I reached the open area in front of the university, stood next to the statue of Mikhail Lomonosov and gazed up at the towers. However dysfunctional Leila had told me it was inside, confirming what Kit had said, it really was beautiful. The symmetry and the pillars were offering something special to the people of Moscow, an adoration of education that reminded me of Cambridge. A group of sportswomen walked past in their burgundy tops, CCCP in white. They were laughing and pushing each other. I felt a little homesick.

I took the page with today's map section from my pocket and unfolded it. I wished I could do this with baking paper and overlay them, but I could do that when I got home.

Someone walked up behind me and spoke in English.

'Hello.'

I turned, laughing. Of all the days to try a provocation. He was stunningly handsome, clear grey eyes under floppy blond hair. A bit like Kit's hair, now I thought of it. Had they used him as a model? He didn't have the military stance of Sergei.

'I'm meeting someone,' I said, turned my back to him and studied my map.

A hand appeared around me and pointed to the map. 'This is a good place.' He moved to stand in front of me, taking the other side of the map. 'Are you going here now?'

'Who are you?'

'Ivan. Hello. Are you going now?'

'None of your business, Ivan.'

I tried to be cross, but his smile was so wide. He even had the same full bottom lip that Kit had. Did they have a whole room full of men to choose from, according to taste?

'I am not rude. There will be thunder soon.'

I looked at the sky. The clouds did have the purple tinge of a storm.

He had such an open face. He didn't look like a spy, but I had to assume he was. Then again, I had missed flirting, and I wasn't sure that I could do worse than I had been by being careful.

'OK, Ivan. What would you do today?'

He looked so pleased and surprised that I was glad I was an idiot. He held out his hand and I took it.

The KGB had chosen well. The hand-holding had convinced me that he was one of them. Russians didn't hold hands. But, if I'd written a description of my ideal date, it would not have included an Elvis fan who would happily sing a tribute concert for one while I sat on the ground and laughed myself silly. He took requests, and didn't quibble at the titles I asked for: 'Suspicious Minds', 'You're the Devil in Disguise'. It was all the same to him, even if the words were, at times, utterly indecipherable to me.

The rain poured, but safe under the arched entrances to Novodevichy Convent, we could watch the lightning and, exhausted, he came and sat next to me. I shivered, and thought how wet our tail was going to get.

'I am very thirsty,' Ivan said.

'I'm not surprised.'

'Maybe we should go for a drink somewhere, when the rain stops.'

'I'm not sure. I should get back.'

Ivan nodded. 'We can go another time.' He looked out at the rain. 'Is someone waiting for you?'

'Yes.'

'I live with my mother, my sister and her husband, and my – she has a baby, a boy.'

'Your nephew.'

He nodded. 'Nephew. My father is died.'

'I'm sorry.'

He shrugged. 'A long time now. Where do you live? Not in Moscow, where else?'

'England.'

His eyes lit up. 'Ah, London. That's good.' He smiled.

'Good films from London. And Japan. I like to go London and Tokyo.'

'Are you a student at the university?'

He looked confused. 'Of course. I meet you at the university.' He took my hand. 'I study engineering for space.'

'That's very good.'

He nodded, serious. 'Very good. Very hard for space.'

I was doubting very seriously now that he had anything to do with spying. His English wasn't polished enough, and he was a genuinely lovely man.

'Ivan, will you get in trouble for being here with me?'

'No. I speak lots of English at university. It's good. They say, talk lots of English. Is good. And you speak Russian?'

'Da.'

He laughed. 'Da. Is all you know.'

Horrified, I realised that Ivan thought I was a student too. That it was all right to speak to me because I belonged there. He could get in terrible trouble.

'Ivan, I really have to go now.'

'OK. It stop soon.'

'No, I really have to go.' I stood up. 'Thank you for a lovely afternoon.'

He laughed, and gestured around. 'Better place next time.'

'Yes.'

He stood too. I reached up to kiss him on the cheek, and lingered there too long. What damage there was had already been done. He turned his face and I kissed his lips. And we kissed again.

27

Between the range of shops we now went to, and the British Embassy, our lives had improved with as much food and alcohol as we wanted. Leila even got used to classical music in the background, as she told us scandalous stories that Seb couldn't get printed, and stories that probably weren't true about the swimming pool being haunted by priests who thought the cathedral was still there. She knew where Kim Philby lived off Gorky Street. Kit fidgeted and looked uncomfortable. She got the map and pointed out Brezhnev's address, 26 Kutuzovsky Prospekt. She talked about the monochrome clothes of the leaders, to stop them standing out from the rest of the population, and about secret cities that even other Russians didn't know about. And sometimes we had cocktails for lunch and talked about Eva Mann.

'Just because the character in the first story is called Eva, doesn't make the author someone called Eva,' she said.

'I know. But the initials and Eva together?'

'She says she doesn't write stories.'

'I don't believe her.'

'So, what do you think it all means? That last story. Where is she in it? England or Russia?'

'I can't decide.'

'You know samizdat, the underground writings that get passed around? They're in Russian. This is in English for a British reader. Do you think it was for you? How did she somehow get this to you in England?'

'Honestly, I've been wondering for months and I still don't have any answers. I think it was a signal which I haven't worked out yet.'

'Is she the type to be too subtle? Or has she overestimated your deductive abilities?'

I punched Leila's arm. 'So, Seb hasn't found her on any records?'

She shook her head. 'The war destroyed so many records that it's not very surprising. You're sure she has a link to Britain?'

'Yes. She was definitely in Britain, and then Berlin. And she speaks,' I closed my eyes to remember, 'Russian, French, German. And Polish. So, I'm guessing she went there after the war as a translator.'

Leila looked at her watch. 'Ah, I have to go. I have a Russian lesson at the Lenin Library. You ready to work out where Eva belongs?'

She paused. I'd been distracted. Ivan had come in and was standing by the bar. Was he angry with me for not agreeing to meet him again? Had he been arrested and questioned?

'Have you got something to tell me? Who's that?'

'No one. Just Ivan.'

'Just Ivan. And you a married woman.'

I forgot I was married. I saw her raised eyebrows. 'Nothing happened.'

'Oh yeah. That's who you stood me up for, isn't it?' She pushed me. 'Come on, I have to go. Say goodbye to lovely Ivan.'

While Leila paid up, I waited for Ivan to notice me. When he did, he smiled. He was OK. It was OK. I wanted to go over and speak to him, but I had somewhere to be and I didn't want him to be noticed by Blue Jacket. If he hadn't been before.

I gathered our coats, hats and scarves. In the bathroom, I took her fur coat, heavy like blankets, and she took my woollen one, and we wrapped our faces in scarves.

'What about handbags?' she asked.

'They won't notice that,' I said. 'How do you know you haven't got a shadow, anyway?'

'I don't know for sure, but they usually don't bother until the last few months. That's when people have to work out ways of staying in touch when they've gone home. So, I'm not certain, but I'm pretty sure.'

I grabbed her arm. 'Leila, this is so exciting.'

'It's just step one. Find out where she lives, and then you have information on her, for a change.' She laughed, pulled the scarf over her mouth and waved. I was to wait five minutes and then, if it had worked, Blue Jacket would be waiting outside the Biblioteka Lenina. For Leila.

The little park by Eva's apartment was empty, and I could sit on the bench. I didn't have to disguise the fact that I was watching her windows, but I made sure that the tree branches obscured me a little. It was about five degrees in the daytime, and the cold was the reason we'd chosen this day. I could wrap up and not look too obvious. I hadn't realised I would be waiting this long though. My body was warm, but my toes were numb.

The lights went on in the apartment and I checked my watch – seven o'clock. Now it was starting to get dark and I was feeling very stupid indeed. Either our switch had been spotted or Eva really did live here. Either way, I was getting ready to give up and go home. I hoped that Leila wouldn't call in on Kit and tell him what we'd been up to, even if it was much later than I'd said I'd be back.

I saw someone moving in the apartment and sat up a little straighter. I waited for the lights to go out, but they didn't. A few people passed and I saw a figure leave her apartment. A figure with a dog.

They passed the entrance to the park and I stayed still, my face buried in the scarf, wondering whether the dog could smell me. Then I stood and saw them walking back to Kalinina Prospekt, crossing the Arbat. I followed them, watching the figure I assumed was Eva place something on a concrete windowsill. Before I could pass it, a couple came from the side road and picked it up. The man put it in his pocket and they walked towards me. The woman's fur coat was pale, almost luminous in the dusk. I kept my head down, my eyes on Eva. Sometimes her hand fell onto the dog's head and rested there, as if for reassurance.

She turned left at the main road and walked away from the centre, the dog keeping pace at her side. I hadn't been this far down Kalinina, although one of the hard currency stores I'd been to was somewhere around here. I saw them walk into the entrance of an apartment block, one of the massive twenty storey ones, but built in two connecting parts, like an open book.

I couldn't walk in there after them. There would be an unofficial guard keeping out foreigners, some dezhurnaya reporting on who came in and out. There was someone on every floor of every building, the secret infrastructure which ensured the Soviet Union persisted. So, either Eva lived here on Kalinina, or she was visiting someone. Either way, I was sure that she didn't live in that imposing apartment.

It was getting very dark now and I was feeling exposed. The lights of the cars made the buildings look like they were shifting, and every building corner seemed to have a man lingering on it, smoking or reading a paper. I shuddered, and turned to walk back to the Metro. At Arbatskaya, I could walk through to Biblioteka Lenina for my line. I pushed my hands further into my pockets and started to walk, before noticing a dog panting behind me. Eva had caught me up.

'You're not being followed,' she said. 'I went inside to check.'

I felt proud that I'd beaten the KGB, but she didn't look pleased.

'I'll have to report this, and then they'll be watching you much harder.'

I nodded.

'Let's walk.'

She headed in the direction of Arbatskaya and I walked quickly. She was much faster than before.

'So, you don't live in that apartment?' I asked.

'No.'

'And you wrote the fairy tale stories?'

'Hardly fairy tales. Folk tales, maybe.'

'Did you mean for me to read them? How did I get them? I don't understand how I was picked and what I'm supposed to do with them.'

Eva paused and looked at me. 'I want to go home. I want you to get me home.'

I stopped walking. This was the other Eva, the unguarded one who had spoken to me openly on the way to the gardens. She walked on, the dog keeping pace beside her. The dog. What would happen to her dog? I hurried to catch up.

'I can't do anything, Eva. I'm just married to someone who works at the embassy. What do I do?'

'You tell the embassy that I want to come home.'

'Won't you be put in prison?'

'I am already in prison.' She touched the dog's head. 'I know things. I am useful. Maybe they will be kind.'

She has no idea, I thought. The British would never trust her again. She'd spend her life under surveillance wherever she was. And what would they think of me, if I became her go-between?

'Can't you contact them yourself?'

Eva shook her head. 'You don't understand. If I just walked up to the embassy, I wouldn't make it to the gate. I'd get sent to Siberia. They don't see me as Soviet. They don't trust me and they never will. We might be being tailed right now. Walk faster.'

We'd reached the Arbat Metro, but she kept going.

'Eva, I don't trust you either.'

'Of course not. That's why I had to get you interested in me before I asked you for anything. If I'd approached you with this you'd have run a mile. But not telling you drew you to me, and that means you feel manipulated.'

'I have been manipulated. I'm still being manipulated. How did you contact me?'

'That was easy. We knew your father's job and name, we've been keeping an eye on him. We also watch out for protests, people who like to challenge the status quo are often sympathetic to what we're doing. And your name was coming up at a lot of them. We even have a photo of you with your friends. We linked your name back to your father. Then your marriage announcement was in the national press. That gave us Kit's name, and we found out his job and his name was on the list of new diplomats, and the visa application for his new young wife. Then it was a matter of seeing where you went and leaving the stories where you would find them.'

'How did you know I'd take them?'

'It's your class. You think you own everything, that you have a right to what you want.'

I stopped. When she realised, she came back to me.

'I can only tell you my story, Marta. You know your part in this.'

'That's not enough to make me help you.'

'It's all in my stories. You've read them. Didn't you understand the message? Who are the wolves?'

I whispered. 'KGB.'

'And the narrator?'

'You. But what happens to your dog if you go? What happens to your daughter? Anything you leave behind will be punished.'

Eva opened her mouth and then closed it. She looked away and slowed as we walked around to the front of the Lenin Library.

'You know everything I can tell you.'

'I know nothing but my interpretations. And if your side got you to write the stories, they must have read them. They must know what they say, on the surface and underneath that.'

'I was hopeful that you would be smarter than them, Marta.' She looked at the statue. 'Lenin lived, Lenin lives, Lenin will always live.' Eva smiled. 'You know that, right?'

'I've heard it. I don't think I know it.'

'I can't escape him by myself. I need help. Please, think about it. I don't see what you can lose, bringing in a lost sheep.'

The words were practised, but the smile was awkward and real. She knew how it sounded. The sheep, chased by wolves across Europe? It didn't suit her at all.

'I'll think about it.' I walked away to the Metro, and turned back. 'Eva? Is any of it true?'

'Nothing is true.' She sat on a bench, her dog resting her head on her lap, the vast columns of the library behind her. 'And, at the same time, it's all true.'

I knocked for Leila to swap coats back before I went to my apartment, to find Kit was already there, looking very relaxed on the sofa. I could see from his face that he knew I'd been up to something.

'I thought you'd be down here,' he said, 'and then Leila had an open bottle. I haven't eaten. And Leila hasn't said anything. Have you, Leila?'

'I haven't said anything.'

She sat on her writing chair and poured another drink for herself and one for me. I nudged Kit upright and sat next to him.

Kit waggled his finger in a way that I could see Charlie doing. He was faking nonchalance. 'But something's going on. And someone has a birthday tomorrow.'

I looked at Leila and she gestured towards Kit. He was supposed to be my husband and I'd never even asked when his birthday was. He saw my face.

'Well, I suspect that this might not have been birthday related then.'

'Do you know when *my* birthday is?' I asked.

'November?'

'Close. October.'

'Do you two actually know each other?' Leila said, handing me my glass.

'We adore each other,' Kit said. 'We're just not very good on birthdays. I'm starving. Drink that up and let's get some food, Martha.'

I downed the wine, and Kit pulled me up from the soft sofa. He put his arm around me and we went upstairs. He didn't speak until we were inside the apartment, with music on.

'So,' he asked me, 'where have you been?'

'Just at Arbat.'

'Isn't that where Eva lives?'

'Yes.'

'And?'

'I think I need to come in and speak to someone.'

'It's choir tomorrow.'

'No. Someone more important.'

Kit sighed. 'I knew something was going on. Did you bring any food?'

'No. We've still got some sausage. I left it on the balcony because it was cooler today than the fridge.'

'Some bloody pigeon must have stolen it.'

'It was inside a saucepan, with a lid on.'

'Ah. Well, unless the pigeon took the saucepan as well, I think we've had visitors. I'll see what we have.'

He'd taken me away from Leila to ask, and I realised that he didn't trust her at all. I regretted involving her now because of what Kit would say. I probably shouldn't have said anything at all to Leila. But it was too late for that.

28

I walked into the embassy, unsure of what was to come. I saw Emily, pearls in place, hovering in the background. I stood, awkwardly, by the entrance. I didn't want to be Eva's spokesperson. I should be isolating her, as the rest of them did.

Kit came down the stairs and gestured for me to follow him. His skin looked yellow in the weak lighting. Outside the clouds were heavy and inside the building the air felt thick with the anticipation of unfallen snow.

The stairs were shallow and swept around, back towards the front of the building. Kit knocked on the wooden double doors and, at a signal I didn't hear, opened the door. Sir Alec was sitting with his back to the window in a low armchair, dark clouds behind him and a feeble beaded table lamp at his side. There was an open file on the coffee table, which he closed before he stood to shake my hand.

'Mrs Hughes.'

He gestured with an open hand to the chair facing his, and I remembered that was my name. I half turned to sit, before realising that Kit hadn't come in with me.

'So, I believe you have something to tell me.' Sir Alec

leaned back in the armchair and pressed his fingers together.

'Yes. I met a British citizen, Eva Mann, and she wanted me to contact you on her behalf. She is currently living in Moscow and wants to return to Britain.'

'We know about Mrs Mann.'

'Right.' I waited. 'What do you know?'

'I know,' he leaned forward, 'that she is regarded as an enemy of Britain and you have been meeting with her regularly. How did you know to make contact with Mrs Mann?'

'I didn't.'

'You weren't aware of her before you came to Moscow?'

'No. I mean – no. I had been given a book of stories, which I now think she might have written, but I didn't know who she was.'

Sir Alec raised an eyebrow.

'Folk tales. Talking animals and things like that.' I wasn't making this better. 'They have her daughter in them, a cosmonaut, and they describe how she fell out of love with the Soviets. She's scared and she wants to go home.'

Sir Alec started to look through his papers. 'She doesn't have any children. Do you have any proof of anything in the stories? Don't you feel it was all a bit of a game to get you to come and find her?'

'I didn't intend to meet anyone.'

'And yet.' He sat back again. 'We have been hearing other distressing news, of course.'

I tried to keep my confusion from my face. Was he talking about Sandra? My report on Charlie? I couldn't guess.

'My wife's choir has been rather short on numbers recently. Maybe you'd like to join her?'

He stood and guided me to the door, his hand near but not actually on my back. He murmured as if someone else was in the room.

'I think it would be a supremely good idea to spend your time with the Britons associated with the embassy. The women here only want to guide and help you. Moscow doesn't have to be navigated alone and shouldn't be. So, let's not hear anything about people outside our little family.'

He opened the door. I nodded briskly, took a step and he closed the door. Kit was waiting. We went downstairs slowly but spoke quickly.

'Well?'

'Some patronising twit has banned me from speaking to anyone who isn't connected to the embassy.'

'That won't be a problem, will it, darling? Eva Mann was clearly deceiving you on the orders of our peace-loving friends.'

'She was interesting though, and she asked for my help.'

'And you tried. You've been a bit silly, but thoroughly decent.'

'But does this include Leila? She's not connected to the embassy.'

'She is connected. She's allowed to come here whenever she needs to. It's all to keep you out of trouble, darling. We don't want to lose you to a gulag. Anything else?'

'I have to go to choir.'

Kit's face fell. 'Oh, Christ. Sorry.'

Silently, he guided me to one of the back rooms. Emily was sitting with her pearly friend, Jessica. Sheets of music were spread out over the table, next to a teapot and cups.

'Ah, Martha. You made it. How lovely,' said Jessica.

'If you've finished, I can come back next time.'

'No, we're just getting started. We're choosing our Christmas carols to get them just right.'

'That's months away.'

'No such thing as too much practice.' Emily took an

empty cup and filled it for me. 'And what else would you be doing?'

I was rescued at lunchtime. Kit extracted me with the lie that we had a reservation at the Metropol, as unlikely as that sounded.

'I need something to do, Kit. I need something that will excuse me from that hellhole.'

Kit put his arm around my shoulder. 'Are you exaggerating, darling?'

'No! It's a terrible punishment for talking to people.'

'It's a sensitive place and time.'

'Why? It's all opening up, now, isn't it? Brezhnev has meetings with Nixon, Nixon visits, they're all allowed to talk to each other.'

'The peace-loving Soviets are always at war in their hearts, and the freedom-loving Americans like to lock people up. But, yes, letting them lie to each other in a polite way is a good thing, I'm sure.'

We passed the pie stall outside the Metropol, but it was too cold to sit around. We went into the restaurant, steamy with the heat of oncoming winter, and ordered wine while Kit persuaded the waiter to admit to what was available.

'The boilers are back on, then,' I said.

'They're saying we'll get the first snow on Sunday.'

'That would be amazing. I always thought Moscow was cold, but it's all up and down. It's like being in London, really.'

'Except for all the restrictions.'

'Really, that doesn't feel a million miles away, either.' Eva's comment about my class had stuck. 'You can't just walk into any building in London. There are shops and offices that are guarded by doormen. Schools and universities are dominated by people with money who know other people with money. And I know I'm talking about myself and I know I've benefited from it. Just look at all those people striking for the right to a decent wage. We're completely corrupt. Freedom isn't a British skill at all.'

Kit sat back and shook his head. 'You can't see the difference?'

I leaned in. 'Well, all the bugging and following is annoying,' and then I raised my voice a little, 'but is it so different making me spend time with old ladies? That's a form of spying and control.'

'The main difference is that you can stand in Hyde Park or Trafalgar Square and tell everyone exactly what you feel about Edward Heath and nothing will happen. The papers can criticise him, the workers can strike and the radio can condemn soldiers killing protestors in Northern Ireland.' Kit drained his glass. 'Five years ago, in Red Square, eight people held slogans protesting against the invasion of Czechoslovakia. One banner said, "We are losing our best friends". These people were sentenced to years in prison, or exile, or Siberia or psychiatric hospitals. Because to criticise the Union is to be insane. That's where freedom begins to look a bit different.'

His face was flushed. Too flushed for the wine he'd drunk, although he was already halfway through his second glass.

'I see.'

'Do you? Because there's a good reason why we need prior permission to go more than fifty miles outside of Moscow.'

He paused as the waiter placed our meals on the table. I wished we'd been talking about the speed of this delivery, rather than having an argument. When the waiter was out of earshot he continued.

'There's people like you all over the place who think that left-wing must be good, that the hard-working peasant really does run this show. And you think a comfortable room with two polite ladies and a pot of tea is a hellhole.'

'You know I was exaggerating.'

'I mean, why do you think Eva wants to leave?'

'If you know how bad it truly all is, why wouldn't you help her?'

'She made her choices.'

He began to eat, and I started to slice up the tough fish I'd been given. It was so overcooked that I suspected we'd been given plates that had been returned to the kitchen. It would explain why they'd been so quick.

I looked up. Kit was glaring at me. I had the urge to giggle. Our first proper married argument.

'Spit it out,' I said.

'It's not a joke. I've known you for years. I never, ever thought that I'd got you wrong. But they were right. You are a communist sympathiser and you're going to destroy my career.'

'I'm not—'

'Do you know that your name is in *The Index*?'

'I don't know what that is.'

'I explained that away, because your father is important and they'd just made a note of you to be aware of who's who, and who may be important. But no. You were in there because you're on their side.'

'Do you know what, Kit, with your stupid childish nick-name? You really need to understand something about me. I don't have a Communist Party card, but I can see that there are possibilities in the theory that we should consider. Because our way is not perfect. And you are as bad as them if you think that I can't have my own opinion on the matter.'

'An informed opinion is one thing. An emotional over-reaction is quite another.'

'I'm not being at all emotional about this ridiculous argument, I'm being emotional about falling out with you. I came here to see new things, but also to be with you. And this whole time here, the attitude of,' I looked around and lowered my voice, 'the people you work with is that men do and keep secret all the important stuff, and the women can keep themselves quiet and tidy and out of the way. But it's boring if you don't have anything to do. I'm not going to be having babies and I don't believe in yetis. So, I've just been speaking to people. Not telling them things, not spying, just interacting in a normal way with strange and interesting people. But, unlike Russia, in Britain it's only women who get called mad when they won't be obedient.'

'Touché.' Kit smiled, and we started to eat again, but there was something that had changed. I just hoped it would go back to normal. I didn't tell him that my blue jacketed friend had been replaced by many more jackets than I could keep track of.

29

Finally, it did snow, but only for two hours. Still, it was enough to do two things. Firstly, I started to get really excited again for a Moscow winter, and all that it promised. Secondly, I realised that I needed to make it to more green spaces and make notes on the parks and forests so I could spend the winter writing about them.

Kit asked me now for a complete account of my day over dinner, and I wasn't allowed to laugh off his requests. He knew what I was doing, so I resented his pretending to ask. I told him I'd been to the Illusion cinema inside one of Stalin's Seven Sisters, the Kotelnicheskaya Embankment Building, and walked along the Yauza river for a while. I watered my jasmine plant and thought up lies.

'What did you watch?'

'I can't remember. It was very earnest. I fell asleep.'

I told him I'd been to the Inturist offices and bought tickets to see the body of Lenin and inside the Kremlin.

'What did you think?'

'It was OK.'

I told him I'd stayed at home, reading.

'So, you had time to cook today?'

'No, I wasn't hungry.'

He'd know that I was lying, of course, but he never said.

'How was your day?' I asked.

'Oh, we just had to extract one of the exchange students from the Lubyanka.'

'What did he do to get arrested?'

'She,' he said pointedly, 'was taking photographs of a protest outside it. It's illegal to take pictures of the Lubyanka, and protests, so that made for a long afternoon.'

I fiddled with my knife. 'Was she injured?'

Kit looked at me. 'She was swept into the prison with a load of protestors by most of the men working there. They weren't asking for passports. I'd say she was injured, yes.'

He left his meal half eaten, and went out to smoke on the balcony. I watched him shivering and I wanted to go out and hold him, but I didn't.

My home-made maps were beginning to fill out with little details. I started to imagine an illustrated book, with the map on a page and a transparent insert. I did think about how I would explain this if I got arrested and thought, everyone thinks I'm a spy anyway. They'd just have to send me home. I started to wonder which side it would be.

Underneath all this walking and mapping were Eva's stories and the story about Eva, as I tried to work out what bits were true and what bits were narrative exaggerations. In the stories, there was a daughter, and she'd mentioned a daughter, so that might be true. Her lover seemed to have abandoned her in the stories, and she did seem very alone. But then, she, too, was now a spy of sorts, hiding herself behind ideas and requests and lapsed Britishness.

The fact that Leila found it interesting, too, made me

feel a bit less obsessive. I had someone to talk to about it. I didn't know whether to believe Eva, but I wanted a reason to.

Then, on the 24th, it snowed for four hours, and this time it settled properly. I was woken by the sound of shovels, and I got up to watch it fall from the balcony onto the fir trees and the last leaves of the birches. It wasn't a proper Moscow winter yet, only three or four degrees, but it held the promise of what was to come. The air was still and hard, cut with the cries of children sliding down the slope at the back of the apartment blocks on bags and sledges.

I wrapped myself up in my winter coat and knitted hat and went outside. Would my jacketed men leave their warm cars and follow me into the snow?

I walked into the woods, seeing the pale blue sky through the birch twigs and the snow on the branches making the shadows underneath look blacker than usual. I put my hand on a striped trunk, but they'd stopped peeling bark like wallpaper.

My feet were starting to ache with the cold of melted snow. The pavements were cleared, but the snow in the wood had soaked right through. Yet I was determined to see the view from the university. From the Lenin Hills, I could see the whole of Moscow, freshly covered, before it began to melt again. I thought of going back for Kit's wellies but decided it would take too long. The lift hadn't worked for a couple of days. I would just walk off the cold. The thought of bumping into Ivan kept me going.

Along Leninsky Prospekt, the trees were beautified, and the buildings had small heaps of snow on windowsills and doorways. I was stopped a few times by women in thick fur coats and rubber boots, who told me to get some proper clothes on.

'Vy zaboleyete.' You will get ill.

'Nichevo.' It's nothing.

I thought of the way my mother used to make me wear two pairs of socks, scarf and gloves. But that was for playing snowballs. Here, everyone had an opinion.

By the time I reached Universitetsky Prospekt, my feet were numb and I didn't feel like an adult at all. I walked down to the observation point and leaned on the balustrade. It was everything I imagined: the tower blocks, the cupolas, the trees, all pristine. There was a strong, cold breeze up here. I kept rubbing my hand under my nose, not knowing if it was cold or running. My feet were starting to hurt. I wanted to stay, and I wanted also to be in a hot bath.

All the voices around me were from Western Europe. Did the Russians not appreciate this, or did they just know there was no rush? There would be a lot more snow to look at. I stamped my feet.

'Hey.'

My immediate hope was that it was Ivan, but the voice was too high. I turned around to see Leila wrapped up in a fur coat, fur hat and some solid looking rubber boots.

'What are you doing here?' she asked.

'I wanted to see the snow.' I was feeling a bit tearful now. 'But I'm quite cold.'

'I'll walk back with you,' she said. 'There's something I need to show you. And we might need some music on for this.'

I stepped away from the balustrade, my hands deep in my pockets.

'You came out in leather shoes?'

'You sound like every old lady I've seen today.'

'But they're right. You can feel that they were right, can't you?'

'I can't feel a thing.'

Leila put her arm through mine and guided me home.

Leila filled a roasting dish with lukewarm water so I could soak my feet. Her fur coat lay backward over my chest and lap. My shoes looked as if they were ready to fall apart, but she screwed up pages of *Pravda* to try to give them some shape. The vodka she'd given me felt too cold in my hand, but hot in my stomach.

'There must be a reason why they drink this stuff, right?' she said.

'I suppose so. It's not for the taste.'

'Do you want another?'

'No thanks.' I held the glass out and she put it in the kitchen. I placed my hand back under the coat and pushed my face into the fur.

'I borrowed the coat, if you're wondering. It's my aunt's.'

'I should have borrowed things from Alison before she left. Her boots, for a start.'

'She did leave you boots, and a fur coat. Kit's got them.'

'Has he?'

'I think they're still in his office. He's probably worried about where you'll go in them.' She smiled sadly.

'When did he say that?'

Leila sighed, and sat at her paper covered table. 'He comes around before he goes home. He's been doing it for a while.'

'Does he ask about me?'

She nodded.

'What do you tell him?'

'Nothing. I barely see you now, anyway. I miss our meals, and I bet you miss my oven.' She smiled weakly. 'I don't know what's happened between you, but neither of you seems happy. Is there a way forward?'

'I don't think so.'

'Are you going to leave?'

I looked at her, and past her, outside, to the Russia I'd been waiting for. 'I don't want to. I can't. Not yet.'

'It won't be easy. He's pretty cross with you.'

'Yeah, I know. I'm cross too. But, right now, I'm worried about Eva.'

Leila raised her finger. 'Let's watch some TV.'

She put it on, some programme about a steel factory, and began to go through the papers on her desk. She pulled out an envelope and sat down close to me on the sofa.

'Someone in Seb's office went over to West Berlin, following some story.' She waved her hand. 'Anyway, I'd given him a name, just to run past some people, see if anything cropped up. And it did. He brought this back. It's a Xerox. He managed to get it back to the office for an hour or two.' She smirked. 'He's ridiculously good-looking. You would not believe what he persuades people to do. Thank God he's in journalism and not politics.'

I pulled it out. It was folded strangely, sections of different lengths.

'He had to fold it to hide underneath a dust jacket.'

I unfolded it. A copy of a two-page document. I scanned through it. Eva, Eva, Eva.

'What is it?' I whispered.

'I can tell you what I think it is. I think it's the beginning of the story of how Eva came to Moscow.'

11.ix.1946

Statement from Miss P. Walsh on the disappearance of Miss E. Ingham, as dictated to Lieutenant Barker.

I moved into a small apartment on Buda-
pestastrasse with Miss E. Ingham in June
1946, and this is my report on events before
she left. I have been asked to make it clear
that this information did not come directly
from conversations I had with Eva, but from
reading her diary in October, something
which I only did because she was absent from
work and hadn't been at the apartment for
two days. I don't appreciate the things which
have been said about my doing this. If I
hadn't, Eva would still be regarded as missing
and soldiers would be looking for her.

Our first months were normal for the
time. We found it hard to eat outside of
the apartment, so we spent a lot of time
together. Sometimes we would meet with
other embassy secretaries and share food
and drink. Eva didn't drink alcohol in those
early months, but later came to bring home
spirits. I now know that she was given these
by a man. There was no mention of what she
did in return for these bottles. She seemed
one of the more innocent of the secretaries,
even though, at twenty-five, she was one of
the oldest of us. I don't know why she wrote
so much about feeling lonely. I was always
there.

In her diary, Eva referred to meeting a West
German man, living in the American sector.

She called him Wolfgang, and he had told
her that this translated as the 'wolf path' or
'wolf journey'. She liked this idea of being
named after animals. I don't know where
they met. I think he was her lover. I don't
know. She didn't tell me anything about this
man, and I did ask her all the time where
she was going. She said she needed to think
and she liked the fresh air. She said she
preferred walking on her own. I thought we
got on well.

They would meet by the bridge over the
Landwehr Canal, and spend time in the
Tiergarten. I think they stayed in the British
section. I don't know who she thought he
was, or what job he told her he had. He must
have said he was involved in the reconstruc-
tion. I know we're supposed to accept that
not all Germans are Nazis, but she must
have wanted more proof than him saying it.

I think his surname must have been Mann,
or Volk Mann, because she practised writing
her name like you do when you're at school
and you like someone. Eva Volk Mann was
the last thing she wrote in the diary.

She didn't come back on Wednesday 30th
October. I reported this to the office, and it
was on the 31st that I searched her room
and found the diary in the suitcase under
her bed. On Friday 1st November, I planned

to hand the diary in to the Sergeant, but it
was gone. Between me going to bed at half
past ten and waking at half past seven,
someone had been into our apartment and
taken Eva's belongings. I had been reading
the diary in bed, but I didn't hear anything
when it was taken from my room. I don't
sleep well now.

I looked at Leila.

She said, 'I looked it up. Volk is Russian for wolf.'

'So that explains the initials in the booklet. Eva Wolf
Mann.' I looked back at the sheets. 'It all seems sad,
somehow.'

'Only if you believe she really wants to go back to Britain.'

'Don't you?'

'It's not what I get from the stories, no. She could have
made contact in a dozen different ways without involving
you. She probably took papers with her, some kind of
information, which would mean she's in terrible trouble if
she does ever go back. There's something specific about you
that means she wants you to be interested in her.'

'Maybe. But you're interested too.'

'I'm all about the story.'

That made me tense up. I wanted to say that she couldn't
let Seb write about me, that I wasn't part of the story. But
that might make her more interested in my part, whatever
that was.

I said, 'Do you think Wolfgang was Russian?'

'I think he was a German-speaking Russian spy, Andrei
or Vlad, sent over from the Soviet sector to collect information. The Communists were regarded as allies then.
They believe they won the war, we believe we won it, and

the Americans believe they won it. I don't think anyone believed that, nearly thirty years later, Berlin would still be split down the middle.'

'Why would she come to Moscow? Wouldn't he have dumped her there when she wasn't useful anymore?'

'She must have made herself really useful. Once she slips from the British side, it's only Eva that could tell you.' She stood up and yawned. 'I'd better go to my lesson. I won't be in later. My absence is becoming a problem so I need to eat and sleep at the university tonight. Meet me on Thursday after classes and we can look for some of your missing forests. Unless you're meeting up with lovely Ivan again?'

'No, I'm not seeing Ivan. I only saw him once.' That hadn't stopped me going back to where we'd met, again and again, in the hope that I would.

30

It took a few days for my feet to recover but, as soon as I could, I got the Metro. I wanted to visit Eva, to see if she still wanted my help. I felt that if she told me about Wolfgang, anything to verify the pages, then she was telling the truth about all of it. I didn't want to have to help her, but I needed to feel all right about it. I'd decided that, if she was convincing, I was going to ask her to tell her story to Leila's boyfriend. As a journalist, it would be easier for him than anyone else to get the story out. However, she didn't keep provocateur hours on a Thursday, so finding her would be tricky. I got on the Metro and changed lines to come up Arbatskaya. The Khudozhestvenny cinema looked to be open again.

I wandered down to the building I'd seen Eva go into, but there seemed little point in going in as I had no idea where her flat was. I went back to Eva's fake flat, checking for jackets behind me and not being disappointed. I tried to open the door which had always been open, but it was locked. I knocked and an old woman answered.

She spoke in Russian. 'What do you want?'

My spoken Russian was still poor, and I could understand more than I could say. I tried pointing.

'Friend.' I indicated the stairs. 'I come.'

The old woman shook her head and closed the door.

I walked back to the small garden that I'd waited in before and looked up at the windows. I couldn't see anything behind them, no lights or movement. I walked over to the Alexander Gardens, to see if she was on her bench, but two old ladies sat there, not speaking to each other. I walked around the Kremlin walls, expecting to catch sight of her, but she didn't appear.

The jackets knew I was here, and she hadn't been summoned. Maybe I wasn't allowed to see Eva again. She wouldn't have told them what we talked about. The British didn't believe what we'd talked about. My stomach clenched. Maybe she'd been taken away, exiled, sent back to the Siberia of her stories. I would never know what happened to her, even if Kit did.

My eyes filled with tears, though I didn't understand why I was so upset. I walked around to Red Square, along the line for Lenin's tomb, which never seemed to get shorter, and looked at St Basil's in the distance. There she was, waiting, with her dog.

I walked towards her, smiling, but two armed soldiers got in my way.

'Dokumenty,' one said.

I said, 'Britanskaya,' and searched in my bag for my passport. I couldn't find it. I looked up, but I couldn't see Eva any more.

'Dokumenty.'

'Hold on.' I started to take things out of my bag and saw it at the bottom. 'Here.'

I held it out and tried to look around for Eva. There was

no sign, not anywhere. I looked up at the soldiers. One was looking at the photo, then me, then passing it to the other. I held my hand out to take it back, but he started to flick through it. I tried not to show I was in a hurry as it was clearly slowing them down. It was passed over again, and then handed back to me.

'Spasibo,' I said, and I started to run towards the cathedral.

One of the soldiers shouted, 'Ne zapuskat!'

I slowed down to a fast walk, but I knew she'd gone. At least she wasn't in Siberia. Yet.

When I arrived back in the apartment, Kit was home early, and listening to the Bolero. Both bad signs. He came out to the hall while I was still taking my coat off.

'Martha.'

I waited, but he guided me into the room before he said anything else. There was a half-empty bottle of red on the table and another, already open to breathe, by the record player. This was really bad.

'Kit, what's going on?'

'Sit down.' He poured me a glass and his face was so serious that I quickly drank half of the wine in one go.

'Is it my parents? Has something happened?'

'No.'

'David?'

'No, there's no news from home. It's nothing like that. It's work.'

'I've only just come in. I wasn't hiding anything. I didn't even speak to Eva.'

'Martha.' He put his hand on mine. 'Darling, we know about Sandra.'

'How she died?'

'Yes, but also about the letter she gave you. We've been told about the letter you passed on and that makes your position—' He sighed. 'The Ambassador thinks you should go home for a break.'

I pulled my hand away. 'No.'

'It's just a holiday.'

'No, I don't want to leave. It's going to be winter and I have been looking forward to it so much.'

'The embassy is worried that you will be compromised. I mean, even more than you have been.'

I finished my wine and looked out past the balcony. 'But when can I come back?'

'Soon,' he said. 'You'll probably be back before Christmas. Not that they have Christmas here, of course.'

He filled both our glasses, and fetched a plate of rye bread, sausage and cheese from the kitchen. We picked from it for a while.

'What exactly am I being punished for?'

'You're not being punished, darling. You thought you were helping out a friend, I expect, and it turned into something quite, quite different. I would never have put you in this position if I'd known.'

'But if I leave, what will change?'

'We are going to force a couple of points with the authorities, ruffle some feathers. They wouldn't like their wives in London being approached like Sandra was.'

I was confused, until I remembered I was just a wife. A dependant.

'Do you know why Sandra died? Was it them?'

Kit nodded.

'Was it connected to the letter?'

'Not directly, darling. Not directly.' Kit shook his head. 'I've loved having you here.'

He smiled grimly. I turned my jasmine plant around on its saucer. It was looking rather droopy.

'It doesn't sound as if I will be coming back, Kit.'

'You are coming back. We will have Christmas dinner at the embassy and frolic in the snow.'

'Do you promise?'

'I promise. Cross my heart.'

He did mean it. I knew he did.

'How long have I got?'

His face fell. 'The flight is booked for tomorrow morning. I think it's been booked for a few days. I swear I didn't know until a couple of hours ago. I'm so sorry.'

'So, it has nothing to do with Eva?'

'I don't think so.'

'Why aren't you asking what happened with Sandra?'

'Do you want to tell me?'

'No.' I finished my wine, and he refilled the glass. 'I won't be able to let Leila know what's happening, will I? Will you explain things to her?'

'Of course. Is there anyone else?'

Eva. Of course, Eva, wherever she was. 'No.'

He nodded, and then pointed to a large black case next to the sofa. 'Do you know what that is?'

I shook my head.

'A Geiger counter. I was given it to test on your clothes and shoes. Sometimes our peace-loving friends use radio-active dust to track people's movements. See where they go, who they see. Our scientists have no idea about the medical implications long term.'

I shuddered. 'And?'

'Oh, I didn't find anything. I just wanted you to know what they are capable of.' He raised his eyebrows. 'For when you come back. I know you're a nice person, and you can forget when you talk to people that they are capable of things like that without thinking twice. That's what the poster was for.'

He pointed back to the poster of the cosmonauts, man and dog, destined for the stars. I remembered my arrival, when I had the whole of Moscow to discover.

I was feeling very drunk by now. I picked at the bread. 'I do love Moscow. I could stay if I wanted. I don't think they can make me go.'

'Pyotr will be here at eight.' Kit tilted his head. 'Play the game, Martha. Go for a holiday, come back when things are settled. Moscow will still be here.'

'I know. Like Lenin.'

'Like Lenin.'

'Metro'

by

E. V. MANN

I keep my eyes on the darkness of the windows so that I don't miss anyone waiting on the platform at each Metro station. I don't recognise my reflection in the glass. It could be either day or night in this underground cosmos as I criss-cross under the city, wander from one line to the next. Sometimes I catch the scent of a wolf and run for the next train.

The faces of women blur together, but I know she'll stand out. I know her better than my own face. I'm scared she won't recognise me anymore. I have been transformed by arctic journeys.

The train doors open and I can smell the wolves which hunt me. I look outside to the rectangular panels of grey marble which cover the platform walls. The matching slender pillars are gently arched, but they've ruined the curve with large electric lights. I mustn't think 'they', I remind myself. We.

The carriage feels too warm, so I loosen my scarf. I think I'm speaking to myself, but I can't hear the words. I have so many words to use up that they wake me at night, eating their way out from inside my brain like maggots. I catch the eye of a woman sitting opposite. She is staring at me. She isn't who I am looking for, and my eyes slide away.

I make an effort to unclench my fists and focus on what I will ask for, if they get me. Just one last word. One word – home. Maybe this time they won't catch me. Maybe this time I'll find her first.

The doors close and, as the station is whipped away, I see something large running alongside the train and then slipping back. Large and quick, like austere fire, and then darkness. I close my eyes. I know that shape. The smell is overwhelming now. I hold my scarf over my mouth and nose. Gradually, the smell fades and I think, maybe we've left it behind.

Maybe, I think, when I get off at Kolomenskaya I can just admire the yellow ceiling and white plasterwork and trail my fingers over the amber treacle of the octagonal marble columns. Maybe I won't think, it's all too much, as I slide underneath the gilt cartwheel chandeliers. Maybe I don't have to fall when they capture me, like before, hands smashing and mouth bleeding on the cold brown tiles. I lay there, wishing I'd fallen on the tracks instead.

The train pulls into the station, and the thick marble columns slow their passing. I stand up and cross the threshold between metal train and cool ceramic and think, oh, there's nothing here. I look around. I can leave, I'm free to leave, I think, and my heart lifts even while the stench is so thick I can taste it at the back of my mouth.

I remember the posters on the walls of my life: 'Lenin is always with us!' My shout echoes from the marble and makes the chandeliers tremble.

Everyone keeps walking. No one turns around.

I walk out of the station and feel the cold air keenly like death in my lungs. My wolf is waiting for me at the entrance, ready to take my arm, and I go with him, as quietly as snow.

31

I tried to enjoy being at home. I had been away for less than a year and I should have missed it, but it was like coming home from Cambridge. A temporary stop-gap. Something to get through.

I missed Kit and spent hours staring out of the window, wishing he had a phone. I wrote letters to him but found their generalities frustrating. I wanted to be back in Moscow before they arrived. I couldn't write about anyone or anything without wondering what the censors would make of it all. I certainly couldn't mention my family. My father, his position and his secrets, loomed behind everything. He could barely look at me when we passed in the hallway.

I tore up the letters, and annoyed Cook by trying to pick up her recipes to take back to Moscow. And I was back by myself while Ma was out selling jam and Pa was 'at work'.

Kit had convinced me to take back all my clothes to give them a proper wash in the machine, instead of half-rinsed in the bath. I liked how much softer they were, but I walked around the town centre looking for seamless rubber boots and warm underwear.

My parents had acknowledged my twenty-first birthday

by getting David over for the weekend. I forced him to go to the pub.

'I've got to get out of this house. I just wish I knew when I can get back there. You haven't heard from Kit either?'

David shook his head. But he didn't look at me, and I knew he was hiding something.

'What?'

'I just don't think it's very likely that you'll be going back.'

'Why? What have you heard?'

'Nothing specific. It's just, people who are sent home like you were don't tend to go back.'

I held my head in my hands.

'It's all right, Martha. You'll find where you're supposed to be.'

I spoke into my hands. 'I'm supposed to be in Moscow. I love it there and there's so much I didn't see. I was waiting for the snow.' I felt David's hand on my shoulder and whipped my head back. 'It's Pa, isn't it? He's put a stop to it to punish me.'

'Why would he do that?'

I groaned. 'I don't know.'

'He doesn't have a say about what happens at foreign embassies.'

'He could do. Do you know, I have no idea what he does and what he has a say in. But they all did.' I gestured vaguely towards Russia. 'They knew.'

David lowered his voice. 'They told you who he was?'

'They let me know that they knew who he was. They probably know him better than me.'

'You know him as well as anyone else.' David exhaled and placed his fingers on the table. 'You need to do something other than waiting. Something you can continue with whether you stay here or go back to Moscow. Read all of Shakespeare's plays, or go back to Classics and remind yourself why you liked them so much. Listen to music, take up knitting, I don't know. Kit said you were doing a lot of walking.'

'So, you have heard from him?'

David slid his fingers from the table and rested them in his lap. He sat back and chewed his lip. 'The world we live in, the three of us, isn't one where we can answer everything. You're not like us. You like to tell people what you know, and that's not a bad thing. You're an open person, but too open sometimes. You're not happy to sit in the background and not ask what's happening. And that can make things tricky, dangerous.' He frowned. 'Do you understand what I'm saying?'

'Yeah. I shouldn't ever have gone.'

'Maybe.' He finished his pint. 'We'd better get back.'

I followed him up Church Street, a little way behind, and thought, he was right. Up ahead was the school and, beyond that, the church. If I didn't watch out, my life would be restricted to this section of road, backwards and forwards. I needed to stop waiting around for Kit to change things for me.

No one would actually say that I couldn't go back. I tried to speak to Ma about shopping for my return, and she turned away. Pa was grim over the dinner table. If I looked at him unexpectedly, I'd see that he looked sad. I was a disappointment. I went through my books, my papers, never knew what day it was.

I started to go back to the library, requesting books on Russia and flicking through the atlas to marvel at its size. I found travel books with pictures of palaces in the middle of parks I'd walked right past, churches I'd missed by not turning a corner, and snow on everything. I sat at the library table and cried at the thought that I couldn't go back. I learned the name of the librarian, Rosalind, and she started to research other books I might like and arranged inter-library loans. She never asked why I was back, and I was glad.

I lay in bed reading Eva's stories, the picture of the Cathedral of Christ the Saviour clear in my eye as the dragon burned it down, the smell of the Metro vivid, and the Apothecary's Garden, drenched with rain in my imagination, wolves in the forests. I realised that I yearned for Moscow how Eva yearned for her piece of England. I understood the last story now, torn between two places and two peoples. I felt it in my stomach. Neither place existed. Britain now was a very different place to the one Eva had left thirty years ago. It had been battered then, but now it was angry, and even in this privileged corner of Gloucestershire, I could feel it.

Moscow wasn't perfect, and even there I was in a privileged position, but it was new to me. If anything, it had made the problems here much clearer. And the propaganda. The national anthem every time the national TV station closed down for the night, the programmes celebrating the lives of the ordinary working man and woman. Willie Turnbull and Hugh Adam Crawford had had their turn at charming the country this month, not to mention all the guests on *Pebble Mill at One* and *Nationwide*. The country was fracturing with people realising that things could change, and the rich didn't have an automatic right to run the world. Who knew how long Heath could hang onto power?

Then there was me, in this house, not even knowing the real name of Cook or the woman who came in to clean five mornings a week. 'That girl,' Ma called her, and in all those years I'd never asked what they were called.

But I could change. I didn't have to be like my mother, coolly dismissive, or my father, upholding the status quo silently in the background. I suspected that he *had* been behind my return, safeguarding what I'd left of his reputation. It didn't make me happy to have intruded on his territory like that. I also suspected that he felt guilty for pulling me back here.

One day when 'that girl' was cleaning his room, and had left to empty the bin, I went in and sat in his chair. The books were sociological, political and geographical. I tried the drawers. All were locked. His letter rack was full of neatly lined up envelopes.

The books and the autumn weather reminded me of the smell of packing for a new year of study. It was the time of leaving home.

I picked up the telephone and called Harriet.

32

I met Kit in London. I knew when he called that this was the end, but I was still happy to see him.

'Darling,' he said, his arms open. I held onto him, smelling the Russian cigarette smoke embedded in his coat. We walked arm in arm from Paddington, through Norfolk Square Gardens where we sat down.

'Tell me everything,' I said.

'I wanted to tell you in person that your chest has been sent back with your things in. I couldn't bear for it just to turn up, and we know what the phones are like.' He grimaced. 'Isn't it nice not to wonder who's listening in?'

'I have no one to phone, and at home my parents would be listening in. Not that I'm at home right now.'

'Yes, I heard you were staying with friends. I'm glad you're not alone. You'll make new friends,' he hesitated, 'and more than friends, of course. I was wondering how you felt about getting a divorce. What would be easiest for me would be to get the no fault divorce after two years. So, it would be dated from when you left Moscow. But, darling, you're the only one who would be wanting to marry again, so I need to know if you are all right with that.'

I tried to hide my face by looking at the pavement.

'You're upset? Martha, I am so sorry.'

'Oh, it's not you, Kit. I know it's inevitable, and not a real marriage. It just feels as if we'll fall out now.'

'Never.' His arm tightened on mine. 'Let's do what we dreamed of for all those months in Moscow.'

'Go to the pub?'

He nodded. 'Absolutely.'

He stood and offered his hand to pull me up. I took it and seeing my wedding band, realised I'd have to take it off. My temporary husband. I would always miss him.

We walked away.

'London feels different, don't you think?' he said.

'Yes. Unsettled.' I looked at him. 'Is it snowing yet?'

'It's going to start next week, according to the reports. I know you think you're missing out, Martha, but it will be below freezing until the end of March. It's not pleasant.'

I thought of the pictures and couldn't bring myself to agree with him. He squeezed my hand as we went into The Royal Exchange. I found seats while he went to get served. It had only recently opened for the day and we were the only customers.

He carried our drinks over, a pint for him and a half for me.

'Kit, when you come home, can I have your tin money box? Or could you get me another one, and I'll pretend it's the same.'

'Of course. I'll give you the poster too.' He smiled. 'Just in case you need reminding.'

I changed the subject. 'How's Leila?'

'I don't see much of her. In fact, I only bumped into her once outside our building. I told her where you'd gone, of course.'

'What did she say?'

'Just that it was a shame. That kind of thing.'

I was annoyed that he would sound so uninterested. Or maybe they were spending a lot of time together and he thought I'd be jealous. I didn't know. I just knew he was lying.

'Have you thought about what you are going to do next?' he asked.

I nodded. 'I have a plan.'

'Oh, tell.' Kit sat back on the bench. I leaned toward him.

'I'm going back to university. I've got an interview at the University of Essex.'

'Martha, why?'

'I need a change.'

Kit's voice went high, 'You haven't had enough of those?'

I laughed. 'No. I'm switching to Political Science too.'

Kit leaned forward. 'This is about going back, isn't it?'

I shrugged and smiled.

'Martha, the whole world is waiting for you. You could always go to Iceland or Denmark. There is snow in lots of beautiful places that are a bloody lot safer than the Soviet Union.'

'It's not just the snow. I really do love Moscow, and I'd like to be able to decide when I'm ready to leave. I couldn't decide anything for myself then, but there's no reason why I can't make my own application to the British Council.'

'They won't give you a visa. Not after the last few months. And you really shouldn't try. They have their hooks in you, Martha.'

Kit looked ashen. I'd really thought he'd be more impressed by the way I was working around problems.

'Didn't you listen to me when I told you what it was really like? All the hypocrisy, all of the lies. Everything you did was orchestrated. Did you listen? If you go back you will never be free again.'

I laughed. 'They don't have anything on me.'

He looked at me in disbelief. 'You have no idea, do you?'

I sipped my drink. 'Is this going to affect your job?'

'I don't know. No. Maybe.' He sat and drank for a while. 'You've been back a few weeks, and all this has happened.'

I finished my drink and went to the bar without asking him. His eyes were glazed over as he worked out something. When I got back he'd formed his questions.

'When do you start your degree?'

'In the autumn.'

He took a long drink. 'What does your father say?'

I moved the empty glasses to the table next to us. 'I'm twenty-one. I get a grant. I don't need permission.'

'You can't get a grant when you've been expelled, surely?'

'I am lodging with Harriet's family while I work. I started as a secretary a couple of days ago in Bayswater. It has a different LEA, so I used her address to apply for another grant. I thought you'd be pleased that I wasn't relying on you to get me back there.'

Kit shook his head. 'After all the money they spent on your schools to get you into one of the best universities, you don't think your parents deserve a say?'

I raised my eyebrows.

'And Political Science? At that hotbed of radicalism?'

I laughed. 'Kit! Seriously?'

The door opened and a group of men came into the pub. Kit glared at them.

'It was radical about five years ago,' I said.

He lowered his voice, 'You remember the Angry Brigade trial last year? The longest trial in history, that one? Two of them were at Essex.'

I whispered, 'I promise that I won't join the Angry Brigade. Maybe the Slightly Patronised by Well-meaning Men Brigade.'

'I am not patronising you.'

'You're saying I'll end up in some bombing group.'

'I'm saying,' Kit hissed, 'that you should consider your father's position before you make decisions like that.'

'If my father wants me to consider his position, then I suggest he bloody well tells me what it is.' I pushed my chair back and walked away.

I left the pub and walked back to Paddington. I was furious with Kit, forgetting that I'd been convinced I would love him forever less than an hour ago. A hotbed of radicalism? That's exactly what Pa would say. And that was why I hadn't told him, or Ma.

In the hour it took me to get home, my parents had been informed. They swore it hadn't been Kit who told them, but some unspecified university tell-tale. The phone kept ringing that night. When Ma had finished, Pa called, and then David. I sat on the stairs to speak to him.

'What have you done now?'

'I'm going back to university.'

'But not Cambridge?'

'No.'

'Why?'

'Because I can, and I can't stay at home. How would you feel?'

'Essex sounds like a good choice. Have fun. If she calls you again, please tell Ma that I'm going out, so not to call me back.'

'Will do.'

I put the phone down and stood up. It rang again.

'David has gone out and I can't tie up the phone any longer. I'm off to bed now.'

Ma's voice was trembling. 'We're not going to allow this to happen.'

'Why not? Because it's a hotbed of radicalism?'

'Because you cannot be trusted. You never know when to stop speaking to people.'

'I really don't think you have a say in this. We could meet for lunch in London and you can interrogate me on what I'm up to.' I sat down again. 'Or we could just talk about normal things, like life.'

Ma sighed and put the phone down. I went to bed.

1974

33

Essex was different to Cambridge in more ways than I could count, but it felt like home. I imagined having a room in one of the tower blocks, almost as high as my home in Moscow, and from it I would see woods, green spaces and a river.

It had been a long day, and the paperwork was complicated. I'd had my interview in the Politics Department, my British Council application was being reviewed and every decision was mine again. If I didn't get the Council exchange, I'd apply for a holiday visa. If I didn't get that, I'd look at something else. One way or another, I was going back to find out what happened to Eva.

There seemed to be many similarities with Moscow at the university when I arrived earlier, but gradually the differences reminded me that I was not there. The blocks of building didn't have guards or dezhurnaya on every door, watching and noting who came in and out. There was laughing and kissing in public. When I ordered food, they had it.

Since I'd been back, I didn't have to eat sour cabbage in vinegar and oil, so I missed it. The fact that almost everyone wore jeans, usually flared jeans, struck me as decadent and wasteful, before I bought my own pair. It was almost impossible to stay in the present, thinking all the time about what came next. But I would try.

At home, I'd scoured the papers for news of Russia. Scotland had had the northern lights for eleven nights, and some snow, and I envied the Scots for being under that northern sky. Here I watched the fog, thick on the fields and river, thin in the weak sunlight. I wished Eva knew that I was where she wanted to be, scanning the stories for clues even now.

I had time before my train, so I walked across the hill that dropped down to the campus buildings and went to the lake. The edge was muddy with footprints and where the geese and ducks had paddled, and I remembered my frozen feet. I still needed rubber boots.

It was late afternoon and the frost was coming, but I wasn't ready to leave. Moscow had introduced me to trees and I gazed at the greens, yellows, oranges and reds, some-times purple leaves, thinking, I should know what that tree is called. I noticed every birch tree like a friend. I noted the oak tree recently hollowed out by lightning, the tree where the earth between the roots had been hollowed out, heard the traffic of the long road to Clacton. I wished for a dog to walk with me.

I started to walk back to Rayleigh Tower. I passed a group of students performing Shakespeare under a tree, *Othello*, and I slowed my pace to listen. Desdemona was about to be murdered. I watched her beg for her life, disbelieving her fate. Maybe I should get involved in something like that. They were bound to put on a Greek play which I already knew. Or maybe I should take up a sport. It might help me sleep. Or just run on my own. I hadn't seen anyone run in Moscow, but here people used the park as if it was purposeful. In Moscow–

I had to stop comparing everything to Moscow. I had to stop shutting myself off. If I was going to get through this, I had to meet people.

I turned back and headed for the square with the rectangular fountain in the middle. I sat on the edge, like a dozen other students, but I was on my own in the dusk. Someone had been chalking slogans on the step: 'art belongs to the people'.

'Marta.'

I didn't turn. That wasn't my name, after all, and there were other people here meeting, talking, making plans. I looked away, through the arch to where it was already dark.

'Marta.'

Slightly closer now. The hairs began to prickle on the back of my neck as the voice seemed familiar. But it couldn't be. I didn't know anyone yet. And that wasn't my name, even if the voice made it sound like mine. I kept my eyes focused on some distant point.

A woman sat near me, the fountain trickled, and the sun continued to set behind the buildings. I shivered. It was like Eva's first story where she sits next to the water and the wolf sits next to her. I couldn't smell a wolf, just the harshness of Russian filterless papirosy and something else, something underneath that.

Close, and very quiet now, one last time.

'Marta, I am with you.'

I could hear the smile in her voice, my wolf, and everything became clear. She'd fed me information I wanted. She'd taken me drinking, got me to talk. And I hadn't stopped. There had been no boyfriend in the flat, not even a pair of trousers that he might have left behind. I went through everything I'd told her from my conversations with Eva, everything Eva had said. I'd spied for the Russians and never even realised. She'd won and I didn't even know I was competing.

'Still thinking about Moscow?' Leila asked. 'I heard you applied for the British Council exchange.'

Everything Kit had talked about came back to me. My hands were shaking and I clasped them together. 'What are you doing here?'

'We know each other, Martha. I know you're going to argue that you don't know some things about me, but you know everything that's important. We got on, and we had fun. And I think that you know this could work.'

'What could?'

'Things need to change. Things need to be shared. You understand that.'

'And what about protest when things aren't right? You claim that it's all for the little people, and then tell them to shut up.'

'There's more than one kind of communism. The Soviets have the one that suits such an immensely vast country and population. Same with China. But Cuba and Britain, they are small islands. It would be a version that worked for us. You have to start somewhere. And it would be people like us making the decisions.'

'And what exactly would I be doing? Censoring books? I read *Doctor Zhivago* before I went, and *The Master and Margarita*. I can't support banning them.'

'Did you read Solzhenitsyn?'

I shifted my legs. 'I tried.'

'Boring, isn't it?'

She grinned and I couldn't help but smile. I had liked Leila. But Kit was right. I was part of a plan so big that I couldn't even see it. They had something on me, but I didn't know what it was.

She opened her hands. 'Look, it's a work in progress. The theory is sound, but the Soviet Union is still progressing towards communism, slowly. They're going to get things wrong. We will too. But what chance do we have as women to change things now? Those men who run Britain don't see us as intelligent people, just future mothers. This is the only way to get true equality. It's what you've been fighting for.'

I knew that look of excited conviction. I used to like the way she'd sweep me up in her arguments. But not now.

I looked at the clouds, as if considering what she said. 'I didn't see any women in the line-up at the Kremlin.'

When she looked up, Leila's face had hardened. 'Again, you're talking about Soviet communism.'

'It's the one I know.'

I leaned back on my hands and stretched my legs out.

'We want you to work for us.'

'I don't know anything.'

'You could find things out. Your father is working on some really interesting projects. Non-secret analogue encryption. Does that ring a bell?'

'I don't want to help you. Look what happened to Sandra.'

'Sandra?' Leila laughed. 'Oh, don't be ridiculous.'

She carried on laughing so long that I sat up properly to look around. No one was watching. She wiped her eyes.

'OK, maybe you didn't kill Sandra.'

'We didn't touch her. That's the silliest thing I've heard. Think about who Sandra was embarrassing.'

Her husband. Of course that made sense, but I wasn't sure.

Leila held her hand out to me, and I took mine away. 'Think about it properly. You really like it there. You fit in.'

'Oh, I do. I love Moscow. But I think I would have liked it under the Tsars too. It's just a beautiful place. Shame about who's in charge.' I stood up and tried to look steady. 'Right, I'll be off.'

Leila smiled. 'It would be so easy. It would just be as if you were chatting to friends. Like chatting to Eva. She sends her regards.'

Eva. Was that what they held over me?

'No, I'm not going to work with you because of Eva.'

I took a step away, back towards the path to the main road, and the bus back to the station. I felt relieved, now that she'd shown her hand. Eva wasn't enough of a pull. She'd made her choices and I had to accept that I wouldn't learn the truth.

She said, quietly, 'Poor Ivan.'

'Ivan?' I stopped and turned back to look at her.

'We had a long chat with Ivan. I think he was hoping that you'd confirm his story. But if we're not going to talk, I don't see how you can do that.'

Oh God, Ivan. His degree and his family, everything at risk because he spoke to me. What had he lost?

She hadn't even stood up. She knew where I was going and where I'd been. She smiled, and I knew Kit was right. If I took one step towards her, my life wouldn't ever be my own again. I wouldn't have the choice to stay or leave, all my decisions would be made for me. Anyone I liked would be at risk.

'Tell Ivan I'm sorry,' I said. I walked away to catch my bus.

'Cliff Pirate'

by

E. V. MANN

At night, I lay in bed listening to the tickle of pebbles and slate. I can always hear it, above the slicing Icelandic winds, or the abrasive Saharan rains which leave red sand on the doorstep. The gentle crumbling of the cliff is louder than everything in my mind.

The front of my house looks the same as ever. The small gate, which still needs painting, guards the pea gravel path. It's the house I used to live in. I remember it from when I was younger, but somehow I am back there, as if I never left.

I don't know if old friends are shunning me or have forgotten they knew me, but they no longer call with their moth-eaten furs and growling voices. My only visitors now explain, a little slower each time, exactly how perilous life is.

As if I wouldn't know.

Sometimes they draw little maps on envelopes of places I would be safe.

'I know it's temporary,' I tell them. 'I do know, but I have time.'

'This house could crumble at any moment,' they say. 'You don't want to be here when it falls in on you.'

I laugh, thinking how silly it would be to be buried alive with all the space of the sea right there, knocking at the back door.

They look sadly at me, and with horror at the disappearing garden. They measure it, maybe slightly shorter than the last time, and leave, crunching away.

Perilous. I like that. It makes me feel like a pirate on the high seas.

The last storm took the garden statue and tried to rattle the sash windows out of their grooves. I pushed them all open, propped the doors wide with furniture, and let the wind pass right through, my hands tight over my ears and the sea spray stinging my eyes. I waited it out and the morning was shiny like a poisonous berry, the sea slinking back.

It was a tough victory. All my books were ruined.

After a storm, I always look down on the people who come in their raincoats, with toy-sized picks and brushes, to search for the stone-hard bodies of ancient creatures, curled around the astonishment of death.

They wonder at the statue of Lenin amid the dinosaurs.

I wonder at them, and call out, 'Lenin is always here!'

I look out to sea, the pirate of my perilous ship. I refuse to curl up and I refuse to crumble. My garden is two steps long now, but it is still there, and I am still here, the only witness to the rocks the sea hurls at me, chipping away angrily at the land. I collect my own rocks and keep them by the door to throw back.

It is my house, my one remaining wind-bent rosemary bush, my land. The sea grumbles away to itself. One of us has to win, but I think I have a chance.

Acknowledgements

As ever, I have relied on many kindnesses in writing this book. Sue Dawes is the best, and most creative, reader any writer could wish for. The talented Bieke Dutoit shared her knowledge of Moscow and the Russian language (any errors are my own). Also thanks to Moira Forsyth, a brilliantly sensitive editor, and to all those at Sandstone Press for their help.

I am also grateful to the women who travelled alone to Moscow and published their experiences: Marguerite Harrison in the 1920s, Santha Rama Rau and Sally Belfrage in the 1950s, and Sheila Fitzpatrick in the 1960s. All braver women than I am. Also in the 1960s, Adrian McIntyre's account of life as a businessman in Moscow added some often bizarre details, as did Martin Nicholson's memoirs of life inside the British Embassy in Moscow.

My husband, Mark, has been both inspiration and solver of plot problems. My children would also like to be mentioned: Alfred, George, Henry and Mabel, maybe you'll read this one.

WICKSY AND THE KING'S SHILLING

PETER WICKS

ISIS
LARGE PRINT
Oxford

First published in Great Britain 2011
by ISIS Publishing Ltd.

Published in Large Print 2011 by ISIS Publishing Ltd.,
7 Centremead, Osney Mead, Oxford OX2 0ES
by arrangement with
The Author

British Library Cataloguing in Publication Data
Wicks, Peter, 1933–
    Wicksy and the king's shilling. - - (Reminiscence)
    1. Wicks, Peter, 1933 - - Childhood and youth.
    2. Great Britain. Army - - Military police - -
    Biography.
    3. Draftees - - Great Britain - - Biography.
    4. Large type books.
    I. Title II. Series
    355.2'2363'092–dc22   11788195

ISBN 978–0–7531–5273–7 (hb)
ISBN 978–0–7531–5274–4 (pb)

Printed and bound in Great Britain by
T. J. International Ltd., Padstow, Cornwall

The Send Off

By
Wilfred Owen

Down the close, darkening lanes they sang their way
To the siding shed,
And lined the train with faces grimly gay.

Their breasts were stuck all white with wreath
And spray
As men's are, dead.

Dull porters watched them, and a casual tramp
Stood staring hard,
Sorry to miss them from the upland camp.
Then, unmoved, signals nodded, and a lamp
Winked to the guard.

So secretly, like wrongs hushed up, they went,
They were not ours:
We never heard to which front these were sent.

Nor there if they yet mock what women meant
Who gave them flowers.

Shall they return to beatings of great bells
In wild trainloads?
A few, a few, too few for drums and yells,
May creep back, silent, to still vintage wells
Up half-known roads.

The Return

By
Peter Wicks

Back down the sunlit tracks they came that day,
To the siding shed
And stumbling, left the train, blind faces, shattered
grey.

Their heads were bandaged white, bemedalled, nay,
These were not dead!

Nurses led them and that same tramp
Stood staring hard.
Watched their return to the upland camp,
Now a haven and that tramp
Blinked, swallowed hard.

Now publicly, our wrongs redeemed, they went
Through dead strewn flowers.
We knew from which front this very few were sent.

Blind, still they yet mock what women meant
Who threw them flowers.

Should they return to beatings of wild bells?
This one trainload.
This broken few, too few for cheers and yells
Now led back silent from that muddied hell
Down longed for roads.

My father, Frank Wicks of Cowley, spent many months in the trenches of the First World War. He was fascinated by my stories of Germany, a country which he had never seen. I asked him what it had been like going to war. He was very reluctant to talk about it, but he did point me to the poems of Wilfred Owen. I was so impressed by his poem *The Send Off*, that I wrote a poem in his style and called it *The Return*.

Frank George Wicks of Cowley
1885–1953, died aged 67

<u>DEDICATED TO:</u>

My father, who inspired me.
My wife, Barbara, who encouraged me
to keep on writing.
Becky Curtis, Kirsty Small and Hannah Barney, of
ISIS, who also encouraged me and supported me.
Julia Buckle, who prepared the manuscripts.
Mike Thomas Palmer and John Colella, without
whose help I might not have finished this book.

The Journey

March had come in like a lamb and was now throwing its weight about in a very lion-like manner. Thursday in March 1950 was early closing day, which was a relief as we had already spent half the morning pushing the shop door shut against the wind, which swirled up and down the high street, blowing over rubbish bins and buffeting cyclists and buses alike. It bowled hats along the pavements, upended umbrellas and ladies skirts with equal abandon, and, every few minutes, it interspersed with flurries of soot pellets and white hailstones.

As it was early closing day, I had hoped to get a game with the Oxford Nomads Rugby Team that afternoon. The Nomads were a team made up of amateur rugby enthusiasts, who played in the Oxford Thursday League. They were mainly comprised of shop workers and college servants and anyone else whose half-day fell upon a Thursday. I knew that I was second reserve to play against the Culham Theological College, and the prospect of being trodden into the mud by this group of oversized, mayhem-loving, would-be bishops did much to diminish my enthusiasm. The prospect of playing in the biting wind, and the thought of having to cycle ten miles to the college, did not help, either.

1

It had been a slow morning with few customers to serve. Ralph Mander had been boring all the young apprentices, me included, with his reminiscences of being a wartime R.A.F. Policeman in Bermuda. Mr James, our dancing salesman, had been practising some new dance steps in the basement cabinet showroom with Elsie, our elderly invoice clerk, for a competition they were entering. Mr Ward, our buyer, was snoring behind a huge pile of invoices, which he was supposed to be filing, and Billy Kimber, our elderly carpet porter, was doing his stand-up cockney comic routine for the ladies of the counting house. Mr Allen, our Director, Neville Coobs, our Despatch Manager, Ray Smith and the van men were playing a makeshift game of darts in the lino cellar. Gordon Hastings of the carpet department and John Phillips of the adjoining linen department were playing a fierce game of chess on one of the glass-topped counters. Mr Mack, the linen buyer, and his assistant, Mr Hopkins, were conferring with a linen goods representative in his office, and David Rivers was chatting to his fiancée, whilst sitting upon the staircase of the soft furnishing department.

Mr Massey, the head porter and timekeeper, rang the bell for closing time, and seconds later, we were racing up to the head of the basement grand staircase to clock out. I knew that I did not have a lot of time, and so I dashed out into the inclement weather and down to the little warehouse in Bear Lane where the staff kept their bicycles. I had a lightweight, waterproof suit for cycling in which I kept in a small compact roll behind the saddle — a fat lot of good when the bicycle was 200 yards away, and it was raining as if it had just been invented.

I was already too wet to bother with the suit by the time I had reached my bike, so I leaped on and headed down towards The Plain and on to Rosehill.

I had bought new mudguards from Halfords on the corner of Long Wall Street, planning to replace the cracked and discoloured white plastic ones that I felt detracted from the appearance of my gleaming gold Hercules Kestrel racing bike. So, the night before (Wednesday), I had settled down to the task and had no sooner removed the old guards, than the heavens opened, and I was forced to retreat into the sanctuary of our warm kitchen, leaving the new, smart, white and gold Bluemel's deluxe mudguards on the kichen doorstep.

I had every intention of fitting them once the rain had stopped, but alas, I had not done so. I now regretted it as the front wheel spun a thin spray of slush up the front of my suit and into my face, whilst the rear wheel threw up another deluge of spray, which covered my back. And, of course, I didn't have my waterproofs on.

"Mum will sort it out!" I said to myself, in the manner of teenage sons everywhere. Yes, Mum would sort it out, and she did.

I reached Rosehill, still pedalling furiously, and there, bicycling along in front of me, was Mr Howse, our local insurance collector. The "green man" my dad always called him, whereupon my mother would sniff and declare that he was just jealous.

"Your father would not know a gentleman if he got up and hit him!" Mother would say, acidly. A confusing remark which always left me puzzled.

Mr Howse *was* a green man. His bicycle was a gold and green painted steed — what was called a deluxe sports model, twice the weight of mine, with enclosed chain case, deep mudguards, and with two headlamps and attached batteries case fixed to its crossbar. It had a kickstand similar to the ones fitted to motorbikes and a buffed brown leather briefcase carried in the front carrier basket next to the two-tone bell. Mr Howse himself was a small, neat-looking man, who always wore green, except for his highly-polished brown shoes and his black bowler hat. He could have been aged anywhere between forty and sixty, though I later discovered that he was in fact nearly eighty. The way he rode his bike always reminded me of a university Don or business executive at a desk — I cannot explain why. He looked like a gentleman; if he had been a street cleaner or a navvy, he would still have looked like a gentleman. The way he raised his hat to all and sundry, his manner of stepping aside to let old people pass, his carefully modulated voice and his pleasant face — it all gave the impression that he really cared about people, it came as no surprise to find out that he was a Methodist lay preacher.

Now, true to form, he was cycling determinedly up the hill, wearing green oilskins with a matching hood that was pulled down over his bowler hat and attached to his chin by a length of elastic. Every so often, the crosswind would catch him under his cape and send him flapping and careering towards the grass verge like a demented crow. Even so, he managed to touch his hood and hat in greeting as I struggled past.

I finally reached home, and what a sight met my eyes! There was my mother, standing on the dining table having hysterics. The cat had caught and delivered to the house a large brown rat, as a gift for her, and Mum, who had once panicked at the sight of a fur glove dropped carelessly on our sofa, was not appreciative. The rat was skidding and leaping dementedly around the room, with our cat in enthusiastic pursuit, emitting feline cries of what probably translated as "Tally Ho!".

Taking the situation in at a glance, I grabbed the broom and chased the rat out of the back door, falling over the cat and twisting my ankle in the process. Both rat and cat disappeared into my father's potato patch, and the coast was clear. My mother was not reassured, however and was adamant that she would not come down off the table until I'd proven that the rat really was gone. I stumbled around on one good leg, banging about under table, chairs, settee, cupboards and beds until she was persuaded that there were no further rodents in the house.

Satisfied, Mother began to descend; she teetered precariously as she attempted to climb down off the dining table and onto a chair, and I was called upon to assist her. Now mother was the first to admit that she was no lightweight, and I had already wrenched my ankle and was using the broom as a makeshift crutch.

To make matters worse, we had a linoleum floor, which was quite slippery when wet, and, of course, I had tramped in absolutely dripping. With my bad leg supported by the broom, I reached up to steady Mother down. She put her weight on my shoulder, and I, in turn, leaned more heavily on the broom . . . and the broom handle skidded across the lino. I was brought almost to my knees, and Mother, with one leg extended towards the dining-room chair, landed her foot heavily on the seat, all her weight bearing down on the medium heel of her court shoe, which cut straight through the somewhat flimsy three ply; she wound up with one leg extended on the table behind her and one leg trapped in the chair frame. She looked a little like a hurdler in a high-speed camera still — except this was not so funny. Clearly in pain, she was unable to move, and, strong though I was, I could do little to help on my own.

It was at this point that Mr Howse came up the garden path. Once a month he collected the insurance premiums along our road — I had forgotten that he was due today. My mother always had a cup of tea and a biscuit, together with the payment book and money, waiting on the front windowsill, where he preferred to stand so that he could chat to my parents for a few minutes before raising his hat and cycling off to his next port of call.

He now rapped on the window and, upon hearing my mother's cry of distress, together with my call for assistance, dashed around to the back door, let himself in and helped ease Mother off the table until she stood on both feet, though still with one leg securely trapped in the frame of the chair.

Mr Howse was an eminently practical man, so after I had got a flat blade screwdriver from my father's tool box, he tapped and lifted each tack in turn until he removed the plywood rectangle from the frame of the chair, then we sat mother at the table, with the plywood still round her leg. There was a large gap in the plywood around her knee, and splinters were threatening to scratch her skin. Mr Howse took two library books and wedged them either side of her knee with the spines of the books running parallel to the crack, then we both exerted pressure, folding the wood panel upwards until it split suddenly in two.

Mother's leg was unharmed, though a little uncomfortable, and she gratefully thanked Mr Howse, then bustled round her kitchen, producing a date and walnut cake (which I must have missed), as well as three great cups of tea.

Whilst the kettle was boiling, Mr Howse, who it turned out also taught first aid, checked my ankle and bandaged it with a support he kept in his briefcase for emergencies. Finally, when we were all settled with tea and cake, my mother asked, "Have you heard how the travellers are getting on?"

"One of our managers comes in from Wallingford, and he saw them being moved on by a police van outside 'Back Hand Mansion'. He couldn't see what happened, except for a brief glimpse, because at that point the bus carried on."

"I take it that C.J. was there, complaining as usual!" said mother, bitterly. She did not like C.J., but then few people did. My mother was a Labour Councillor, and

7

she had often crossed swords with C.J., who was a man totally obsessed with money and power. He was always trying it on with the Council; one of his last stunts was to put a fence around several acres of Common Land and to have it patrolled by men with dogs. Having held the land for seven years and a day, he was able to register the land as his because of some old law.

He had once visited our school and given us a lecture on business practices. He described himself in glowing terms as a "highly successful business man". I wondered if he knew that most of south Oxfordshire referred to him as "Scrooge". He treated his tenants badly, and few stayed in his employ for long. The only remark my father made when I had described his somewhat boastful lecture was, "Nobody worships his creator as much as the self-made man!"

"He may have a lot of money," said my mother, "but otherwise his life is a mess. He's had two wives walk out on him, and I believe the third one is about to go the same way. He has no true friends, and his favourite saying has always been, 'Your best friend is your pocket'!"

This then was C.J. — a small, squat man, who habitually sat on a cushion to make himself appear taller. No one had ever seen him smile, and he had deep worry lines on his face, presumably caused by worrying about money and the acquisition of it.

"If he can't take it with him when he dies, I reckon he won't go!" said Dad, who rarely said a bad word about anybody.

8

"Back Hand Mansion" was the name given to his home by the locals. It was a large country house with an imposing drive facing onto the A40.

But what was this about travellers? What did they have to do with C.J.? Who were they and why did C.J. call the police? I had heard rumours at work of a strange couple slowly making their way along the London to Oxford road. According to eyewitnesses, this couple were progressing slowly, rarely covering a mile a day.

Had I been able to ride to the rugby match as intended, it seemed that I would have passed the couple coming the other way. But as it was, I couldn't, I didn't, and Mr Howse kindly offered to leave a message with our vicar, the Reverend Claude Buckwell, who would phone the Theological College on my behalf, though it transpired that the match was cancelled anyway due to flooding on the pitch.

With nothing else to do but sit and hold skeins of knitting wool for my mother to roll into balls, I pumped her for information regarding the travellers.

According to my mother, with her inside Council information, Oxfordshire and Berkshire social workers were very concerned about the strange couple, but they seemed to have declined all offers of help. It seemed that they were attempting to move all their worldly goods by hand. Having started off in the east end of London some months before, their party consisted of an enormous man, slightly older than me, a crossbreed Alsatian dog and an old and frail lady in an ancient wheelchair. They also had an old costermonger's wheelbarrow piled high with old pieces of furniture and carrier bags and half a dozen sacks and an old bicycle upon which the sacks were hung.

It seemed that the man would wheel his bicycle, complete with sacks, to a point several hundred yards on, deposit the sacks, then cycle back to the handcart. After roping the bicycle to his shoulders, he would push the handcart to the sacks. Meanwhile, the dog sat guarding the old lady. When the man had reached his drop-off point, he would whistle, and the dog would race down to take up station under the cart. The man then cycled back and, again roping the old bicycle to his shoulders, wheeled his mother slowly down to where their baggage lay. Both couple and dog were in a poor state. He was finding it difficult to walk and had rags tied under his shoes with baler twine, presumably to make the going softer.

When they stopped for the night, they pulled the handcart into the shelter of a friendly hedge, and stretched tarpaulin out across the wheelchair to make a temporary shelter for the night.

Quite a few people had tried to help, but they were mistrustful of everyone, and their dog was overprotective. Another problem was that neither spoke much English. He had a cleft palate, which made speech almost unrecognisable, and when she spoke, it was in a tongue that only he seemed to understand.

It was unfortunate that they chose to park up for the night opposite "Back Hand Mansion". Unfortunate, too, was the fact that when C.J. rose that morning, having looked out of his bedroom window over his purloined acres, the first thing he saw was the humble little shelter set up on the pristine grass verge fronting his property, and, insult of all insults, their tarpaulin was tied to his elegant railings. Almost apoplectic with fury, he had dashed out in his dressing gown, in spite of the rain, to confront the couple.

It appeared that the dog had been hunting during the night, for there on the grass were two rabbit skins and an appetising stew was heating up on a little wood fire. According to one of the servants, who had no love for him, C.J. kicked the stew over and tried to rip the tarpaulin off, exposing the travellers to the driving rain.

At this point, the dog went for him, and he claimed that he had been badly bitten by the animal. Doris, the servant girl, maintained that the dog did nothing of the sort, and certainly there were no marks to prove such a thing had happened.

In due course, having been called by C.J., the police appeared, and, having taken statements from C.J. and Doris, the police took the dog away in their van, and the couple were forced to move on in the driving rain, minus their protector.

That morning, C.J. dismissed Doris without notice for disloyalty.

"There was no way I was going to carry on working for a lying creep like him, especially when he couldn't keep his hands to himself! It was just that he got in first."

I got home late on Friday night because I had had to travel by bus (my ankle was still playing me up). There,

11

waiting for me on the dining-room table, was a buff-coloured envelope — my first O.H.M.S. communication. I was to be called up for National Service. This meant I would have to take time off from work and report to a set of offices in New Inn Hall Street in the centre of Oxford city, there to attend a medical to make sure that I was fit enough to join the army.

The following Monday saw me hobbling up a steep rickety staircase and into a very large room, which presumably had been some sort of old warehouse. The building was so old and decrepit, that it seemed in imminent danger of collapse.

"Pray that the woodworm don't stop holding hands!" said one wag. "Otherwise the building will collapse, and then we are all in trouble."

There must have been fifty or so lads of my age gathered around the floor in small groups when a very small man in uniform came into the room carrying an enormous megaphone. He could not have been over 4' 6" tall. I well remember that he had enormous black shiny boots.

"Look at the size of those feet!" said the wag. "He wouldn't need to shoot the enemy; he could trample them to death! What's more, all those medals! If he had any more, he would have to wear them on his back!"

It was true; he wore so many campaign ribbons on his diminutive jacket, that there hardly seemed room for pockets.

The soldier with the megaphone now addressed us. He had an unusually deep voice, and it seemed to vibrate up from his boots.

12

"Those aren't boots!" said the comedian. "They're echo chambers!"

"Right gentlemen!" he roared. "I am going to call out your name, and as I call them out, you will answer, "Here Staff!" and then form a line in the middle of the hall."

He duly called out our names, and then a young, and very pretty, Royal Army Medical Corps nurse walked down the line and handed each of us a sheaf of papers, a paper sack and two small bottles. Just as we were casting around to ask one another what we should do, there was a clatter on the stairs. The door burst open, and in tumbled my old friend John "Ginger" Thorne.

"Brandy!" he croaked. "Give me brandy! These stairs are a killer. No one told me that I had to climb a parachute jump."

Then he saw me, and a broad grin lit up his freckled face.

"Well, if it isn't my old mate, Wicksy. What are you doing old chap?"

"Same as you by the looks of it," I responded.

"What did you do to your foot?" he asked. I told him. "With a bit of luck you could dodge this. Me, I've got too much to do to get called up. As far as I am concerned, it's a bloody waste of time."

"Mind your language!" said the pretty young nurse, severely.

"Don't tell me you haven't heard worse than that before," John replied in a loud voice. "I'll wager that you yourself have used far worse. I've been out with a

13

lot of nurses in my time, and what they get up to is no one's business."

"That's nice for you," she replied sweetly. "And when you grow up, perhaps your mother will let you come out by yourself!"

There was such a roar of laughter from her audience that the tiny staff sergeant came out to see what all the laughter was about. Was Ginger discomfited?

"Not a bit chap," he said with a broad grin, blowing her an elaborate kiss. "I think I am in love!" Turning to me he asked, "How did you get here?"

"By bus," I replied. "How did you?"

"By military policeman!" he answered, grinning. "The army has been after me for weeks. I wanted to come, but I kept forgetting the dates. But these two Redcaps turned up at our ma's, and now here I am."

I walked across and peered out of the grubby window down to the street. Sure enough, there were two large military policemen sitting in their jeep, puffing away on two small cigars.

"Play your cards right, and I'll get you a lift," said Ginger, unabashed as usual. The rest of the room was looking at him with unconcealed respect. "It's a waste of time anyway; there is no way I could get through a medical. My doctor reckons that I am a mystery of medical science; it's a wonder I'm alive. You name it, I have it!" I looked at him — five foot eight of muscular body, so ginger you could almost light a fire off him and glowing with health, he looked the fittest person in the room.

14

Now, we were all instructed to strip off to our underpants, putting our clothes into the sacks provided for that purpose. For some minutes we stood, a shivering shambling line, unable to look one another in the face, dejected and miserable whilst, from a room next door, came the sounds of hearty laughter and the unmistakeable chink of crockery.

Eventually, after what seemed like an eternity, the army doctors trooped in, each attended by a uniformed nurse, and took up positions at desks placed at intervals around the room. Then it started.

One by one we filed round, going from one desk to another in turn. We were prodded, poked and, in one embarrassing moment, ordered to cough whilst being tested for a rupture.

Ginger, it has to be said, looked positively ill; he swayed at one time, had a glass of water brought for him and complained plaintively. I realised that he was making a serious attempt to fail the medical. He was so convincing that I almost believed it myself. He took twice as long as everyone else — and then came his master stroke! He began to foam at the mouth. We were alarmed — the nurses clustered around him, and then he was rushed into the other room. He returned looking pale and shaken just as we were putting our clothes back on.

"What happened?" I asked

"The crafty bleeders only put a stomach pump on me!" he answered, bitterly. "Where is the trust I should like to know."

At that moment, the staff sergeant called us to attention, and, one by one, we learned the results of our examination. With one exception, we had all been graded A1, whilst Ginger had been graded A2. In other words, we were all fit for military service. Ginger was appalled.

"What if I had been passed A3?" he demanded.

"You would have been dead!" came the smug reply. "We gave you A2 status because we believe that you have a mental problem."

I duly got my lift home in the military police jeep. This was quite strange really, because six months later, I became a military policeman.

Just as we were leaving, the staff sergeant crooked a finger at Ginger. "A word to the wise, son," he said. "Next time you try the old froth in the mouth trick, try Pears soap — it doesn't taste so good, but you get more convincing bubbles."

Miss Franklin had a pony cart. She was a familiar figure on our estate of Rosehill and also in the neighbouring villages of Cowley, Littlemore, Iffley, Sandford and Botley. She was a source of admiration to many and an equal source of irritation to others, for she was what is now called a Jehovah's Witness. Several times a week, in fair weather and in foul, she would crank up the large gramophone she carried on the seat beside her and play Bible tracts and talks which were delivered in strong mid-west American accents by the individual commentators.

16

She had trained as a nurse and was always to be found where the sick and destitute needed her the most. She and her sister owned a large farm by the Oxford-Henley Road, just outside Sandford upon Thames. Their father, who at a very young age had won the Military Cross in the Flanders trenches during the First World War, had registered himself as a conscientious objector after he had become a Jehovah's Witness in the 1930s. He had been thrown into prison for his beliefs, where he had died, a victim of prison abuse and pneumonia, only to be followed several weeks later by his wife, who died of a broken heart. So it was that in 1943, the girls had found themselves running a large modern farm, with a great deal of success.

Because the farm had been deemed to be of national importance to the food industry, the girls had had half a dozen Italian prisoners of war billeted with them to provide labour, together with a retired farm manager to advise them. Such was the level of expertise shown, that by the end of the war, they owned the adjoining farm as well. Both farms each had a set of fine labourer's cottages, and these were now occupied by groups of Italian families in such happy profusion, that the locals renamed the area "Little Tuscany".

Harry Smith had arrived at the farms the year before — a real mystery figure. No one seemed to know much about him, and if the Misses Franklin knew anything, they kept it to themselves.

Curiously enough, no one had ever heard him speak, or even make a noise, so it was generally assumed that

17

he was dumb. He attended the clinic at the Littlemore Psychiatric Hospital once a week, and it was said that he had attended Lady De Pomeroy's Care Home in Wallingford, both as a patient and, latterly, as a gardener. Although he had an English name, many of us suspected that he had not been born in this country, for long words seemed to baffle him. He did not live with the single Italian men at the big house, but rather lived like a hermit in a converted barn at the edge of the estate. He did not mingle or associate with anyone, but he was a good worker for all of that.

At about the same time that I was attending my National Service medical, Harry was clearing a flooded ditch by the main road when he heard a female voice calling out in a strange tongue. He looked around, but not seeing anyone, went back to work. However, he could not shake off the memory of the voice or the worry that something awful had happened.

He put down his spade and walked down the road to have a look — and then he saw it; a body lying motionless in the long grass of the verge, face down.

A wheelchair was wedged on its side in the flooded culvert and an old lady, with water already up to her shoulders, was desperately struggling to free herself from the wheelchair, which was locked as it was in the concrete "V" sides of the culvert.

Without hesitation, Harry leaped into the icy water. The torrent was so fierce that the shock of it took his breath away. Rotten twigs and drowned rats piled up against his chest, driven by the force of the rapidly rising water.

18

Summoning all his strength, Harry fought to dislodge the wheelchair, but his attempts were hindered by the bags festooning the chair, which, as they swelled with water, served to further lodge her in.

After what must have been a superhuman effort, he managed to drag the old lady, still in her wheelchair, to the safety of the tarmac road.

It was at that moment that help arrived in the form of the Misses Franklin and their pony cart.

They quickly assessed the situation, and, with a decisiveness that made them the admiration of every single man in the village, they sprang out and immediately applied artificial resuscitation to the old lady, who by now was fading in and out of consciousness. The ladies lifted her into the pony trap and made her as comfortable as possible.

The older Miss Franklin, Annette, now turned her attention to the body in the grass — the lady's son. Against all odds, she discovered a weak pulse. It transpired that he had passed out from sheer exhaustion, probably aggravated by lack of food and his efforts to get his mother out of the driving rain.

Dr George Balassa had been driving up from Wallingford Hospital when he approached the scene and was waved down by Annette. His partner, Dr Julia Keane, was with him, and she transferred into the pony cart to assist Miss Franklin, whilst Doctor Balassa stayed to render assistance to the son.

Harry helped lift the unconscious man into the car, and the doctor sped him to the Radcliffe Hospital, where he was placed in Intensive Care.

19

The old lady was installed in one of the main bedrooms in the Franklin house, where she hovered between life and death for over a week, during which time the two Franklin sisters intensively nursed her, taking it in turns to sleep in a camp bed by her side. Time after time, the old lady would call out in a strange language which was unintelligible to the sisters. This left them most distressed inasmuch as they could not tell what she was saying or what she wanted. There was one word that she called out so many times, the sisters came to recognise it — "Gethsemene!" But they had no idea what it meant.

On the second night, the whole house was woken by a furious barking. When one of the household's men went down to the front door to investigate, he was confronted by a large, unkempt and fierce-looking dog. The creature bounded past him, running straight up the stairs, where it clawed frantically at the sickroom door.

Susan Franklin, fearing that the door might be irrevocably damaged, lifted the latch, and the great dog burst in, leaping on her patient's bed and licking the old lady's face and hands in great distress. Then came a miracle; the old lady opened her eyes and tried to sit up.

The dog settled down protectively at the foot of the patient's bed, who was now looking about her in wonder at the magnificent room. She was tearful with joy at being reunited with her dog.

C.J. had started the day in a particularly foul mood, having discovered that his flower garden had been destroyed during the night. Apparently, it looked as though a herd of cows had trampled the beds, but he was at a loss as to whose; Not his, surely, he reasoned, for they were in a field half a mile away. The hedges were good, and the gate was new, and, although it was not padlocked, it had a good latch.

As he looked on, a young bull hove into view with half a line of ruined washing caught round his horns. One of his young bulls! It was almost certain that someone had opened the gate during the night and driven the whole herd down the road and into his garden.

Daylight examination showed only the prints of a large dog among the cattle, but no human footprints.

C.J. rang Wallingford Police Station and was told that he would be prosecuted for leaving cattle on the road unattended (apparently Saunder's milk float had collided with one of the other steers. The animal was unhurt, but the float was extensively damaged). This made him furious. Remembering that the dog was taken to the pound, a shaken C.J. demanded, "Is that dog still there? Has it been destroyed as it should have been?"

"The dog is no longer with us," was the tart reply. This was no officer that C.J. could bribe, although to give him his due, he did try. Six months later, he received a six-month prison sentence, together with (according to my mother when she related the events to me when I came home on leave) some very unwelcome publicity about his dealings.

Apparently, the dog had settled calmly into the little shed where the police constables kept their bicycles. The door had a latch some four feet off the ground. The dog ate a hearty, well-deserved meal, and then settled down for the night. But during the night, the latch had been softly lifted, and the bird had flown. Strangely, the door had been softly closed again. The loss was not discovered until 8a.m. the next morning, and by then, they were too busy to worry about a runaway dog, which no one (apart from C.J.) considered to be even remotely dangerous.

Henry Smith

But what about Henry? He had risked his life rescuing an old lady from certain death. The old lady was being cared for at the big house (there were actually two big houses — one at each farm, but only the one where the Franklin sisters lived was known as *the* big house).

Still soaking wet and shivering from the cold, he had collected the bags of possessions from the culvert and placed them in a soaking pile on the other side of the farm hedge, carefully concealing them from curious passersby. He then took up the bicycle, swung his ditching tools in a sack around his shoulders and made wet and unsteady progress to the big house.

Much to the delight of several giggling housemaids, he was promptly ordered by the formidable housekeeper into a large zinc bath placed in front of the kitchen log fire. The lady had lost a son in the Italian Resistance, and she saw a strong resemblance in Henry and had kept a motherly eye on him ever since he had arrived at the farm some months earlier.

One of the girls was sent to his cottage to fetch a fresh change of clothes, and yet another volunteered to launder the clothes he had been wearing.

Later on, washed, dressed and warm, he was in the great kitchen, where the enormous table was laden with beautiful china and delicious dishes of food. He was feted in style by every one of the farm staff who had come to shake the hand of their hero, and Dr Julia Keane had popped in to give him a quick checkover and pronounced that "no ill effects were suffered".

About half past two, the local district nurse called in to see the new patient. Annette was telling her the story, when the nurse suddenly said, "You did not say anything about the handcart. I am sure that someone told me that they also had a handcart."

The two sisters had not been aware of the missing item, and so two farm labourers were despatched to find it. It was duly discovered pushed into a lane in Nuneham Courtenay, where it had been concealed in a wooded entrance. One of its wheels had partially jammed on its axle, and, stacked as it was with old suitcases, boxes and a brass bedstead and a horsehair mattress, the two of them could barely shift it.

Now, a few weeks earlier, the sisters had taken delivery of not one, but four new tractors — the latest thing in modern farming, and the Italian labourers, with whom the tractors had proven to be a big hit, needed no urging to bring one of the machines up to tow the cart slowly and carefully into the farm coach yard.

The six magnificent shire horses had been put into well deserved semi retirement on the farm, where they were growing fat and lazy.

The tractors had proved to be a great hit with the Italian labourers, any one of whom needed no excuse to service or drive these wonderful machines, as Mr Wyatt the farm manager remarked. It seems that every Italian male has motor oil running through his veins; they were so keen to show what these machines could do that productivity went up by 200 per cent.

Many a late night, Italian housewives came out to drag their husbands into cold dinners on tables laid several hours earlier and with children sound asleep in their beds.

The situation got so involved, that in the end the dozen aspiring mechanic drivers were put to a test, the winners would each have a tractor under their charge.

It needed no urging to bring a tractor up to tow the cart slowly and carefully into the farm coach yard, and it was when it was being unhitched, that one of the axles, notably the one belonging to the wheel that was jamming, gave up the struggle and collapsed completely.

Apart from the horsehair mattress, everything was dry, having been tied down under the tarpaulin. The whole load was packed by willing hands into a particularly dry corner of the large Georgian coach house which was empty apart from Bertolli's workshop and a beautiful gypsy caravan which was being slowly and meticulously restored by that craftsman.

Bertolli, or "Bert" as everybody called him, was a sixty-year-old Italian craftsman, who had, he boasted, worked on Milan Cathedral. He had come to England to stay with his son, Mario, and his family, who had come to the farm as a prisoner of war, and was now, some ten years later, the senior foreman of both farms.

Bert had lost his wife to cancer some five years earlier and was now, it was rumoured, romantically involved with a widow in Littlemore Parish.

He acted as maintenance man to the two farms, and the sisters had extensively equipped the coach house with an array of the latest woodworking machines, as well as a small forge and blacksmith's shop. This was Bert's kingdom, and he was probably the happiest man in England; he had around him his family and his grandchildren, who all adored him. For years, he had lived in a poor and rather grimy district in Milan, and now he lived in the elegant coachman's cottage on the estate, with swans at his front door, wood pigeons in the woods behind him and a little cabin cruiser moored into the backwater at the end of his kitchen garden.

It was soon to be Annette's birthday, and the whole household wanted to give their beloved mistress a celebration to remember.

For many years, there had been a real Romany camp at Sandford upon Thames, just down the road. The gypsies, who for generations had acted as fruit and potato pickers on the farms, had sold Mario the aforementioned gypsy cart that Bert was now restoring and transforming into a wonderful work of art.

The Franklin sisters protested that they did not celebrate birthdays or Christmas, but "Little Tuscany" would have none of it.

"I'm rather afraid that it is a case of liking it or lumping it," Annette had said to Susan. They had tried, in vain, to explain to their extended family that their beliefs did not allow them to celebrate Christmas or birthdays, only wedding anniversaries.

This had, unfortunately, upset the children, who had been looking forward to meeting Father Christmas. In the end, the sisters had capitulated, and the children had had their way; although, of course, the sisters had not joined in the celebrations.

Annette was well aware of her proposed birthday present, and often went to watch Bert at his labour of love. In the end, the sisters hit upon a solution.

"British kings and queens have two birthdays — an official one and a private one. I shall put my birthday a week ahead, and that will be my official 'unbirthday'. Hopefully no one will suspect a thing," Annette had said.

Bert had extended both the body and the shafts of this wonderful vehicle. He had replaced the wooden wheels with the latest in motor-van wheels, a brake pedal and a handbrake placed by the driver's seat, plus a modern electrical system to make the caravan road legal. The interior was a model of design. Cunningly designed cupboards and wardrobe doors concealed all those implements needed for living on the road. The wives had painstakingly sewn beautiful curtains and cushions. The interior surfaces were elegantly veneered in Fiddleback Mahogany, and there was even a tiny kitchen galley with a wood burning stove and a working water tap.

It was because the weight had been nearly doubled, that the vehicle had had its shafts extended to take not one, but two, of the great shire horses.

Henry Smith spent a lot of time either training the horses to work in tandem or helping Bert with the painting and polishing. Bert had a fine tenor voice and fancied himself as an opera singer. Henry had a guitar, and he was not long under Bert's influence before his confidence began to blossom, and the pair started to give impromptu concerts on the lawn in front of Bert's cottage.

There was one incident when Henry and Bert had gone to the house of Bert's intended, and, creeping outside her window, had serenaded her by moonlight. Unfortunately for them, the lady, who had taken a sleeping pill, was quietly snoring in the back bedroom. Her old and somewhat cantankerous mother was asleep in the front bedroom, and hers was the window they had chosen to serenade under.

At least a dozen neighbours, attracted by the noise, had come out into their front gardens to watch. Bert, who had dressed himself in a borrowed "Pirates of Penzance" costume and had glued on a stiff waxed moustache for effect, sang for at least half an hour, whilst the neighbours cheered and clapped each aria.

Fuelled by a bottle of red wine, he sang until it looked as if the sash around his waist, tight as it was over his portly frame, would burst. But there was not even a twitch from the bedroom window.

"Give me a sign, my love!" he called, beseechingly.

And then the sash window flew up. Spreading his arms joyfully and raising his face towards the window, he cried, "She is here! My love! Will you . . .?"

Before he could complete the sentence, he received a cascade of water in his upturned face.

"Let that be a lesson to you, you Italian varmint! Disturbing an old woman's sleep at this time in the morning; hop it before I call the police!"

A malicious gnome face appeared at the window, hair in curlers looking like a barbed-wire fence and a face covered in white face powder. It was a face you could frighten rats with.

"Be off you heathen, or you will get another one!"

They left hurriedly, whilst his lady friend slept on, blissfully unaware.

The Bully and the Bedsprings

I awoke early, having barely slept. Today was the day I joined the army. Not as a volunteer, but as a national serviceman. I could hear Mum downstairs getting the family breakfast and my father, who was a First World War veteran, scrubbing up his old army kitbag, in which I would carry my spare clothes, etc. Mother presented me with an almighty breakfast, convinced that I was going to starve on army fare. Dad presented me with my shoes, buffed to a high shine.

At 7.25, I pried myself from my mother's tearful embrace, and Dad and I set out for Littlemore Railway Station, Dad pushing his old bike, upon the handlebars of which was balanced the kitbag. Dad was as proud as a dog with two tails, raising his cap to all our neighbours, for this was the day that I, his son, came of all.

The railway station was roughly about half a mile from the house. My dad always swore that the British railway system was the finest asset this country had ever had. Every UK destination was now no more than a 20-minute walk and a train ride away. Anyway, there we were, striding out to the railway station, me carrying a brown carrier bag with enough sandwiches for a

30

fortnight, and my father with his freshly scrubbed kitbag balanced upon his bike.

We had not gone two hundred yards when we saw a small figure dodge behind a large bush in a neighbour's garden.

"Jimmy Twp!" we both exclaimed. At that moment he took to his heels, an object clutched under his shapeless coat.

"At least that explains who has been stealing the milk," said my father. "Poor little devil!"

We all knew Jimmy Twp (pronounced "Tup"). Ever since I could remember, he had been a fixture around the streets of Rosehill.

"Carry your shopping for tuppence missus?" and he would bob and clutch his cap, twisting it in two grimy hands, eager to please. Less that 4′ 6″ in stature, he moved everywhere at a sort of high-speed hobble. Although Dad reckoned that he was in his thirties, he had a simple, child-like mentality. I don't know if he had a father; we never saw one. His mother, with whom he had lived, had been an elderly, diminutive little lady, habitually dressed in black, and who kept herself to herself. Her house had been neat as a pin, like herself — windows, hung with floral curtains, sparkled; tiny lawns, smooth as velvet; and a garden with such a profusion of vegetables and flowers, even father was envious. Six months ago, Mrs Twp had died, leaving Jimmy to fend for himself. Either forgotten or overlooked by the local authorities, he and the house in which he lived were slowly descending into wrack and ruin.

We headed on past the church and my two old primary schools, over the bridge and down the long slope to the railway station.

Littlemore Station was a jewel in the crown of the Great Western Railway. The painted surfaces around the building and its bright wicket fence sparkled. The two porters and the booking clerk, immaculate in their railway uniforms, were busy polishing the many brass handles, whilst the lady booking clerk was watering the baskets of flowers which hung in such profusion around the platform, which appeared to have been thoroughly scrubbed earlier. Such was the standard of cleanliness at the station, Father swore that the stationmaster's wife had been polishing the rails with silver polish, and there were those of his friends who believed him.

The stationmaster now appeared, resplendent in his uniform of gold-braided peaked cap and brass-buttoned jacket, stiff starched collar and shiny boots.

"Morning Frank," said he. "This the big day for the young master?"

I blushed furiously, as I thought, "Condescending old fool!"

My father saw what was in my mind, but as I said it, my furious retort was completely lost in the stentorian bellow of our railway engine as it emerged from under the bridge, much to my father's relief.

Our transport consisted of two streamlined diesel cars which were brightly painted in the Great Western livery. Both cars were identical and were what Doctor Dolittle might have referred to as a "pushmi-pull yu". All the driver had to do at the end of his journey was to walk down from his cab, drop into the rear facing driver's seat and he was ready to return home, without having to turn the train around.

Father quickly pushed my kitbag up onto the seats just behind the driver. The interior was similar to a bus.

The stationmaster boarded the carriage behind us.

"Good morning, Mr Belcher," he said to the driver, producing a large silver pocket watch. "This won't do!" he said sternly. "One minute and twenty-seven seconds late! This is the second time in two years. That time you were two minutes late! Absolutely disgusting. We shall be getting a reputation for unreliability if you don't pull your socks up my man."

Mr Belcher scowled. "Don't blame me, Mr Clifton; blame Thames Station! The idiots up there left the ladies lavatories locked; someone mislaid the key. I had to pull up in a cutting to let the ladies relieve themselves behind the low bushes."

"Right," said Mr Clifton, studying his watch. "You have exactly one minute and seventeen seconds for departure. You will leave directly upon my whistle!"

Meanwhile, the two porters were dashing along the length of the two carriages slamming their doors, finishing up with the door I was seated against. The stationmaster raised a small green flag and there was an impressive blast from his whistle. The driver responded with a toot from his engine's horn and two raised fingers at the stationmaster's retreating back, and we were off.

I waved from the open window to my father, who managed to keep pace with the train for nearly twenty-five yards on his old bike, going at such a pace I was afraid that he might ride off the end of the station platform. He did manage to stop however, and a second later, he was lost from sight.

We passed a gang of railway workers all standing back from the track and who, as we passed, saluted us with mugs of what I presumed was strong tea. A minute later, we were sliding across the river Thames, over the black bridge and powering down to Oxford.

Bicycles littered the gangways, trilby-hated gentlemen studied newspapers and chomped upon cigars, and several knots of ladies, dressed in their Sunday best, chattered excitedly, presumably looking forward to an exciting shopping expedition. There were two backpackers, all sun-bronzed knees, gleaming teeth, and earnest expressions as they studied guidebooks and maps. There were also half a dozen lads of about my age. In due course, I was to discover that they were, like myself, conscripts to the King's army.

We passed the mainline signal box. One signalman was hanging out of the high window cleaning it; a second one could be glimpsed at the signal levers, and a third one was sat upon the outside platform on the tall steps of the signal box, checking a list. Seconds later we had crossed the bridge, and we were at journey's end — Oxford station.

We all got off. There were quite a lot of people milling about on the platforms and there must have been at least sixty young men congregated just inside the booking room. All were of my age, and each carried either a suitcase or a backpack. In my case, I had a kitbag. It dawned on me that these were to be my new travelling companions.

A very impressively uniformed army Sergeant materialised in our midst. "Right gentlemen! I will call out your names, and as they are called out, you must answer, "Yes Sergeant," and then form a line at the north end of the platform."

The roll call was made in alphabetical order, and so I was last to join the line. We were then informed that we had twenty minutes before our train arrived, and, when it did, we were to take the first two carriages in the order we were called up in, and that we could fall out for a smoke. I did not smoke, so I popped into the buffet shop on the platform and got a very welcome cup of tea. The Sergeant also had the same idea, and he generously paid for the beverage. In the course of our conversation, I learned that we were to entrain to the Royal Artillery Induction Camp in Oswestry, Shropshire.

The train rushed through the countryside at sixty miles an hour. We sat in subdued blocks of six, our luggage stored under the seats, with small bags and boxes above in net hammocks. Every so often, a smoky blast of air would enter through the top sliding windows, so that we were slowly being covered in black smuts. After a couple of hours, I shared out my sandwiches to the seated compartment. It seemed that my mother knew what she was doing, because I seemed to be the only one to have brought food with me.

All too soon, we arrived at Oswestry, and there, again, we had to detrain and muster on the railway platform, complete with luggage. There must have been well over one hundred of us, and now we were required to get onto three coaches, obviously hired for the purpose. With the luggage loaded, we were again on our way.

My first impression of the Royal Artillery Camp was that of a dozen or so modern hangar-like buildings, each covering around an acre of concrete flooring, some open to the sides. There were lethal-looking dark-green field guns everywhere, with neat canvas hoods over their barrels and stacks and stacks of artillery shells. Squads of denim suited men marched everywhere, barked at by over-enthusiastic Sergeants and their assistant Bombardier, whilst their victims struggled to comply with their shouted commands and, occasionally, even managed to march in step.

The largest of the buildings was what they designated a dining or "mess" hall. It was similar to the other buildings, except that it had four permanent walls with a stage platform at one end and, at the other, a huge kitchen with cooks toiling away. In the middle area were long lines of trestle tables and chairs.

Again, a roll call was taken, and we then had to file past an elderly tea urn to collect a none-too-clean battered tin mug and a dollop of strong, brown and mysterious liquid.

"Is this tea or coffee?" we asked.

"It's whatever you want it to be!" came the smug reply of the soldier manning the tea urn. "One thing though — drink this, and you will forget all about women. The only oats you will get in this establishment is porridge, salty as the Irish Sea and great for polishing your brasses!"

There now came an announcement from the overhead loud speakers for us to take our places at the tables, upon which we would find neatly printed cards bearing our names. We were not to sit down, but were required to stand to some sort of attention whilst dozens of Sergeants passed behind us, each carrying trays of beer in half pint glasses. These were placed upon the tables in front of us, with the admonition that they were not to be touched before the order was given.

As we were standing at right angles to the stage, we could now see several impressive-looking Officers upon it, the chief of which now addressed us. I forget the actual words, except that it was a welcoming speech, stressing the traditions and benefits of being in the Royal Artillery. When he had finished, we were then addressed by the Padre or Army Chaplain, who, irrespective of individual beliefs, led us in a short prayer. The Adjutant now stepped forward, and he pronounced the oath of allegiance to God, King and Country, which we all repeated line by line and word for word. Finally we were ordered to drink a toast to the King and then to the Regiment. We stood facing the stage, and following the example of the Regimental Sergeant Major, we each raised our glasses in our right hands and took two hearty swigs. At the bottom of my glass, something could be seen glinting, and upon further investigation, it proved to be an old silver shilling piece — the King's Shilling! Now having drunk the King's beer, we were deemed to be new members of the Royal Regiment of Artillery.

A large stack of tin trays was now placed at the end of each table, and these were passed along one by one until each seated man had received one. I looked at mine curiously. About the size of a domestic tea tray, it had shallow compartments hammered into it, the reason for which soon became clear. We were then passed a battered enamel mug and a clip containing a knife, fork and spoon. I found myself lining up in front of the food server. Two men stood on the opposite side of the table behind a large steaming dish of carrots and another one of boiled potatoes. The scene was repeated at regular intervals along the table, with pairs of soldiers doling out dollops of carrots, peas, cabbage and turnips, together with a very watery looking stew. Beyond these were another two stations serving up bread and margarine, rice pudding, custard and apple crumble. The resulting mess in each tray looked revolting. So speedily was each item slopped into the tray, custard intermingled with potatoes, gravy crowned the apple crumble and stew covered everything else and dribbled over the shallow edges of the trays. To add to the general chaos, scores of sparrows and starlings flew around, or roosted in the high-girded ceiling and let their droppings fall with depressing frequency, much of which landed in the food. The tea was pretty awful as well; black as tar, it had been brewed up in a huge vat, to which condensed milk had been added together with the tins, which were simply split in half with a fireman's axe and dropped straight into the noxious brew. The tins were presumably collected when the vats were cleaned out.

We were given ten minutes to finish our meal and then were required to clean our dishes. By the exit doors was a large water tank, half full of hot water, into which half a sack of soda crystals had been dropped. Above it, dangling on cords, were half a dozen scrubbing brushes for cleaning our "eating irons". Woe betide anyone who dropped an item and had to grope around in the tank's soupy depths.

Once we'd washed up, we were allocated our sleeping quarters. These were wooden buildings called "spiders". They were huts joined at right angles to a central section which contained lavatories, wash and shower rooms and a scrubbing room for kit cleaning. Each room contained twenty beds, ten on each side of a central aisle. The beds were situated at regular intervals and were flanked on either side by a metal wardrobe and bedside locker. Once inside, we chose our beds, slid our bags underneath, and put our names on the cards affixed to each frame.

A Sergeant then summoned us back outside, and we lined up in our alphabetical order. Thus arranged, we marched to the Quartermaster's store, which was a huge building with a long counter spanning its length. Behind the counter were rank upon rank of lockers and shelves. These contained all sorts of army clothing: boots, belts, haversacks and other webbing. Manning the counter were about a dozen soldiers, a Sergeant and an Officer. We were instructed to file slowly down the length of the counter, stopping at each store man. I saw no sign of a tape measure — the store man simply measured us up with a practised eye. Step by step, we were issued with two pairs of everything: shirts, ties, underpants, cellular vests, socks, trousers, battle dress blouses and all sorts of essential equipment. Eventually, loaded up like donkeys, we staggered to the end of the counter and out of the door.

Once we'd arrived back at our respective barrack rooms, the bargaining began in earnest. There were a great many different body shapes on view — tall, short, fat, thin — and it was soon found that very few of my companions had been given uniforms that remotely fitted. I myself had received a battledress two sizes too short and trousers that flapped over my shoes. The swapping and bargaining continued until we were all reasonably attired in the uncomfortable khaki battledress (we soon discovered that whatever the material had been treated with brought many of us out in an ugly rash, myself included), by which time we were due to return to the mess hall (so very aptly named!) to eat an indigestible liver and bacon dish, liberally spattered with brown Windsor soup, followed by apple and rice pudding.

On our return, the Bombardier instructed us to write a letter home on the notepaper that he was now issuing. My neighbour was distressed, because, as he quietly explained to me, he had no writing skills. I told him to tell me what he wanted to say, and I wrote it for him.

For some time, I had been uncomfortably aware of a youth, slightly bigger than myself, who seemed to have taken a dislike to me. It transpired that he came from

Nottingham, and, according to him, he was a member of a particularly violent and sadistic gang. He seemed to go out of his way to barge into me "accidently". I recognised the situation for what it was. My father had warned me about the barrack-room bullies.

"The world," he used to say, "is divided into victims and predators; be neither."

I took care to avoid the youth, but the more I tried to ignore him, the worse he became. He sneeringly referred to me as the "Oxford Ponce". Anyway, I was not particularly perturbed by him; I had spent my early years as a grammar schoolboy defending myself against some of the roughest gangs in the Midlands, and, as a result, I had not only represented my school in the semi-finals of the Amateur Boxing Association at Eton College, I could also hold my own in the more brutal "no holds barred" street fighting culture of the day; so I did not feel unduly threatened.

A quarter of an hour before "lights out", having made my bed and stowed my things neatly in the locker, I went for a shower. When I returned, I realised that something very strange had happened. The excited chatter, which had so filled the room when I left, had been replaced with an expectant, deathly hush. Feeling all eyes upon me, I ventured deeper into the room, and realisation dawned; the old days were not consigned to the past — I would have to fight my corner, yet again.

There upon my bed lay the gangster. My clothes were strewn all about the floor, and my kitbag had been upended into a rather smelly wastebasket.

For a moment, I shook with white hot rage, and I took a step towards the offender. Then I recalled my father's voice.

"Calm right down. Think the situation through, and then humiliate him so much that you will destroy his credibility; never get mad, get even!"

Somehow, I kept my cool, nigh on impossible though it was, and I meekly gathered up my possessions into a pile in the middle of the room.

"This is my bed now, Ponce; you go down there."

There were some sniggers from our companions over my apparently wimpish behaviour. But how best to respond? Then it came to me. Whilst still an apprentice in house furnishing at C.P. Webbers, I had been required to assist the porters in delivering, and assembling, several hundred bedsteads, mattresses, wardrobes and lockers to New College, Oxford. This was a particularly arduous job, because hundreds of twisting, worn stone stairs had to be negotiated, and hefting both the metal divan and spring interior mattress had demanded a certain degree of strength.

Those beds, I'd suddenly realised, were of a similar make to these army beds. My decision made, I walked over to his bed, picked it up, and strode over to where he was lying with a silly, self-satisfied smirk upon his face. It was unfortunate for him that his eyes were closed, otherwise he'd have seen it coming, as I lined up the bed and simply dropped it. The divan legs dropped over neatly, and he was pinned

"You've forgotten your bed!" I said loudly, as I added my fourteen-stone weight to the snare. The pain must

42

have been considerable, as he screamed, shouted and swore, utterly incapable of relieving the situation.

After about five minutes, I relented and lifted the bed off; too soon, it seemed for he still had some fight in him. He launched himself off the bed, and I met him with a straight left, followed by a right cross. He dropped like a sack of potatoes.

"Who's next?" I demanded loudly, looking about, but there were no takers.

I picked up his equipment and threw it out through the nearest window, then I herded him back to his corner, where he sat, defeated, in the dark.

The following afternoon, we discovered that he had deserted, and I never saw him again.

Redcap

The next morning, after a breakfast of porridge and bird droppings, we were given our first taste of marching drill or "square bashing" as it was called. Drill took place in one of the cavernous hangers, from which the field guns had been hauled out in order to give us the space to develop our marching skills. A brigade of guards we were not. Most of the first session was spent trying to distinguish the left foot from the right. Inevitably, when trying to execute a "Right Turn" or even an "About Turn!", some confused individual would turn the wrong way and the rest of the squad would collapse into them. Our drill parades proved to be a great source of entertainment to the various cooks, A.T.S. typists and off-duty drill instructors, many of whom cried tears of laughter upon viewing our shambolic endeavours.

The rest of that day consisted of interviews, written examinations, lectures, a forty-minute run and then more marching. Lance Bombardiers visited the various dormitories that evening, in order to instruct us on such things as how to clean our kits, spit-polish boots until they gleamed like black jewels, polish brasses and the correct way on how to lay the uniform trousers beneath a mattress to gain the immaculate creases so beloved of the army.

* * *

The camp was surrounded by huge potato fields, and we were required to volunteer our services, collecting stones from the fields and gathering the crops themselves, such as potatoes, carrots, cabbages, depending on what was in season.

We were also required to learn our eight digit number, unique to each man, to such effect, that sixty years on, I can still bring it immediately to mind.

During that first week, like all my fellow recruits, I was interviewed by a bored lieutenant in order to ascertain what my particular duty should be in the King's Army.

The following Monday, I had my answer; I was to be sent to Rhyl to train as a Technical Assistant (field guns) — apparently a plum post, but I was horrified. It had been assumed that, because I had been a scholarship boy, I was good with figures. Not so! I am dyslexic, not with letters, but with numbers, to such an extent that mathematics was quietly dropped from my itinerary, and I took extra French instead. I had such faith in my incompetence that I visualised all sorts of awful tragedies, such as shelling the wrong positions, or getting the shell charges wrong.

I was quietly desperate when I confided my fears to the Bombardier in charge of our hut. He in turn spoke to the Drill Sergeant, who in turn spoke to the Regimental Sergeant Major. The Sergeant Major, or R.S.M. as he was called, interviewed me at length and, after giving me a simple (to him) geometry test, passed me on to the Adjutant. As I waited outside the Adjutant's office, I studied a poster on the wall. This was of an immaculately turned out Military Policeman on a motor cycle. There were also smaller inset figures of M.Ps on horseback, with dogs, jumping from aeroplanes, aboard boats and driving jeeps.

I had been told that the corps of Royal Military Police (or C.R.M.P.) never recruited directly, but only from regiments of the British Army and Royal Marines. I had always wanted to drive a motorcycle or a jeep and I saw this as my opportunity to learn for free. Accordingly, I spoke to the Adjutant and, after conferring with the R.S.M., he said he would give me a decision in good time.

Anxiously, I waited for his decision, but nothing happened. Day after day passed and still nothing. Two weeks later, our transfer papers came through, and I was still expected to go to Rhyl. Despondently, I boarded the coach with a group of fellow soldiers, resigned to my fate.

The coach started up and we were off! I don't suppose we had travelled more than a mile from the camp gates when a Military Police jeep swung into the path of the coach, forcing us to a sudden stop. A red-capped Sergeant appeared at the front of the gangway.

"Private Wicks," he shouted. "Come forward!"

It appeared that I had got my transfer after all, though by the looks I was getting from my travelling companions, I fear they may have suspected that I was some master criminal, arrested in the nick of time.

Soon I was transported to the Oswestry railway station with my kitbag, handed a set of papers and a rail ticket and sent on my way to Inkerman Barracks, Woking.

Legend had it that Inkerman Barracks was an old lunatic asylum, built for the criminally insane. The sign that hung over the guardhouse aptly illustrated this high-walled, grey-stone building, which was set all around a vast echoing square. Worn with age and barely discernible, it read, "Abandon Hope All You Who Enter Here". Some wag had written beneath, "Never Forget Where You Left Your Trousers!"

I was required to sit in the high-ceilinged waiting area of the Orderly Room office, alone at first, but soon joined by other soldiers, all from various regiments. There were Royal Marines and guardsmen, gunner, infantrymen and even a horse guardsman. There were 120 men in all. A few were national service recruits like myself, others were seasoned soldiers with campaign medals, and a few wore stripes, denoting non-commissioned officers. However, because we were now of one rank only, probationer M.P.s, the badged N.C.O.s had to remove their insignia. Some were old soldiers who had left the army, hadn't liked what they'd found, so had joined up again.

The first thing that struck me about the place was the noise. The curious high pitched yelps that echoed across the parade square made it remarkably reminiscent of a dog kennel; then I realised it was coming from some half a dozen drill instructors who were parading sweating groups of soldiers up and down the grey-cobbled surface.

We were divided into three separate squads of approximately forty men apiece. Each squad was under the control of a Sergeant and two physical training instructors or P.T.I.s as they were known. The P.T.I.s were sadistic brutes, who tormented us through unarmed combat and physical training. Within several days, we realised that they were power mad. One of their favourite ploys was to order each victim to have a haircut. I had had my hair cut short by an Oxford barber before joining up, but now I had to have four close-cropped haircuts within the space of three days, and I was not the only one. Every day there were long lines outside the camp hairdressers, to whom we had to hand a scrawled chit and one shilling and nine pence for a short back and sides. Several men, including myself, rebelled and were put on a charge for failing to comply with a direct military order. We were paraded in front of the Adjutant. We were not allowed to speak in our defence and were all given two hours late drill, including a full kit inspection, plus Sunday afternoon camp duties. Our particular camp duty, I recall, was to scrub about 9 square yards of gymnasium floor with a toothbrush — a common punishment. It turned out we were softly treated compared to those who had to scrub the toilet cubicles using their own toothbrushes.

Unarmed combat was the worst. We would be segregated into pairs, one soldier as the aggressor, the other as defender. If the P.T.I. felt that not enough pain was being inflicted upon the person receiving the hold, he would apply extra pressure. As a result of this, one

48

man's wrist was broken, and he was sent away for 4 weeks leave.

The P.T.I.s also took great delight in pushing us into muddy trenches filled with water which we were traversing on the end of a rope.

The biggest brute of the lot was our drill instructor, a Northern Ireland Protestant from Belfast — Sergeant McShane (not his real name, I hasten to add). The grapevine told us that he had once been married, but his wife had divorced him after only three weeks. He was a man with a chest full of campaign medals and a mouth so foul, it was like listening to the screams of the damned trapped in hell. Unfortunately, one of the officer's wives objected to his strident epithets which carried over the parade ground in full hearing of the children's school run, and he was duly dressed down by her in front of us. After she had gone, he turned to us and said,

"Well, you heard the lady — does anyone else object to the King's English?"

I was not used to foul language; I worked in an environment where people did not swear. Rough as the district was, our neighbours did not swear, and my father and mother most certainly did not swear.

"Anyone objections to my language?" he asked again, in his sneering Belfast accent.

There was silence from the ranks, and then my brain switched off, and my mouth took over.

"Yes Sergeant, I do."

"What was that probationer?" he demanded.

I recalled my father's words that people who swear do not have the brains to express themselves properly; only cretins fill in the blanks with swear words as it makes them feel clever. In reality, they are uneducated slobs.

I relayed this information to him, while the rest of the squad sniggered. Two minutes later, I found myself on a charge marching between two escorts to the Adjutant's office, the Sergeant leading the way.

As we came to stand outside the Adjutant's office, we heard the shrill tones of the lady who had complained to sergeant McShane; obviously she was not happy with his response.

Sergeant McShane flushed an angry red, and, as the office clerks came outside to hear what all the commotion was about, we all grinned. Eventually, the door opened, and the lady emerged. Giving Sergeant McShane an icy stare, she stalked off, leaving him visibly shaken. Turning to myself and the escorts he shouted, "Caps off, belts off," and I was escorted into the Adjutant's office. We had to march into the office in double quick time, and our rapidly thudding army boots were so loud, they threatened to dislodge the ceiling plasterwork. The Adjutant, who was well known for liking a couple of snorts of whisky at lunchtime, put his head in his hands and directed at Sergeant McShane a look of pure malevolence as he listened, stony-faced to the Sergeant's charge of insubordination. I was not allowed to speak in my defence, and my punishment was to be confined to camp for one month, plus four weekends of kitchen fatigues.

I had come off lightly, although I did not appreciate it at the time. The Sergeant was ordered to stay behind, and it seemed that he also received a severe dressing down, because for a few days after, his language was severely curtailed. I, however, had made an enemy, and one who I could not fight. In his twisted mind, I was the reason for his downfall, and I became a target to his circle of cronies. Every day I was singled out for harsh criticism: My bed was half an inch over the white painted line; there was dust on the light fitting which hung a good ten feet above my bed; the shape of a button sewn on the reverse of the lapel had been pressed into visibility on the front side; crushed fibres had been imprinted by the smoothing iron — I got extra night fatigues for that one.

It was inevitable that I should stand out from the others because of my treatment, and those who wished to curry favour with their instructors took full advantage of it. I was having a pretty bad time of it.

There were in our group, six recruits from Liverpool, all of whom had been police cadets with the Liverpool Constabulary, and I began to hate them. If a cruel trick was played upon anyone, they were inevitably at the bottom of it. On one occasion, one of the gang had to clean out the general office, and he took it upon himself to snoop into the probationers' confidential records. He discovered that I had boxed in the interschool's boxing championships and that another probationer had also done the same in Yorkshire. It was therefore planned to pit us against each other to afford some illegal barrack entertainment for the rest, but I was sick of fighting, and Frank felt the same, and so we became good friends. This did not suit the Liverpool "mafia" at all, who branded us cowards.

Finally, we hatched a plan. We would fight (but we carefully avoided saying "each other"). The set-to was scheduled for Easter Bank Holiday in the gymnasium. There was one condition — the match was to be refereed by the person who had accessed our records. This, he was delighted to do.

The day dawned, and we hammed it up like the great enemies we were supposed to be, but of course never were. "Scouser", the ref., grinned broadly as he bowed to his audience and informed us that he wanted a good clean fight. The bell was rung and we advanced upon each other. Scouser hopped around us like a demented rabbit, and, on cue, we hit him simultaneously. He dropped like a rock.

"Anyone else want to get involved?" Frank queried. Five minutes later the Liverpool "mafia" were fighting each other and everyone else, going at it with such ferocity, the ring threatened to collapse under the weight of bodies. Frank and I stood back and admired our handiwork.

"Fancy a char and a wad?" asked Frank. "My treat." And we strolled arm in arm to the N.A.A.F.I. for a cup of tea and a slice of cake.

If I had it bad, there were many others who were considerably worse off. One such lad was from Dublin, Ireland. It transpired that his father was English, and although he had never been to England before, he found himself in our squad in Inkerman Barracks. His father had been a guardsman, and without actually seeing him, the army decided that he should become a member of the Irish Guards. Unfortunately, no one had taken his dark skin tone into account (his mother was a second generation West Indian, and it was because of the prejudice shown to his wife, that the father had moved his small family to Dublin). Fearing the repercussions of a black face seen guarding Buckingham Palace, the army hierarchy had rapidly transferred "Paddy" into the camp.

Sergeant McShane led the witch hunt against him.

"Why don't you desert," was his constant taunt.

The Liverpool mafia, taking their cue from Sergeant McShane, used every cruel trick in the book to make his life miserable. His bed was carried out and left in the middle of the parade ground; his kit would frequently be vandalised; the P.T.I.s took great delight in putting him down, often addressing him as "Nigger Pat".

One day, he snapped and laid one of the P.T.I.s out cold. No one spoke up for him, and he was escorted to the guardroom. That night, four instructors entered the guardroom and beat him so severely that his spleen was ruptured. There was an immediate whitewash, and a statement was issued to the effect that he had suffered peritonitis, and we never saw him again.

As a result of this incident, however, the culprits were all swiftly packed off, and we received a new Sergeant, Sergeant Bennet, who was a far more humane figure; stern but fair and always approachable.

He was a medium sized, thickset man, with a cheerful expression and always, even on parade, accompanied by a small Springer Spaniel, whom he had trained to walk impeccably by his side. Legend had it that the dog had saved his life by sniffing out a booby trap. Under his tuition, our group prospered, and I began to enjoy the army.

I did not enjoy the cooking, though. We had plates and mugs, but only a sadist could have produced the meals which were dolloped out. The Corporal in charge of the canteen was an old soldier, who had been a prisoner of war in Japan during the last conflict, and he was still showing some bizarre behaviour. Every now and then, something would trigger him, and he would throw pots, plates and anything else that came to hand. He would often drop kick loaves of bread across the kitchen, aiming them to land in large wicker baskets behind the servers. Most of them missed, landing on the wet tiled floor. Unfortunately, these would then be served up with our meals. A young Second Lieutenant, who was called the Officer of the Day, and the Orderly Sergeant would sometimes make an appearance during the meal.

"Any complaints?" he shouted.

"No sir!" we shouted in unison, unable to take our eyes off a large moth caterpillar, all of three inches long, inching his stately way across Scouser's plate, intent upon a lettuce leaf. Scouser, meanwhile, was so intent upon talking and cramming food into his mouth that I do not believe that he was even aware of the caterpillar. A little while later, after some kindly soul had pointed out his misfortune, he headed at a rate of knots to the medical room, where he was put on a stomach pump. As Frank said afterwards, "it couldn't have happened to a nicer guy."

Our squads of 40 men each had been divided into three sections: the first section would receive motorcycle training; the second one would receive vehicle training; and those who already possessed current driving licences would undertake advanced heavy vehicle training, or P.S.V.

During this period, we all had to do a forced march from Woking to Salamanca Barracks in Aldershot, a matter of some fourteen miles. It was a matter of honour between each instructor as to who would get there first. Unlike the other Sergeants, who travelled up by jeep, Sergeant Bennet led by example. He strode out in front of his men, his faithful companion at his side. Half way along, we made an illegal stop at a pub, where he treated us all to a cold Shandy. We were worried. "You can't afford this Serge — you being a family man an' all. All these drinks must cost a fortune."

"Don't worry," he replied. "I've got fifty quid riding on this race. I know the other instructors — they won't have the sense to stop and will run their men into the ground. We shall have two more stops, and then we will leave them standing." And we did. We passed one group with two miles to go. The other group were in sight of the winning post when we ran past them. They had no response, and we were as fresh as daisies. Our Sergeant bought us all another one that night.

Sergeant Bennet had been posted in from Cairo, Egypt. Before the war he had been a young police constable before joining the wartime Military Police. In Cairo, he had been a Company Sergeant Major, but had taken a voluntary reduction in rank in order to return to the U.K. where his wife was receiving critical cancer care. Sergeant Bennet was a gentleman — he did not curse us, or put us under stress. He led rather than drove us, and as a result we became the top squad in the depot. I especially benefited, to such an extent that on a Sunday church parade, I was approached by the great R.S.M. Britain himself and informed that I had been recommended for an officer's course.

After the fourteenth week of training, we were required to yomp on a forced march with full equipment to Aldershot, some fourteen miles away, to take part in vehicle training.

"Yomping", by the way, is a mixture of fast marching and running — incredibly tiring. It was with great relief that we turned into the old cavalry barracks that was to be our base for the next month. There were three courses open to us, one of which was driving, usually a Bedford 15 cwt lorry, or a motorcycle. Our squad was to learn how to ride a motorcycle.

The barracks, or horse lines as they were called, consisted of some dozen Victorian buildings and were basically stables with barrack room accommodation above in the long two storey buildings. Although the horses were long gone, the barracks absolutely reeked of horse manure. Our sleeping accommodation consisted of one bare room, in which were four lines of basic metal beds with a green metal locker for each one. There were no curtains, so one dressed behind the open door of one's cabinet. The floor was of rough scrubbed pine. There was no heating, which was just as well considering the smell of horses, mingled with the overpowering reek of petrol and oil fumes.

Our barracks would have been a modern Health and Safety Officer's nightmare. At each end of the room was a single door, behind which was an external iron staircase, which was lethal when it rained because of the smooth iron steps. Eventually, one staircase was roped off and used, instead, to store petrol containers.

Below in the old stables, sixty odd motorcycles were jammed into the confined spaces. Cigarette butts littered the floors. It was a miracle that there was never a serious fire as everybody seemed to smoke, and I even saw a mechanic working on a motorcycle with a lit cigarette dangling from his mouth, completely oblivious to the fact that there was an open petrol tank within just a few feet of him.

For the next month, we were to receive 4 hours per day motorcycle training. Sergeant Bennet still took drill training and police lecture, but every morning we would spend hours learning to ride the heavy B.S.A. girder forked motorcycles. These were slow, ponderous brutes with side-valved 500 c.c. engines that sounded like tractors and a sump clearance so low, that when doing cross-country training over rough terrain, they would suddenly stop on severed tree branches hidden in the long grass. It was a common sight to see a motorcycle travelling at thirty miles an hour stop abruptly, pitching its unfortunate rider into a graceful swallow dive into the rough grass beyond. We learned how to dismantle and replace a carburettor in seconds with a machine gun firing a few inches over our heads. We rode on handle bars, or dropped behind our moving motorcycles, whilst endeavouring to hit a moving target towed behind Sergeant Bennet's jeep with the most inaccurate pistol in the British Army. As our Colonel said, "They may not frighten the criminals, but by George, they terrify me!"

Attached to our squad was a Royal Signals Corporal named Corporal Moon, who was a large, beefy individual. He was aptly named as he had a big round face and a stomach which preceded him, or sat comfortably over his petrol tank. He was not well liked, as he had a cruel sense of humour. He was responsible for our motorcycle training, but he was an idiot. Nobody laughed but him. One day, the parade ground was set around with obstacles — beer barrels and the like. Each man was required to negotiate these obstacles, while riding at a walking pace, twisting around and between them whilst avoiding each one by less than three feet. We had to ride round and around the obstacles until he was satisfied that we could control our bikes before going out on the open road.

We all wore dispatch rider helmets, made of heavy steel, without visors. The trouble was that my helmet, in accordance with the army custom, was at least three sizes too big for me and there was no opportunity to change it. We wobbled around the course until Moon decided to relieve the boredom by producing a police-issue truncheon and hitting each rider on the helmet as they passed him. The result was that instead of maintaining concentration, several ran into the obstacles, with at least one person falling off.

Galvanised by this success, he grew even more enthusiastic, and as I passed him, he hit me hard on the helmet with all the force of his muscular arm. To me, it was like being in a dustbin whilst being hit with a sledgehammer. The interior of the helmet's webbing gave way and the helmet jammed down firmly over my eyes and nose. I lost control, but before I did, I managed to steer the motorcycle front mudguard into his bowed legs. Yes, I was hurt, with a broken wrist and a searing headache, but his injuries outweighed mine. Moon's riding jodhpurs were ripped to shreds, and he was cut in a particularly sensitive area. As I lay in the medical centre waiting for my wrist to be set, I had the satisfaction of listening to his shrieks as his wounds were treated none too gently with iodine.

My accident meant that my motorcycle training was finished. It was decided that I would assist Sergeant Bennet as much as possible, the result being that I came top of the written examinations. After two weeks, having lost so much in motorcycle training, the decision was taken to put me on a Bedford 15 cwt lorry in order to obtain a driving licence. All Military Policemen had to be proficient in the use of either the two wheeled or four wheeled vehicles. Sergeant Bennet had had the use of a Bren Gun Carrier and a jeep during his short stay in Cairo.

Whilst living in Cairo, Egypt, he had jumped upon his motorcycle, which was parked outside his married quarters, only to discover that a young cobra had crawled along the top of the bike's exhaust system for warmth during the night.

"I had a plastic windscreen on that bike, and I must have vaulted clear over the top of it," he told us.

I passed my driving test, scraping through the test for four-wheeled vehicles in a little military pick-up truck.

All too soon, the summer had passed, and it was time for our passing out parade. We spent all our free time polishing our brasses with near industrial levels of Brasso. We cleaned our brass buttons using a small nailbrush and a brass slide under the button to protect the uniform fabric. We rubbed our cap badges on pieces of cardboard liberally splashed with Brasso, until they were abraded so much that the fine details on the badges were flattened, producing a highly lustrous surface.

The camp tailors visited us, and we were issued with a new uniform, each one tailored to fit. Each jacket sported the single stripe or chevron denoting our new rank and the plum red badge of the C.R.M.P. Old soldiers showed us how to treat the inside of trouser creases with hand soap, which would produce a sharp, permanent knife-like crease. Our pistol holsters, belts, haversacks and gaiters were blanched white so many times, we were in danger of snow blindness.

Every night, we would sit around in groups, polishing our boots to a mirror shine. We achieved this by first smoothing out the leather using a hot silver spoon, which had been heated over a candle, and half a tin of Cherry Boot Polish. The resultant shine was produced by applying thin multiple layers of spit and a tiny quantity of polish applied with the forefinger and a soft duster. Chin straps and gaiter straps also received the same treatment. All our packs were neatly squared off with pieces of cardboard for fillings. Our pistols were so liberally oiled and polished that if we were to draw them in an emergency, they would most likely have slipped out of our grasp.

The anti-snake gaiters were the worst — they had a tendency to ride up over the tops of the boots with normal use, causing painful welts on the backs of our legs. We countered this by hanging lead weights inside the folds of the trouser bottoms, which helped to keep the gaiters in place, but having lead weights around your ankles is not the cleverest thing to do, as many ex-national servicemen still bear the scars of this dangerous practice. True, they made the trousers hang correctly, but that's about all. Probably the worst thing was the use of strips of leather in place of the usual bootlaces; they had the tensile strength of wool and were always breaking during drill, but substituting normal bootlaces in place of these standard army issue thin strips of leather could earn you a night's fatigues.

On inspection days, our mattresses were squared off with boards to give a flat, boxed-off appearance, likewise our two blankets and one pillow. Our kit also had to be displayed on the bed for minute inspection. It was common practice to set the whole thing up before going to bed at night, then sleeping on the bare boards underneath our beds to avoid disturbing the displays.

Our barrack room had a large grate, and this had to be scrubbed clean even into the chimney flue. There was a highly polished brass coal scuttle and each piece of coal set therein had to be carefully washed, dried and set back in place. Floors and walls had to be scrubbed till our arms ached. Piles of coke for the canteen had to be set in geometrically precise pyramids within painted white lines to denote their boundaries.

Windows were washed so many times that it was commonplace for birds to fly into them. We balanced precariously upon one another's shoulders to clean light fittings and cross beams. We hid the old brooms and scrubbing brushes and replaced them with new ones protected in cellophane. Heaven help anyone if a Sergeant Major came in, and wiping one finger upon a hidden ledge, came up with a single speck of grime upon one white gloved finger. No wonder men collapsed from exhaustion on the parade grounds on the following days' passing out parade.

Passing Out Parade

We woke to a beautiful September morning. This was the day that we would officially become Military Policemen. Practically all of us were awake and about well before the reveille buglers' call. We jostled each other to shave in the too few washbasins before the hot water ran out. Military washbasins were not equipped with drain plugs to the basins, and some old soldiers had learned to keep rubber bungs in a trouser pocket. The usual practice was to let what little hot water there was run free and unused straight down the wastepipes. We scraped at stubbly beards with single edged heavy-duty galvanised razor blades and used the army issue all-purpose hand soap in lieu of shaving foam. This soap was also used for scrubbing our kit and washing what little hair we had. The soap itself was a curious khaki colour and proved more hazardous than beneficial, as quite a few developed skin complaints after using it.

Sergeant Bennet came in to give a last minute pep talk.

"Chins in — chests out!" he said, and, "Bags of swank boys — bags of swank!"

Finally, after inspecting one another with a critical eye, we trooped out, bandy legged (to avoid damaging our boots and white gaiters by contact with each other) and stiff as marionettes (to keep our neatly pressed uniforms in pristine condition, and also because of the military white belts, worn so tight that they were as unyielding as a corset) onto the parade ground.

We duly paraded under the eagle eye of Sergeant Bennet, and then at 10.00a.m. precisely, in marched the lone piper of the Scots Guards. The order to march was given, the echoes rebounded back, and we marched once round the full parade ground and then out through the archway of the main gate and guardroom, where the full military band of the Scots Guards awaited to precede us.

Down the road we marched. "Bags of swank boys!" Sergeant Bennet had said, and bags of swank we gave it. We looked good, and we felt even better.

The children of the school came out to wave little Union Jack flags at our passing, and young mothers with pushchairs tried to keep up with our marching. The lone piper slipped away behind the trunk of a big chestnut tree for a crafty drag on a cigarette, and the band played on.

We wheeled smartly onto the big sports ground at the side of the barracks. In the middle of the field was a platform, upon which were set two dozen odd chairs and, in front of that, a "saluting" lectern. Around this were masses of flowers in pots and troughs and, all hung side by side, the flags of the Union Jack, the C.R.M.P. and the General Officer Commanding Aldershot District. Around the roped-off boundary were hundreds of chairs occupied by hundreds of spectators. Behind these lines were pavilions, first aid posts, beer tents, and latrines, to name but a few.

The Provost Marshal himself was to take the salute, and we marched past, half strangling ourselves to give an "eyes right" and at the same time not stumble upon the soft grass. Eventually, we were up in ranks in front of the Colonel and one by one we had to march smartly towards him. Saluting stiffly, but smartly, we had to shout out our serial number, rank name and initials, before being presented with the official M.P. armband and Redtop. Having put these on and saluted smartly yet again, we strode back to the ranks.

How I wished that my father could have seen my moment of triumph. There were masses of my colleagues' relatives and girlfriends present, many of whom had arrived by private car or taxi, but I knew that there was no way that my family could hope to afford the coach or train fare. I was so disappointed, and then felt ashamed of myself. I didn't know how far Woking was from Oxford, but I did know that it was an awfully long way.

We were marched back to our barrack room to take off our white accoutrements and to return our pistols to the armoury, and then it was off to the canteen for a surprisingly half-decent meal. Afterwards, we were free to do whatever we liked.

I couldn't face the happy faces of my comrades inundated as they were with families and girlfriends, so I retreated moodily to my bed.

I had just dozed off when there was a crash at the barrack room door, followed by the stentorian bellow of Sergeant Bennet.

"Lance Corporal Wicks, stand by your bed!" And to my astonishment in strode Sergeant Bennet, but no longer a Sergeant, for he was now wearing the insignia on his forearm of a Company Sergeant Major. This was surprising enough, but the most amazing thing of all was that there, stood next to him, was the diminutive figure of my father.

I almost fell over with shock — I could not believe my eyes. My father, who if he had a shilling in his pocket, always gave it to us kids in preference to his own needs. I knew that he had no money and was always too proud to ask. How had he done it? My wonder only increased when I learned that he had bicycled all the way! My father in his mid-sixties, with a chest so bad that sometimes only willpower had kept him alive, had cycled all this way to see his second son receive his promotion. No longer did I feel envious of my mates and their families — I had a father to be proud of.

Dad had left the day before on his old bicycle, with his best suit, boots, razor and towel, clean shirt and two loaves of bread and a bottle of water, all packed into a clean sack tied over the handlebars. He had slept in an empty barn the night before and, upon reaching Woking, had changed and shaved in the public toilets.

As we were marching onto the sports field, I had half thought that I had caught a glimpse of a blue-clad figure, wheeling a bike through the spectators. No, it could not be, I'd told myself, but I was wrong. Man! I was so proud. What man ever had a father like mine?

Tears rolled down my cheeks, embarrassing both of us as we hugged and slapped each other awkwardly on the back. The Sergeant Major turned away and strode out of the barrack room. It transpired that my father had remembered the name of my Drill Sergeant, and, after we had marched back to the barracks, he had asked for Sergeant Bennet.

There were several persons being presented with medals and other decorations by the General. The usher had pointed out Sergeant Bennet and afterwards took my father over to speak with him. The new Sergeant Major had been very impressed by my father, who, it has to be said, was wearing all his medals for the occasion, and took him to the Sergeant's Mess as his guest for a well-deserved meal.

He escorted us round the various displays. There were races between the Royal Mounted Military Police and the motorcycle team over a short distance, which amazingly, the horses won, scoring a complete whitewash. There was a display of police dogs, including one by a large Alsatian, who not only rode pillion on the back of his master's motorcycle, but leapt off whilst the vehicle was in motion and captured a running make-believe thief. There were demonstrations of dogs sniffing out explosives and drugs. There were also demonstrations of physical training, judo, basketball and a comic fancy dress football match. Sweating squads of men stripped down two motorcycles into their various component parts and then, dividing the parts between them, scaled a wall, a huge net, and crawled through big sewer pipes, before finally swimming across a large pool, to assemble the bike on the far side. The winners being whoever could fire it up and then do a complete circuit of the field carrying all members of the five aside team.

We viewed some of the more grisly exhibitions in the marquee of the Special Investigations Branch and watched a demonstration of parachuting. Military Police took part in a static military map reading exercise, which carried a small prize for the winner, and which, to my amazement, was won by my father.

Sergeant Major Bennet had a word with the Entertainments Officer, and my father was put up for the night in the Officer's Mess. When I saw Dad the following day, he looked slightly the worse for wear. It turned out that the Colonel, being a keen amateur gardener, had monopolised my father all evening, buying him several schooners of vintage sherry. As my father rarely drank, he was feeling somewhat out of sorts the following morning.

The Sergeant Major then sprang another surprise on us. He had been to see the Rail Traffic Warrant Officer and presented me with the rail warrants "Didcot to Littlemore via Oxford". I had been worrying about my father riding back, and was both relieved and grateful until I realised that they were from Didcot.

"That is not a problem," Sergeant Major Bennet replied. "I shall take you to Didcot myself. I have to go to the Reading Hospital to see my wife, and the Welfare

Officer has kindly loaned me a jeep from the motor pool."

He was as good as his word. The bike was slung on the back of the jeep, Dad rode in front, and I sat in the back, slightly encumbered by the bike, one kitbag, two suitcases and a bored Springer Spaniel. My father treated us to a great fish and chip meal, paid for by his winnings, and eventually we arrived at Didcot Station.

I took them both into the refreshment booth for a cup of tea, but to my surprise, the manageress refused to accept payment. Finally our train appeared, and Sergeant Major Bennet made his goodbyes and collected the dog from a group of admiring children who had been feeding him biscuits.

The bike was loaded into the guard's van, complete with my kitbag, and we embarked on the last leg home.

We arrived in the same way that I had left all those months before — Dad pushing his bike, with the kitbag balanced on the handlebars. Mother rushed down the garden path to greet me and almost suffocated me in the process.

I was home!

Home On Leave

I awoke back in my own bed to the smell of eggs and bacon. A few seconds later came the call of my mother.

"Peter — breakfast!"

I threw open the bedroom window whilst simultaneously struggling into my old dressing gown. I was amazed to find out how much it had shrunk, or more likely, how much I had grown.

It was a glorious morning. I could hear the solitary insistent "Dong! Dong!" of the Littlemore church bell calling the faithful to early morning communion. I had belonged to its church choir since I was seven years old, and I decided that I would go to the eleven o'clock morning service. I had successfully come through what was possibly the worst twenty-two weeks of my life, and I thought that it would be appropriate to offer a prayer of thanks.

I washed, dressed and ate my first home-cooked breakfast in months. Afterwards I went outside to get my beloved bicycle. Before leaving for training, I had carefully wrapped it in cardboard and greaseproof paper to protect it, and then hung it up in the beams of my father's shed out of the way. Imagine my shock to find that it no longer hung there. My little brother had availed himself of my absence and had taken the bicycle for himself. I finally found it, crushed under a disgustingly dirty rabbit hutch behind the shed and in a woeful condition. The beautiful frame was deeply scratched; bits of cardboard were stuffed into the wheel spokes to make a noise; the front wheel was buckled and both tyres were flat and split beyond repair. The beautiful Lucas dynamo set had been swapped for a pair of roller skates.

But what was the point of complaining? My mother, who could deny him nothing, had given him the bike to borrow until my return, on condition that he looked after it. My mother, who was nearly blind, but would not admit it, had been totally taken in by him, as usual. I contented myself by clipping him around the ear and prepared to walk to church.

There were lots of faces to greet me at church. Jack Hudson and his brother Les, Gordon Knight, Rosemary Clinkard, the Beckets — father and son, Bob Miller, the vicar Reverend C.C.L Buckwell, Mr Quelch the choir master and Mr Tanner who was now a sidesman, and many others — too many to mention. After church there was a wonderful surprise. Outside, waiting to greet me was Paula McGillick and her soon-to-be fiancé Michael Kelly and his brother Jim. These three went to the Roman Catholic Church, a couple of hundred yards down the road, and they had seen me going in.

I had a very good friend called Paula McGillick, she was an Irish girl. We met when travelling on the bus to Oxford. She was a very pretty girl too, with a lovely personality, she had come over from southern Ireland to join her father, who had a job in a car factory. She soon became very popular in my circle of friends, joining us in football and cricket.

I had had a very uneasy relationship with my sisters and she became a very good friend and confidant, more than they could be.

Most of my male friends were hopelessly attracted to her. One of her great talents was playing the piano, every few weeks or so my friends and I would be crammed into her front parlour gathered around her old piano with its couple of wonky notes, singing a collection of Irish songs in exaggerated Irish accents. On of my good friends, Mike Kelly, who was also Irish, was her boyfriend and later they were married. On her sixteenth birthday we held a party for her at her house and it was there that I had met Shelagh Bennett.

Shelagh was tall, slender and blonde, with a striking resemblance to the Hollywood actor Tony Curtis' wife, Janet Leigh. And although younger, the similarities were startling. I escorted her home that night and that was the start of a very strong relationship. We went everywhere together and I worshipped her, it was an innocent relationship, neither one of us knew the facts of life. This was common in the 1940s and I always envisioned that we might get married one day.

Mike and Paula had come to welcome me home on my first leave, but Shelagh was noticeable, for her absence.

Paula was distressed to hear that I had not received even one letter from Shelagh in all the time I had been away. Was she aware that I was home on leave? I did not think so. Paula offered to go over to Shelagh's house with Michael that same afternoon to see what the situation was.

It turned out that Shelagh had met someone else, and I was history. Paula and I cried together. I cried for myself, and she cried for me.

I felt as if my heart had been ripped out of me, and despite the surplus of would-be girlfriends, I had no enthusiasm for it.

I decided to visit my old school, Southfield Grammar School for boys, so one afternoon, a few days later, resplendent in my new uniform, I walked over. The school day had just finished when I walked through the gates. A few of my old classmates, now elevated to the upper sixth form and cramming for university, were still in attendance, and they greeted me with open arms.

I had badly wanted to go to university, but my parents' situation made this impossible, and I did not want to add to their burden. My mother had been upset when I decided to leave school and get a job, but I think she was also relieved that I would now contribute to the upkeep of the family. As we talked, several of my old teachers came out of the school gates, including my old form master, Mr Brashour and my English master, Doctor Freeboirn-Smith, a man who had been convinced that I would become a writer of books. It turned out that he was right, though it took nearly sixty years for me to put pen to paper.

We chatted happily for ten minutes or so, and then the headmaster, Mr D.G. Perry appeared. In all the five years I had spent at the school, the great man had never condescended to utter one word to me; I was the lowest of the low — a scholarship boy.

"Wicks is it?" he asked.

I was surprised that he even remembered my name.

I replied, "Yes, I am." I felt proud; I had achieved my first stripe.

Then, looking at me with contempt, he maliciously said, "Of course, you are really only a Private. That one stripe is just a make-believe rank! All your colleagues have obtained King's Commissions — is that all you could manage?"

I wished for the ground to swallow me up. I turned and headed blindly down Granville Road and out of the school gates for the very last time. I perceived that I would never walk into them again until I had done something of merit in my life. I have never returned or joined Southfield Old Boys Association. I had always felt like a pauper amongst princes, and that one moment, those few words had brought it all back.

The rest of my leave I spent helping my dad on his three allotments, or walking with Paula and Mike. They did their best to cheer me up, but it was almost with a sense of relief that I headed back to the army.

Fate had not finished with me, however. My mother had decided to iron my uniform. I was not allowed to wear civilian clothes in public, besides of which, it is doubtful my old clothes would have fitted me. As she was ironing my trousers, a knock came at the window — it was her neighbour with a bag of apples for her.

She turned her back to speak with Mr Hallett, as my sisters, Betty and Joyce, came into the room fighting over a skipping rope. My mother had left the electric iron sitting on our dining table, upon which she had placed the trousers.

Seconds later, the iron was flat on its face, having been knocked over in the argument, and was sizzling directly onto the uniform fabric. An enormous scorch mark was imprinted right across the seat of the trousers.

We spent all day trying to get the scorch mark out, and even tried rubbing it with a half-crown piece, but, although we did succeed in reducing the burn mark, it made the material as delicate as tissue paper. I did have an army greatcoat with me, and, when I went out, I was very careful to wear this to conceal the damage. The trouble was that that month was one of the hottest we had had for decades, and I almost collapsed from heat exhaustion.

The worst bit, however, was when I got back to barracks. When I reported my return to Inkerman Barracks guardroom, the greatcoat was peeled away, the damage was revealed, and I was arrested. My punishment was to be demoted for one month, all leave and privileges stopped, two hours of kitchen duty every night and extra drill Saturday and Sunday. I also had to buy a new uniform and cover the cost of the damaged uniform *and* pay for stores replacement, plus tailoring costs. Although only the trousers had been damaged, I also had to pay for the jackets.

What little money I received was stopped to pay the bill, and it took me 6 months to clear it. C.S.M. Bennet spoke up for me, but it was like they said — "Rules is rules!"

The Sea Crossing

One week later, I was posted. Several of my colleagues were posted to Northern Ireland, a cushy post at that time. Others went to Cairo, Egypt, or various locations in the United Kingdom. Some were sent to Malaya, which was then a hot spot, and for this they had to endure jungle training in the woods behind Inkerman Barracks for six weeks. The woods were full of non-venomous snakes, all imported for the purpose, and other creepy crawlies. The biggest posting was to Korea (I lost one of my school friends to that war; he was caught out by a booby trap). One of us was sent to Paris, and I, with some twenty others, was posted to Germany.

A week later, our little party had embarked upon the troop ship that ran a ferry service from Harwich to the Hook of Holland. We crossed at night. The ship was uncomfortably hot and stank of diesel. It was the first time I had actually seen sailors in army uniform, and I was surprised to find that the army actually ran boats and even aeroplanes.

It was October, and the crossing was rough. As this was a night crossing, we had all just been fed a greasy evening dinner of indigestible sausages, carrots as hard as bullets and a strange sort of reconstituted potato,

77

masquerading as mash. Old hands, who had made the trip before, solemnly advised us to eat a hearty meal — for reasons no one seemed prepared to explain.

At 10p.m. we set sail — if that's what you'd call it! The boat seemed to travel crabwise in a series of sickening lurches across the tops of enormous waves. The wind shrieked and howled as we were catapulted down into one trough and up again, only to plunge into another. Everything vibrated, wires, steps, stanchions etc., to such an extent that it seemed the old ship would shake apart. It didn't help much when a rumour arose that one of the lifeboats had vanished.

Soon, we were fighting for space at the railing.

Rain hurtled down in sheets, and, now and again, a flash of lightening would enliven the proceedings. Some of us, me included, doubted that we would ever see dry land again.

We had a choice; those who had nothing left in their stomachs to bring back up could lay down on damp bunks, steaming like wet dogs, and pray for unconsciousness, or, if still wracked with nausea, we could stagger outside onto the main deck to be jolted, soaked and bashed about by a storm that was clearly enjoying itself. Feeling that I wanted to die, I crept into a top bunk and was soon unconscious.

I awoke just after dawn. Sunshine was streaming though a porthole level with my face, and the ship was steaming into harbour on a millpond surface as sedate as the River Thames.

Even as I focused, I caught my first glimpse of Holland. A battleship-grey post jutted out of the sea, and on top of it, a herring gull preened its feathers. I slithered down from the bunk and crawled out on to the deck.

During the night, my peaked cap had dropped onto the floor and someone had been neatly sick in it. I could not accuse anyone; for all I knew, it could have been me. I held it in the toilet bowl and pulled the lever. It worked well enough, but I almost lost the cap, the pressure was so great. Had it not been for the cap badge tangling with the chinstrap and jamming within the S bend, I would have lost it for sure.

I saw one of the army sailors coiling a large howser.

"Not a bad crossing," he called. "One of the smoothest we've had for a long time. Hungry? They do very good bacon, eggs and fried bread in the harbour canteen."

My reply was lost in my precipitate rush to the nearest guard rail.

An hour later, several hundred men in a vast variety of uniforms, were paraded in various groups on the jetty, whilst a roll call was made. There we waited, in a great pathetic steaming mass, to be led through the cavernous customs hall.

After a while, a military police lorry turned up, and, amidst the catcalls and boos of our disgruntled fellow passengers, we were taken to the little military police house. Here, we were allowed to shower, change into dry uniforms and drink hot, sweet tea or coffee before we were dosed with some green concoction.

By 9a.m., we were recovered and somewhat surprisingly, hungry. We were taken into the little mess

79

room, where two attractive Dutch waitresses served us a lovely meal. There was gleaming white and silver chinaware, starched tablecloths and ivory handled cutlery. It was obvious that the meal had been carefully chosen — not a hint of grease in sight.

Germany

At 10a.m., our small party was driven to the railhead. There, before us, stood a gleaming brown and gold steam train. As befitting our new status, we were placed in the carriages marked "Officers and N.C.O.s only". Presumably, before the war, these had been first class carriages, and the white-coated Dutch steward assigned to us took great pride in telling us that these had once belonged to the Orient Express.

We travelled through a country so flat that I could scarcely believe what I was seeing. For mile upon mile, we thundered through the golden October sunshine, between russet fields. Cities stood out in the far distance like islands, but there was not a hill in sight.

At every rail crossing, there were hundreds of people on foot and on bicycles waiting patiently to cross. Girls in flowery skirts, young men, bronzed and golden haired, in pale blue dungarees, all chattering and waving as we went past.

Here and there stood a windmill with sails lazily turning. Upon the sail of one, a Union Jack fluttered in the breeze.

We passed a canal, where great, patient carthorses towed enormous flat-bottomed barges. The captain sat with his feet dangling inside the stern cockpit, puffing contentedly on a white clay pipe as he steered the enormous tiller, his wife on the middle deck pegging out clothes, which waved like bunting down either side of the vessel. The captain's wife, or "first mate", blew us a kiss as we passed, and the baby, in a little play pen behind her, waved his rattle. The captain's sons, or "crew", led the two great dray horses along the canal path, whilst a young woman, who could have been his daughter, rode a bicycle a few hundred yards ahead, presumably to warn anglers, of which there were many, of the barges' imminent approach. The train driver gave two toots on his whistle in acknowledgement.

We passed many white-painted houses, with their curiously "flap-eared" roofs, that reminded me of a legion of cocker spaniels, all sitting to attention.

The white-coated steward came through and informed us that we were in the first sitting for dinner, and we followed him into the immaculate dining room, where there were chefs with tall white hats and pretty waitresses who were in formal black dresses with starched white aprons, cuffs and collars.

There was no menu, but that was the only thing missing. The meal was a chef's delight. We ate with silver cutlery and gold banded china. I heard afterwards that the cutlery was carefully counted before the other ranks arrived, and both cutlery and china were replaced by basic N.A.A.F.I. eating irons and earthenware.

We came to the border town of Aachen, where the train stopped, and two German customs officials, resplendent in grey and green uniforms, climbed aboard. They walked through the train, checking the manifest lists and challenging various individuals in perfect English to open their bags. They were accompanied by two medium-sized spaniels, which passed amongst us, sniffing excitedly.

Whilst we were there, one of the spaniels, his tail wagging furiously, suddenly sat down in front of a sergeant from the tank regiment. The two officials immediately took him under arrest, and we did not see him again. I learnt afterwards that the dogs were used to sniff out marijuana and other drugs, and that the troop trains were a favourite method used by the drug smugglers to get drugs into Germany.

As we left Aachen, we saw lots of poles, each having a small platform fixed to it. These, we were informed, were for storks to nest upon as an alternative to their favourite nesting sites — chimneys. Quite a few people had died as a result of coal gases not being able to escape up the chimney when it was blocked by the birds. We saw many of the storks, which were so big that one wondered how such a large bird could perch without damage to the roof.

Eventually we steamed into Germany, which had a spectacular rolling countryside of lakes, farms, woods and villages. I was struck by the fact that there were few tractors about. I saw men in short-sleeved shirts with scythes, cutting hay, horses pulling goods wagons, and even a horse-drawn tram. On the main autobahns, great diesel juggernauts, towing as many as three trucks, thundered through the countryside.

I remember that we passed by what had been a main road bridge that had been bombed so precisely, that it was as if some giant hand had scooped out the centre, and left houses and a church totally unscarred.

At mid afternoon, we were called for coffee or tea if required — this time served in N.A.A.F.I. earthenware mugs. As we rolled through the countryside like lords, I was struck to see how few factories had survived — acres upon acres of skeletal, burnt-out factories, sheds and city centres. There was grey dust and rubble everywhere, and amidst it all were people toiling like ants. Every so often, a great, gleaming, ultra-modern building rose up through the devastation. Although I did not recognise it at the time, this was what politicians described as the rebirth of Germany.

Just as the streetlights were coming on, we arrived at our destination — Bielefeld. We disembarked, and the train pulled out. We were met by a military police sergeant, together with a German driver in a big scammer troop carrying lorry. Soon we were jolting through the busy cobbled streets, heading eastwards to the outskirts. Twenty minutes later, we had arrived in, what was then, a tiny village.

We travelled up a charming lane surrounded on all sides by apple tree orchards, and passed a pub (or café as they were called in Germany), where several older men in leather shorts toasted us with steins of lager, and a plump barmaid blew us a kiss.

Finally, we arrived at a picture postcard building, which was one storey high and had a thatched roof. It was surrounded by flat fields containing goats and horses, all grazing contentedly. We found out that the building had acted as the village school, but the children were now at a very large, modern school in the district, and that the council, with a sharp eye to business, had hired the empty building to the military police. It was ideal, inasmuch as it had four airy classrooms and an assembly hall, whilst the army had built a prefabricated cookhouse and dining room to the rear. Two of the classrooms had been turned into dormitories for our small party, whilst the assembly hall continued as a lecture room, and when the chairs were pushed back, as a gymnasium.

Original children's paintings still decorated the walls, and the children's toilets and basins were still in place — a drawback when many among our party were well over six feet tall.

This was to be our home for two weeks, and we spent our days wandering the sun-lit lanes, with occasional visits to the café and on one occasion to see Stewart Grainger in an English historical film at the local cinema. I was amazed to find that almost everybody, except the very old, spoke English, and this probably had to do with the fact that almost all films were from Hollywood, and of course English pop songs predominated.

Every morning, we sat through interminable lectures from old soldiers, mainly concerning sex, booze, fish and chips and precious little else. In the afternoon we were taken out, complete with sandwiches, on tours of the towns and points of interest.

Every night two of us would be called upon to man the office as per army regulations. It was the first time that I had ever worked through the night. We sat up in a small, comfortable office in the over-stuffed chintz easy chairs next to the telephone in case of emergencies, but it never rang in all the time we were there.

Sitting in front of a roaring log fire in what must have been the teacher's common room, with its thick Persian carpet and book-lined shelves, I discovered the *Wind in the Willows* by Kenneth Graham, and not having read it before, I sat enthralled by the adventures of Mole, Ratty, Badger and Mr Toad. I did two nights on night duty, in which time I managed to read the book from cover to cover.

On the second night we were there, we were all awoken by a resounding crash from the kitchen, and we all dashed out in our pyjamas. There, in the middle of the tiled floor, at three o'clock in the morning, stood a large goat with a basket round its horns. Pots, pans and two trays of cutlery were on the floor, as well as several half-eaten loaves of bread, which had been in the basket. It transpired that the door had a faulty latch, and the goat had formerly been the children's pet.

On the second Sunday, a small party of us were taken into Bielefeld to a small green-painted tin shed, which was a small chapel built by British prisoners during the last war, and now adopted by the British army of the Rhine.

We returned at 4p.m. for tea, and there, to my surprise were two M.P.s who had come to collect me. It turned out that they had escorted a military prisoner to the glasshouse (the nickname given to his majesty's military prison) at Bielefeld. Apparently, I was to join the strength of 102 Provost Company, based in Dusseldorf. The two Lance Corporals were staying the night, and I was to leave with them the following morning.

Monday morning, I had said goodbye to my former companions and was sat huddled up in my army greatcoat in the back seat of an open-topped jeep.

After three hours of fast travelling, we arrived at the outskirts of Dusseldorf, via the autobahn. My companions told me that, because the road had been laid in 21 foot stretches of concrete, each ridge of concrete would cause the tyres to clump, something similar to the rails of the old British railway line, with their hypnotic clickety clack. It further transpired that a great many accidents occurred when drivers travelling at high speed fell asleep at the wheel. On the way, I was regaled with macabre tales of crashes they had attended.

I was impressed by the magnificent town of Dusseldorf. Wonderful green copper-domed buildings fronted the splendid Rhine River, along with gleaming shop fronts, as elegant as anything in New York or London, beautiful parks and a magnificent wide boulevard named Konigsallec, all patrolled by elegant ladies stationed every twenty yards or so. It was some time before I realised that these were ladies of the night.

Great modern stores, including Woolworths and Macys, ranged either side of the boulevard with their flower gardens and ornamental fountains. There were elegant clothes shops, pavement cafés, art galleries and lighting shops, a magnificent railway station, all surrounded by glass and steel office blocks.

Trams clanked along the black-cobbled roads. Bells rang, cars hooted and parked across pavements, and people shopped, walked and chattered in one vast, heaving mass. Yet, just behind this front, the old commercial heart of the city was a bare wilderness; a huge plain of derelict earth, flattened by warplanes and now being dragged clean by huge crawler tractors and lines of lorries and carts.

Two things that struck me most were the young children doing cartwheels for pennies and the overpowering smell of cigars. It seemed that every able-bodied male in the town had a cigar permanently clamped between his teeth.

"Oompah" bands predominated, and every corner had its pavement artist or accordion player, often both. A clown on a unicycle handed out leaflets, and German policemen in old-fashioned black uniforms and strange leather helmets patrolled the streets.

Birds! There were birds everywhere! Mostly pigeons, strutting amidst the crowds of feet that threatened to crush them. At one point, I saw an old lady trundling along the pavement, chatting excitedly to her companion, a large French stick poking out of her heavy shopping bag, and perched there, unnoticed by the two ladies, was a grey town pigeon, contentedly pecking at the loaf.

It seemed that there were almost as many birds as people; great grey, white and blue birds, strutting across the roads in front of the fast moving traffic, and upon one tram clanging its way down the Konigs Allee, half a dozen pigeons were comfortably ensconced on its roof, like six old ladies taking a well earned rest.

102 Provost Company C.R.M.P. was situated in a residential district of Dusseldorf. The building was set in a leafy, middle-class district of substantial houses, directly behind a large Catholic girl's school on the road named Graf Adolf Strasse. The building itself was a long, honey-coloured building, obviously erected in the grounds of the small house in one corner of the plot. The story was that the building had been put up as a party raising venture by the local Communist party some two years before, and that they had been unable to make it pay. 102 Provost Company had taken it on a short lease on very advantageous terms.

The building was long, without decoration of any type, flat roofed and five floors high. There was a small yard at the back, where we kept our odd vehicles, and which directly backed on to the girl's netball courts of the adjoining school. The close proximity of so many teenage men and young girls must have been a nightmare for the several burly nuns trying to supervise their well-heeled charges. I remember one nun, a Sister Mary from Donaghdee, Ireland, had a demeanour and voice so fierce, that Hans, our interpreter, said that even the Gestapo backed down in front of her.

The house had been converted into workshops, in which several sign writers, an upholsterer, three seamstresses, a tailor and a cabinet-maker plied their trades. There were even three gleaming Volkswagen Beetle cars, complete with smartly uniformed German chauffeurs. I had not realised that the British army was responsible for rescuing the Volkswagen Car Company from the ashes, and these were impressive little cars.

There was a basement in the main building and this contained the boiler room, kitchens and storeroom, with the N.C.O.'s dining halls on the ground floor. Also on the ground floor, reached by several wide steps and a modern glass panelled door, were the offices of the Commanding Officer, Major Brook, the Regimental Sergeant, Major Causon, and the second in charge, Captain John Betty, a well-known motorcycle racer and motocross champion. Further along was the General Enquiry Office, manned by the Duty Sergeant and two Lance Corporals. Further down the polished, tiled corridor was the shared office of Lieutenant Bill Sykes and Second Lieutenant John Stokes, who coincidently had been a scholar at Magdalene College, Oxford and who lived less than a mile from my house.

At the furthest end of the building was a strong room, full of equipment racks, loaded with arms, ammunition, tents and other such items. This was the kingdom of Company Quartermaster Staff Sergeant Harrison, otherwise known as "Q". Here, he reigned supreme with his two Lance Corporal stores assistants. It was said that he did his training with the Inland Revenue. He was so tight, that if you required a new pencil, you had to produce the old stub and sign for it. Heaven help us if we lost anything, for we never heard the end of it.

On the opposite side were the Pay Office and Orderly room, manned by a Sergeant, two clerks and the very beautiful shorthand typists. Next to that was the office of the Anti-vice Squad, which premises was shared with the two German interpreters.

The next two floors were a series of two-roomed bedrooms. Originally, each unit had consisted of a bedroom and sitting room, each being connected by a single door. In the interests of economy, however, both rooms had been turned into bedrooms, each containing one single bed, wardrobe, bedside table, small writing desk and easy chair. The main staircase ran up through the centre of the building and adjoining it, on each bedroom floor, were washbasins, toilets, baths and showers in a communal block, and that old army favourite, the Army Equipment Blancoing Room.

On the top floor, to the right of the N.C.O.'s bar and stores, occupying one half of the building, was the recreation room, used for exercising and dances, and occasionally for a court martial. This floor was ruled over by "Hooch", the best known dog in the British army and the official Military Police mascot. Officially, he was a drug sniffer dog, and he had had some successes, but, he loved beer (with a definite preference to Pilsners Lager), and it had got the better of him. Faced with a cache of drugs or a pint of lager, he would go for the beer every time. When I arrived at the Company, Hooch must have been about seven years old. No one was sure of his history, but it seemed that he had been rescued from a battlefield as a very small puppy. With the exception of Q and the Alsatian next door, he was a friend to everybody. He was sixty parts Dashund, with the long nose and body of that breed, and forty per cent Bull Terrier. He lived with the barman in a basket behind the N.C.O.'s bar on the top floor of the building, and he was a familiar sight in the town, riding in the back of a military police jeep, with a little custom-made red cap on his head and a khaki dog coat sporting a Lance Corporal's stripe and a long service medal. He looked the part of a real police dog.

R. S. M. Causton

Regimental Sergeant Major Causon was the lynch pin upon which the whole company of almost one hundred men and officers revolved. A few years back, the BBC made the hugely popular *Dad's Army*, and in Captain Mainwaring, it was almost as if R.S.M. Causon had come back to life: The same build as the Captain, remarkably similar facial features and matching voice. I have often wondered if the creators of *Dad's Army* had met the R.S.M. during the war somewhere. As I say, the resemblance was amazing. The only difference was that he swore — boy, did he swear! It had grown into such a habit, that I do not think he was even aware of it.

His wife, however, in total contrast, was a graceful brunette, half a head taller than him. She dressed elegantly, was charming, (even to us minions) spoke beautiful English and would close her eyes and shudder fastidiously every time her husband swore.

On the day the toilet system blocked up, I overheard the R.S.M. tell our Commanding Officer, Major Brooks, that the lower toilets were ankle deep in manure. The men laughed when we heard Mrs Brooks, the C.O.'s wife, say to Mrs Causon, "My dear, can you not get him to say 'sewage'?"

"I only wish I could," came the reply. "It's taken me twenty-five years to get him to call it 'manure'."

The Sergeant Major had an encyclopaedic knowledge of army law.

"I was a barrack room lawyer," he said. "I proved to be such a thorn in the army's side that they had to promote me."

He did not suffer fools gladly, and it was generally admitted that his bark was not as bad as his bite. He was a scrupulously fair man, and as I discovered later, had immense personal courage, and when my beloved grandmother died suddenly, he was kindness itself. Our afternoons would often be enlivened by his shout of, "Where's that bloody Q?" And the Quartermaster Staff Sergeant would come running to his master's voice. The Sergeant Major ran what is called a "tight ship". 102 Provost Company was a very busy military police station indeed, and all of us were overworked and distinctly underpaid.

Major Brooks, our Commanding Officer, was a tall, well-built, smart man, with the studious air of an Oxford Don. He and his wife were so alike in demeanour and looks they could almost have been twins. Our C.O. had one overriding fascination, and that was life after death. He questioned me at length concerning my beliefs, and I discovered that most of my colleagues had received similar grillings. He was an agnostic, who was interested in all forms of religion. He could talk at length upon Sikh, Moslem, Lutheran, Buddhism, Roman Catholic, Shinto and Hinduism.

Rumour had it that he was studying for a degree in comparative religion.

Captain John Betty of the Gloucester Regiment was our Second in Command. I said from the Glousters, because all officers in the military police were all seconded from certain regiments. There was only one true military police officer, and that was the Depot Quartermaster. All other officers wore the rank and insignia of their mother regiments. Captain John Betty was a motorcycle champion. His personal transport was a B.S.A. Road Rocket, with unbelievable acceleration and road holding. I rode it once, and it scared me half to death.

The official strength of the company was 10 sections of ten men apiece, together with one Sergeant and one full Corporal. In practice, there were only seven sections due to staff shortages. One section was based at the Hook of Holland depot, mentioned previously. One was based in the town of Wuppertal. One section was based at Krefeld and a further section at Munchen Gladbach. The rest of us comprised one, two and three Headquarters Section. The outside sections were all commanded by a Sergeant, assisted by a full Corporal and an interpreter. Each section also had one army chef, who in turn had two civilian kitchen assistants/ waitresses, a maintenance man, two typists and a chauffeur with an olive green Volkswagen Beetle bearing army markings. Each policeman also had a motorcycle. The Sergeant had a jeep and the Corporal a 15CWT Bedford "Paddy-wagon" truck. There was also a small contingent of part time cleaners, gardeners and mechanics.

Headquarters Company had a similar set up, except that each Lance Corporal at Headquarters was responsible for no less than seven vehicles each. In my case, I was allocated six motorcycles and a jeep. Each vehicle was required to do a minimum of 70 miles a month.

I believe that the idea was that, should there be an escalation of problems, cold war wise, and because every National Service man had to serve five years with the Territorial Army, forces could be made up and fully prepared in a matter of a few days.

Overseeing this vast collection of vehicles was "Tiffy". He was a Polish man serving with the Royal Electrical and Mechanical Engineers. His name was so unpronounceable, I don't think I ever heard him called anything but "Tiffy". Incredibly though, he ruled his German assistants like a martinet. He was still only a Private, but heaven help the Sergeant or Corporal who provoked his lashing tongue. He was also Captain John Betty's chief racing mechanic. In his view, every army vehicle had to be mechanically perfect, and if it wasn't, why not? A small, intense-looking man, I never once saw him in anything but oily dungarees, hands and face liberally smeared with oil. When Tiffy said, "Jump!" we merely enquired, "How high?"

By contrast, the Company Quartermaster Sergeant, "Q", was a large man of some twenty stone, and like Tiffy took his duties seriously. He trusted nothing and no one. He was said to leave coins under mats in his stores to check to see if the cleaners were honest. If a Sergeant requested six items for his section, he would supply five. Thus, the R.S.M., irritated by the complaints of the Sergeants, would bellow down the corridor, "Where's that bloody Quartermaster?"

Q was also convinced that the way to promotion was dependent upon the amount of charges or misdemeanours he could prosecute against his fellow man.

Every day, two or three of us would be lined up outside the R.S.M.'s office on the flimsiest of charges. We would be double marched, with cap and belt off, into his small, overworked office, our boots thudding in double quick time. The R.S.M. would be wincing behind a pair of pince-nez glasses as each thud reverberated throughout the building. We were always found guilty, and the standard punishment was to be demoted to the ranks for two days. Basically, this entailed removing the stripes from our uniforms and then sewing them back on two days later, or getting the Company tailor to do it, who was charging a small fortune for the job.

Ultimately, someone had a brainwave — stick them back on with wallpaper paste, and guess what — it worked! Yes, it worked well, and for some weeks we marched about with our uniform stripes glued on with flour and water paste, made up for us by one of the waitresses.

Disaster soon struck, however. Some 50 of us, Officers and men, had to attend a large church parade for Remembrance Day at the B.A.O.R. church at the Rhine Centre, a massive showpiece park on the outskirts of Dusseldorf that had originally been erected by the Nazis as a tribute to Hitler. It had numerous playing fields and athletics tracks, concert hall, cinema, restaurants and a very modern church.

We were required to attend to the car parking of an enormous number of vehicles, both military and civilian. All went well until we were caught in a massive deluge of rain, at which point, to the amazement of the onlookers, the glue holding on our stripes dissolved, and they peeled away in a soggy, floury mess. We were undone!

There was no love lost between the R.S.M. and Q Harrison. Having had half his Company paraded in front of his desk, having had to cancel two days local leave when he had planned to celebrate his wedding anniversary, and after a tense interview with Colonel Bowers, the District Provost Marshall, he was most definitely not happy.

"Where's that bloody Q?" he bellowed. "On parade! Double quick march." And the portly Q heaved up to his office, enormous carpet-slipper shod feet flapping like two great paddles (he was excused boots), with his enormous stomach bouncing one way and his matching bum wobbling the other.

Our Chief Clerk, Sergeant John Forrest, had secretly been training our Company mascot for some time, and as Q shot past the Orderly office, Hooch barked at his heels in perfect timing — LEFT, RIGHT, LEFT, RIGHT!

Whilst we all roared with laughter, Q tried to kick Hooch away, but the dog promptly responded by snatching one of Q's slippers and haring off down the corridor with it. We subsequently found it dumped in a pile of coke. Hooch was truly a remarkable dog. One afternoon, however, tragedy struck. Hooch was sat in the back of the jeep, whilst the driver and his mate went to investigate a break-in at a local N.A.A.F.I. They were some time, and on their return, Hooch was gone. His lead had been unclipped.

The Company had broken up a dog fighting ring some months before, and these people were suspected, but of course there were no witnesses. Appeals were made in the local press for his safe return. Pilsners Lager Company offered a reward, and he was even given an appeal slot on B.A.O.R. Radio. All to no avail.

Three months passed, and still nothing happened. Then one day, the R.S.M. and his driver were sitting in a jeep, waiting at the traffic lights in one of the sleazier districts of the city, when a small body came hurtling across the road and shot into the jeep. It was Hooch, barking excitedly and wagging his tail so furiously, that he almost seemed in danger of taking off.

He was in a sorry state; his claws were broken, and he had lost over a third of his body weight, plus his smart coat and hat were gone. He had a length of twine tied tightly around his neck, which he'd obviously chewed, in order to escape. He was covered in bites and bruises and the theory was that he had been used as a punch bag to train illegal fighting dogs. The former dog fight gang was suspected, but nothing was ever proved. In time he recovered and became his lovely self once again.

★　★　★

The first duty I copped was to guard the motor transport garage. It was probably the least-liked duty we were given. The garage was sited on the other side of town, about 5 miles from the headquarters. The garage or "MT Lines" as it was called, was sited on the grounds of a huge hotel, which had been destroyed by fire; only the blackened skeleton still stood. We learned that a lot of people had died in the fire, and, situated as it was on the banks of the River Rhine, the place was an eerie sight, even in fine weather. At four o'clock in the morning, it was a very strange place to be; the river mist swirling around the orange halogen lamps in the compound, the screeching of banging doors and the loud creaks from the old building, together with the wind howling across the compound like a myriad lost voices.

Oddly enough, the compound itself, which, according to locals, had been an old Jewish cemetery, had not been touched by the fire. About 100 yards square, it was bounded by an old-stone, two-metre high wall, which still contained the mounts of plaques which had been torn from the walls, and in one corner, on its side, was the sculpture of a large dog. This appeared to be very old and probably weighed several tons. The area was completely concreted over, and it was probable that many old Jewish graves were still underneath. On the southern wall was a large prefabricated shed, and it was a regular occurrence for rats to chase across the roof girders in full sight of the unfortunate viewer beneath.

My shift was from 5p.m. Saturday night to 7a.m. on Sunday morning. In Tiffy's office and behind his desk,

100

was a small fold-up camp bed, a flask of tea and, on the wall, a telephone. I was about halfway through a lurid paperback novel I had found on the desk, when the telephone rang — an insistent "BRR BRR" in the chill atmosphere of the office. I climbed off the camp bed and picked up the phone — there was nothing. All of a sudden, though, I heard the unearthly wailing of seagulls. I shouted like a fool down the receiver, but of an answer, there was nothing. I dropped the telephone receiver as if it was hot; I had never heard of seagulls flying about at night.

Apprehensively, I went to the door and looked out over the compound. Some thirty feet away, a huge bank of fog, fantastically lit by the overhead orange lamps. I looked to my left at the blackened skeleton structure, which stood out in the moonlit sky, where the stars were like frozen diamonds of light. Rising up out of the rolling bank and half way up the building, in what must have been one of the hotel corridors, was a nightmarish green blue glow that seemed to hover in the empty window space, and then it was gone. Incredibly, there was not a sound; certainly no seagulls wheeled and cried in the frozen air, no cars moved, no lights glimmered in the sleeping city, and I felt as if I was the last living being on the far edge of time.

I rang the B.A.O.R. switchboard, of which this telephone was an extension. A very irritable and sleepy operator answered. After a taut conversation, he advised me — (a) that no one could possibly have rung me without his knowledge and (b) to take more water with it! I told my colleagues about my experience, and

101

frankly they scoffed; the worst problem that anyone else had encountered was the discovery of a fat rat jammed into a teapot. Luckily, I was never asked to do the duty again.

I was questioned at length by our Commanding Officer about my experience, to which he listened intently, but made no comment.

Two days later, I had worse things to worry about. I was ordered to report to Colonel Bower's office. He was the District Provost Marshal and the head of all military police units in B.A.O.R. 4 District. His office was in the middle of a modern office block, and I was directed to the lift for the second floor. I jumped into the lift just as the doors were closing. There were already three occupants inside as I entered: a middle-aged man and two women. To my surprise, they also were headed for the office.

Eventually, I was called into the inner office and not only was the Colonel there, but also the District Chaplain. The Chaplain started the proceedings, and after saying a prayer for divine guidance, proceeded to lecture me on honour, morality and duty. I stood there totally bemused, but it was only when he told me that it was my duty to marry the lady, that the penny dropped.

"But this is impossible!" I cried desperately. "I cannot possibly be the father of anyone's baby — it is not me!"

The Colonel sighed, and, rising to his feet, crossed to the outer office. He opened the door and ushered in the three people I had seen in the lift. The man glared at me and rapped out an unpronounceable barrage of words that had the office typist in the outer room covering her ears. The other woman glared and looked accusingly at me, whilst the third woman was crying. I now saw that she was young and in the advanced stages of pregnancy.

To my intense relief, the situation was cleared up easily enough in the end; it turned out to be a case of mistaken identity. We had a sister company, the 2nd Infantry Division BOAR Provost Company, and somewhat amazingly, they also had a Peter Wicks. The army seemed incapable of differentiating between us, and this was to lead to a great deal of confusion in my army career.

The first month I was there, I spent all my working hours in the main office, stock taking in the Quarter Master's Stores, or attending lectures in the mess hall on map reading and forward planning, moriarty English civil law and even religious instruction. I also had to look after my motorcycles. By 5 o'clock, we were exhausted, but our day rarely ended there.

However, during my fifth week, I copped for town patrol duty with three other comrades. At 6.30 in the evening, we paraded into the main office, collected our pistols and paraded in front of the R.S.M.'s critical eye like self-conscious fashion models. The R.S.M. was acting duty officer that night.

We were driven to the centre of Dusseldorf and dropped off in various city locations, where we were given our beat instructions before being left to our own devices.

Because it was my first night, I was accompanied by Corporal Jacques, an old soldier of vast experience.

Our beat was down either side of the Koenigs Allee with its gleaming shop fronts and crowds of late-night shoppers. Kids were doing cartwheels in front of us, amiable drunken old soldiers thrusting forward through the crowds to shake our hands, and hordes of young urchins diving around us on skates, mapping our measured tread along the wide pavements. The prostitutes were the worst however, and we dreaded walking past them. They would be stationed every twenty-five yards along the pavement and took great delight in propositioning us — actions speaking louder than words.

My most abiding memory was of the two of us trying to walk steadily down the main street with an enormous German man, who must have been at least six feet six inches tall, draped around our necks. He was breathing whiskey fumes so strong, I was beginning to feel lightheaded.

What was amazing was that we met an awful lot of friendly old soldiers, claiming that they had only fought on the Eastern Front against the Russians. I remarked to Helmut Schmidt, our interpreter, how friendly everyone was, and he told me, quite seriously, that before the British came, people lived in a nightmare of fear and now they had been given a new lease of life.

Despatch Rider

Life continued pleasantly enough for several weeks, and then a bombshell dropped. As previously mentioned, military policemen were expected to be proficient drivers of either motorcycles or jeeps, which, by pure fluke, I was, having passed my driving test in a Bedford 15CWT truck. However, the aforementioned "other" Peter Wicks was a proficient motorcyclist, and here lay the problem. There had been several incidents of mistaken identity. There was such confusion that at one time the War Office insisted upon calling me "Wilkes" — army number notwithstanding.

Once again, they'd got us confused, and orders came through appointing me as the official dispatch rider to Embassies, outlying stations etc., a wonderful job, except for one small problem — I had only ridden a motorcycle once or twice previously, and that was only round a barrack square. I had never gone above second gear.

Frantic calls were made to the British Army of the Rhine local office, but it appeared that the army's mind was made up — official courier I was appointed to be, and official courier I was — there could be no argument.

Accordingly, after several fits and starts on a foggy November morning, I drove my unaccustomed motorcycle out of the main gate and to my first call; there were fourteen calls in all. My predecessor used to complete his run in less than five hours. I was grateful for the fog because few passersby would notice my predicament — a smart policeman on a highly polished motorcycle, screaming down the high-speed autobahn in second gear, at a mind boggling twenty-five miles per hour. Whenever I could, I practised changing gears up and down, until my left foot on the gear change lever was in danger of dropping off.

It took 15 hours to do that first day's run, but eventually after some six months, I was able to complete the run in four hours. I will never forget the excitement I felt when I crossed the 60mph barrier; the empty stretch of autobahn in front of me, dead straight for many miles, a keen wind at my back thrusting me down the shallow gradient, the road surface dividers clunk-clunking against my wheels. The heavy old motorbike flashed down the road at almost 80mph. I could almost visualize crowds cheering and a brass band playing, but all I got was an annoyed "CAW" from a disgruntled pair of crows, whose roadkill dinner I had interrupted.

All that winter, I persevered, and no one guessed my secret. By March I was thoroughly proficient in the handling of my machine, and motorcycling became a pleasure rather than a burden. I got to know the roads around Dusseldorf pretty well, and upon one occasion was overtaken by a gang of Birmingham Hells Angels on their way back to Holland. They were so delighted to see me, an English man, that I was practically dragged into a riders' café, where we all consumed copious amounts of Schnapps and Vodka. This resulted in me returning to the depot wearing the uniform of a Hells Angel, and with a German army helmet in place of the usual army crash helmet that I habitually wore. The upshot was that I had to apologise to the civilian staff for the upset I had caused by entering the kitchen in such a costume. I was also busted down to Private for seven days. Riding a motorcycle was not so much fun after all.

In the winter, there was no peak on the helmets to protect one's eyes from the driving rain, and the heavy motorcycle gauntlets we had to wear soaked up the rain like sponges. It became routine that every hour I would stop and let the engine idle for ten minutes, whilst I dried out the gloves on the exhaust pipe of the bike. The motorcycle great coats we were expected to wear were as stiff and unyielding as tank armour and almost as heavy. As for the army riding breeches . . . words fail me. Every time it rained, the breeches, which were already tight, would shrink, and they would shrink so much, I found it difficult to walk. Add to that the riding boots, tight to the calves and full of water, and woollen socks shredding themselves round the ankles, and you had an ensemble that was both uncomfortable and ridiculous, as-well as difficult to take off. It usually required two good friends to assist in tearing off the offending articles. The worst bit however was that the knees of the breeches had to be blanched white on the inside with white tennis shoe whitening cream.

Whenever it rained, it would leave both biker and motorcycle in pools of white shoe cleaner.

One day, whilst driving down an icy lane with a frozen stream running alongside, my feet down to maintain balance, I came across a crowd of people all skating or sliding on the hard ice surface. I was greeted with much mirth and enthusiasm. It turned out to be some sort of feast day being celebrated with nuns and clowns on ice. There were school children in fancy dress costume, and the town's silver band accompanying them for all they were worth. The mayor was there, together with his corporation. There were sledges, wine barrels, hot chestnuts and even a quartet of leather-trousered, back-slapping German dancers.

A very pretty, laughing Rhine maiden flagged me down, and I was led to meet the mayor. Coincidently, it transpired that his daughter was a doctor at the Radcliffe Hospital in Oxford, the very hospital in which I was born.

An hour later, having received some very extravagant hospitality, I was on my way.

One late November day found me riding back to H.Q. The temperature was in the minus degrees, the winds were buffeting the old motorbike, and the handlebars seemed to have taken on a life of their own. Several times, I rode perilously close to a ditch. Despite the minus degrees of cold. I found myself sweating under my heavy despatch rider's great coat. To make matters worse, I was travelling over bare heathland, without a

108

tree or a bush in sight, and I was desperate for a pee; if I could have ridden the bike cross-legged, I would have done.

Then it started to rain. I would have gone by the side of the road, but there was too much traffic streaming past, and my clothes were highly visible. I gritted my teeth and rode desperately on.

At length, I came across a tall stone wall behind which was a steep sugar loaf shaped hill. A row of dark, forbidding trees led up to a steep path flanking a gravelled roadway. The wind howled through the treetops like a wild animal, and the trees themselves bowed and genuflected like living dancers trying to lift their toes up out of the sticky mud.

I pushed the bike behind the wall, and then realised that I could still be seen from the road. I looked into the embrace of the clutching trees, then I gritted my teeth and trudged on up until I came upon the brow of the hill. There was almost a full moon, and the grass leapt and dashed against the knoll like a silver grey sea of pounding waves. I looked down onto a most curious building. I had once seen a building like this in West Wycombe, Bucks; a part of the notorious Hell Fire Caves. As far as I could tell, this building was no more than a wall of arches set in a hexagonal shape and approximately some 60 ft in diameter. There were many monuments around the walls. Obviously the building was many years old and had been in use as a graveyard for some considerable time.

Even as I looked, there came, borne upon gusts of wind, the awful stuff of nightmares, a sound so familiar

109

to my youth, a voice of hate, so malignant, that for a second or two I was paralysed with fear — it was the voice of Hitler!

And then something struck me on the helmet — a smooth round pebble from a slingshot. This was followed by another, which hit my goggles, somehow missing the lens, but breaking the metal nosepiece. Several other stones thudded into my body, the heavy great coat absorbing the impact. Through streaming eyes, I saw them; about a dozen black-clad figures coming out from behind the monuments. Several carried slingshots, the rest appeared to be carrying crude clubs. All were advancing upon me, their intention obvious. My fear suddenly vanished. I heard the panting voice of hysteria, with its message of hate towards the Jews. I thought of my school friend, Neville. I had been there when his parents had received the news that his grandparents, cousins and aunt had all perished in Auschwitz Concentration Camp.

A blind, unreasoning fury overtook me. I had a lightweight Sten gun slung across my shoulders which I was taking back to the armoury for repair as the cartridge clip was jammed onto the gun. Because to all intents and purposes the gun was still live, it had been unusually decided to return the gun with me. I also had my trusty old six shooter with me, and I now drew it; but it was all a bluff. We were not allowed to carry bullets, and, since an article revealing as much had appeared in one of the so-called newspapers of the day, they most likely knew that we were not allowed to carry ammunition, let alone fire a gun without having filled

110

in forms in duplicate, triplicate and most likely in quadruplicate as well, it meant that I was a sitting duck.

As they got closer, I saw that most of the group were wearing some sort of black uniform consisting of flat leather caps and American style black army boots over black overalls. I had heard of such groups before, but had never seen one. These were the self-styled guerrillas of the Third Reich — Hitler's werewolves.

I noticed that a tall dandified creature wearing a black opera cloak with scarlet interior and a large swastika armband seemed to be leading the attack. I waved my pistol threateningly, which seemed to stop them for a moment, and then seeing that I was not in a position to fire, they crept forward again.

I reached behind me and took off the Sten, and then using the classic firing position, I waved them forward.

It was at that moment that a rock caught me across the head, and I fell to one knee, jolting the Sten gun, which sprayed forth its lethal hail of bullets. I saw the leader go down with a shriek of agony (he had taken two bullets to the leg), and the rest of the figures ran.

I performed what first aid I could then dragged him over to a pillar set centrally in the graveyard and forced his arms around the base, securing him with my handcuffs; it was my intention to leave him until he could be picked up. I then realised that I still needed to pee! The phonograph was still pouring out its message of hate, and so I decided to relieve myself on it whilst in full view of my enemy.

So much for the best laid plans of mice and men. What I did not see in time was the live cable powering the phonograph. There was a flash, and I felt as if I had been kicked in the stomach, such was the force of the electrical shock I had generated. I staggered back to my bike, leaving my prisoner crying piteously.

The trouble was that I had lost my bearings, and it was two days later before a German police patrol found the scene of the incident. The prisoner and my handcuffs were gone; his friends must have sawn through the handcuffs to release him.

All was not lost, however, for two days later, he was picked up in a local hospital with a shattered leg. They told me that he had blubbered like a baby. He was one of the nastier pieces of Nazidom, and he lost no time in giving up his fellow gang members. As far as I know, he died in prison.

Dress Rehearsal

The following spring we had a visit from Governor Dwight D. Eisenhower himself. This was of course before he became President of the U.S.A., when he was still our Supreme Allied Armies Commander. It was decided that 102 Provost Company, in other words us, were to form the guard of honour at the airport.

It was probably the worst decision ever made — we were hopeless! Why we had been chosen and not the Irish Guards or the Black Watch was a mystery to me. Some of my colleagues had not stamped on a parade ground in several years. True, we looked smart, but as for drill — we were like broken puppets.

We had just two weeks to learn the routine. Those of us who had recently come from the Depot were not too bad, but I'm sorry to report that Sergeant Major Causon, (who was probably at the time the Army's most efficient policeman) was as hopeless a drill instructor as could ever be found in the British army.

Sergeant Major Causon was a proud man, and, like so many old soldiers, he had been drafted into the army during the Second World War. For years, he had been a village constable, with little or no need for parade-style duties, but such was the need for military policemen, he had been fast-tracked into a position of great responsibility. Then, when the war ended, he had opted to remain with the corps. The problem was that his training in parade drill had been overlooked.

The Sergeant Major took up his stance at the head of the parade, and he certainly looked impressive. He shouted a command. The command should have been:

"PARADE BY THE LEFT — QUICK MARCH!"

But whether he was suffering from stage or parade fright, the command rang out:

"PARADE BEST FOOT FORWARD — MARCH!"

There was chaos. Several soldiers, totally baffled as to which was their best foot, stopped still, other marchers cannoned into them, with the result that several were buffeted over the pavement.

Hooch tore himself from his master's grasp and laid into his mortal enemy, the Alsatian from over the road.

The old German Servicemen, who lived in a hostel directly opposite, laughed almost fit to burst. Relations with them were friendly enough; in fact, at least half a dozen of them were found sitting upon the low wall opposite, playing cards or chess with noisy good humour whilst drinking copious amounts of home-brewed beer, which was so strong that even our dog Hooch couldn't stomach it.

The Sergeant Major, face as red as a beetroot, shouted, "COLUMN ABOUT FACE!" Which was a command totally unknown in the British Army. I shouldn't wonder if it wasn't a direct result of watching a Colonel Custer American Army film. As a result, some turned about to the left and stumbled, because the order had been given forcing them to turn on the wrong foot. Many of them stood stock still, whilst their comrades at the rear, who had not heard the order, ploughed resolutely on until the Sergeant Major was backed against a high strong wall.

It was probably unfortunate that this was the time of day when hordes of young mothers passed our building to collect their offspring from the infant's school just up the road. Word swiftly got around that something was going on, and suddenly we were besieged by hordes of onlookers. It was pandemonium! Children ran unrestrained around and among us, and at least one old soldier laughed so heartily we had to call an ambulance, fearing that he had had a heart attack.

For three days, we went through the hideous embarrassment of parading in front of our neighbours, and then, on the fourth day, it rained.

We were all congregated in the junior dining room when the Church Army mobile canteen appeared outside our front door. Twice a day we were visited by the refreshment van belonging to the English Church Army, which was a similar organisation to the Salvation Army, run by a Major and two lady helpers. Whilst he was in the hall serving out buns, shoe laces and razorblades, someone asked him how he was doing with the Church Lads Brigade. He ran a very impressive and popular band of church lads' volunteers, who had a first class brass band and were made up of a mixture of sons from the married family army estate and some German boys. I had seen them on several occasions at their church parades at the Rhine Centre, and they were impressive. Their average age was only about fourteen, but they could put a formation of guards to shame.

The problem was presented to the Reverend Major (I forget his name). He came up with a stunning formation. Five N.C.O.s were chosen (of which I was not one), and these were interspersed along the length of the column. There were to be six manoeuvres, each to be preceded by a blast from a whistle. Orders were to be whispered down the ranks and on one whistle blast from a chosen soldier in the ranks, the whole formation would turn, advance and check with perfect military precision.

It worked! That afternoon we paraded again, and to the astonishment of the old soldiers, put in a perfect performance full of confidence.

The next day we marshalled again. The trouble was that one old soldier had spotted our ploy and introduced his own whistle into the proceedings, blowing with marked abandonment, causing us to halt, stumble and stop until we felt dizzy.

There was another problem. When the assembled company came to attention, it sounded like a rattle of machine gun fire. The Reverend Major was consulted again.

"Does anyone play a drum?" he asked. I told him I could, so a side drum was borrowed from the Boy's Brigade and camouflaged by a 102 Provost Company sign to cover its original logo. I practised drumming so hard that my colleagues were volunteering for extra duties to get away from the noise, but it worked. Because he could no longer sabotage us, our whistle

116

blower gave up in disgust. We still blew our whistles, but these were now enveloped by the sound of a drum roll from my furiously bashed drum.

It was then that our saboteurs pulled another stunt to upset our equilibrium. Three of the old soldiers came goose-stepping down the pavement in front of us dressed in their old army uniforms for the benefit of the laughing crowd. With uniforms tightly stretched at the seams, they goose-stepped daintily as a duck at first waddle. All their uniforms were old and obviously made for men much thinner in a previous life. They looked ridiculous as they smirked at their audience.

We were nonplussed, then someone suddenly started impersonating geese with a loud, "HONK, HONK, HONK!", and as one man, we all joined in. The ladies mainly clapped and cheered, and some even joined in with the honking chorus, as did the three old German soldiers we used to call Laurel, Hardy and Kaiser Bill, for want of their real names.

Laurel was tall and very thin, whilst Hardy was so small and fat that the kids called him Humpty Dumpty or Mister Egg. Kaiser Bill, named because of his drooping walrus moustache had a pronounced wobble, and looked as if he was about to burst into tears at the drop of a hat. All three of them were as tight as frogs (born out by the empty bottles on the opposite pavement), and to great applause from the watching crowd, the trio joined in and goose-stepped as delicately as a set of overweight chorus boys.

It was a shame that on the same side of the road, but hidden from the rest of us, appeared a young lady

117

pushing a toddler in a pushchair, accompanied by her small toy poodle bitch. Behind her came Hooch's sworn enemy, showing a marked interest in what Hooch considered to be his girlfriend. With a throaty growl, Hooch hurtled towards his enemy, with his lead streaming behind him; unfortunately, as Laurel goose-stepped past Hooch, his delicately pointed toe caught in the dog's lead. Somehow or other, Laurel pivoted on one foot, spun and kicked Hardy in the stomach, before collapsing in front of him.

Hardy went down over Laurel like a felled ox, whilst Kaiser Bill, who was obviously in an alcoholic daze, sat down upon the pavement and proceeded to take his boots off.

Meanwhile, the dog fight continued apace with neither gaining the upper paw, until both were booted back by their irate keepers. The poodle eyed the combatants disdainfully and proceeded upon her way. When Hooch swaggered up to her, as befits a champion, she bit him hard on the ear.

Further revelations were to follow when Hardy was unceremoniously yanked to his feet. It proved that his too-tight uniform had given up the unequal struggle with his voluptuous curves and split down his spine from shoulder blades to builder's bum and beyond. Upon rising, it could be seen that his whole back was tattooed in glorious colour with a fox hunt in full cry and the fox disappearing with only his tail visible.

That night, peace was declared between us and the old soldiers, and they all came over with their carers to what is termed in army parlance "a glorious peace op".

The Inspection

At last, the great day dawned. The tailor and his assistants had worked overtime to smarten up our Sunday best, and we were now on our way to the airport in a big military troop carrier. It promised to be a hot day; the sun shone, and, stiff as tailors' dummies in our uniforms, we sweltered.

Eventually, we drew up in ranks of three in front of the red carpet laid down where the plane was to land. The carpet, though impressively long was of a lightweight, flexible material, and was clearly unsuitable for the purpose, for now a warm breeze had sprung up and begun to ruffle the edges of the said carpet.

Dust started to blow around us, and our newly whitened webbing belts, holsters and straps were looking decidedly grubby. We tried to protect the gleam of our highly polished toe caps by rubbing them on the calves of our trousers, so that we must have looked like a gaggle of flamingos.

After some minutes, the plane landed, and just as the fuselage door opened, the carpet developed a life of its own and flapped gently down the runway, with several airport staff in hot pursuit (we heard that pieces of it were found on the autobahn several days later).

From the plane poured a solid phalanx of soldier bodyguards, all above average height and completely obscuring the smaller General Eisenhower. The assembled "brass" took a chance upon which section of bodyguards the General might be surrounded by and led their parties in determined forays through the human forest, in order to shake the great man's hand.

The General swept by us like a dose of salts, straight into the reception hall. It transpired that there had been a threat upon his life and his bodyguards were taking no chances. All that work we had put in with whistles and drums was for nothing. Just to show that we could do it, we did a quick demonstration of our newly acquired skills for the benefit of the main onlookers and then we headed for the nearest bar.

One week later, a bombshell was dropped which made up for our disappointment at the airport. We were informed that we had been chosen for a snap inspection and stock take. The following morning, two enormous American automobiles arrived at our front gate and disgorged a dozen very smart and keen-looking American officers, complete with briefcases and slide rules.

To say that we were caught on the hop is no understatement. The duty Sergeant was sitting shirt-sleeved and braced at his desk behind a high fence barrier in the outer office, reading the *Daily Mirror*, whilst Hooch snored peacefully in a basket at his feet, when the officers burst in.

Sergeant Matthews leapt hastily to his feet, knocking his mug of tea all over his newspaper, whilst stubbing

120

out his cigarette on the "no smoking" sign prominently affixed to his desk.

It seemed that all these officers were specialist officers in their own right. We learned afterwards that the officer who inspected the fabric of the building and the Quartermaster's Stores had in his previous working life been the manager of a large hotel.

The Sergeant Major, who had been planning a day off, arrived unshaven, and a keen observer would have been able to see that he still had his pyjama jacket on underneath his battledress blouse.

We were awakened by the strident clangour of the fire alarm and struggled bleary eyed outside to the back yard, where we stood shivering in a strange assortment of sleep attire.

A roll call was taken, and then we were all sent back to our rooms to change; there would be no breakfast that morning. All our kit had to be laid out for inspection on our beds, and these were critically assessed by the keen-eyed American officer. Afterwards, all available personnel, other than those on office or night duty, were ordered to the garages for a motorcycle and jeep inspection.

We duly paraded up to the old burnt-out hotel on the banks of the Rhine, where we were split into sections of ten apiece, with one of the American examiners allocated to each group.

As I may have mentioned, we had enough vehicles for four times our size, all of which had to be kept in perfect running order. First of all we were requested to start up all the bikes. Tiffy first poured a thimbleful of

121

some mysterious liquid into each tank; he called it his elixir. Whatever it was, the engines exploded into life with just one kick. This was surprising, because the engines were normally very difficult to start, sometimes taking several minutes to tick over sweetly. The American officers were impressed, and when we knew the secret, so were we, for Tiffy had poured a thimbleful of whisky into each empty tank before topping up with petrol.

We were quizzed individually upon each of the machines under our care. Vehicles were inspected critically by each officer, who had a big check list. Drivers sweated under the bonnets, and even the undersides of the jeeps were checked. In some cases the wheels had to be removed to inspect the brakes.

We had a special section containing the highly polished jeeps, complete with sirens. These were used for motorcade escort duties only. Olive green, with gleaming brass accessories, they sported very powerful sirens, flashing lights and loudspeakers. Next to them stood my Embassy bike which had only just been delivered.

Up to this time, all the army motorbikes had been B.S.A. 500cc side-valve motorcycles, which were slow and ponderous with girder forks. The matchless 3 GL had only just been introduced into the British army, and I was one of the first to ride one on duty. It was a dream machine; lighter and smaller than the old B.S.A. bikes. The 3 GL was equipped with the new telescopic front forks, which made for a more comfortable ride. Although its engine was only 350 cc in capacity, it could leave much larger bikes standing, both in top speed and acceleration. The Americans were most impressed, and one even rode it around the yard.

It was after that that the bombshell dropped; we were all told to produce our driving licences for inspection. Not a problem you might think, except that I did not have one! It was humiliating when I had to explain that I had never been issued with one and had not even been on a course — the whole sorry saga was trotted out. There was an anxious, high-level conference, and the result was that I was issued with a licence on the spot, signed by the General himself.

Even Hooch, that sagacious dog, proved he was no ornament by leading one of the officers to a corner of the yard, where four dead rats were laid neatly side by side.

The following day, Hooch was promoted to Corporal, although he was not as impressed by the extra stripe as by the beer ration.

Petra — A Damsel in Distress

Early October found me and Ken Stone travelling along on the autobahn in Ken's jeep. It was about ten o'clock at night, and the fog was so thick that the visibility was down to a mere ten feet. I sat frozen upon the flat bonnet of the jeep, like some old ship's figurehead, trying to guide Ken with some very original hand signals in an effort to keep the vehicle on the road. I had never seen fog so thick. Not even the London pea-soupers could compete with fog like this; it was a complete white out.

We were on our way back home, having been out to take statements following a particularly nasty accident — a battle tank had pulled out during the night and crushed a tent full of German service organization personnel. We ourselves were not called out until two days later, by which time we could do little more than take statements from witnesses, and there were not too many of those.

Anyway, there we were, freezing to bits in a vehicle with no heater and only a canvas roof, travelling along the autobahn at a mind-boggling five miles an hour, sometimes drifting towards the left hand verge and, at other times, the right hand verge. Occasionally, great German lorries would thunder past us, festooned with arc lights rather like ships in the night. But for the last half hour or so, there had been nothing.

Then, suddenly, a shape loomed out of the haze before us. Ken swore and stamped on his brakes causing me to slide off the bonnet. We were scared out of our minds; the autobahn at night is a pretty spooky place, and to see this ghostly shape materialise, having just interviewed the survivors of the tank accident, sparked our imaginations and shook us up, to say the least.

We clung to each other in terror for a brief moment, before common sense prevailed. What our weary and edgy minds had viewed as a ghostly shape, turned out to be an old eiderdown. A closer look revealed two small pairs of feet.

I walked round to the other side to investigate, and there, underneath the eiderdown, were two small figures — a young woman around twenty years old and a little girl about six years old. My first impression of them was of two frightened pairs of eyes. Both were dressed in rather curious clothing that had obviously been made for a much older woman and had been inexpertly tailored to meet their needs. The woman was dark skinned, presumably from a life on the land, and the girl, who was barefoot, was shivering uncontrollably. As I came towards them, the woman pushed the girl behind her and produced a large knife.

She was obviously terrified and wild, like an animal; it took a great deal of persuasion to get both of them into the jeep. The little girl was like a zombie, and all the time she was with us, I didn't hear her utter a single

125

word. Anyway, we clad them in our uniform great coats and took them to the Salvation Army hostel to see the Reverend in charge.

The pair were extremely anxious throughout the journey and the woman clung to her knife, waving it threateningly in our direction every three of four minutes. We were intensely relieved to deposit them in the Salvation Army's care. We said our goodbyes and headed back to our depot.

We had a typist called Elsie, a beautiful girl, very religious and moral, and she was walking out with a Salvation Army Major. It was she who told us what had happed after we left the hostel.

The woman had taken a meal there and then abruptly run away, taking the girl with her. They hunted high and low for her and eventually found her hiding in one of the big wheely bins. It was a worrying period, as it was apparent that the little girl had contracted pneumonia. The woman was persuaded to leave her daughter in the good hands of the Salvation Army whilst she took on a small part-time job waitressing to support them both. As far as we were concerned, that was the end of it for us, but then Elsie told me a remarkable story.

The woman's name was Petra. She was of Dutch descent and had been a member of the Communist Party. The German Nazis had taken her family and transported them as slaves to East Germany, where, as a girl of barely sixteen, she had been grossly mistreated. She had been put to work on a farm owned by a local Nazi official, where she was kept in a stable by the man and forced to eat pig swill from the trough. He had taken great delight in tormenting her and had raped her daily, so that she soon found herself with child. His wife had hated the girl and covered her in cigarette burns.

In due course, the baby was born, and he placed her in an orphanage. For four more years, Petra continued to suffer, but she clung to one great hope — that she would be re-united with her daughter.

In time, the child was given to a prominent German family to be brought up as their own daughter, but Petra was determined to get the child back.

In 1944, the Russians entered the area, and the farmer's wife, who had so badly mistreated Petra, came to her, begging for protection from the Red Army, who it was said were doing dreadful things to Nazi women. The farmer had vanished, leaving his wife to face the music alone.

Petra took his shotgun and marched the wife into the stall where she had lived for so long. She tied her hands behind her back, stood her in the pig trough and then placed a noose around her neck before tying it around an overhead rafter, forcing her to stand for many hours. Then as a final gesture, she stabbed her in the leg with a carving knife and left her in agony.

Petra packed a small suitcase with the Nazi couples' valuables, grabbed what clothing she could find and fled. She knew where the orphanage was because her master often collected pig swill from there. But when she got there, it was empty and deserted — the occupants having fled.

Beds and furniture were still intact, although much of the furniture had been turned upside down by the Russian troops looking for loot.

The office was also still intact, although anything of value, such as typewriters, had been taken. The filing cabinet had been forced open, and many of its papers destroyed, but wonder of wonders — lying half-burnt in the grate, was the register of the people who had adopted the children, and even their addresses.

Whilst she was searching the papers, she heard a noise behind her. Turning she found a Russian soldier with a Tommy gun pointed straight at her.

Petra was led in front of a Russian official and despite her protestations that she was not a German, was put in a hard labour camp for 12 months, where she was given a hard time by the other prisoners. It was during this time that she acquired the knife for protection, and it soon became apparent that she was prepared to use it without compunction.

At the end of the 12 months, she was shown the gate. Returning to where she had carefully hidden her suitcase, she was overjoyed to find it still intact. The next thing was to locate her daughter.

Careful enquiries elicited the information that the would-be foster parents had been tied up to the railings in front of the house and burnt to death. Whilst she was combing the ruins of East Berlin, she came across small bands of feral children, who lived among the ruins.

Then she saw her — her daughter! She had not the smallest doubt it was her; there were certain physical

128

similarities and defects which proved to her that this really was her child.

There was now the problem of getting the child back to her. A fourteen-year-old boy whose range of survival skills was limited led the little gang of waifs and strays. A short confrontation and the production of the knife convinced him to hand over the reins of leadership to Petra. He was fed up with the responsibility of leadership anyhow and stepped down to become her second-in-command.

Under her leadership, the group soon prospered. In fact they became feared among the citizens of East Berlin. The little gang had now grown to fifty, and Petra became their modern day Fagin. They survived by using their criminal skills: shoplifting, mugging, intimidation, and any other criminal activity that would bring in money to the small group.

The headquarters was a large cellar in a bombed-out site. Although the group prospered, Petra's daughter was still unable to speak; it was believed that she was traumatised by the brutal deaths of her adoptive parents.

Some eighteen months into Petra's leadership, one of the children came to her and told her that one of the "creepos", as they called the Communist Police, had taken one of the girls into his hut and was attempting to rape her.

Petra burst through the door and told the child to run — which she did. The man's lascivious attentions were now focused on her, and, being much larger and stronger than her, he managed to get behind her. She

129

bent forward, and as she did so, took the knife out of her boot and, stabbing upwards behind her legs, succeeded in castrating him.

Obviously the "creepos'" would now be after her, so she decided to leave Berlin, leaving her second-in-command in charge.

The first problem was to get out of the Russian zone, which she succeeded in doing by crawling with others under a mass of barbed wire fencing.

Once she and her daughter were safe in West Berlin, she had hunted for transport to take her into the western zone. A Swiss lorry driver was found who, for an extortionate sum, was prepared to take both her and her daughter through to Amsterdam.

Accordingly, she and her daughter rode in the high cab for many hundreds of miles. In the cab was an old eiderdown, which the driver normally draped over the engine to keep it warm. Petra and her daughter wrapped themselves in it in one corner of the cab and slept during the drive.

Shortly before we had met her, the Swiss driver had tried to force himself on her. Fighting back, she had produced the knife and stabbed him in the arm. With blood pouring from his wound, he had literally kicked her out of the cab and onto the concrete, before driving off with both her possessions and her beloved daughter.

About two miles further on, he had pushed the child out and, in a fit of remorse, had left the eiderdown on the road with her. Neither Petra nor her daughter had shoes, and all their money and possessions had gone with the lorry driver. It was in this predicament that we had found them — cold, hungry, wet and shoeless.

Although Petra lived in mortal fear of Germans, our typist, Elsa, succeeded in taking her under her wing, and the couple settled down to a spell of relative happiness. Petra had her job in the hostel as a waitress and kitchen hand, and Elsa, who was a dab hand with a sewing machine, produced many fine clothes for the pair of them.

The little girl soon began to speak, and it was some twelve months later that we heard that Elsa had managed to secure them a train fare to Amsterdam, and that she had later received a letter from Petra to say that she had found her grandmother, although her parents were long since dead.

We had a Sergeant, Sgt. Barnum (not his real name), and he was a crook. Every soldier in B.A.O.R. was allowed to purchase, for his personal use, 200 cigarettes at a much reduced price — literally for pennies. The good Sergeant was in charge of allocating duties to us poor mortals, and we soon discovered that by allocating our cigarette ration to him, we could avoid some of the more onerous duties that we could be saddled with.

British cigarettes commanded a high price in Germany, and he ran such an extensive operation, that he saved all of his pay and purchased two Mercedes Benz taxis, which he operated with civilian drivers all over Dusseldorf.

And that wasn't the only scam he had going. Once a week, he travelled down on the troop train to the Hook of Holland port with our interpreter, his partner in crime. The scam was small but inventive and brought them in a great deal of money. Helmot, our interpreter, would walk the length of the train offering packets of pornographic playing cards to the squaddies going on leave, knowing they would have money to burn. The Sergeant, passing as a civilian worker dressed in mufti, would follow at a discreet distance and make a careful note of all the purchasers.

At the port, he would reappear in full Military Police rig and arrest all those who had purchased the pictures. The purchasers, who had already spent an expensive sum, now found that the pictures were confiscated and were given the choice of either being arrested, with all the scandal that that would involve, or paying an exorbitant price to the Sergeant to avoid prosecution.

The whole process was repeated on the way back, resulting in the two men amassing enough money to start a dubious nightclub in Dusseldorf, which was nicknamed the "Snake Pit". Both men ran this scam quite happily, without fear of detection, for months . . . until they got greedy.

As each passenger embarked for the night sea crossing, they were issued with three blankets: two grey and one blue. In the corner of each blue blanket, the scammers, along with the issuing store man, burnt a cigarette hole on the edge, so as to be almost invisible and detectable only to a very keen eye. Non-smokers were annoyed to find that they were being charged for causing fire damage to the blankets, but they could escape prosecution by donating a sizeable contribution in the "Barnum Friends Society's" collection tin. All such contributions went directly into the pockets of the Sergeant and his associates.

Eventually, the pair picked upon a Sergeant Major in the Special Investigation Branch, who was a dedicated non-smoker and who had photographic evidence of the store men burning the holes. One by one, each store man confessed, divulging the names of his co-conspirators.

One thing led to another, and the Sergeant was Court Martialed and finished up in the military prison, where he still continued to run some inventive scams.

Desperate Manoeuvres

In November, it snowed so heavily that it lay thick upon the ground. It was then that our masters decided that the British army should undertake our first major military manoeuvre in arctic conditions. Our section was called upon to drive to a remote spot in the Black Forest and pitch our little open-ended tent in a clearing next to a forest crossroads.

I had with me the matchless 350 O.H.V. GL38 motorcycle, the suitability of which I was meant to be assessing for the British army.

We huddled together in our little tents, which we cunningly packed around with snow for greater insulation. The Black Forest was aptly named; it was a huge, menacing, shadowy forest, crisscrossed by paths of perfect white show and collapsed branches.

Our headquarters was set up in an ancient, long-deserted pigsty, and it was in its walls that our cook had set up a paraffin cooker and, together with his assistant, was very soon brewing up tea using melted snow, in which floated the occasional acorn. We ate tinned bacon, stew and beans and even twenty year old tinned chocolate. We ate snow, washed in snow, bathed in snow and even shaved in snow.

The first night we were there, in accordance with army customs, it was decided that we would all guard the camp in shifts of two hours a piece. My shift was due to take place at 2 o'clock in the morning, so I went to bed at 6p.m . . . and slept until 10 o'clock the following morning.

I awoke to the birds singing and snow falling off branches — but otherwise, all was silence. I thought, "This is strange!"

I had slept straight through, and nobody had woken me. Why? I hopped round to the cooks' mess, still encased in my sleeping bag. To my astonishment, the camp was deserted. It turned out that my motorcycle, the one I was so proud of, had vanished, along with two army jeeps.

Apparently, my so-called comrades had taken it upon themselves to go for a drink or three, to which end they had taken the two jeeps some half a dozen miles along one of the tracks to a traditional Black Forest cafe.

It all boiled down to the fact that four of my friends (one Sergeant in charge and three corporals) were due to leave the army the following week, and they were suffering from a condition known as "demob happy", which induced them to take liberties that, under normal circumstances, they would never have done.

Anyway, as was quite normal with these communities, they were welcomed with open arms and were given large quantities of Schnapps, one of the most potent drinks known to man. It appears that a lot of friendly banter had arisen between the two parties, that is my friends and the German drinking population, over the merits of the German BMW motorcycle and the British Norton. It culminated in one of my inebriated friends driving back down to camp and loading my motorbike, which was not a known model in Germany, onto the back of the jeep and then demonstrating its versatility, presumably to win a bet. One of the Germans brought down his big old BMW, and they raced around the clearings, showing off, as was all too common with British troops.

By midnight, they were totally skint and well into their cups. Money had to come from somewhere to provide more Schnapps. And that's when the unthinkable happened. An old local farmer who had been admiring the bike, offered to buy it. At that time they had amassed a counter bill of nearly one hundred marks and, unfortunately, they had no money to pay. The motorcycle was worth considerably more than 100 marks, so the deal was done. They sold it for 120 marks — the 20 marks being my share.

Needless to say, there were some pretty sore heads by the time realisation dawned the next day. I was innocent, but I would have to bear the blame. To say that I was not happy would be putting it mildly. Our initial problem was that we did not know the name of the person who had bought the bike, though one of the café regulars was under the impression that his son worked in a factory about 20 miles away and that he had purchased the bike for his son to ride to work on.

We were in a real fix. If we had gone to the civilian police, I would have been Court Martialed for sure. Eventually, a plan was hatched, and we drove down to

136

the nearest town, in which there were a dozen factories, and we hung around outside the factory gates.

Eventually, the son of the purchaser was seen to enter a factory gate on my motorcycle. We waited until late afternoon, then approached him. We offered him 120 marks for the motorcycle, which was what his father had paid for it. He refused point blank; he wanted at least 500 marks for it. This we had not got. He also threatened to go to the local newspaper. He had us over a barrel. A lot of telephone calls were made to sympathisers both in B.A.O.R. and the Depot, with a result of us raising 540 marks, which he accepted, and I rode the bike back to camp.

It was decided that it was too risky to have the bike outside Dusseldorf as it was attracting too much interest, and so I returned to Headquarters, and the duty driver took my place on the scheme.

The Arab

I was settling down to a quiet relaxing Saturday afternoon off, when the telephone rang — it was Q ringing up for transport. Q had a charmed life as a soldier, because every time something unpleasant materialised, such as manoeuvres in the snow, he claimed leave of absence on various pretexts, and while the rest of the Company was sweating or freezing, depending on the weather, he would be sitting nicely ensconced in a warm study, drinking lager and eating sausage and chips.

Under normal circumstances, his request would not have been a problem. Duty drivers rarely had to do anything more taxing at the weekend than pick up the occasional piece of mail or shoot down to the local wine merchants for a bottle of wine for the Officers' Mess. Even if I had to pick up a passenger on the pillion of the bike, providing I carried a spare helmet, there was no problem.

Anyway, Q rang to ask if I would collect him from the "Woes and Joes Club".

"Certainly Q; I'll be there in 10 minutes," I said.

The Woes and Joes Club occupied the top floor of the very modern *Presidium* (Police Station), which was a large imposing building rented to the British Army, and it presented one small problem which had totally slipped my mind. On the second floor were the medical offices of the police headquarters and on the fourth Saturday afternoon of the month, the ladies of the street were required by law to attend for medical examinations. I had the dubious pleasure of having to walk through them, being propositioned at least 100 times on the way. This may have seemed bad enough, but there was worse to come.

I duly presented myself at the Woes and Joes Club, and the Steward informed me that they had a large party there and as Q was in need of sobering, I was advised to wait.

While I sat waiting, the steward offered me a small plate of caviar and a glass of champagne, which I accepted. I cannot pretend that I enjoyed the caviar, in fact it tasted horrible, but I could not complain. Ten minutes later, and after what seemed like several trips to the lavatory, Q appeared. I could not believe my eyes — in place of Q was an Arab Sheik. He looked as if he had slept in the Arab costume for at least a week, and he stank of booze. He had been sick, and his clothes were in the laundry. I nearly had a fit when I realised that I was going to have to take him on the back of my motorbike in all his regalia. I did ask them if they had something to cover him, but they had nothing.

There he was, this man with an enormous paunch, hook nose and with a 5 o'clock shadow, waddling towards me. I couldn't decide whether to laugh or cry. Apparently, he had not been home for three or four days, which did not help. His wife was not happy, either.

I decided to try and sneak him down the back stairs and get him home as quickly as possible, as he only lived a mile away. I was trying not to arouse curiosity, but unfortunately I walked straight into a hoard of ladies of the street, who literally mobbed us as we came round the corner. My passenger was collecting cards as if there was no tomorrow. The next thing I knew, he had vanished into one of the lifts with a very large lady, leaving me standing like a fool, surrounded by women.

He finally reappeared with his turban disarrayed, so that it kept hanging over his face like a pair of curtains. He was more unsteady than ever. I escaped the clutches of the ladies, but not without losing my armband and half my tie. I was also covered in lipstick. I finally managed to get the great fool out to the rear courtyard, where the bike stood.

After several false starts, I managed to get him seated upon the pillion of the bike and finally, having been push-started by scores of high heeled young ladies, and with him standing up on the back foot rests, swearing undying love and blowing kisses to the cheering mob, we were on our way. He continued to wave and call after every pretty girl he saw; frequently leaning over so far that we were in imminent danger of crashing. Every time I had to turn the bike to go right, instead of leaning his body into the angle of our ride, he resolutely balanced his body the opposite way, so that the bike steered an erratic course between kerb stones.

I toiled down the street at the awe-inspiring speed of ten miles an hour. Unfortunately we caught the attention of all the kids in the area who were doing cartwheels for tourists. Many of them reached up to touch him, and the silly fool pushed money into their grasping little hands.

"Just another hundred yards," I thought, "and this nightmare will be over."

The block of high-rise apartments in which he lived was just around the corner. "Just a few more yards, and I can drop him off, then I'm home and free."

Was I heck!

At that moment, the large staff car of the Provost Marshall himself pulled up alongside us. I groaned inwardly. I had already escaped one Court Martial that week, now it looked as though I was in danger of another one.

The driver wound down his window.

"Compliments of the Colonel, he would like a word."

I managed to get my passenger off the motorbike, and he stood and swayed, while I went around to the back door of the Colonel's compartment, aware that I was covered in lipstick, armband gone and what remained of my tie half way round my collar. I saluted him as smartly as I could.

"What's this man?" asked the Colonel. "Are you some circus freak show?"

I thought hard. Meanwhile, Q was still handing out money to the kids and swaying gently.

"Who is this individual?" he demanded "And what's he doing on your bike?"

I lied desperately. "I was ordered to pick him up sir. I understand that he is an Arab delegate at the Conference (there was a big peace conference going on in the town) and his transport has let him down."

The Colonel looked at me suspiciously. "Umph!"

The next moment he addressed Q in what I believe was Arabic.

Oh my goodness, I thought, that's torn it. Then miracle of miracles, Q answered in the same language like a native born. You could have knocked me down with a feather. They chatted for a minute or two in Arabic, and then the Colonel got out and bravely saluted Q and shook his hand.

"Well done," he said to me, and then he was gone.

I felt weak at the knees. We had just a few yards to go, and then we were at the front gate of his married quarters.

He seemed to sober up rather suddenly, and I soon found out why. We staggered drunkenly up the garden path, falling into the flowerbed just the once. Suddenly the front door flew open with a crash, and there stood the lady of the house.

Q insisted that I come inside. Meanwhile, his other half hovered around like a small, black thundercloud.

For 2 hours I was stuck there, during which time I learned that Q had been in the Palestine Police before transferring to the British Military Police — hence his expertise in Arabic. Having been forced to look through photographs of Q in his Palestine Uniform, I eventually managed to make my escape, and, as I tiptoed over the doormat, I heard the first sounds of shattering crockery.

Anti-Vice Squad

In the last half of my second year, about October, I was promoted to the Head of the Anti-vice Liaison in B.A.O.R. 4. It sounded great — however it was not all that it was cracked up to be. The Anti-Vice Squad consisted of one person — me — plus the services of a part-time interpreter. I spent most of the time running around on my motorbike, chasing forms. What sort of forms you might ask? These were questionnaires supplied by the Local V.D. Hospital and filled in by soldiers who had been infected by local prostitutes.

It was my job to interview these soldiers; the idea being that we could identify the ladies who had given the soldiers the infection, then report them to the German Police Vice Squad, who would insist that they have a medical examination, with the hope that they could be cured.

The problem was that, even if we found them, it was purely voluntary on the part of the ladies concerned whether they had treatment or not. Quite a few refused treatment, and all we could do was to warn the local soldiers.

The forms also presented a problem, as they were filled in by infected soldiers who had invariably been drunk and so could only recall sketchy details of the

144

episode. A good clear description, as far as we were concerned, was that she was a woman in a red dress called Matilda. She was short and fat, sometimes tall and thin, and aged between 15 and 75. This description applied inevitably to the same woman who had infected a dozen soldiers in the one evening. It was a well known fact that the Russian side was sending these ladies down into the west to infect as many soldiers as possible, and I have no doubt that the Americans were doing exactly the same thing on the other side. (Thank goodness it was not AIDS at that time, or half the population would have died.)

It was a thankless, boring job. I trucked around the countryside on a motorcycle with these forms, staying at various camps overnight as the fancy took me.

There was not a large variety of drugs about, *but there was* a little heroin and a lot of cannabis. The cannabis was a pretty bad one as it caused an awful lot of paranoia. I once saw a woman throw herself through a plate glass window under the influence of this drug. It was also the cause of a lot of fights, especially when combined with beer. Once addicts were hooked on it, they were really hooked. Most of the drugs came in from Holland, and the drug gangs seemed to have control of everything; Amsterdam was the most notorious hot spot. We did the occasional raid, but it was pretty obvious that we were trying to tackle a mountain with a tablespoon.

My most abiding memory of being on the Vice Squad was walking with a female German officer across a large plain of demolished buildings at the rear of

Dusseldorf city centre. In the middle of it was a large set of steps leading down into a complex of cellars in which were a series of furnished rooms, occupied by prostitutes. The people used to call it "The Warren".

The officer and I sat in a waiting room like a pair of lemons, waiting to interview a woman, whilst men were dodging about all over the place, trying to avoid us. I think we ruined that afternoon's trade.

There is, however, a more pleasant memory of that period. Christmas Eve — the last Christmas I had in the forces, when everybody in the Company who was able to go, were taken to a big burnt-out cathedral, which was minus its roof, together with hundreds of German civilians. There, we listened to a glorious choral thanksgiving, whilst the snow swirled down through the open roof.

All too soon it was time to go back to Civvy Street. My two years' National Service almost up, we went back on the troop train into Holland, and then took the boat to Harwich, U.K. Another train took us to Woking, Surrey and Inkerman Barracks. When we reached the depot, we were prepared to be demobbed.

We were there for two days. On the last day, representatives of police forces around the country came and tried to recruit us into various civilian police forces. I myself took a chance and was recruited into the police force in Oxfordshire.

I had to go to Aylesbury to be demobbed, which meant going on the train from Woking to the Territorial Centre, where I had to give in my cap, belt, flashes and badges. The basic uniform I was allowed to keep, otherwise I would have gone home naked. They gave me a beret and badge saying "Queens Own Oxfordshire Hussars", and then I was put on a bus and taken all the way home to Oxford — a journey of about an hour and a half.

My dad was delighted to see me, so was my mother. My brothers and sisters, however, couldn't have cared less. Then my dad came up with something special, a homecoming present. While I had been in the army, I had been sending home £1 per week, which was quite a lot when you consider that I was only getting 30 shillings a week. Instead of spending it, he had saved it and bought me a motorbike. It was a B.S.A. Bantom 125 cc 2 stroke — not new, but in extremely good condition. It was my pride and joy! I was so grateful to my father because when I came out of the army, apart from a few shillings, I was skint. I was now mobile.

I had six weeks to wait until I could take a job, so I wandered around the countryside, enjoying my new toy. One glorious morning, I found myself heading towards the home of the Misses Franklin.

I arrived at the long drive of the Franklins' farm with its white-painted picket fence. The horses, now very fat, were romping in the hay meadow, and I stopped the engine for a few moments to admire the view and to listen in silence to the sound of larks, wood pigeons and, from the green and gold of the Cumner Hills, the first call of the cuckoo. The river ran past the bottom of the drive, a light bluish flash across the landscape. The cottage stood, picturesque, on the bank, and Bert's little motorboat was tied up to the old willow tree. Bert himself was digging in his front garden.

The great grey tractors were crawling around the main farm house, dragging all sorts of implements around the fields. I could see two housemaids cleaning the windows and a third pegging out clothes.

I caught the flash of green and blue Kingfishers diving for fish in the slow running stream, and a little further on, two majestic swans chivvying a small family of indignant ducks.

Could this be paradise, I thought to myself?

I saw Susan Franklin come out onto the front steps of the large house and, on seeing me, came towards me with delighted cries of welcome. Taking me by the hand, she led me into the big kitchen, where Henry Smith and Bert, who had by that time gone into the house, were busy with the kitchen sink, obviously re-plumbing it.

Moments later, Annette came into the kitchen and gave me a hug. I noticed a strange thing about Henry — he had totally lost his foreign accent, and he spoke with the local burr. Bert, of course, was still the same. It had transpired that he had married his lady love and was now living in his cottage upon the banks of the river.

We sat around the big table drinking coffee and tea, the others bringing me up to speed with all the things that had been happening whilst I had been away.

I asked Susan what had happened to the travellers. Apparently, the old lady still lived in the house, where she had been nursed back to health, and the estate had employed the son.

"What about the strange language?" I asked.

"Oh, that was quite simple," replied Susan. "The poor dear could only speak Welsh."

She explained what had happened. The lady's husband originally came from the North Pembrokeshire area, where he was a railway man. At the beginning of the war, he had been transferred to London. They kept themselves to themselves and only spoke Welsh within the family, as she was not able to converse in English. Her son, who had a cleft pallet, could converse in English, but it was impossible for him to be understood.

When their house was totally destroyed by a V2 Rocket, the husband had been killed, and the old lady was placed in a nursing home, where she was unable to get anyone to understand her. Consequently, she was ignored by the staff there.

Her son had been placed in the YMCA, where he was bullied. Eventually, he managed to trace his mother, and they decided that he should go to a specialist unit to learn a trade. He'd also had an operation for his cleft pallet and was now making himself understood.

Although they were still there, they really wanted to go home to their roots.

Mrs Beppo, (who we met in a previous book) the lovely Italian, Welsh speaking lady, had become very friendly with the Franklin sisters, and it was she who pointed out to the others that their guest could only speak Welsh. She therefore acted as interpreter.

"So what about Gethsemene?" I asked. "What did that mean?"

"Simple — it is a little hamlet above Fishguard, where they were born. They still have an old cottage near the cliff path there that has been empty for many years. Seeing you has given me an idea. For some time we have been planning a trek up the A40 to take the old lady and her son back home. How would you like to come with us? We would pay you well, and you would be the courier for our little party. Bert has built not one, but three magnificent caravans, each one pulled by two Shire horses. We shall also take one of the tractors with a long cart, upon which we shall be carrying our tents and chairs. What do you say?"

"I say — Great!" I said.

We celebrated with a drop of sherry and shook hands.

Susan said, "Here's to the good companions!"

Excited as I was, I just knew that it would be an eventful journey.

Also available in ISIS Large Print:

Return to Wigan Pier

Ted Dakin

"One Saturday night when the alehouse was busy, we hopped over the yard wall, gathered a few pop bottles from the bottom crates and over the next few days handed them back to an unsuspecting landlord for money."

Ted Dakin's third memoir is filled with more tales of his childhood in Wigan. In *Return to Wigan Pier* Ted also compares today's weather with winters past, housing then and now, gambling habits, the recession and even the habit of Church goers. On a more personal note Ted also shares tales of games of spin the bottle and grief in the community, which led to wrestling lessons in the name of helping a close friend.

ISBN 978-0-7531-5269-0 (hb)
ISBN 978-0-7531-5270-6 (pb)

We Waved to the Baker

Andrew Arbuckle

"I wished I had asked Mum to buy my most recent favourite food, a raisin-filled slice of cake that the baker called a 'fly cemetery'. This was rather a strange name because I never saw any dead flies when I was eating it."

We Waved to the Baker is an evocative and heart-warming collection of stories from Andrew Arbuckle's youth in Fife. Through the fresh gaze of childhood, he depicts the rugged hard work of life on the farm, while capturing the essence of growing up in a boisterous family and close rural community. We follow the young Andrew as he deals with the trials and tribulations of school, older brothers and plucking chickens, while throwing in as much mischief as possible.

ISBN 978-0-7531-9590-1 (hb)
ISBN 978-0-7531-9591-8 (pb)

Bitter Fruit

Rod Broome

The first twelve months of my career proved to be highly eventful. I was appointed to teach at a junior school . . . succumbed to a nasty dose of pneumonia caused — everyone said — by living in a cold, damp, rented flat; and on Christmas Eve I became engaged to Anita, the most wonderful girl in the world!

In the final part of the "Broome" Trilogy, Rod Broome describes his early days in teaching; a head teacher who died in post, his first position as head teacher in a new open-plan primary school and how this caused staff to learn new methods of teaching. He recalls the day the school got its first computer, and the afternoon when the caretaker dressed up as a snowman!

ISBN 978-0-7531-9582-6 (hb)
ISBN 978-0-7531-9583-3 (pb)

Wicksy and the Concert Party

Peter Wicks

"In many ways, certainly for the first couple of years, I was to find that I was a square peg in a round hole."

Peter Wicks returns to tell his hilarious tales of being a teenager. Having been awarded a scholarship Peter attended Southfield Grammar school in Oxford alongside fee paying students who at times endeavoured to make school life difficult for young Wicksy. Peter remembers vividly each school building, its every twist and turn and the personalities of the teachers who brought it to life.

Early days at the school were a struggle for Peter but when he makes a drastic decision and his pet dog Pat bounds defiantly after him, he learns how life can take an unexpected turn for the better and begins to push himself to the top of the class.

ISBN 978-0-7531-8378-6 (hb)
ISBN 978-0-7531-8379-3 (pb)

Wicksy

Peter Wicks

"On my fourth birthday, I was presented with a beautifully made, yellow painted, pedal car. I remember that it had a horn, battery operated lights and a proper hand brake. I grew so attached to that car that I insisted upon having all my meals in it."

Brought up in and around Oxford, Peter Wicks brings his memoirs to life with a riot of colourful stories. From picnics with his parents via school days and bullies to spending summer holidays with his grandmother, Wicksy's tales are a charming look at a wartime childhood.

He also touches on the difficulties faced at the time, with air raid sirens, gas masks and wartime shortages, and the sad death of a childhood friend.

ISBN 978-0-7531-9502-4 (hb)
ISBN 978-0-7531-9503-1 (pb)

ISIS publish a wide range of books in large print, from fiction to biography. Any suggestions for books you would like to see in large print or audio are always welcome. Please send to the Editorial Department at:

ISIS Publishing Limited
7 Centremead
Osney Mead
Oxford OX2 0ES

A full list of titles is available free of charge from:

Ulverscroft Large Print Books Limited

(UK)
The Green
Bradgate Road, Anstey
Leicester LE7 7FU
Tel: (0116) 236 4325

(Australia)
P.O. Box 314
St Leonards
NSW 1590
Tel: (02) 9436 2622

(USA)
P.O. Box 1230
West Seneca
N.Y. 14224-1230
Tel: (716) 674 4270

(Canada)
P.O. Box 80038
Burlington
Ontario L7L 6B1
Tel: (905) 637 8734

(New Zealand)
P.O. Box 456
Feilding
Tel: (06) 323 6828

Details of **ISIS** complete and unabridged audio books are also available from these offices. Alternatively, contact your local library for details of their collection of **ISIS** large print and unabridged audio books.